CONFLICT OF INTEREST

Liam was moving before he even realized his intentions. He reached for the hand on her purse and circled her wrist, using it to pull her closer. Her heels tapped out two steps as she was compelled forward until she bumped into him like a car in a carnival ride. They were chest to chest now, as Liam's hand slid into the small of her back, his broad palm spreading open. He could hear her breathing increasing in tempo. He could feel the tips of her breasts rubbing against him. He could also feel the pressure of her warm, taut belly along the shaft of his rigid cock.

"You come that willingly? You know almost nothing about me," he managed to rough out. "You walk into my arms, with your body so exposed . . ."

"I know what I feel. And I know what you feel. For the moment, that is enough."

DANGEROUS

JACQUELYN FRANK

WRITING AS
JAX

ZEBRA BOOKS
KENSINGTON PUBLISHING CORP.
www.kensingtonbooks.com

ZEBRA BOOKS are published by

Kensington Publishing Corp.
119 West 40th Street
New York, NY 10018

All Kensington titles, imprints, and distributed lines are available at special quantity discounts for bulk purchases for sales promotion, premiums, fund-raising, educational, or institutional use.

Special book excerpts or customized printings can also be created to fit specific needs. For details, write or phone the office of the Kensington Special Sales Manager: Attn. Special Sales Department. Kensington Publishing Corp., 119 West 40th Street, New York, NY 10018. Phone: 1-800-221-2647.

Zebra and the Z logo Reg. U.S. Pat. & TM Off.

First Zebra Books Mass-Market Paperback Printing: September 2014
ISBN-13: 978-1-4201-3445-2
ISBN-10: 1-4201-3445-0

First eKensington Books Electronic Edition: September 2013
First Zebra Books Electronic Edition: September 2014
eISBN-13: 978-1-4201-3663-0
eISBN-10: 1-4201-3663-1

10 9 8 7 6 5 4 3 2 1

Printed in the United States of America

Chapter One

"Why do I get the feeling I'm about to have a really bad day?"

"Dunno. Did you look in the mirror when you woke up again?" Inez queried with earnest concern, even going so far as to blink the lashes of her bold blue eyes a couple of times in affected worry.

Kellen crabbily reached out and smacked her in the back of her head, Inez's helmet protecting her from all but the impetus and the sound of the strike.

"Hey!" she complained, grinning good-naturedly as she whacked him right back, a little harder than he had done.

"If you two are done?" came the dry query over their headsets.

"Sorry, Leader," Kellen apologized for them both as he exchanged knowing humor with Inez using eyes alone. Inez made a low hand signal near her hips that indicated what she felt their Field Leader needed in order to snap him out of his present bad mood. Kellen had to cover the thin microphone near the corner of his lips to keep his laughter from bursting out over the open channel.

"Inez, you are going to have a real hard time hitting your targets if I snap that smart-assed hand off at the wrist."

There was an instantaneous end to all horsing around when the boss made threats in *that* tone of voice. They both sobered up quickly as Inez gave him a contrite, "I read you, Leader." She covered her mic as well and whispered, "I swear that man has X-ray vision."

Kellen raised his brows and nodded in sympathy.

"Alpha Team, prepare."

Kellen and Inez became instantly serious, each disconnecting their sidearms from their holsters, nimbly checking their ammunition status both by digital readouts and by examining their chambers and clips. They holstered with precise movements so closely synchronized, it looked like the sequence had been practiced a thousand times.

It had been practiced well beyond that.

Both took a single-knee stance, side by side, each reaching to smack the front of a fist against the other's, a ready signal of team connectivity. Then they simply crouched and waited.

Liam Nash watched them, feet braced hard apart and arms folded over his broad chest as he kept his face completely unreadable. He didn't want any of the other occupants of the observation booth getting the slightest impression of restlessness from him, so he kept very still, his breathing steady. It wasn't that he was anxious. He knew his teams. He knew each one was going to perform up to expectation and beyond.

What he didn't care for was going through this horse and pony show in the first place. The only thing this ridiculous display proved, he thought with disgust, was that his crew could hit targets while on the move. The local police training grounds were romper rooms compared to the facilities he trained his people in.

However, under no circumstances would he allow civilians

into the NHK complex. He sure as hell wasn't about to let them see the specifics of how they trained. Fortunately, the reputable name Nash, Harper and Klein alone was usually proof enough of capability, and stunts like this weren't required. Unfortunately, Carter Spencer, the jackass intent on hiring them, had an enormous bug up his ass and had insisted on an exhibition.

Liam understood why Inez and Kellen were screwing around. He couldn't blame them, really. It was one thing for them to execute observed maneuvers to try to meet *his* knowledgeable standards, or even those of a guest from one of the specialized forces communities, but to perform like tots in a kindergarten play for the clueless approval of a certified asshole? It was degrading for soldiers of their renown and skill to be put through their paces for an ignorant civilian.

Spencer had been sent by one Devon Candler to evaluate and gather an opinion on their outfit. To be fair to Candler, Liam could respect sending out a forerunner to gather a report before wasting valuable time interviewing potential fly-by-night operations. Also, if Candler was in a situation where NHK's services were needed, it was probably safer all around to send out someone else.

On the other hand, Candler shouldn't have sent out a moron like Spencer who, in this instance, had decided to get into a dick-swinging contest with Nash. Liam's normal instincts would have included a lot less tolerance and a lot more anger toward such idiocy. However, Micah Harper, the business-minded partner of their triad, had made him promise not to do anything to purposely lose NHK's chance at this valuable client. Since Micah wasn't there to court their prospective client's representative with his usual charm and endless patience, Liam was forced to take on a diplomatic role while Carter Spencer lorded it over those he knew were twenty times the man he would ever be.

And that was just Inez, Victoria, and Marnie, Liam thought with a grin.

He kept his eyes on the field below, not needing to look to his right to see Spencer. The other man's smug face was reflected quite clearly in the observation booth glass. He was currently making low-voiced disparagements to his two flunkies, pathetically puffing himself up as superior even though he stood eight inches and at least 100 pounds shy of the man next to him, who could squash him like the little insect he was.

Liam took in a slow breath, cooling his temper as he forced himself to devote 100 percent of his focus to Alpha Team.

"Alpha, ready?"

"Ready," came the sharp reply over the cutting-edge headsets. Liam raised his stopwatch, not willing to depend on the field clock's accuracy. He nodded to the control chief.

"Alpha, execute," he commanded sharply.

"Is this a team with a female?" Spencer asked, sliding his hands into the pockets of a suit that had to have cost an arm and a leg. Still might cost him an arm and a leg if he kept mouthing off, Liam thought with a feral internal smile. "I see no wisdom in using a sex proven to be physically inferior in strength, size, and speed, equal opportunity be damned. You shouldn't kowtow to the feminists or any other affirmative action group because you fear legal reprisal, Nash. Your reputation might suffer."

Liam just stood quietly and watched Inez Flores and Kellen Gordon enter the field. Inez took point as usual, her movements like lightning even in heavy armor. Once the first round was fired, the rest, as they say, was history. They tore the hell out of the course in record time.

"Jesus," the chief exclaimed, tapping his chronometer as if something had to be wrong with it. "They beat the SWAT record."

Liam already knew that. He had made it his business to

know what that record was. He didn't say anything; he just let a small curl touch his lips in one corner and said, "Beta, you're up. Alpha, stand down."

Inez whipped off her helmet, the sunlight briefly gleaming off the laser-etched hologram of her little boy on the protective gear's forehead. She claimed he was her guardian angel and the sole reason why she'd never been seriously injured in the line of duty. Her partner watched her shake out a ream of ebony hair, grinning as he thought it more likely had to do with the fact that Inez was the fastest moving thing on two legs. Kellen took off his own helmet, tucking it under his arm as he started to unsnap the locks on his body armor.

"Tsk. You were low on the last two, champ," he taunted her.

She flipped him off, making Kellen laugh, and then she reached to help him with the rear shoulder catches of his chest plate. He could do it himself, but it was easier to let his partner do it.

"Better too low than too high," she said cheekily. "Which I will deny saying if you repeat it to Liam. You know Nash has no sense of humor when it comes to performance."

"Nez . . . I've worked under the man for ten years. You think I don't know that by now? Turn." Inez turned so he could hit her clasps. "And by the look of him, I'd say he could boil water in his bare hands at the moment."

Inez followed Kellen's gaze up to the observation booth. "Yeah, well, we haven't had to show off our skills to a potential client in a long time. Liam's rightly insulted. What does a civilian know about what we're doing down here? I mean, he has no military background. Not so much as a merit badge from the Boy Scouts. What does that *pendejo* think he's looking at?"

"He's looking at Nash to see if he can push his buttons. That either makes him really smart or really stupid." Kellen and Inez shrugged out of their armor in tandem, the same way they did just about everything else.

"I'm going to vote really smart," Inez speculated as they shouldered their torso armor and walked toward the three Hummers parked imposingly along the Academy drive. "From what little I've heard, Devon Candler doesn't strike me as the sort to hire idiots. Especially not for a personal secretary. I bet Spencer has direct orders to yank the boss's chain. Like you said, to see what riles him and how quick he is to lose his temper."

"Nash would rather wear nothing but women's lingerie in Times Square than let anyone purposely make him lose it," Kellen noted. "Spencer's in for a huge disappointment. C'mon. Let's ditch this stuff and see if we get back in time for Charlie team to go through. I have a bet with Victoria that we'd kick their asses time-wise."

"Easy money," Inez laughed, shaking back her midnight hair so she could kiss the picture on her helmet.

Liam finished dismissing Delta squad and stripped off his headset. He angled a cold, calculated look at Spencer, who was trying to find something disparaging to say. Liam was on to the game by now, so he waited patiently for the useless B. S. to come. He turned his back to the field and leaned against the console, crossing his combat-booted ankles.

"That's four squads, Spencer. The next four I bring out here will be more of the same," he said evenly, "but I would prefer if I didn't have to shame the local SWAT with four more record-breaking times. They'd start begging me to train their men; there'd be embarrassing groveling, and I might even be in danger of having my ass kissed. I'd rather spare myself the inconvenience."

The control chief snorted out a loud laugh and nodded his head as if that was exactly what would happen. Since the location had been arranged entirely by Spencer, Liam couldn't be accused of buying that reaction. It pleased and amused him.

"Well," Spencer said, stopping to clear his throat loudly, his hands fishing in and out of his pockets twice. In Liam's opinion, nothing looked more pathetic than a man who didn't know where to put his hands. "Thank you for your time, Mr. Nash. I will discuss my observations with my employer. You will be notified—"

"Not so fast," Liam barked, making the secretary freeze, including his agitated hands. "I want to meet Devon Candler. No decision can possibly be made when there has never been a meeting between the principal parties. Your job was to see if we were legit, and now you know we are. This is clearly a matter of life and death here, so let's cut through the bullshit and get this done."

"I think you should allow me to decide when and if it will be time for you to meet my employer," Spencer said, almost as though he were lecturing a teenager in need of guidance. "Candler International has a certain way of doing things, Mr. Nash, and if you find that so difficult to adhere to just during the preliminaries . . ." He trailed off meaningfully.

"Then perhaps we aren't suited to each other," Liam finished for him, matching his contemplative tone. "You know, you may actually have something there." He stood up straight, making certain his imposing 6'5" frame towered over the other man. "Nash, Harper, and Klein stands on its reputation, yet I have accommodated you today with patience and alacrity. Your employer came to us because there was a need, and we're the best when it comes to satisfying that need. When you can respect what you've seen here today, and what everyone else in this line of work already knows, then we'll be able to talk business. Until then, I have other clients and a training schedule to maintain."

Liam leaned toward the glass, knowing someone had an eyes-on at all times, and whipped his hand around in a fast signal for them to wrap it up.

"Mr. Nash, this process is hardly over," Spencer scoffed.

"Um," Liam made as if he were contemplating that, "actually, Spencer, it's as over as over gets." Liam turned to the other men in the room. "Chief, Casey, Ryan, thanks for your assistance."

Liam reached to shake hands with the three techs who had helped measure the field performances. He maintained good relationships with a lot of personnel in law enforcement all over the world, but in his hometown it was 100 percent first-name basis. It was crucial to cultivate associations so that the NHK compound didn't clash with the local cops. Besides that, a lot of the SWAT and ESU team members for metro, county, and state came to NHK for consultations on everything from high-tech weaponry to the newly patented body armor he and Veronica Klein had developed. It was now the only thing on the market able to withstand piercing ammunition *and* the vicious attacks of the Morphates. It was also three times lighter than the hard-shell armor his troops were currently wearing to train in.

"Here's how I see this, Spencer," he said negligently. "Someone is gunning for your boss. I've got the equipment and the trained personnel you need to keep Candler alive. You don't hire me, your boss dies . . . and you," Liam tsked hard, "are out of a job. But until you hire NHK, it's not my problem, so . . . good luck."

Liam swung his gear bag up onto his shoulder, sliding on a pair of sunglasses, but not before he turned his back on Spencer and winked at the three cops running the control room. He walked out amidst their amused chortles.

He made it all the way to the line of Hummers in the drive before Spencer came huffing up in his wake.

All eight of Liam's recently displayed crewmembers lounged lazily outside of the vehicles, leaning against steel wherever it was available. Inez was even sprawled along one of the hoods in a way that was only missing a revealing bikini. Instead, she was in her regulation blacks, the sleeveless tank and heavily pocketed pants covering all but her arms. Everyone wore identical outfits, right down to the sunglasses, combat boots, and dog tags.

Inez sat up alertly when Spencer came running up at Liam's back. Liam had a thumb hooked under the strap of his gear bag on his shoulder, which allowed him to discreetly cut a finger across his throat, negating any action from his wary people. Everyone continued to lounge in place, though he knew eight pairs of eyes watched attentively.

"Nash! Wait!"

Liam took his time, reaching to stow his gear in the back of the lead Hummer. When he heard Carter Spencer reach the drive, he turned and leaned casually on the warm black metal of the truck.

"What is it, Spencer? I've a busy day and you already wasted my morning."

"Well, I hope you have time free at three o'clock. Devon Candler would like to see you if you're available."

Spencer was all amiability and excitement, as if he were bestowing a great honor on Liam and his partners. In a way, he was. Devon Candler was a notorious recluse and personal interviews were rare. That would be useful to Liam if he eventually took on the security detail for Candler. It was harder for enemies to gun for someone when the target hardly ever exited their secured environments, gave away no personal information, and rarely allowed photographic images of themselves to be caught. On the other hand, it also made for a severely limited amount of information on his potential client. Liam didn't like mysteries, especially when the lives of his people were a factor.

"Inez," he called over his shoulder without looking away from Spencer, "tell Mr. Spencer if my three o'clock is available."

Inez sat forward with a grin, pretended to consult her memory for all of an instant, and then said dutifully, "His three o'clock is already booked." She smiled. "However, you are available for the next two or three hours, boss."

"But I was told . . ." Spencer sputtered. "You can't just—!"

"You're the secretary. Isn't it your job to move things around? Upload the directions to this number and tell your boss I'm on my way." Liam reached for a card in his pocket, flicking it at Spencer, who barely caught it as he frantically pulled out a smart phone that no doubt had the exact details of Candler's schedule on it. Liam frowned when Spencer accessed the device without so much as a password or thumbprint for security. *That*, he thought, *will be the first thing to go.* "Flores, Gordon, you're with me."

Inez and Kellen hopped into motion, swinging into the truck's front seats. Liam climbed in the back after dismissing everyone else to their regular schedules back at the NHK compound. Inez started the truck while Kellen turned on the SatNav system that would take the directions Spencer was about to upload. The satellite navigation system would pinpoint the exact location of the address and the quickest way to get there, as well as tracking fuel stops, hospitals, local law enforcement, and dozens of other vital stats that always came in handy. However, thanks to Roni Klein's inventive genius, they had the added bonus of having SatNav keep track of known and evolving Morphate clan locations, as well as other potential hotspots in the areas they would be passing through.

These types of clever programs, as well as inventions like the new body armor, earned NHK lucrative contracts. Between their facilities, private security services, and the research and development, NHK was a well-rounded success.

They could afford to indulge in tossing a little arrogance in Spencer's face.

"Where to, Liam?" Inez asked cheerily.

"Head north, champ. I'm thinking the thruway," Liam

speculated. Inez knew enough to trust his instincts and she obeyed without hesitation.

"So, you think we'll have any trouble getting an appointment?" Kellen asked with a grin as Liam pulled out his laptop and began to negotiate with the SatNav wireless system. It always took a while for Roni's encryptions to engage, but it was also the only way of ensuring the highest level of privacy during transmission, allowing Liam to work freely without fear of being hacked.

"I don't see why not," Liam mused a little absently, scrolling through screens quickly while he waited for his connection. He drew up the NHK schedule and began thinking about how much personnel, time, and equipment was going to be needed to guard Devon Candler.

He would personally be in charge of this operation. Leo White Crow and Kadian Corelli, the other two Field Leaders in this region, were involved in other assignments. He was fine with that. He'd just returned from a training seminar at Langley, and his team was itching to get back into the field. They trained hard while he was away, but his people needed the adrenaline of real action and reaction. They were just hardwired that way.

"So, what work are you two looking for?"

"Initial," they chorused.

"That's a 24/7 haul the first week, Inez. What about your boy?" Liam asked.

"He's staying in San Francisco with my folks for the next two weeks. I am free, free, free as a bird."

"Translated: She's bored, bored, bored out of her everloving skull without him," Kellen chuckled. "Put us on days," her partner requested for them, "both for initial and afterward for when the little man comes home." Liam made note of it, knowing that Kellen knew everything Inez required, and that the reverse was also true. The pair was the best-meshed team he'd ever worked with, and they were best friends besides.

"Did we get that upload yet, Kell?"

"Yeah. You were right about the thruway. It'll take us about an hour more to get there. How'd you figure Candler was north of us?" Kellen asked him.

"Candler's reputation for seclusion. The far edge of the Catskills is ideally suited for privacy and anonymity, and yet within easy travel to the resources at the leading edge of the mountains and New Manhattan. Spencer also dropped some clues earlier."

"What're you expecting?" Kellen wondered.

"Honestly?" Liam shrugged a large shoulder negligently. "I wouldn't be surprised if the property gave the NHK compound a run for its money."

Inez snorted at that likelihood. "We never get that lucky. I'm betting on a modern showplace with enormous windows and brilliant interior lighting. Not to mention a whining, wealthy brat to help create a security nightmare. Did you catch the dork and the fancy smart phone? The thing comes with powerful pass protection imbedded and he doesn't even use it."

"Yeah," Liam said grimly, even more annoyed with that safety hazard now that Inez had also noted it. "But Spencer is one thing and Candler another. Just because Carter Spencer is a pompous ass doesn't mean his boss will be."

"Let's hope not," Kellen muttered, not sounding at all hopeful.

Chapter Two

"I should have put money on it," Liam mused as they drove slowly up the winding drive to Devon Candler's mansion. There were extremely high brick walls surrounding the entire property, he was already counting security cameras, and they'd come through a security gate that actually lived up to its name for a change.

"I don't get it. What are we needed for, exactly?" Kellen asked in perplexity.

"Physical equipment isn't everything," Liam reminded him as Inez parked the Hummer. "C'mon, let's find some answers. Keep your opinions, speculations, and conversation to yourself from this point on, okay?" Without knowing what they were getting into, Liam didn't want them spewing information. Of course, he didn't think his people would do that, but it never hurt to speak reminders out loud.

"Got it," Inez agreed for them both.

Liam led the way. Each watched their surroundings warily as they were led through an enormous foyer and into a room at the front of the mansion.

"Well, the butler just let three heavily armed people into the house without so much as physically checking our identification." Liam turned to cock a wise brow at Kellen. "Whether we're expected or not, that's an unforgivable lapse. Beginning to see why we're needed?" Kellen nodded, his hand absently resting on the butt of his main pistol.

Liam was prepared to wait a while, considering their precipitous arrival, but a servant entered the room within only a few minutes. It actually pleased Nash to know Candler wasn't going to play games with them, like Spencer had tried to do, by making them wait.

"You may have an audience alone, Mr. Nash, and your companions may make themselves comfortable until they're needed," the butler instructed carefully.

Liam nodded shortly in acknowledgment and he looked back at his team. He touched his watch and silently made a sign meaning "fifteen minutes." They would make contact one way or another by then; comprehension was in their eyes.

Nash turned and followed the manservant out of the room and up a sweeping staircase that was the centerpiece of the entryway. From the tumbled travertine marble beneath the fine indigo carpet protecting it, to the highly polished brass banisters, it spoke of art and style as much as function.

He took note of everything he passed, counting rooms and hallways, marking exposures and exits. It wasn't much of an assessment because he was shortly led into a large room little different from the one he'd left Inez and Kellen in. It was another parlor of sorts with plainly upholstered furnishings in a very spartan style. There were minimal pieces, making the hung artwork the central focus. Liam noted a second set of doors at the opposite side of the long room and at once realized this was where his future client would enter.

He wasn't disappointed. When he heard the click of a turning latch a few minutes later, he faced the approach with nothing between himself and the door. This left a long expanse of carpeting to act as a runway, and he would use the span to observe his prospective client. The doors opened with a burst of energy, a no-nonsense movement and confidence, and in walked Devon Candler.

Time suddenly ground to a halt for Liam. Every single muscle in his heavily powered body contracted abruptly with shock.

Devon Candler was a woman.

She entered the room with a display of powerful presence, blatant femininity, and the most mouth-watering curves Liam had ever laid eyes on. And just like that, in the breadth of a nanosecond, Devon Candler robbed Liam Nash of his peace of mind.

If there was one thing Nash prided himself on, it was his unwavering professionalism. Even when he was off duty he had to maintain a constant level of control. These were dangerous times and there was no telling what troubles could crop up unexpectedly. Considered a deadly weapon even if he were stripped naked, Liam had always taken his responsibility to exercise caution and discrimination very seriously.

His entire morning had been spent in high gear Field Leader mode. That meant that nothing, *absolutely nothing*, could distract him from his obligations and purpose. Devon Candler shouldn't have made any impressions on him other than what was necessary for divining her intent in the coming transaction.

However, Liam's reaction as she crossed the threshold to enter the room had nothing at all to do with professional focus. She floated in on a confectionary cloud of white silk and deep, dark sable hair. Her thick mane rippled down her back in long waves like ribbon candy, billowing around her elegant face and collarbone in a fall that exhibited its extraordinary body. Liam felt his fingers twitching as a rapid-fire fantasy of plunging his fingers into that rich drape of dark chocolate hair spat though his mind like a burning acid.

She drew his attention with ever-increasing focus as she began to move toward him, crossing the long span from the doorway just as he'd planned. Or perhaps it was her plan, a part of his analytical and distrusting brain tried to whisper to him. And yet he ignored himself. Didn't even hear himself.

She wore a white dress, if it could even be called a dress. Its halter top caressed the back of her neck, falling over each breast with a neckline that plunged all the way to her navel, and then met up with an ankle-length skirt that fluttered like a banner against her hips and legs as she walked. She might as well have not been wearing anything at all. The material was so damn thin that he could see the dusky tips of outstanding breasts, the thrust of her nipples wickedly apparent even at such a distance. The white lines of her panties promised she wore nothing more than a thong. He could see every inch of her peach skin through the gauzy fabric, from her long graceful neck to her roundly curved hips and thighs. Her waist tucked in right where a decorative but perhaps unreliable scarf tie kept the sheer silk dress in place on her body, and strong, beautiful bare feet made alternating appearances as she strode toward him. She moved like a dancer, with precise and measured poise in every step.

Finding himself gawking at her body like a callow teenager, Liam quickly shifted his attention to her face. It didn't help much. He wasn't even sure if he could call her pretty at first. Elegant and sly, her features reminded him of a feline . . . or a vixen; a sweeping nose the center point, with the cheeks, chin, and brow all curved back and up toward her hairline in a way that was as graceful as it was unusual. She had a mobile mouth shaped for ready smiles.

But it was her translucent jade eyes that gripped him above all. The almond shape, the corners tilted up into the gliding lines of her bone structure, combined with dense, soot-black lashes to give her an exotic look. They stood out sharply, vividly, and boasted a keen intellect behind them that was as much a turn-on as everything else about her.

Yes. It *was* a beautiful face, Liam realized quickly.

As she approached, he was swift to realize that her physical beauty only scratched the surface. She displayed a highly sensual nature, this fact broadcast in the absent way her hands caressed her own body. A simple drift over waist and hips, a glide against her throat. Each and every self-stimulating stroke, no matter how unintentional, sent heated signals to Liam's senses, making tight muscles clench even tighter and aware nerves twang tautly to attention with unholy expectation.

Liam struggled to regain control over the volatile responses of a body turned unreasonable traitor in a span of thirty seconds. He had no business responding so carnally in such an unpredictable situation. If he started thinking with the wrong head he could get his entire team in trouble. A beauty she might be, but could she be any more obvious? Her mannerisms and her clothing were a blatant invitation and there was no way in hell he was going to fall for it. If he wanted to get off on that type of thing, there were a hell of a lot of strip joints around town selling the same damn thing for a lot less cost in complication.

Firmly refocusing, Liam reminded himself that he still didn't know her intentions, if they were honest, or if there was something hidden behind all of this that he ought to know about before he considered endangering the lives of his teams. The thought drew him harshly back into reality just as she came within his reach. She stopped, tilting her head back to meet his hard eyes. She was a good seven or eight inches shorter than he was, though still tall for a woman. An anticipated flirty smile flashed at him as she extended a long, refined hand.

"Good afternoon, Mr. Nash. I'm Devon Candler, and I'm very pleased to make your acquaintance."

Liam was instantly struck by the polished cadence of

her speech and the elegant manner of her movement as she reached for his hand. It was so straightforward, so matter-of-fact, and not at all the dance of coy flirtation he'd been expecting from her. Liam reached out and grasped her offered hand, simply holding it as he studied her contradictory signals slowly and carefully, trying to figure her out. She was incredibly warm, the heat of her body radiating notably against his palm. He had expected her hands to be perfectly soft, as soft and smooth as the rest of her skin appeared to be, but as he absently stroked his thumb over the range of her knuckles, and his fingers against her palm, he noted the characteristic toughness of calluses.

"Good afternoon, Ms. Candler," he greeted her cordially, using the politesse as a way to keep himself from assessing her body for its physical fitness. He would wait a minute, wait until he was back on solid footing before he indulged in that potentially risky curiosity. "The pleasure is reciprocated," he assured her.

Her smile bloomed, displaying a pearly white collection of straight teeth. Brilliant reflections of light flashed in her eyes with her expressed approval. "I have heard a great many things about you and your organization, Mr. Nash. Long before I found myself in need of you, I had heard of the rescue of Jonathan Greening from his kidnappers. And the failed assassination attempts on Minister Michelle two years ago, and the renowned Joseph Florin this past June. They owe their lives to you. In a time when assassinations, kidnappings, and murder have become par for the course for anyone in the public spotlight, there is some measure of reassurance to be found in you."

She closed her opposite hand over the back of his, the gesture strangely intimate for a first encounter, yet it was obviously natural for her. He knew instantly that this was no ploy or affectation for the sake of flirtation. He would have felt that difference quite keenly. It left him a bit stunned and bemused.

Liam was very rarely caught off guard by anything anymore, it being his business to expect the unexpected, but she was already nothing of what he had anticipated.

He had built up too much expectation on too little information and the deliberate misrepresentation of one Carter Spencer. Then he had jumped to on-sight conclusions based on how she was clothed. Devon Candler's audacious presentation of herself and her warmth of personality were in contradiction with what one would expect of a recluse.

"I, on the other hand, have heard nothing about you, Ms. Candler. But this is by your design, so you would expect that," he returned, finding his tone as warm and companionable as hers was. She'd made a damn easy conquest of him if she could make him forget a whole morning's worth of aggravation with a pleasant greeting. He gave himself a mental shake and withdrew his hand from hers. He absently rubbed at his palm as it cooled quickly in the room's air. "I'm sure we both have very busy schedules, so we should cut to the chase."

"Yes. Carter told me you're very direct when it comes to business and you don't appreciate delays or dancing around significant issues." Her eyes narrowed on him slightly. Liam realized he was frowning darkly in response to her use of Spencer's given name. Damn it, he knew better than to show reactions like that. What in hell was the matter with him? Was he trying to blow this deal for NHK? "You don't care for my Carter?" she asked, sounding very amused. "He is something of an acquired taste," she said with a chuckle as she glided toward a serving tray set on a table.

"Is that what you call it?" Frankly, the man left nothing but a bitter taste in Liam's mouth. He wasn't exactly thrilled with her phrasing for that matter. What did she mean 'my Carter'? If there was something sexual . . . something intimate between them, that could alter the whole dynamic of the situation and make things far more difficult than they needed to be.

Devon laughed in a rough, sexy rasp of delight that

erupted from deep in her lungs. She had a low voice for a woman, though not mannish. Voice and laugh both belonged on the opposite end of a phone-sex number. She would have made a fortune at it, Liam thought.

"Just look at him like a trained monkey," Devon urged, this time making him grin in spite of himself as she filled glasses from a pitcher and then turned to serve one to him. "He does everything I ask, even the things I find distasteful, but he can be a surly little bastard sometimes. Here. Peppermint iced tea."

Liam accepted the glass and took a seat beside her on a large sofa after she had glided onto it. She crossed her legs, giving him a fine idea of how long they were in spite of the light fabric draped over her.

"Thank you," he said, immediately setting the glass aside, "but ma'am, if you don't mind, I'd like it if we could talk about you and why you feel you need NHK."

"Carter didn't explain that my life is in danger?"

"That was all he said. That sentence and no more. It doesn't tell me what I need to know."

She frowned, a soft line tugging down between her dark brows. "I'm sorry. He's trying to protect me. However, he does a poor job of it, being too cautious at the wrong times and not cautious enough at others."

Liam had to bite off a query about why she associated herself with someone whose incompetence and shortcomings she clearly recognized. It made no sense that she would allow such faults in her private secretary. Something wasn't co-pasetic about that entire relationship, Liam thought quickly. He would have to remain observant.

And alert, he reminded himself. It was easy to feel relaxed around her, with her surprisingly easygoing humor and per-sonality, something he absolutely should not be. She was so at ease and so tranquil, not at all the vision of a woman in fear for her life. The realization sparked suspicion into the back of his brain again and he sat up a little straighter.

"What's going on, Ms. Candler?" he asked her directly, adding some sharpness to his tone in an attempt to bring them both to the point.

"Devon," she corrected easily, "if that's not too awkward for you. And it's simple, really. My enemies have made a target of me, putting a price on my head. A very large price. Enough of a reward so that when they themselves rest from trying to harm me, others jump readily into their place. There have been six attempts so far, two that were extremely close." Devon reached to lift a folder from the near table and handed it to him.

The first photograph was an eight-by-ten of a sandstone and terra cotta mansion engulfed in flames, the second photo showed only stone, burned black, remaining. Liam could tell that nothing would have survived a blaze of such proportions. The next two were burned-out cars, the destruction looking like bomb work. It was the fourth that took his breath away. It was an undated photo of a bedroom in an undisclosed hotel. The bed was covered in blood and it had been violently shot to shreds. His eyes swept up to hers, then burned over every inch of her body in search of scars or telltale markings that would identify that blood as her own. She graciously complied with his silent investigation and lifted the hem of her gown all the way up to her thigh. There, still rather freshly healed, was the pocked marking of a gunshot wound that sliced through the rear thigh muscles. It wasn't going to be much of a scar, he could tell, but her remarkable healing abilities didn't make the injury any less dangerous or compelling.

"Why have you waited so long to get protection?" he demanded through tense vocal chords, his blood seething with an inexplicable rage when he thought of her sleeping like that, ignorant of an approaching danger that had nearly succeeded in ending her life.

"Because I thought the house and the first car fire were accidents. Afterward, when I became more aware, I thought knowledge and caution would see me through." She stood up and paced a thoughtful circuit before him, the shadows of her body dancing in transparent white silk playing merry hell with his concentration. The thin straps of that damned thong drew his attention every single time to the curve of her bottom as she turned or passed. "Unlike many women, Mr. Nash, I am capable of protecting myself." Now that he was looking for it, Liam could see the limp that hampered her pace. It was the faintest thing. She was too proud to show an obvious weakness. He could see that in the straightness of her spine and the rigidity of her statement. "No one was in that bedroom but me and the assailant. I assure you, he's come to regret that."

Polished and refined she might be, but Liam didn't doubt her for a heartbeat. In order for her to have survived, there had to be something as tough as steel running through her. Add her fierce pride to it and it probably irked the hell out of her that she had to go to others for help. Yet, she did it with dignity and aplomb.

"You could get any number of people to guard you," he stated at last, studying her stoic features very carefully. "There are some fine firms out there. Why did you pick NHK, Ms. Candler?"

"Devon," she persisted gently. Then more directly, "I prefer your . . . umm . . . style."

"And what style is that?" Liam asked, a thrill of anticipation shooting down the back of his neck as he realized there was potentially a lot more going on here than the average babysitting job.

Devon stopped and looked at him. She suddenly kneeled

before him in a graceful sweep of silk, her knees settling
between the toes of his boots and her hands resting lightly
on his bent legs. Their eyes locked with an instant sense of
intimacy and he held himself very still as he tried to decide
how to react.

"You dislike my being this close. It makes you uncomfortable. If I close the distance, the discomfort increases . . ."
She demonstrated her point by sliding her hands up his
thighs and leaning her body in toward his.

For Liam, it was as if he'd forgotten how to breathe. Or
move. It was as good as having her kneeling naked in front of
him, an image he had no trouble conjuring in his active mind.
She'd been hot-wiring his senses from the minute she'd entered the room, and now she was about to drive the car right
off the showroom floor. He felt her ribs sliding against his
inner thighs, the soft weight of her breasts a torturous brush
over the material of his blacks. Devon's scent flooded up and
over him with a hint of orange citrus and some unidentifiable
spice that blended deliciously with the smell of warm, sexy
woman. On the back of that scent came heat. It was a body
warmth that, as she leaned even closer, swept in fast and furious waves over his thighs, groin, and belly, methodically
seeking its way up his chest. Completely out of his control,
Nash's body responded to her lure, hot blood pulsing low into
his hips until he was hardening in answer.

Discomfited, Liam reacted by dropping the folder on the
floor and grabbing her shoulders tightly.

"Defense," she said quickly to make her point. "You've
stopped me from doing what you don't want me to do. But
this is basic physics. You have to continually expend effort to
keep me where I am. The threat stays, your energy is uselessly
spent keeping me constantly at bay, and this doesn't change.
Not until one day when you weaken, or when you aren't
paying attention . . ." She marked her line of reasoning by

sliding her unimpeded hands all the way up the insides of his thighs until her fingertips flirted just shy of discovering her effect on him. "One day something gets by you and you're victimized. There's only one thing you can do to stop it. Only one thing, or you must face the inevitable." Her hands twitched and he felt the brush of stroking fingers along the rigid length of his fly.

Liam exploded off the couch, hauling her up and shoving her backward. All he wanted in that instant was to get her as far away from himself as he could reasonably manage before . . . well, *before*. He wasn't expecting her to stumble back awkwardly, landing hard on her bottom on the floor.

"Are you out of your goddamn mind?" he bellowed as he marched to tower over her, knowing that at his height and in the peak of fury he was beyond imposing. He told himself he didn't give a damn as his hands rolled into mighty fists. He fought not only his temper but an agonizing pulse of blatant sexual arousal. *What in hell was she thinking?*

"Offense," she gasped out, her expression folding into a taut tension. "Don't you see?" she panted softly. "Offense is the only true defense, otherwise you'll always be fighting to protect yourself."

Liam stilled, his anger bleeding out of him so swiftly he was left a bit at loose ends, his body swirling with direction-less urges and emotions. He suddenly and sharply compre-hended the point she was making. He looked down at her, his entire body vibrating with tension and a keen awareness he didn't want to feel. Devon was flushed so deeply that he could trace the coloring along her skin beneath her sheer dress. She was breathing hard, with strain tightening every part of her body. Her lips had become less mobile, pressed firmly to-gether, and he realized it was because she was in pain.

Liam remembered the bloody sheets in the photo and the scar on her leg.

"Christ! Devon, that was a stupid thing to do!" he spat out as he bent to scoop her off of the floor. "Touching a strange man like that! When he could take it for a damn invitation and overpower you easily? Especially after showing him your vulnerability? I didn't mean to, yet I still re-injured your leg!" He swept her over to the couch he'd abandoned and settled her onto it. He went to one knee beside her and pulled up the silk skirt of her dress so he could gently probe the angry wound. She sucked in a fast breath and he frowned darkly.

"I just didn't want you to tell me no," she said tightly through her teeth. "I wanted to make sure you understood exactly how I feel."

Liam looked up and met the penetrating jade of her eyes, his big hands resting around her warm thigh. "I do understand. But you could try asking first, straight out, and then attempt shock tactics *after* someone says no. It's a sounder plan of action."

"I don't like being told no and then having someone change their mind later. It raises too many doubts. At least now you know what I'm capable of. I'm no precious damn porcelain princess who will stand idly by while someone tries to shoot me to shreds."

Liam actually couldn't help grinning at that. She also refused to play the ignorant wilting flower, and that was going to be a key factor in saving her life one day. She faced her dangers proactively. Nash was the last person who'd condemn proactive behavior.

Provided it didn't get her killed or raped along the way. Liam's smile disappeared and his anger fumed up around him again when he thought about what she could have opened herself up to.

"Yeah, well, you're damn lucky I'm not a closet rapist. Going around and . . ." Nash wasn't shy, but he'd be damned if he was going to start talking about it out loud when he wasn't exactly over the memory of that ghostly erotic touch in the first place. "Talk about handing the mouse a big ass wheel of cheese," he grumbled as he turned his attention back to her leg. He slid his hand between her thighs, drawing out her knee so he could see the healing exit wound. He ignored the eddy of incredible heat she gave off as it bathed his fingers and his aching palm. He was trying to keep the craving twitches in his fingertips down to a minimum as he rasped out, "Especially after showing up in a dress like this."

"You don't like my dress?" She sounded genuinely upset as she studied the chic garment for flaws.

"Oh, I like it," he muttered gruffly. "It's just a little overt."

"Is it?"

Liam watched her frown and nibble on a corner of her bottom lip thoughtfully. The pensive expression told him she was honestly debating his opinion. Nash quickly began to regret his remarks. Who was he to judge her? He'd stepped into her world barely ten minutes ago. Why should his opinion even matter to her? The dress was no different from hundreds he'd seen before on other fashionable women. Why did it rattle him in this situation when it was forgettable window dressing everywhere else?

Then he recalled the enormity of the task she wanted to hire NHK for and the daunting responsibility that came with it. She didn't just want protection from her enemies; she wanted her enemies eliminated. It was a cold and ruthless decision, but as she had so aptly demonstrated, it might well be the only option to save her life.

Liam ran gentle, thoughtful fingers over the wound along her inner thigh and asked matter-of-factly, "Devon, who is it that you've made enemies with? Who would go through all this trouble to try to kill you, and why?"

She opened her mouth, hesitated, then said, "I hold the key to the lives and deaths of a lot of people. Those who hunt me also hope to remove the hold I have over them." She took a deep, unsteady breath. "I can't be more specific, I'm sorry. But you don't need to know the finer details. What you do need to know is that, besides those in search of a huge bounty, my main enemy is a Morphate."

Chapter Three

Devon was expecting his reaction, but still she jumped when he exploded up to his full height in an awesome rushing wall of bone and sinew that flexed and bulged with dozens of tautened muscles. She looked the long way up into his deceptively understated amber eyes, marveling at the glints of gold within them that flashed when his temper was aroused.

Morphates was a word no human being liked hearing.

She imagined Liam Nash had grown to hate it more than most. His personal knowledge of Morphates was one of the reasons she was so determined to have him.

It was also quite possibly the main reason why he might turn her down.

"Are you telling me that you have *Morphates* gunning for you?" Nash ground out in a voice so low and dangerous it was practically a growl.

"To be precise, it could be the leaders of a couple of different Dark Cities," she said firmly, keeping her eyes steadily attached to his. "Whoever it is, he wants me to suffer . . . or submit. I have a lot of information the Morphate leaders feel is quite valuable."

Devon did not blame Liam for his stupefied expression. Morphates themselves were stupefying. Once humans, Morphates had been created by a mad scientist named Eric Paulson a few decades back. His experimentations on the indigent, the criminal, and others had resulted in the people who now called themselves Morphates. Well known for their savage instincts, their ferociously sexual natures, and the fact that they were, by agreement with the government, supposed to limit themselves to the Dark Cities they had volunteered to live in, they were more recently thrust into human awareness because there were upstart Morphates who no longer wanted to be trapped behind the walls of those confinement camps. The Dark Cities were huge metropolises that had been overrun by the refuse of humanity—gangs, criminals, the homeless. Ultimately, humanity had thought it best to wall off cities like New York and Chicago, give up on them and let the criminals have them. They wanted to pretend that would be the end of the matter. When the Morphates had come on the scene, their leaders, their Alphas, had struck a bargain with the humans, agreeing to live in the Dark Cities. Agreeing to make themselves responsible for them. Agreeing to quietly keep to themselves along with all the other things that frightened mainstream humanity.

But that had been before they'd begun to breed new generations, before it had become obvious they weren't going to die off like normal humans did—before mainstream humanity had realized that Morphates couldn't be killed, not even by time or the aging process

The only thing that could control a Morphate was another Morphate. The Alphas, to be exact. The Alpha hierarchy was an absolute one. If you lived in their City, you obeyed and respected your Alpha . . . unless you felt yourself capable of challenging that Alpha and taking over his or her position. In the thirty-five years since the Phoenix Project, that had only happened once . . . in Dark Houston. All the other Dark Cities were still run by their original Alphas.

The Alphas themselves were controlled by an Alpha Council. Each Alpha answered to the political and legal power of the Alpha Council. Ideally. But recently two Dark Cities had broken away from the Council's control, had decided to start living by their own rules, and Morphates had started bleeding out of the Dark Cities. Some had gathered into new enclaves that occasionally liked to intimidate and bully the humans they considered inferior to themselves in so many ways. Luckily, for the most part, they paid humans about as much mind as they might a stray animal. They were more interested in fighting amongst themselves for power, feuding for control.

Just the same, there were hostilities between the two species. Morphates didn't respect humans, and why should they? Humans were inferior creatures compared to Morphates, with the abilities and power that they wielded. Humans feared and despised the unstoppable prowess of a species that could potentially wipe humanity from the face of the earth.

To further complicate things, Morphates could easily pass as normal humans if they wanted to. Some people thought that they *were* still technically human, but many humans and most Morphates disagreed with that, each finding it to be a little bit insulting. Still, the Constitution protected American Morphates just as it did anyone else, and all laws applied. Then there was that little thing called immortality. You could put a bullet in a Morphate's brain and it would still survive, healing from the wound completely intact.

Oh, and there was one more little thing . . . that little thing about drinking blood . . .

So she wasn't surprised by Liam's reaction in the least. It was to be expected.

"I chose you because you have experience in this kind of altercation. Your people have the equipment needed to hurt them, to slow them down, as well as the training specific to fighting Morphates. I'm not asking you to burn them to the ground, although in a perfect world that might be nice, but I do need you to make enough of an impact that you get the message across: to leave me alone."

"Last I checked, assault on that scale is still illegal," Nash reminded her stiffly. "My people are bodyguards, not mercenaries. Oh"—he smiled sarcastically as he folded brawny arms over his chest and settled in a firm stance—"and it's common knowledge, you can't kill a Morphate."

"You've killed a Morphate, Mr. Nash." She took satisfaction in the way his breathing froze into silence, the superiority on his face falling away in a rush of shock. "And the only reason the incident is even on record is because you reported it to your C.O. in the Secret Service as a matter of protocol. It wasn't as though there was a body left behind." She threw up her hands and made a poofing sound to indicate the vaporous cloud that occurred when a Morphate was finally, truly dead, its body dissolving into its basic gaseous components.

Liam stared at her as if she'd grown an extra head.

"How do you know that?" he demanded. "How did you find out about that?" His eyes narrowed to amber slits when she didn't respond immediately. "There are only a handful of people who know how to kill a Morphate. Even fewer know what happens to them when they die," he said in a low voice full of threat. "Now I ask you again, Ms. Candler, how do you know that?"

"Hmm." She contemplated her answer for a moment, watching as his huge hands dropped to his sides and curled into tightly clenched fists. "I suppose I don't have a choice," she mused.

Devon was testing his patience and taunting him, and it probably wasn't at all wise to do so, but there was something fascinating in the way Liam Nash reacted to her. She had seen hours of video files on this man, everything from interviews to reports, and even supremely stressful tests of strength and mental fortitude. In each and every one he had remained as still as stone and even less expressive.

Not anything like the man who stood before her now, clenched tight with suppressed storms of emotion.

The man whose extraordinarily fit body, in spite of its forbidding solidity, had quivered like a taut bowstring when she had boldly touched him.

Devon concealed a shiver as her fingertips burned with carnal memory of the all too brief caress against his blatantly aroused cock. It had been a shocking surprise in spite of her bold tease. She had never expected him to respond to her as a man does a woman. Not after everything she had seen, read, and learned about him. She had assumed that as well trained as he was, a veteran of every tactic known to man, he would have been completely dispassionate. Completely immune to . . . well, to her.

But he had been hot and hard . . . and he had scolded her for wearing an "overt" dress.

Devon lowered her eyes lest he see the smug amusement blooming in them and twitching against her lips. She liked the idea of having him a little off center. She didn't know why. She just liked it.

"Candler International," she said quietly, "has a military contract. Research focused on stopping Morphates both temporarily and permanently. Specifically, creating viable weapons."

"And you succeeded," he breathed in unabashed awe the instant comprehension dawned. "That's why they are after you. That's why they all want you dead." He dropped quickly to his knees again, swiftly energized, his amber gaze gleaming with anticipation. "Tell me, how are you carrying the main component? What's your delivery system? The bullets we're using now are hazardous for humans to handle and too unpredictable. How did you get around the toxicity factor?"

Devon laughed at him, unable to help herself. He was like a kid on Christmas morning. His hands and inspection returned to the wound inside her leg almost absently and she felt them actually shaking.

"I've never seen anyone get so excited about a new weapon before, Mr. Nash," she teased him.

"Liam," he corrected. Devon sucked in a sharp breath when his probing fingers hit a painful spot. She hoped she hadn't pulled her hamstring muscle again during the fall. She'd done it once already and it was a damned nuisance as well as painful. Incapacitation irritated the hell out of her.

Then the sadist squeezed her thigh again and she threw her body back against the cushion, her hips lifting reflexively as she moaned long and low.

"Something I can help you with there, Nash?"

Nash twisted around when someone spoke from across the room. Devon turned her head to see a man and a woman standing there, fully armed and wearing outfits identical to Nash's. The woman was a Latina beauty with insanely gorgeous hair, but the man was almost prettier than she was. He was about six feet tall with golden hair cut short and neatly fashionable, and dark, almost black eyes. He looked more like a model than a soldier, even though he was clearly the latter. With a Roman nose, chiseled lips and cheekbones, he probably melted hearts everywhere he went. The body he maintained in order to perform his job only improved the package. Plus, the mischievous smile and amusement dancing within his eyes instantly made her want to return his good humor.

Devon realized what she and Liam must look like. When Nash merely turned back to what he'd been doing, she was momentarily impressed with his composure. But that was only until she realized the so-called hard ass soldier was flushing slowly from the neck up, and she bit her lip as she stifled a giggle. His eyes shot to hers and he gave her a look that could have killed even a Morphate.

"Gordon, we got a medpack in the Hummer?" he asked evenly.

"Of course," Gordon snorted as if he couldn't believe Nash had asked such a thing.

"Bring it up." He added sharply, "Double time!"

Devon watched as the man and woman exchanged looks of humor, but the male did move quickly out of the room to obey the order.

"Devon Candler, this is Inez Flores," he introduced without looking at his coworker, but raising a hand to beckon her forward. "Flores, this is Devon Candler. Ms. Candler was assaulted not too long ago and has a healing gunshot wound to the thigh. She fell and has re-injured herself. Could you take a look please?" Nash turned to Devon. "Do you mind? She's an excellent medic."

"I don't, but I wish you wouldn't make so much of a fuss."

Nash just gave her a look that asked her to indulge him so she lay back with a sigh and tried to brace herself for the pain of more probing. Flores kneeled beside her commander. "She's already starting to swell," Nash indicated softly as he turned Devon's leg with incredible gentleness for such daunting looking hands. She could feel the roughness of his calluses gliding over the skin along her inner thigh and she suppressed a shiver. She had reacted the same way the first time he had touched her, an unexpected thrill from an unexpected source. "It's the exit side I'm worried about. How long ago were your stitches removed?" he asked her.

Devon smoothed back her hair on one side and told him her first lie since they had met. "A couple of days," she said vaguely. "Please, I wish you wouldn't . . ."

His quelling glance worked. Devon's heart danced with a flutter in her breast when he mastered her so easily in spite of her own assertive personality. She was instantly fascinated, probably as he had been when he'd first seen her. He'd been obviously taken aback, though she was certain he hadn't realized how transparent his expressions had been. She'd gotten used to the reaction from those who expected Devon Candler to be a man, or some sort of old gray warhorse instead of a young, thriving beauty, but there was something more to Nash's response than there was with others. She'd been studying him ever since.

"No bleeding. Not at the edges of the wound anyway. The bruising isn't darkening yet so I don't think she tore anything inside," Flores mused as she gently probed from one side of the wound to the other. "Too soon to tell for certain, but nothing more than swelling as far as I can see. Actually, it looks pretty good for a recent injury."

"I've always been quick to heal," Devon dismissed easily, finally losing patience and brushing away the hands touching her leg. She sighed with relief when she was able to pull the skirt of her gown back into place. She didn't sit upright, however, her leg too sore now to withstand the pressure of sitting directly on it. As if reading her mind, Nash picked up a pillow and placed it under her calf and knee, raising her thigh from the couch and supporting the weight of her leg, instantly making it feel even better.

Soon after that, the fair-haired Mr. Gordon came bounding back into the room, breathless enough to have run the entire way back and forth. He handed a nondescript black box she assumed was the med kit to Nash, who laid it on the ground and popped it open. Gordon stood with feet braced and arms across his chest as he watched his commander pull out a white chemical pack. Nash crushed it in one hand and shook it rapidly to combine the chemicals that would cause it to become instantly cold. Then he pushed it under her elevated thigh.

"Let me know if that's too cold. We can put a towel between the pack and your skin," Nash said as he closed the kit.

Flores had risen to her feet, but Nash remained kneeling beside her.

"So tell me something," Nash asked thoughtfully. "Who is currently doing security for you? You have to have someone manning those cameras." He paused. "You do have someone, don't you?"

"Of course. I have two private guards for the interim. Once you bring your people in here, all security becomes your domain. My only exceptions are the obvious. No cameras in my bedroom, private sitting room, or office. No personnel inside any of those places, even on rounds, when I'm not present at the manor. I deal with a lot of sensitive documentation and it's out of the question when it comes to confidentiality. You can do whatever you like surveillance-wise along the boundaries of those rooms, but nothing that views the interiors through the windows or doors.

"You'll also have to maintain surveillance on my offices at Candler International. That's here, London, Japan, and Kuala Lumpur. I have permanent residences in all those cities except Kuala Lumpur, where I stay at a hotel, but I will give warning of travel at least two weeks in advance if I can at all manage it, and you can have parts of my schedule up to several months in advance if you consult with Carter—"

"Okay, as to that," Nash interrupted her with a staying hand, "I don't want you planning your schedule beyond two weeks. Also, Spencer has your entire schedule on an unsecured smart phone. Anyone can take it and get your schedule in advance without even breaking a sweat."

Devon's eyes went wide with surprise at that bit of information. She was shocked that Nash had already made such a pertinent discovery for her benefit when he hadn't even accepted the job yet. It impressed and pleased her, confirming she'd made an excellent choice in him, for many reasons.

"That shouldn't be," she said with a frown. "Carter knows how finicky I am about securing all electronic devices.

Specifically for this reason." She began to tap her long nails against her thigh, realizing she was projecting her irritation, but not really caring. A feeling of chilled trepidation crept through her and she began to nibble on her bottom lip. She looked up into eyes of amber and found comfort in the fact that she could read his thoughts, and that they were following the same unthinkable path as hers. "Carter has been in my employ for a very long time," she argued softly, knowing that it was an emotional excuse and not a logical one.

"And yet, all of a sudden your enemies have incredibly detailed access to you that they shouldn't have," he reminded her gently, his hand resting over the top of her thigh in a dreadfully effective indication of her recent wound.

"Morphates don't work with humans, though. They detest them," she said, reminding him of the powerful prejudices between species. Yet, she knew it wasn't universally true, just as she knew why her enemies could never send a Morphate in to spy on her undercover . . . or even to covertly assassinate her.

Because she was Morphate, Devon would have sensed one of her own kind instantly.

But that wasn't information she was about to impart to one of the few men in the world who knew how to kill a Morphate.

The next day, Liam turned in his office chair to look down on the traffic moving through the compound drive. As usual, someone was always coming or going. The compound was a hub of activity from dawn to dusk, and beyond, if they were training in night tactics. At the moment, his team was swarming around the equipment shed, gearing up for the initial installation at the Candler manor house. Liam could see the warehouse from his window and the activity moving smoothly along.

After the main Candler residence was secure, he would send a team on to her primary offices and others to her secondary residences. There was a helicopter and associated pads on the tops of her business buildings, and a private jet, also for convenience. And secrecy, he noted. He was beginning to see why it was so easy for her to conceal herself when she barely set foot onto unfamiliar or uncontrolled grounds.

Securing the secondary and tertiary offices and residences would be organized according to Devon's future plans to visit them. There was also a fleet of cars to take into consideration.

While she had been extremely open to all of Liam's suggestions so far, Devon was finicky about her privacy in certain understandable ways. He'd had no arguments with her so far, but he was certain to step on her toes eventually. He invariably clashed with clients on the issue of where security ends and where privacy begins. It was inevitable.

And she most definitely was now his client.

It had been the photograph of her blood spilled across that bed that had committed him. The idea of her fighting off an assassin *while she'd been shot* had won him over in a heartbeat. There was nothing more impressive to him than a tough woman who knew how to handle herself in a moment of supreme danger. Especially when she came in such unexpectedly elegant packaging. Incredibly sexy packaging. Much too gorgeous to risk losing on a 'next time' possibility where she might not make it out with her life.

Liam groaned when he realized how unprofessional and sexist that sounded, even if it was only in his own brain. He threw down his digital pen and watched it roll across the top of his desk. The neglected schedule he was supposed to be working on flashed on his tablet in irritable reminder of his slacking. He ran both hands over his head, raking his fingers through his short-cropped hair.

The trouble was, he couldn't get their first meeting out of his head. That wicked dress she'd worn, so casually showing off a perfect body, her obvious wit, and the strange exotic beauty of her features. The feel of her hands on his thighs. Warm palms he'd felt burning through the material of his blacks even though the cloth wasn't exactly thin. Then that teasing stroke of her fingers . . .

Liam cursed aloud as his entire body tightened with the memory, mimicking his initial reactions perfectly. He brushed his hand across his fly, adjusting himself away from his sudden discomfort.

"Clients are off limits," he reminded himself aloud, as if it would change the aroused state of his body, not to mention the memories of her that were haunting his mind like teasing wraiths.

He turned back toward his office window, leaning forward to watch Inez and Kellen spar in a little hand-to-hand on the lawn. The pair often had philosophical arguments about different maneuvers in their differing forms of martial arts and it invariably ended up in a sparring match to prove the winning point. He ought to reprimand them for goofing off when they had other duties to perform, but he had a hard time doing that when they were goofing off over training techniques.

Liam believed that Inez and Kellen were his best team for a reason, and that reason could very well be the way they constantly challenged themselves and each other. Inez was determined to prove that a single mother with a child could flourish in this career choice without neglecting her kid, and Kellen was determined to prove he was more than just a pretty face. Inez had been denied SWAT, and though they'd never say it right to her face, it was obvious that being a single mother had been the reason. She'd quit the force because of it. Kellen had made it all the way through FEDOPS training and three years of active missions before resigning for what he simply called 'personal reasons.' Then he'd been surprised to find that the civilian world had a hard time taking him seriously on account of his looks and laid back personality. Employers mistook all that natural charm and easygoing attitude for weakness. It made the pair of them a couple of very serious overachievers, forging the perfect team, and also the perfect friendship. Liam had never had a doubt about either one of them.

His eyes then sought out Colin. Colin was doing equipment checks before final load, testing lights, cameras, sensors, and the like. He was the only doubt Liam had ever had in all of his hires, and he would probably continue to doubt himself until the day he died . . . or the day his baby brother did. Considering the considerable danger on this pending assignment, Liam thought he was probably more sensitive to his doubts than he might normally be. It wasn't that he questioned his brother's skills in the least. Colin was a fine soldier, and an excellent subordinate. He'd been born to take and follow orders with a sense of duty and precision that would make any commander proud and fully trusting of him.

It was more a matter of Liam feeling the weight of the responsibility he had taken on every time he gave Colin an order or duty that could cost him his life. However, he'd made a measure of peace with himself about it, especially after a night not too long ago when he and Colin had kicked back with a couple of beers and had a heart to heart about it. Colin had reminded him that there was more danger under someone else's command than there would ever be under Liam's experienced hand. Since Colin was determined to be in the business, it was actually safer for him to be under Liam's watch.

Liam's phone buzzed, tugging him out of his contemplations.

"Nash," he greeted.

"Devon *friggin'* Candler! You sonofabitch, I didn't think you had it in you!"

"What's up, Micah?" he asked, smiling at his partner's

usual enthusiasm. He had known that Micah was going to orgasm when he heard about NHK landing the Candler job. Micah loved to make money, and Devon would be paying out a great deal of it over the next few months.

"When this gig came up, I thought for sure you were going to blow it. I thought, *'Sure! Ripest plum to ever plop in our laps and I'm stuck in Milan, leaving the man with the personality of the Antichrist to seal the deal!'* But Glory just told me you handed in signed contracts good for six months of 24/7 coverage, *with* an option to pick up. Now, we both know it wasn't your winning charm, because you don't have any when it comes to handling business, so how'd you get the contract?"

"Oh, we have an expertise no one else can claim," Liam told him, taking no offense whatsoever to Micah's colorful description of the facts.

"And that is?"

"Something I won't discuss long distance, Micah," he said directly.

"Ah. No problem, I'll catch up when I get back."

"When is that, by the way?" he asked, grinning into the phone and knowing what the gist of Micah's answer was going to be already.

"Is Roni still mad at me?"

"Let me put it this way," Liam said with a laugh, "when you come home and you can't find your car in long-term parking at the airport, don't call the cops."

"Oh, hell! She didn't!"

"Would I lie?"

"Crap!" Micah added a growl of frustration. "I'm going to kill her."

"Then it's a fight to the finish. Are you going to tell me what you did to piss off our usually mild-mannered partner?" Liam fished hopefully.

"Are you going to tell me where my Jag is?"

"No."

"Then no."

Micah hung up with a loud click.

Liam hung up his end with a low chuckle. The phone buzzed before he could take his hand away and he rolled his eyes, already knowing who it was.

"Yeah, Roni?" he greeted.

"Was that the no-good twerp you call your partner?" she demanded.

"You call him your partner too," he reminded her gently.

"Ha! He'll be lucky if I call him anything with more than four letters in it ever again!"

"Veronica Klein, are you ever going to tell me what this is about? I don't exactly feel comfortable with dissention in the ranks." Actually, he knew his partners well enough to know it would blow over, but it wouldn't blow over until Roni got the problem off her chest. Since he was going to be deeply involved in the Candler assignment soon, her venting resources would be limited. Micah could end up banished to Milan until Leo or Kadian came off assignment.

"I was thinking of inventing a chemical that will melt his current paint job, imbedding itself into the steel of the body so it would then perpetually do the same to every subsequent paint job he attempts to get afterward. Clever, huh?"

"Extremely clever. However, it's not appropriate to do it with company funds or equipment, babe."

"Well! Since when are *you* the numbers geek around here?" she demanded huffily. "The geek is off hiding from me, so who cares who does what with company funds? It would serve him right if we go bankrupt while he's hiding like the chicken-shit wiener that he is!"

"Now, Roni . . ."

"Don't you 'now Roni' me like I'm some hysterical twit PMSing and in need of a pat on the head and some Ben and

Jerry's to get her through the crisis! It's just like you men to stick together!"

She hung up with an angry growl into the phone.

Liam sighed. The world was in a sorry state, he thought, the day it depended on him to be the diplomatic voice of reason.

Chapter Four

Devon was tapping her nails against the desk in a slow, rhythmic pattern. She watched the camera monitors as the small fleet of trucks and Hummers wound their way up her driveway. She wasn't at all upset by the intrusion this installation promised to be. Nor was she nervous about having humans around the house constantly. After all, she had been fully human once upon a time. And, unlike some of her brethren, she found humans to be useful, wonderful people. Like Liam Nash, for instance. He was an extraordinary individual. He was clearly a hardnosed soldier from teeth to toes. Yet she was already aware, after such a brief amount of time in his company, that he was so much more than that. While she wasn't going to claim to be an expert on him after so limited an exposure, she had noted one very important thing. He had a gentle side. It had been in the delicacy of his touch, the abundance of his concern, as he had put aside his righteously earned indignation at her uninvited touch in order to tend to her well-being. The contrast between those two facets had kept her thinking about him frequently over the past couple of days.

Even though the images on the screens were distorted by

the camera angles, Devon knew him the moment she saw him jump out of the back of a truck. There were men and women running around all over the place now, all dressed in what she assumed was identical black, but still she recognized him. How could anyone mistake a build like his? His height alone was astounding, even to a woman of her 5'9" stature. Add to it pounds of muscle in beautifully strategic places, a rugged but surprisingly handsome face, and strange amber colored eyes with gold and umber flecks in them. Devon was unaware that she lightly licked her lips as she admired the broad field of his chest and the sinew roping down his arms. His black T-shirt clung to both like a second skin. She licked her lips again, wondering if he had any body art. Human body art was fascinating to her. Because of the way Morphates healed, their bodies refused to hold the ink of any tattoo not acquired before their transformation into Morphates. The art would fade, like any other foreign injury, within a few days. She really rather wished she'd been the type to get tattoos before she'd had her run-in with Dr. Eric Paulson. On the other hand, living with artwork forever seemed like a very long time, and right now it didn't look like Morphates were ever going to age.

Devon let her eyes move over Nash as he hauled things off the truck, his huge body twisting and bending with fluid ease. His strong, muscular legs glided and bent as needed, showing no hint of error in movement despite the awful leg wounds he had suffered during the previously mentioned encounter with a Morphate while in the Secret Service.

Devon wondered if his crew knew he was the first human, the first *person*, to ever figure out how to permanently destroy a Morphate. His report had claimed it to be a stroke of luck, and so it might have been, but it wasn't as though the weapon were a mainstream material or, as he had mentioned, anything a human being would willingly want to touch for fear of its toxicity.

Irradiated mercury.

Devon had gleaned from her conversation with Nash that his team could be appropriately armed with mercury-filled bullets. She had to assume that meant they were trained in the handling of them as well as their purpose. The toxic ammunition, while instantly fatal to Morphates, was potentially just as poisonous to anyone who handled it. Mercury broke down body tissue on contact no matter what the species. Radioactive mercury . . . well, that was a no-brainer.

Mercury ammunition was ineffective without a way for the liquid metal to break out of the bullet. Often, when a bullet impacted the internal bone structure of the body, it would deform on impact, which would release any substance contained within the bullet. However, just as often it would remain intact. The shooter couldn't depend on those odds when in a fight for his or her life. At present, those who knew about the effects of mercury on Morphates used bullets tipped with a wax-like substance. It held the mercury in during storage, as well as for the duration of the trip down the gun barrel and to the target, but dissolved quickly at body temperature. The result was effective and deadly, culminating in a gaseous cloud of Morphate remains.

However, accidents were frequent and misfires dangerous or deadly. The ammunition couldn't be used in the summer safely when high temperatures threatened the special wax plugs. Carelessness could end in mercury leaking everywhere, poisoning the weapon's carrier. The delivery system, as Nash had pointed out, was flawed and unstable and had needed dire improvement.

Devon had seen to it that the military would court Candler International for the solution, and she was in the process of providing one. The first prototypes were resting carefully in the armory behind the surveillance room she now sat in. She would introduce Nash to them shortly. She smiled when she thought of how his face would awaken with excitement, just as it had when she'd told him she'd come up with the solution in the first place.

Just like it had when she'd touched him.

Mmm, an unsafe thought, she scolded herself as she watched him move and speak with his team. He was a beautiful specimen of masculinity, there was no denying that, and part of her itched to get a peek at the underlying sexuality she sensed within him, but unfortunately they were going to have a working relationship and she always felt that it was best if work and play remained separate. Besides, it was one thing for her to work with, make friends with, and come to rely on humans, and quite another to sleep with them.

Oh, it wasn't unheard of. There were humans out there who could tolerate the savageness of Morphate lovemaking. In fact, some sought it out specifically for its roughness and, of course, the blood drinking aspects. But it was something of an unspoken understanding among lawful Morphates that humans ought to be avoided whenever possible, especially in this respect.

However, there were also unlawful Morphates. Morphates who looked on humans as lesser individuals, with no more or even less value than a domesticated animal. That led to a frightening devaluation. Those Morphates thought it all right to use humans and discard them cruelly. So far such activity had not been discovered by mainstream humans, but rumors were beginning to circulate . . . even more so now that Dark Phoenix had broken free of the Alpha Council and its laws. And if humans knew just how savage and psychotic these unlawful Morphates could be, relations between the races would devolve into chaos.

But in the present climate of Morphate rebellion and feuding, discovery was only a matter of time. That was why it was so crucial that Morphates and humans alike discover ways to protect themselves against the superhuman strength and savagery of the unlawful Morphates. Perhaps just knowing protection existed would help curb the unlawful Morphates.

As for herself, Devon wasn't fond of lying and passing herself off as just another human. Nor would she ever use a human in such base and evil ways. She found humans to be spirited and beautiful. She, unlike some, remembered that she had once been a human, and she remembered what human cruelty had felt like when she had been stripped of all her rights and been experimented on by Dr. Paulson until she had become what she was now.

If she ever did indulge in relations with a human, it would have to be with the truth between them. Otherwise, she would be no better than the beastly worst of her arrogant brethren.

And *they* disgusted her.

Morphates had the potential to be a wonderful species. Devon believed that with all of her heart and her soul. But things had gotten out of control, the decades of focus spent on trying to rebuild Dark Cities that had devolved into chaos and filth had been unbelievably hard on both the original Morphates and their new generations.

Devon remembered those days all too well.

But that had been a very long time ago. Many things had changed, and now she felt it was time for a little equalization between Morphates and humans. Before it was too late. Before humans found themselves overrun and overpowered and all their best ideals stolen from them.

And yes, she had a private agenda. Devon was playing a dangerous game, and now she was dragging more innocents into the fray by protecting herself with the humans from NHK. But she couldn't use a Morphate protection force, not considering the details of her research and its purpose. For although Nash thought he was protecting her, what he was actually protecting was her research and the prototypes. But NHK at least would have a far better chance than anyone else. Why not with Liam at the helm? After all, he was the only human she was aware of who had experience killing a Morphate. Besides, if she had surrounded herself with loyal Morphates, it would have made for just another clan in a war full of bickering clans. No. When she had her victory, it would be with humans by her side. They deserved to fight for their liberties as they traditionally always had. Except this time, they wouldn't quite understand what they were fighting for, or even necessarily that they were part of an intense war.

The playing fields were about to be drastically altered.

Devon had been working in secret for decades, hiding from her enemies as she had strived to make her plans come together. She needed to fulfill her obligation to the mortal military, bringing her people down a peg by placing in human hands the means to level the field. It was a slippery slope. What would then keep the humans from mounting an all-out war against Morphates and using their new weapons to eradicate the interlopers entirely? But she could ask the same of Morphates who had guns. Good or bad, she had committed to her course and she would stick to the outcome. She refused to allow herself to consider what would happen should she fail. Things were already rising to a head between the feuding clans, as well as the racist Morphate and human factions. She knew she was racing against time.

The idea of losing the race woke her up at night screaming in terror and soaking in sweat.

She laughed nervously under her breath at herself, shaking her head and shoulders as if shedding water; only she was trying to shed her sensations of gloom and doom. It did no one any good to get fatalistic. She simply needed to concentrate on one stage at a time. It was the best she could do. Right now that meant concentrating on helping Nash and his people settle in, discussing routines, and sharing other details she thought pertinent. Devon didn't doubt that Nash would be inundating her with recommendations as well. She found herself looking forward to spending time with him. Perhaps over the next six months she would get to know him a little better.

In fact, she wanted to get to know everyone a little better. Including Mr. Carter Spencer. She had trusted him all of this time. Could he be a traitor? Had he actually allowed that murderer into her bedroom at the hotel, telling her enemy how, when, and where to find her? The mercury-filled bullet had gone completely through her leg, minimizing the damage, but leaving enough traces of the deadly metal behind to make healing excruciatingly slow even for one of her rapidly healing species. Her people could even heal themselves after decapitation if the body and head were reunited, no matter how long afterward. They did not decompose, their flesh immune to earthly bacteria and unappealing to flora and fauna that usually tried to break remains down. So long as the parts were joined and blood flow reestablished, there was nothing short of radical bombs that could do what one little dose of irradiated mercury could do.

She had been damn lucky that night. When she had disarmed her opponent and held his neck beneath her foot, he had gloated that she was as good as dead anyway because there was a ten-million-dollar price on her head. She had shot him repeatedly with his own weapon until her foot passed through nothing but vapor. And here it was a week later and she still hurt when she sat and limped when she walked if she wasn't paying close attention.

Infuriating.

When she got hold of whoever was behind the attacks . . . their days would be numbered. Alpha Council was going to pull them in quite sharply. And Liam Nash was going to help her do that.

There was a scuffing sound to her right and she looked up to see the devil himself looming in the doorway. He had struck a casual arm up against the doorframe, making all the muscles and lean lines up and down his left side flex in orchestrated male beauty. It took her breath away. Maybe that was why she had to inhale so slow and deep. It shouldn't have anything to do with her trying to get her fill of his incredible scent. Soap, sweat, and the bold aroma of the outdoors, all combined with that unique factor that was only Liam; that unique factor that made him so irrepressibly male. It swirled in her senses and set her nerves tingling at their ends. She couldn't help but smile.

Liam watched as she turned from her study of the monitors and speared him with those lichen green eyes, their polished surface gleaming with quick, intense thought as she recognized his presence. There was something almost predatory in her expression for the smallest second, but just as his chest tightened with an excited anxiety, she let a smile grow slowly over her pale pink lips. She straightened from her observations and turned to face him fully. Liam couldn't resist running his eyes down the length of her. Not just because she was so fantastically designed, but also because it was an ingrained habit to observe everything he could about everyone, making life for him and those for whom he was responsible safer.

Devon Candler had a way of wearing clothes as though she were born in them. Last time it had been loose, transparent white gauze, this time it was elegant, calf-length black silk with no sleeves and a modest dip of her neckline to just about an inch below the start of her stunning cleavage. The silk was so soft it clung to every single curve from neck to calf, and it was spun with a shine so it gleamed and glittered over every deep swell, drawing attention to every movement. She was wearing stilettos and no stockings. The heels tightened her calves, raised the thrust of her backside and forced her shoulders back so her breasts were gorgeously prominent.

Liam felt as though he had just walked into a wet dream. His blood boiled fast and hot and he began to grow hard just

from the sight of her. He gritted his teeth together, furious
with his inability to keep his body under his own control
when she was around. He *never* behaved this way around
women! Even if he was attracted to them, he didn't get an
instant hard-on just by the look of them. Christ, that hadn't
happened to him since high school and here she'd already
done it to him twice. More, if he counted just thinking about
her over the past couple of days.

"Are you going out?" he asked roughly, forcing himself
back on task as he registered the formality of her attire, as
opposed to the way it clung to her semi-erect nipples.

"Yes. I have a business dinner date," she informed him,
lowering her eyes. Lowering. And lowering. Then they climbed
back up, slowly but surely, after giving him a very thorough
once-over that singed just about every hair on his body. Did
the woman have any idea how much raw sexuality she
exuded? Was she purposely playing some kind of game?
Looking for a fantasy with a bodyguard like in some cheap
Hollywood film? If so, he'd be setting her straight damn
quick. She was hot, but she wasn't hot enough to burn away
his integrity or his moral sense of self.

"You shouldn't leave the house until we've finished with
our initial insertion, worked out a schedule, and begun to
comprehend how you maneuver throughout the day. I thought
I made that clear when we signed the contract."

"I'm not about to hold you responsible for my life when
you've only been here for ten minutes. I'll be gone for three
hours at most. You'll hardly notice my absence."

"Trust me, I will," he assured her darkly, standing
straighter to brace himself on both feet in the doorframe, as if
he had every intention of blocking her from leaving. "You'll
never leave this house without a full escort. I'll determine the
meaning of the word 'full,' by the way. The minute you signed
that contract, Devon, you became my responsibility, and I
take my responsibilities very seriously."

"As any good leader must do. I understand that. However, this is an important meeting and I won't cancel."

"Then I have no choice but to change my clothes and accompany you. Flores will attend also. I need the others here for now, but in the future you'll have anywhere from two to four of us near you at all times when away from the house." He reached up to touch the nearly invisible patch of pink under his ear. "Flores. I need you dressed and prepped VIP, ASAP, copy?"

"Give me ten, Leader," she responded.

"Gordon."

"Leader?"

"Go over the limo with a comb, ASAP."

"Copy that."

"Will my team be lodging in the east wing?" Liam asked Devon. "I assumed that since that wing is the farthest from your private quarters, you'd prefer it. I'll want a west wing room, however. I'll sleep better if I'm within shouting distance of you."

"You have the run of the house, Mr. Nash. I gave you my exclusions. All else is open to you and your personnel, including the recreation facilities and the training room. I'm certain you will enjoy them."

"It's Liam," he said, disliking her use of the formality for some reason. "That's kind of you, but we have facilities at the NHK compound, and after this initial week, I will be the only one living here 24/7."

"Then I invite you to use whatever would make you feel at home, Liam."

It was quite an invitation, being made in that dress with that purring, throaty pitch of voice she had. Not to mention that certain way she stood, hands roaming her belly, hips or thighs in minute, absently erotic movements. The double entendre in her invitation couldn't be a mistake of his mind. He ignored the physiological responses of his throbbing body and decided to set her straight right off the bat. He glanced around and then entered the room so he could close the door.

"I hope I'm not overstepping myself, Devon," he began as politely as he could manage. "I just want to make sure you understood that this is a business arrangement. I keep business and pleasure absolutely separate. Do you understand?" He gave her a meaningful look, hoping she'd get it and that would be the end of her innuendo.

"I see," she mused with one of those mysteriously compelling smiles. "And you think I don't adhere to that same ethic, Liam?"

Abruptly put on the spot, Liam cleared his throat. "It's just that there seems to be this . . . sometimes I get the feeling that . . ."

"That there is a connection between us so arousing and disconcerting it's like sucking on a lightning bolt?" she provided helpfully.

"I . . ." Liam leaned back against the door, as if something had deflated him halfway. "Yeah. That's an accurate description," he admitted with a low laugh.

"You needn't worry," she reassured him. "I am quite capable of maintaining boundaries. Did you think I would throw myself at you? Make a nuisance of myself?" She stepped forward and reached for her purse. "I find you to be a very vital and attractive man, Liam Nash, but you're . . . not quite my type."

That had just become a damn shame, Liam thought as his libido began to career off its axis. When she had stepped forward, her gown had shifted, and Liam had rapidly realized it was entirely transparent. *What the hell was it with this woman and her fabrics*? Didn't she own anything that was more than a micron thick? Liam swallowed hard as his eyes drifted over the shadowed curves of her breasts and their pronounced, jutting nipples; followed the span of her belly to her navel; then lower, only to find the silk had been tauntingly thickened with a thin crescent of embroidery that stretched from one hip to another, dipping dangerously low against bare and beautifully feminine places. He knew she was naked beneath because there was no such embroidery along her side and he saw no sign of panties. It made him wonder if there was any modesty to the rear of the gown.

Liam's eyes darted back to her face, where that smile was still in place, but he instantly realized it was forced and that her face was flushed. He shifted his gaze lower and saw her pulse beating rapidly in her throat. Then he went lower again so he could reconcile what he'd just seen with something he already knew. The thrust of those pretty, dark nipples was there because she was excited. *By him*. Even though she claimed he was not her type.

Liam was moving before he even realized his intentions. He reached for the hand on her purse and circled her wrist, using it to pull her closer. Her heels tapped out two steps as she was compelled forward until she bumped into him like a car in a carnival ride. They were chest to chest now, as Liam's hand slid into the small of her back, his broad palm spreading open. He could hear her breathing increasing in tempo. He could feel the tips of her breasts rubbing against him. He could also feel the pressure of her warm, taut belly along the shaft of his rigid cock.

"You come that willingly? You know almost nothing about me," he managed to rough out. "You walk into my arms, with your body so exposed . . ."

"I know what I feel. And I know what you feel. For the moment, that is enough."

"And everything we just said about working boundaries?" he asked hoarsely as her body snuggled tighter against him with just one little shift in the bend of her knee. He groaned deeply, the feeling so much like a lock fitted with the perfect key. Because he was such a big man, he had always considered the experience something that would be forever outside the realm of possibility for him. He'd even thought people were overrating the sensation. But he was now faced with the evidence of how shockingly wrong he'd been. It shook him considerably, how incredible it felt to have her locked to the length of his body so perfectly. It was eerie, how she seemed made to fit him. His mind leapt ahead, wondering hotly in what other ways she might make a perfect fit for him.

The raw sexuality of the thought stabbed through him and Liam suddenly released Devon, stepping back so unexpectedly that she swayed for balance a moment. She caught herself by laying a hand on the security control console.

And then she laughed at him. But it was so bemused and kindly a sound that he felt no embarrassment.

"Liam," she said, his name so inviting on her lips that he regretted letting her be so personal one moment, and then wouldn't have it any other way the next. "Why don't we just relax as best we can around one another and acknowledge that it will be a challenge to maintain the boundaries we would normally impose on ourselves? I don't want to feel that I've broken my word if there should be," she raised a palm, gently waving two fingers to indicate their close proximity, "lapses."

"I disagree," he snapped. "There will be no more lapses."

Devon watched him turn sharply on his heel and leave the room, probably expending a mighty effort not to slam the door behind him. She exhaled as if she hadn't breathed in ages, sagging against the top of the control desk. Lord, but that man had some powerful sex appeal. The thing was, she didn't think he knew it.

What she did know was that a man like Liam Nash was going to need an outlet for his volatile feelings, but he was going to have to put it off until after tonight's meeting was over.

Since he didn't appear to be the sort of man who took well to sitting on his temper for long periods of time, he would probably be a very dangerous person to be around come the end of the night.

Why that thought gave her such a thrill was completely beyond her.

Chapter Five

Inez Flores had known Liam Nash for three years, so she considered herself just familiar enough with him to know when something was wrong. Unfortunately, she didn't consider herself familiar enough to ask him about it. Liam was a wonderful employer, a stellar trainer and a good man in general, but he didn't let his companions get too close. It was an aspect of his personality that had taken some adjustment at first.

Inez had been used to cops who shared close personal relationships, who considered each other family. Like the partnership she had with Kellen. Her seven-year-old, Parker, called him Uncle Kellen. Her partner practically lived on her sofa during their off time, even though he had a gorgeous condo of his own to go home to. For all his machismo, Kellen didn't like being alone. A large extended family and life in the military had gotten him used to being around a lot of people. Inez supposed one rambunctious boy could easily dispel that sense of loneliness.

It was likely that Liam felt he had to remain aloof in order to maintain his command, but it was more than that. Or rather, less than that. He was used to working in a team, finding a rhythm so everything ran in perfect synchronicity, but she suspected that individual personal relationships baffled him. Even his relationship with Colin, his own brother, seemed distant. Oh, no one doubted that Liam would walk through the burning fires of hell for his brother, but he was no closer to Colin than to anyone else under his command.

Inez sat at the restaurant table across from Liam, dressed in one of the designer dresses she was allotted every year so that in situations like this she could blend in unremarkably. Technically, she and Liam had been out on about a hundred dates over the last three years; just like this, sitting as though they were a normal couple instead of heavily armed and alert bodyguards. She watched exits and distant persons; he watched the principal and those near her.

Frankly, after learning exactly who was after Devon Candler, and that they had what Liam termed 'a powerful motivation' to obliterate her, Inez would have felt more comfortable with more backup. Kellen had been left in charge of the house in Liam's absence, and she felt naked without him. Not that she wouldn't trust her life to Liam in a heartbeat. Because she would. However, she had a connection with Kellen that couldn't be duplicated.

But for the moment she was dependent on Liam, and Colin was their only backup as he waited outside under the guise of their limo driver. As a cop she'd faced down a rare Morphate or two and it had been a terrifying experience. She'd once emptied two 9mm clips into one, and that had only slowed the perp down long enough for them to make an arrest as quickly as they could. By the time they got the Morphate back to the station he'd already been conscious and healing.

Inez's dress was black and fell to just above her knees. It was conservative around the neckline and sleeves because she had to wear her new NHK armored vest under it. She loved the new vest. It was so light and perfectly fitted to her to accommodate her busty proportions. Most armor smashed her boobs down and that was a bitch to handle for eight- to ten-hour shifts. Veronica Klein was a genius, and anyone who said different was a jackass. Liam was brilliant in her book as well. He'd had a strong hand in the ergonomics of the design; like the part about tailoring it to fit the individual. That thoughtfulness inspired devotion and loyalty from one's troops, so it really perturbed her to see Liam out of sorts, knowing she couldn't do anything about it.

If Liam had heard her describe him as 'out of sorts,' he would have found the description woefully insufficient. He sat facing Devon, who was only two tables away from them. He could see her, as well as her smarmy date, quite clearly. He had to admit, the man was a classic. Tall, dark, handsome, and positively oozing charm. He was also constantly finding reasons to touch Devon. On her hand over the table, rubbing her back as he seated her, or touching her neck and face in an obvious flirtation whenever they got up to dance.

Whenever they danced, Liam pulled Inez into his arms and joined them so he could keep closer watch. The dress Devon was almost wearing caught a great deal of attention, so it was very difficult to sort out carnal interest from potential threat. An attacker's intent was always in his eyes first as he tracked and mentally pinned down his victim. Just about everything in the room with a penis was tracking and mentally pinning Devon Candler down as her luscious body slid with grace under the gossamer silk. She wasn't the only woman dressed in the risqué diaphanous fashion, but Liam was convinced she could have drawn the same attention in sackcloth with her knockout build and the way she exuded pure sex.

At least she seemed to be taking their protective presence in stride. She hardly ever looked in his or Inez's direction. What Liam wanted to know was, what had been so damned important about this dinner? She'd called it a meeting, but it looked more like a seduction. Was this clown what she considered her 'type'? Liam couldn't imagine how. Sure, he had looks, charisma, and the ability to sit prettily in what he imagined was her social circle, but that was outside appearances only. There was too much going on beneath all that perfect peach skin for Devon Candler to be satisfied with such artifice. In fact, the more he watched the couple, the more he could see she was wearing out her escort's façade, testing his social skills to the fullest. He began to make little errors, and Liam watched those pale green eyes of hers make quick note of each and every one before becoming perfectly inscrutable. Their conversation was making her date increasingly uncomfortable or nervous. Liam hadn't decided which one it was yet.

The barricade behind her exotic eyes was also a hint of an anomaly. Even after so short an acquaintance, he had come to understand that she allowed her emotions to play easily. At least, she did when she was behind the walls of her home. Was it just this man, or was it the exterior environment? He wished he'd had time to prepare for this 'meeting.' Time to get to know her better psychologically so he could read any signals of distress she might send purposely or inadvertently. He would have researched this guy down to his jockey shorts and made certain he wasn't a threat to Devon.

Liam narrowed his eyes when she pulled her hand away from her companion for the second time in as many minutes, but before she could clear her water glass, her escort grabbed her by the wrist and jerked her forward slightly, rocking the liquid in the glasses as he shook the table.

"Kienan, you will release me and discontinue making a spectacle of us this instant," Devon hissed softly.

"I won't be dictated to in this manner, Devona," he jeered over the table.

"I make no dictates, only requests and arguments of logic, which you fail to see because you can't get past your masculine ego! Why must this be about your pursuit of something you'll never have, Kienan? Is this the only reason you've come here tonight?" she demanded.

"But of course not," he backtracked quickly, smiling with charm as he ran his fingernails over the inside of her captive wrist. "Nevertheless, you can't deny the attraction between us. You reek of sexual desire, Devona. I can smell that juicy little—"

"Excuse me." A throat cleared from far above their seated positions, cutting off what promised to be a truly crude remark. Kienan would never know how lucky he was that Liam had interrupted it. "I was wondering if you'd mind lending me your partner for a dance?"

Nash didn't wait for an answer before gently drawing up her free hand and pulling Devon to her feet. Kienan persisted in his grasp for an indecisive moment, but Liam's quelling, patient stare made her escort laugh and let go. He leaned back in his chair and waved his hand in dismissal.

Liam placed a hand on her back, feeling silk and the warmth of her skin against his fingertips and palm once more, just as he had done so briefly in the security room. He led her to the floor, his eyes flowing easily over everyone surrounding them, over her abandoned date, and then to Inez, who was making her way over to Kienan to fill Devon's empty seat. He strategically kept Devon's back to the small intervention that would occur, drawing her closer until she lightly brushed the length of his body with hers.

"You look quite handsome in silk," she complimented him, reaching to slide one lapel of his jacket between her fingers. "You have an excellent tailor. Most don't know the best way to fit a man of your proportions."

He knew she was right and he laughed shortly to reflect his surprise. "Not many people would realize that. Know many large men?"

"No," she said simply. She didn't elaborate and it made him smile with genuine humor, sarcasm deleted.

"Are you well?" he asked. "He had quite a grip on you." He reached up and slid her hand down to his chest from his shoulder, rubbing warm, calloused fingers over the reddened skin of her wrist.

"I'm fine, thank you. There was no need to rescue me." She smiled as she looked up at him. "But I'm glad you did. It was a better way of defusing the situation than what was about to happen."

"Are you saying you would have been so unladylike in public? In a place like this?" He cast his eyes around the opulent restaurant. He was grinning though.

"You tease me about my manners?" She sniffed. "Although I must say you may have the right to. Your manners have been flawless all evening toward your escort, even though it's a guise. And you dance very well."

"Now," he confided meaningfully.

"Are you saying you weren't the best of dance students?" she teased.

"Up until I realized dancing meant I could have a legitimate reason for holding beautiful, unattainable women close," he admitted.

She laughed aloud and Liam watched over her shoulder as heads turned to look at her. She was oblivious to her effect on the room. "What do you mean 'unattainable'? There isn't a woman on earth who would deny a man who looks this sexy in a tuxedo."

"I've had my share of rejections, I assure you."

"Then again, women can be foolish, capricious creatures," she said dismissively, smiling when he chuckled. She tilted her head and studied him for a moment as he turned her into the light steps of the dance. "I must say, I'm amazed by your lack of awareness about how much sexual magnetism you have."

Said the pot to the kettle, Liam thought. "Perhaps it's just a matter of my having discarded that awareness because I'm on duty," he suggested.

She watched him smile a bit slyly and she knew he was full of it. "I think it's more a matter of it making you uncomfortable, so you discard it as unimportant and unworthy of your attention unless it can be used as a tool. A means to an end."

"Ouch." Liam winced. "That sounds terribly cold."

"I suppose so," she agreed unexpectedly, making him laugh. "But bear with me a moment. You are, at heart, a soldier. Your dedication is proven by the fact that you plan to live at the manor 24/7 in order to supervise your staff for the length of my contract. That's six months, Liam. It's bordering on obsessive." She lifted a soft finger to his lips when he parted them to protest. "Taking your dedication into consideration, it's smart to conclude that you are used to perpetually plotting your every move, and how to most effectively control the actions of others around you in order to obtain your goals. In this instance, seeing to my safety. Now, if in the course of your 24/7 work you might need to use your sex appeal to gain an advantage, you will. It's an asset and you're aware of it, from what you claim, so why not use it as a tool?" She dropped her hand from his mouth and patted her fingers against his biceps. "It's no different from muscle or a gun. And I mean no insult. I use the tactic myself."

"Is that what you've been doing tonight? Because I might point out it has gotten you in trouble already," he said, frowning slightly.

"Would you like the truth?"

Liam felt a strange twist in his belly. It was clearly a warning, as if he might not like what he heard. Liam didn't relish hearing she was actually attracted to that asshole at the table, because, frankly, he thought her smarter than that. He didn't want to learn otherwise. Then again, maybe a little truth was exactly what he needed to distance himself from this unadvisable connection he kept succumbing to.

"Of course. I prefer honesty and bluntness at all opportunities," he said. "As you pointed out, I'm a soldier. My needs are uncomplicated and I prefer it that way."

"I didn't mean for the observation to be used as either an insult or a limitation," she told him with a frown. "You are, I imagine, far more complicated an individual than either of us realizes."

He dodged that bullet smoothly. "So tell me the truth about your date tonight."

Devon knew she couldn't tell him everything, but that fell under omission, not lying. She drew a breath. "I was highly aroused before I even arrived here. I merely borrowed on that tension within myself to try to warm an otherwise uncomfortable evening. I don't like Kienan very much, but I do need him."

Through Kienan she hoped to manipulate one of the two largest factions that had withdrawn from the Alpha council. He was not an Alpha himself, but he was second in command to one and she needed to use him in order to obtain the ear of the one who mattered. He'd been after her for some time, and she'd borrowed on that to get her foot in the door. Otherwise he would never have taken her meeting.

Liam stopped still at her declaration, suddenly unable to make his feet move as he stared down into her jade eyes. Her implication rang through him like a crystal bell, bringing his nerves to attention.

She had been already aroused.

He couldn't miss her reference to that brief moment when he'd held her earlier. Especially not while holding her just as closely now. Her heat burned his hand at the small of her back; her scent rose all around him and there was a slight increase in the tempo of her breathing. The same as earlier, only this time they were in public, her date and his co-worker watching them. It was enough of a reminder to force him back into the rhythm of the dance.

"You're definitely blunt," he said gruffly. "I'm going to have to get used to that. Women usually have an art to their speech that makes conversation with them like trying to find your way through a maze."

"I prefer to make myself undeniably clear," she said. "I don't like—"

She stopped so suddenly to whip her head around that Liam was instantly on guard. He swung her behind himself, placing her nearest the least occupied corner of the room, tracking the direction she'd been looking in.

"Explain," he demanded shortly, quickly scanning eyes around the room for trouble.

"I . . . I heard something," she lied awkwardly. "I thought someone said my name and . . ."

"Got it," he said grimly. He glanced at Inez, who swiftly rose to her feet and joined his visual scan. He touched that little pink spot beneath his ear again. "Let's get her out of here," he instructed Inez. She nodded, moving quickly to them.

"I've given your regrets to your companion," she told Devon gently.

They each took one of her arms and led her to the back of the restaurant.

"Colin's meeting us in back."

Liam didn't draw his weapon until they were in the kitchen. Devon was relieved that he did because she knew there was another Morphate in the area. She could smell whoever it was, unfamiliar and feminine. She found herself in the awkward position of having information she couldn't share with her protectors without giving herself away, and she simply couldn't risk disclosure. Would he suspect a woman as quickly as he would a man? The Morphate was close. Very close. Devon's heart pounded, adrenaline and defensive instincts roaring to the surface. She pressed her lips together as her fangs began to lengthen in reflex, and curled her hands to hide the growth of her nails.

Liam felt tension and resistance in his principal. It wasn't good. If she didn't cooperate, it could make things difficult. He pushed open the outside door, checking all corners quickly and looking for Colin. He ducked back inside.

"It's clear," he told Inez. Inez knew he wouldn't expose Devon to the exterior until he heard Colin pulling up.

Liam looked down at Devon and her wide eyes, realizing he could see the pounding of her heart against the silk covering her chest. "You'll be safe in a minute," he assured her softly against her ear.

"No," she breathed, panting in quick bursts. "No."

He thought she was having an anxiety attack for about two seconds. Then he realized that she just didn't seem the type. His hackles rose instantly and he turned his back to her and scanned the kitchen. He felt her hands grip his jacket for just a moment, but she let go quickly before he could warn her not to entangle him. He could've kissed her for being so bright even though they'd had no time to train her on the rules.

Liam heard the limo pull up and he moved to the door again, checking all directions quickly along the sight of his automatic pistol. Then all three of them, Colin, Liam, and Inez, surrounded Devon and drew her, huddled, down to the rear of the car. Suddenly Devon snapped upright and spun around, shouting, "Liam!"

The female came at them like living darkness, starting nowhere, ending nowhere, but everywhere at once. Inez was struck with blinding speed, her body thrown back into the side of the limousine. As she whiplashed from the force of it, her impact sending fractures through the tinted glass, Devon could see the front of her gown had been torn away, revealing her armor and four distinctive furrows in the outer fabric of the protection.

Liam took the opportunity to grab Devon. He caught mostly fabric, but it was enough to propel her back into the rear of the limousine, where she would be safe. He ignored the tearing of the silk, his eyes hunting for his enemy. Colin had time to arm himself even as he reached to lay a hand over Inez's chest to steady her and keep her from falling.

"Nez! You okay?"

It shook Inez out of her shock and she shrugged him off viciously as she grabbed for the weapon strapped underneath her skirt.

"Fucking *puta*!" Inez spat, whirling around to find her target.

"A woman?"

"Brunette, my size, strong as hell," Inez barked. Liam wanted to smile that Inez had caught sight of something that fast. Then again, she'd gotten quite a close-up.

Then he was drawn fully to focus on a second attack, this time singling out Liam. It was a big mistake. Liam remembered the feel of Morphate claws all too well, but he knew as soon as he heard the fabric of his jacket rend that he would be feeling a painful reminder in a second or two. The claws were so sharp the wounds were like paper cuts that he wouldn't feel for the better part of a minute. He used his minute to discharge his weapon. Colin and Inez followed the beam of his laser sight to react as well. Three and then six mercury-filled bullets flew into the target. Liam heard the ricochet of at least two misses. That was the darkness and the target's speed working against them. The assailant dropped down right on top of them, and Liam saw a red sight point appear on Colin's forehead. Liam grabbed for hair and jerked the deadly bitch back into the impact of his rising knee in the center of her back. Her shot went wild. Inez leapt right in and fired her gun point blank into the woman's chest. The impact drove her down to the pavement, her vicious fangs flashing dangerously close to Inez's arm.

"Shit! She's wearing Kevlar!"

They barely registered that before the assassin was whirling back up to her feet, grabbing Inez by the throat. Deadly claws folded over Inez's carotid artery in the time it took Liam to aim.

Nash fired once.

The assassin whipped back, an expression of shock in her eyes as her hand slipped uselessly from Inez's throat. "No Kevlar there," he noted as blood oozed from the hole in her forehead.

The female adversary dropped like a stone. Colin and Liam stepped up and emptied four more rounds into her. When the spasms started, they stepped away and watched as the body dissolved into streams of gas, finally ending in an explosive puff before dissipating, leaving empty clothing and a pile of personal items behind.

"Cool," Colin murmured. Inez nodded in agreement. It was the first time they had actually killed a Morphate and seen the end result.

"Colin, drive. Inez, shotgun. Keep your eyes peeled. Let's get the hell out of here before someone calls the cops."

Liam bent to scoop up the Kevlar vest and clothing left behind, gritting his teeth as his shoulder pulled the wrong way against the slices through his skin. Quickly he tossed the telltale remnants of the deadly encounter onto the floor of the limo as he jumped in. It wouldn't do for the local cops to come across the empty outfit and start asking questions that could invite a world of trouble.

The car screeched out of the alley, tossing Nash back hard against the seat next to Devon. Gun in hand and at the ready, he shoved himself up and watched the windows as they tore away from the restaurant. When they were speeding along the highway at last, he finally relaxed back with a mighty exhalation.

"First thing, we're putting bulletproof glass on this limousine," he said with disgust. "That was too damn close. Inez is lucky her head is still attached." Liam holstered his weapon and winced with a sharp intake of breath as the movement pulled open the rents left in his shoulder by the assailant.

"You're injured!" Devon exclaimed, noticing his reaction right away. She reached across his lap to his opposite shoulder, a cloud of thick hair swishing over his nose and lips as she tried to pull his jacket back.

"Ow! Shit!" Liam shouted as she pulled the skin. He felt blood rolling down his arm, chest, and back.

"Sit up," she commanded. "Take that jacket off."

"Stop worrying about me. I'm fine. Are you okay?"

She gave him a dirty look for his attempt to divert her attention from his injury. Her nose was inches away from his, her vivid eyes flashing cold green fire so fierce, it was just about the most beautiful thing Liam had ever seen. He instantly became pliant to her wishes, not even thinking to be curious about the atypical response. She slid his jacket down his arms, being much gentler this time. She found herself faced with a shoulder holster that kept her from stripping him of his shirt as well.

"Don't even ask it. The gun stays," he grumbled darkly when she looked at him askance.

"Of course. I was going to ask if you have a knife."

Without hesitation, Liam pulled one from his jacket pocket and handed it to her. She expertly sprang the switchblade and he raised a questioning brow at her skill. "I told you I know how to take care of myself," she reminded him with a mischievous smile when she caught the look.

"So you did," he mused.

Devon sliced through the silk shirt until his shoulder was fully exposed. Blood was seeping from the furrows freely now and she cut away the entire sleeve of his shirt to use for a pressure bandage. She folded it quickly, pressing it against him hard to stop the bleeding. When she leaned her weight forward, Liam sucked his breath in through his teeth. Her position over his lap brought her cheek brushing against his. She could feel his whiskers against her skin, her hair clinging to them as she pulled back in order to make herself look at the pain on his face. She was responsible for this, she thought, and she must face it. She needed to face it. It kept her grounded deeply in the grave reality of her world.

She watched Liam's initial pain fade, and she bit her lower lip hard when his amber eyes finally opened and focused on her nearby face. He searched her expression for a long moment. "It's not your fault," he said, his voice soft in the quiet of the limousine's rear seat. The tinted, soundproof partition between driver and passenger compartments created an intimate privacy.

"Then whose?" she demanded. "Never once absolve me of blame in this, Liam Nash. I accept your role and the fact that you may die saving my life, but I won't accept lack of blame. Do you understand?"

Liam thought he did. She was too proud for false assurances, and too brave for her own good. He saw the hard courage she was hanging on to and he admired her for it. Few people could accept these circumstances, and accept reasonable responsibility for them while they were at it. She was truly a remarkable woman.

He reached up to brush back her hair, tucking it behind her ear for a moment while he ran his thumb along a baby-soft cheek. She wore no base, no powder, only those wicked accents of darkness lining the edges of her eyes, making their exotic slant even more pronounced and her irises more intensely green.

"I won't make the mistake again," he assured her, dragging

his thumb down to her lush lips and passing over the lower one slowly. "Now please answer my question. Are you okay?"

"I'm fine," she rasped out, not sounding too convincing. "I would be lying if I claimed to be unafraid, though," she added, turning her attention to his shoulder so she wouldn't have to look him in the eye as she tried to cope with her volatile feelings. Her emotional reaction was a symptom of mild shock. She was normally so composed that Liam was a little bemused by this vulnerability. As if she'd read his mind, she said, "I don't think I'm quite recovered from the last encounter I had with a Morphate assassin."

Of course not. She still had a healing bullet wound in her leg. One he'd uncharacteristically forgotten about as they'd danced, he realized belatedly.

"We were lucky tonight," he said roughly. Perhaps he should be more reassuring, but she wasn't that type of woman. "The assassin wasn't expecting a bodyguard contingent, and she wasn't expecting us to be armed with mercury. Next time they will be more prepared for us, if not the mercury. I assume that they'll anticipate that too since they seem to know you've created weapons against them."

"Oh, they know. But to them it's still worth a try. If they get me, they get vengeance. The one thing Morphates truly excel in is revenge."

"Yeah, I know," he said with a deep sigh of regret. "There's no logic to this, you know. It isn't as though you hand developed these things on your own. You have an R&D department that does it, just like NHK does."

"That's only partially true," she corrected him, her cheeks turning rosy in the shifting light as she lowered her eyes a moment. "I did hand develop them. I personally designed each one, drew up the schematics and built the prototypes in my labs. My team helped with molding the prototype casings, but I wasn't willing to risk any of them with the responsibility of creating the designs. Specifically for this reason. Besides, for confidentiality reasons it was best to minimize exposure."

Liam was fascinated and stunned all at once. She was another Roni. A brilliant mind wrapped up in a gorgeous personality and beautiful package. She was perhaps less volatile than Roni could be, he thought with an inner smile, but no less ingenious. An inventor. A weapons inventor at that. "Do you know how they found out about the project?" he asked her.

"The usual espionage, I'm guessing. I was so very cautious, but in the end it was all for nothing."

"Not for nothing," he assured her, tilting up her lowered chin with his thumb. "Those weapons will change the balance of power in the world. Mainly for our unfortunately overrun and outgunned law enforcement. I know a lot of cops who will worship the ground you walk on for this."

"Will *you* worship the ground I walk on?" she asked with a laugh as she leaned to peek at his wound. Again her hair drifted like sweetly scented silk over his face, warm and womanly just like the body leaning across him, and he swallowed back a groan. "Did I hurt you?" she asked worriedly when she heard the repressed sound. She pulled back to look at him and he heard her breath catch. That was when he knew how obvious his hunger was on his face, and, try as he might, he couldn't even make the attempt to conceal it.

"No," he responded hoarsely. "I'm feeling no pain."

"You will," she said after a delicate clearing of her throat. "Morphate claws hurt like a . . ." Devon stuttered when his thumb drifted across her bottom lip again, but it was the fixation of his lustrous amber eyes that truly did her in. There were leaping gold flames of desire within them, which she saw even beneath his low-lying lashes. "Liam," she whispered as they mutually drifted closer to each other.

"God, I love hearing my name on those luscious lips," he said without even thinking, his entire being gripped in such intensity of attraction that he would've said anything that came to his mind. He felt her across his lap, a warm sensuous weight that leaned eagerly forward, and nothing seemed to matter anymore.

"I like saying your name," she breathed softly against his lips, the tease of her breath pouring warmly over his face and into his mouth. "I will say it whenever you like. However you like." The blatant invitation was accompanied by a slow resituating of her weight in his lap.

"Would you?" he growled as he reached to tightly hold the back of her head. "Christ, Devon . . ."

He took her. It was sweet surrender for both of them, but an agonizing concession on both their parts as well. Liam swept his mouth against hers with a reserved, shuddering aggression. He didn't want to attack her like some crude grunt with no finesse. She'd been right when she'd said he was more than that. He was more than willing to prove it to them both. He brushed her mouth firmly with his, feeling her rapid breathing like the deepest of compliments, even though it was more due to her exquisite responsiveness than anything he was doing. Her lips had parted already to accommodate her excited need for oxygen, inviting him to delve deep, but he'd been obsessed with her lower lip for far too long now to pass up the opportunity. He nibbled at it, ran gentle teeth over it, and then painted it with a light, teasing brush of his tongue. She caught her fast breath for a cluster of seconds before releasing it in an exultant sigh of pleasure that flowed over him like warm water after standing in the frigid cold.

Devon was in the awkward position of having both hands pressed to his shoulder, so her body was twisted and one arm was crossed between their chests. It was like being bound away from him. She couldn't let go, she couldn't touch him as she longed to, and she couldn't rest flush or even comfortably against him. She had to be satisfied with just his mouth and the feel of his big hand sliding possessively into her hair.

She touched an eager tongue to Liam's artfully teasing mouth, stepping up the exchange in hopes of matching the fire of anxious need broiling within her. Liam got the hint very well and in that next instant Devon's mouth was filled with him; the flowing passion of his tongue, the crush of his hot lips, and the exclusive deliciousness that was Liam. His flavor was crisp and male. It was just Liam, as bold and stimulating to her senses as he was.

He took her mouth, feeling her accept him with enthusiasm, but he could feel her need to shift into a more assertive role in the kiss. However, her contortionist's position in his lap hindered her. He took shameless advantage of her submissive posture by pushing his will onto her with every possessive nuance he could convey. When her eyes flew open, he knew she was well aware of his advantageous terms. Soon, however, she didn't seem to care much either way. She groaned soft sounds of pleasure as he slowly studied the form and function of her mouth with thoroughness enough to impress. She tasted like heaven; his heart pounded harder with every passing second of pleasure it gave him. Her hair slid all around his fingers as he held her and it felt like divinity.

More than all of that, however, was the incredible feel of her body. She was vibrating with pent up energy and unexpressed desire. Forcing it all into the outlet of a kiss was impossible for someone as naturally sexual and sensual as she was. She didn't merely squirm around in his lap; she flowed in those small shifting movements that struck him like eddies of intense heat. She was radiating her desire to be flush with him, to surround him and to touch him.

"Let go," he gasped against her lips. She fished for his tongue once more and he was swept into her wild need again for a long minute before he could break away and repeat, "Let go, baby."

"I can't," she panted softly, nibbling at his lips until she just about drove him crazy with the teasing lure of her flickering tongue. She had quite a way with her mouth and it made him insane to think of it turned loose on the rest of his body.

"Let go." This time he reached up with his free hand, the one on his injured side, and grasped both her wrists in his fingers. The message was clear. He was prepared to strong-arm her if she didn't obey, knowing full well that the struggle would do more damage to him than bleeding would.

"Stubborn bastard," she muttered furiously as she let go. There was humor in the fact that she instantly slid her hands over him to embrace him after the epithet, one scraping up his neck and into his crisp hair, the other curving over his healthy shoulder.

"Stubborn bitch," he shot back readily as he used his now free arm to bind a forearm around her back, dragging her flush to his chest. Without the weight of his jacket in the way, he could feel the pressure of her generous breasts and their pebbled tips.

He was also about to feel the vented pressure of Devon's restricted passion. Her bottom lifted from his lap briefly, raising her torso up high enough to tease his mouth with the brush of a breast. She threw one knee over him, settling herself snugly in a straddle over his hips and thighs. Liam's head dropped back, his throat working as he released a groan.

"God, you're hot," he choked out as his hand slid down to her hip. She was very, very hot. He felt her body burning through his clothing until he broke out in a sweat.

She decided she wanted to devour him, starting with his mouth. Her bottom lifted into his hand so she could find and capture his lips, dragging his attention back to their excellent kisses. Soon they were both breathless and panting, forgetting where they were completely as he slid his hand from her hair, his fingertips stroking her neck and throat until she actually purred.

"Hmm, I'll remember that," he murmured as he lowered his mouth to her neck to see if it would draw a similar response. It did. She even slid herself deeper into the well of his lap as she shifted with abandoned pleasure. By now he already had an all-star erection, but the rub of hot female flesh he knew was completely open to him was devastating to his equilibrium and threatening to the reliability of his fly.

He squeezed his eyes shut tight for a moment, trying to ignore the pretty scent lifting from her body and how badly he wanted to learn those tempting breasts of hers. But he needed to inject some reality into the situation, and damn quick too, before he lost control and did something unforgivably stupid. Something he was already considering even though all he had done was kiss her. But God, her kisses were ten times more potent than sex with most women.

"Liam?" she queried softly when she noted his stillness. Damn it. He was going to go crazy every time she said his name from then on. He just knew it. She couldn't help it, but the way she said it just went straight to his libido.

He was trying to figure out what to say to her when the pain hit.

Because he was so distracted and completely unprepared for it, his entire body convulsed as he roared out with the searing agony cutting across his chest from the site of his wound. He ended up bucking Devon right off of him, sending her sprawling on the floor of the limo, arms and legs akimbo. To her credit, she recovered quickly, grabbing a bottle of vodka in the bar as she scrambled back up to his lap. She held him down with her body weight as she dumped the bottle of vodka onto his wound.

This time when he went to buck her off, she was prepared for it. His second roar of pain had drawn the attention of the others and the partition dropped quickly.

"Venom?" Colin asked. Over the years those who were up

on their Morphate information knew that some Morphates excreted a nonlethal venom through their claws. Nonlethal, but not non-painful. Apparently their attacker had been just such a Morphate. Inez turned to lean in and view the situation. She saw a wild-haired Devon, armed with alcohol and pinning Liam down, as well as any woman could pin down a giant like Nash. The bodyguard grinned.

"I think Ms. Candler has it under control." Directly to Devon she said, "We're almost home now."

"Thank you," Devon shouted. "And call me Devon. You just saved my life and nearly got a boob job in the process. I think first names are called for."

"I think you're right. Inez and Colin works for us, too," Inez agreed with a chuckle. "Has he got a fever yet?"

"He isn't deaf, goddammit," Liam growled through clenched teeth.

"Sorry, Nash," she said with a click of a sympathetic tongue. She sat back down in a hurry, leaving Devon to the ogre he'd suddenly become.

"Crap," he gritted out as he warily eyed the still-armed woman leaning over him. "Lady, put down the Smirnoff and back away," he barked in the tone that could convince the world to disarm rather than face his wrath.

Devon immediately dropped the bottle to the floor, although she didn't move away. In spite of his pain, Liam had to smirk. She honestly didn't care about objects or material things. No woman he knew would let alcohol pour freely over the floor like that and not think twice about it.

"When we get home, I'll tend this. I know—"

"I've been through this before." He ground his teeth as he recalled those days of horror, but the damage to his leg had been much worse and he'd been clawed in multiple places that time.

"Yes, but . . ."

"We're home," Inez called back to them.

"I want you to go right into the house where it's safe, got it?"

"No."

"Devon!"

"Don't you yell at me! You're my bodyguard, not my father!" she snapped right back at him. "I'm not going into the house leaving you out here like . . ." she stumbled awkwardly over her words and he saw her glance self-consciously over her shoulder toward Inez and Colin, " . . . like nothing has happened," she finished in a softer tone, though it was still fiercely meant by the look in her eyes and the tightness of her jaw.

"Okay, okay," he said with less impatience, as he tried to figure out whom she was trying to spare with her concealment of their kisses—him or herself? "Let Colin and Inez help me inside." He paused as pain burned over his back this time, the venom spreading. He cursed mightily between his teeth as she leaned against his arching body to hold him safely in place. "Then," he panted out as rivers of sweat began to roll off of him, "you can change and so can I. We can meet in the middle."

Devon sighed. Either he thought she was an idiot, or he really was deluding himself. He'd be lucky to make it into a bed, never mind a change of clothes. Then a fact from her blended cultures, both Morphate and human, settled into her awareness. Morphate men and human men could be equally as proud and stubborn when it came to showing weakness. She could actually respect that. She hadn't at all enjoyed being injured in front of others. It was an infuriating experience. So when the limo stopped, she nodded in acquiescence to him and climbed out the minute Colin opened the door for her.

Chapter Six

Alda rolled over in bed, stretching and yawning with provocative exaggeration. Her long, nude body with its dark skin, red wine tipped breasts, and taut curves drew her lover's instant attention, even though he'd already had her twice in the past few hours. He was dressing, however, and didn't wish to be sidetracked, even if it was by his divinely sexy mistress. Alda had the sexual appetite of a cat perpetually in heat. All Morphates did, really. If he catered to their every sexual whim or need, he'd never get anything done. Luckily, Alda also had an appetite for variety. They both did. That understanding, combined with a shared bloodthirsty nature, made her the perfect mate for the ruler of Dark Phoenix.

At least, for the time being, Ambrose amended mentally as he buttoned the cuffs of a blue velvet shirt.

"Come, pet, and dress yourself. By now our assassin will have made her presence known. I wish to be ready to receive her when she arrives."

Alda sighed with exaggerated boredom. "Provided she has done any better than the others. If not, a gaseous cloud has no stories to tell." Alda sat up, her hair tumbling in thick, springy black curls around her face and shoulders. Her beautiful mouth flashed a white smile that was just as pronounced as the unusual sea-green brightness of her eyes. Her striking looks still fascinated him. Their type of Morphate, Morphates that had been derived from Dr. Paulson's reptilian experiments, could alter their appearance if they wanted to in minor ways, like forcing a change of eye color or simple skin pigmentation. But there was a natural state they reverted to when at rest. Alda's natural state was unique from the usual stock that filled Ambrose's Morphate ranks. It was what had attracted him to her to begin with. That and her other special talents.

"So you've no faith in my latest choice?" he asked her archly.

She laughed a full-bodied chortle, fangs flashing. "Ambrose, my darling," she cooed, her heavy patois accent making her all the more exotic, "I always delight in the wisdom of your decisions. However, Devona has proved a deadly, unpredictable adversary. Only those who make arrogant assumptions will fail, and you have no such assumptions. This latest assassin . . . she is skilled, but far too cocky."

Alda swung out of bed, her long, sleek legs gleaming in the lamplight as she towered to her full six feet in height, a mere two inches shorter than himself. Diminutive women bored Ambrose. This graceful, powerful Amazon with all of her cunning made him hard just watching her movements as she rose to full-scale glory. It was as though he'd never spent himself, as though she weren't already covered in his scent from his claiming of her. She was Alpha female to his Alpha male, but their breed was not inclined to the possessiveness, the exclusivity, and the territoriality of the other Morphates. And that was just fine in his book.

"We'll see if you're right soon enough," he mused, shrugging the matter off as though he didn't care.

But Alda knew as well as any of the other Phoenix Clan members that the destruction of Devona was Ambrose's singular obsession. Even to the point of the unthinkable. He'd offered rewards to *humans*, creatures he despised and looked forward to subjugating one day. He didn't actually expect any of them to succeed, so the exorbitant bounty would forever remain unpaid, but he did expect them to run her ragged, wear her down. The weaker they made her, the easier for his assassins to eventually figure out how to kill her.

And it was possible to kill her. Thanks to her, any of them could now be killed. Granted, her method of destroying her brethren Morphates had not yet gone mainstream, but he had no doubt that it would be only a matter of time. And he had discovered the basics of her key component for himself shortly after the human government had solicited her to develop specialized weapons to be used against the Morphates.

The problem was trying to get a Morphate to use the mercury bullets with their cruder, more quickly devised weapons, especially when they realized the bullets could be turned on them and spell the end of their immortality. Here again was where humans came in handy. They had no such qualms, even though the bullet in question could be just as harmful to them, and in several different ways. The radioactivity alone, though low grade, could still be quite toxic in the long run. Certainly toxic enough to cause the specter of cancer to loom over the victim's future. But amusingly enough, humans were quite short thinkers for such a fragile and mortal species. They were very apt to put themselves at risk for a good paycheck now and worry about the rest later.

Ambrose had expected a certain amount of initial failure, but he was beginning to get impatient. Time was against him. If Devona brought her prototypes to human weapon makers, the humans could have the means with which to slaughter all Morphates everywhere, no matter what clan they were from, lowest ranking to highest. It was the ultimate betrayal, one he'd never conceived her being capable of. Hell, even he would never have dared to threaten giving away the secret to Morphate vulnerability. But Ambrose had underestimated her cunning and had never seen her ferocious need for the wealth and power that would come with such a critical sway in the balance of power between Morphates and humans. Then again, when she had belonged to the Dark Manhattan Clan back in the day, she had taken part in Kincaid Gregory's feverish search for just such a weapon.

Ambrose frowned and left his suite without so much as a glance back at Alda. She would make her way down in her own time and he was impatient for some good news. Just as he entered the large receiving room, Tansy was coming through the main door, shaking out her claws and fangs with an audible sigh of relief as she passed out of the world shared with humans and relaxed among her brethren.

She made a beeline for Ambrose, but the fact that she was alone boded ill, and he roared out his frustration before she even reached him. Those gathered in groups in the hotel ballroom that had been converted into something very similar to a regal throne room quieted to a breathless silence as the Alpha of the clan vented. Anything that wasn't bolted down vibrated with the power of his vocalized fury. The crystal chandelier clinked and tinkled long after the roar had faded and the memory of its impressive impact remained. In its wake was the purity of silence, all attention centered on their Alpha, some in awe and respect, some in fear and submission.

Ambrose snarled at Tansy as she came near, but the warrior woman merely kneeled at his feet and exposed her neck to him in a gesture of submissive loyalty. This mollified him in a minor way, enough to keep him from tearing the room apart.

"Greta has failed?" he demanded, his words little more than guttural grunts.

"She is dead, my Alpha," Tansy informed him regretfully. "Devona has surrounded herself with humans for protection."

Tansy spat in disgust at the idea. She had hardly believed her own eyes when she'd seen it.

"Humans! Bah!" Ambrose was only voicing what the murmuring crowd around him was thinking. "She sidles up to a nest of impotent vipers. What she sees in those pitiful creatures is completely beyond me."

"Alpha, they were armed with mercury," Tansy added. "I watched from the alley rooftop as Greta evaporated into nothingness."

"So! She has begun the next phase of her betrayal," Ambrose hissed, his copper colored eyes gleaming as he turned the information over in his head. "She gives the cattle weapons to destroy us!" This he shouted for the vast room to hear, although the Morphates were already more than attentive. They all became restless, some angry and some alarmed as they thought of the implications. "Now do you see why she must be destroyed at all costs, as I've said from the start? She's eluded us for too long, finally succeeding in her plot to begin the destruction of her own kind. But I will stop her. I will stop her if I have to go and hunt her myself."

"There is no need for that, my lord," came a soft-spoken contradiction.

A rustle went through the room as everyone shifted to look in the direction of the speaker. Tansy rose to her feet and turned around toward the door she'd entered a moment ago. The sigh that rippled through the room echoed her feelings.

For Jacan stood there.

Jacan was a marvelous specimen of a male Morphate. His muscular build and stunning height aside, it was his coal-black sheet of hair flowing down to the middle of his back and the obsidian glitter of his eyes that riveted all attention whenever he entered a room. Those black eyes held the chill of a true warrior within them. He was dressed in faded blue jeans that clung to every muscle with well-worn familiarity. He wore no shirt, only a buttery soft leather vest worked to a natural beige that was almost white, which covered the expanse of bronzed skin across his chest. His magnificent arms were bare, except for the lone braided circlet of leather he wore around his upper left biceps, a beautifully crafted piece made of a much darker leather, painstakingly softened and woven. Small, curving sparrow feathers rimmed the lower circumference of the band, making a perfect soft brown ring around his arm that swayed with every movement or breath of air.

Tansy felt her heart pounding in delight as her beautiful mate moved into the circle of Morphates loosely surrounding Ambrose. Everyone waited with patience, knowing what would come even before he displayed obeisance to his Alpha. The gorgeous warrior reached to wrap a possessive hand around the back of Tansy's neck and he dragged her against him for a hard, hungry kiss. As he kissed her, his hand absently wrapped her long red braid around his fist again and again. Finally he reached the end of the rope and used his hold to tug her back away.

Jacan glanced away from his woman to look at Ambrose. The Alpha was watching them with obvious pleasure and a small hint of revulsion as well. Pleasure because his sister had wed the most powerful Morphate man in all the clans who wasn't an Alpha, the one man who might give Ambrose concern if it ever came down to a contest for his position as Alpha; but the revulsion was actually because he would never understand the feelings they had for one another. Nor could he stomach the idea of monogamy.

Jacan smiled at his clan leader, a small quirk of compressed lips. He released Tansy and made his obeisance with a kneel. He rose quickly, holding out an arm to Tansy, who slid herself against his side like a holstered weapon. Knowing

Tansy for the cutthroat fighter that she was, he thought it a very accurate piece of imagery.

"Tansy and I will obtain this target for you," he said at last, finishing his leading entrance statement.

Ambrose flared up like a Siamese fighting fish, but instead of gills fanning out, he took in a breath of indignation and flexed his not inconsiderable muscles. His face flushed a rosy hue of outrage that clashed terribly with the bright redgold tint of his hair.

"Jacan, we have finished this conversation and I won't tolerate . . . !"

"I hardly call you spouting dictates based on emotional whim to be the makings of a conversation."

One could have vacuumed the world with the sudden intake of breath in that room. Very few people stood up to Ambrose, and none dared do so in public. But Jacan was no ordinary Morphate. If not for the fact that Jacan was completely loyal to Ambrose, the Alpha leader might consider him a dire threat. His sister's mate, it was rumored, was even more powerful than he was. However, Ambrose's first lieutenant was devoted to his lady, and therefore her family as well. He would do nothing to hurt Tansy.

"Tansy won't be put at risk," Ambrose said with finality, although in a far calmer tone than was expected.

"I'd never risk Tansy, you know that well enough. But if you continue to send these lesser assassins instead of your best, then you'll continue to get less than satisfactory results." Jacan's tone turned casual as he moved to take a seat in a comfortable chair, tugging Tansy in his wake until she slid into his lap and wrapped her arms around his neck. It never ceased to amaze the Dark Phoenix Clan members how openly affectionate these two deadliest of creatures could be. There wasn't a Morphate among them that didn't fear the wrath of either one of them alone; as a united team they were an unstoppable force. "Tansy, my lover, wouldn't you like to kill the Morphate traitor?"

"Oh, ever so much, my darling," she breathed with excitement flashing in her mocha colored eyes. Her hands slid forward over his face to cradle it, holding him for her slow, sensual kiss. She smiled as she pulled away, turning to look at her brother as she pressed her cheek against Jacan's. "However, I'm also willing to stay here making love to you, amusing ourselves by watching the next few failures."

"Good point, minx," he laughed with delight. "My woman has shown me the error of my ways, Ambrose. I'll wait patiently for you to conclude you require us."

Jacan hurled himself out of his chair, sweeping up Tansy in the same movement. Without even another word or glance at their Alpha, they took to the halls, heading for the suite they occupied. Ambrose watched them go with a mixture of irritation and amusement, and then his attention shifted to Alda, who passed the couple as she moved smoothly into the room and then toward him. She was wearing white, his favorite color on her because of the fascinating contradiction to her ebony skin.

Ambrose chuckled in spite of his earlier temper. He held out an arm to Alda. She took it, letting him lead her deeper into the reception room. Seeing his good humor return, his clan relaxed back into what they'd been doing.

The clan headquarters was an enormous skyscraper that, once upon a time, had been a luxury hotel with all the finest trimmings money could buy. Then, after the gangs had overrun Phoenix, the hotel, like all the other grand buildings of the city, had been left to fall into disrepair. But the Morphates had rescued it from such a sad fate. The main body of the second floor, which had once been part of the convention rooms, was now a clubroom. There were pockets of chairs grouped against corners, walls, and surrounding gaming tables. There was a long bar that filled the entire room with the rich scent of exotic coffee roasts and other unusual treats.

"Perhaps this calls for a temporary relocation," Ambrose mused aloud. It was an unwritten law that Morphates must remain inside their territories, but he didn't see Devona adhering to that law, and since he had never agreed to the law, he didn't see any reason why he should either.

They would relocate to his property in the lower Adirondacks. 'They' meaning his entourage of the moment, his security forces, and a few more of those assassins Jacan had been speaking of. It would put him within striking distance of the traitor, making her more easily accessible.

Privacy and security would also be provided by their location in the farthest reaches of the Adirondacks. It was a property with acreage that stretched for miles in all directions. The main house was for gatherings and served as residence to the upper echelon of the clan; extended wings held suites for those closest to Ambrose by blood or by favor. The vast property held a number of smaller buildings, houses, and cottages to contain the rest. In all, the crème de la crème of his clan ran almost to 400 brethren. In Dark Phoenix his clan was known for being the largest grouping of Morphates around, and therefore the most powerful. Splitting away could weaken his position somewhat. But he felt it was a risk he had to take.

"So what do you think, Alda? Am I foolish to want to keep Jacan and Tansy away from the danger the traitor poses?"

"Considering the weaponry she terrorizes us with, I think you're wise to show reserve," she commended soothingly, smiling as he led her to their prominent seats at the head of the room. "However, you must also consider that there are none so skilled, nor so ruthless as your baby sister and her beloved."

"As always, the measured voice of reason, pet," he said expansively as he pulled up her hand to kiss her knuckles. "And you've always had that keen vision of the future, haven't you?"

"Ambrose, I've already told you what I've seen of the future," she said.

"Yes. I have seen it too," Ambrose mused, stroking his beard.

Soon, very soon, he'd subjugate all of the other Cities, forcing them to name him undisputed leader of all Morphates. All Cities would become *his* clan, and he would be Alpha over them all. There were six major Cities to contend with, but although his was the largest, his enemies were also powerful in their own ways. Lucky for him their ideals prevented the other Cities from ever forming true alliances. They depended on their Alpha Council to keep things calm and orderly. But neither he nor the Alpha of Los Angeles had found following the rules to his taste. And Ambrose was quite close with that other Alpha. Quite close indeed.

As for the sects that had broken off from all of the Dark cities, he thought them of little consequence. They were neither large enough or organized enough to be worth his time or interest.

"You have no specific advice or opinions on this issue?" he coaxed her as they settled in and a servant hurried to set out footstools and provide the little comforts they usually desired.

"Only what I've said. Devona has betrayed her own breed with mercury. She will clearly become aggressive toward you." Alda's attention seemed to slowly fade out, her patois thicker as she turned contemplative. "She must be stopped soon before she gains any footholds within the Morphate political structure."

Ambrose almost scoffed aloud at the idea. No Morphate would side with her once it became widely known what she had done to betray her own people.

"This other thing *is* different." Alda tilted her head thoughtfully. "By taking the humans under her hand, she surrounds herself with an unusual resource."

This time Ambrose couldn't contain his derision. "Ha! I hardly call them a resource! I give them credit for stumbling into the schemes of the one Morphate who could give them a real weapon against us. But all prey has defenses. It will only make the hunt more worthwhile." Ambrose waved her comment off with another huff.

"Don't be so quick to dismiss this resource," Alda warned him. "It could make the difference in Devona's campaign for power. Perhaps you should consider sending Tansy and Jacan. Send them now while she's still vulnerable."

"Humans will make no difference in her vulnerability," Ambrose sneered. "She's alone in the world. The only thing she's had on her side is luck and damnable determination. There are other assassins who will do well enough. In fact, you will help me choose," he suggested.

Alda frowned with irritation, as she always did when he didn't take her seriously. Ambrose was unpredictable in what advice he chose to listen to. He had a terrible blind spot when it came to humans, seeing them as nothing more than food, slaves, or entertainment. Alda, however, was convinced that Ambrose ought to be more careful about dismissing them. But she knew he wouldn't listen to her.

Once he destroyed Devona forever, Ambrose would attain awesome preeminence. Letting Alda decide on an assassin was potentially a historic occasion. If she chose successfully, it would always be remembered. She eagerly began to consider his question. There were many great assassins in the clan, some a little insane and unpredictable, like the berserker Ambrose had most recently sent, and some like Jacan who were cold and flawlessly methodical. Since she could not choose Jacan or Tansy, Alda named the closest parallel.

"Send Torque," she suggested smoothly. Those who were listening to their exchange made noises of approval when they heard her choice. "And Rhiannon," she finished, eliciting gasps of amusement and a small smattering of applause.

"Jacan's idea of sending a team has strong merit. They are powerful individuals, but have the ability to work in tandem should you decree it. Rhiannon has that savagery required to tear a swath through Devona's human defenses, and Torque won't be deterred from his main target."

"Hmm. Excellent choices," Ambrose concurred with a sly smile that put gleaming confidence in his eyes. "Devona will never be expecting such a combination. Or any combination for that matter. Morphate assassins usually work best alone. Devious, devious girl!" Ambrose laughed, grabbing her by the back of her neck to force an enthusiastic kiss on her, which she took most readily. "Call them to me at once!"

Devon strode into her bedroom, kicking off her heels and stripping off her ruined gown with furious determination. She walked naked to her closet and snatched up a skirt and sweater. She wriggled into the blue crepe skirt, settling it in place low on her hips, and then slipped into the white sweater, the long sleeves covering half her palms and the hem baring her midriff. Feeling warmer and sufficiently no-nonsense, she padded barefoot to a large locked chest at the bottom of another closet. She keyed in the code and it sprang open. After withdrawing supplies, she shut it.

Devon marched across the hallway, knowing instinctively that Liam would pick the room closest to hers. She found the door ajar and smiled to herself that she knew him that well already. Anybody else would've gone at least one door down to afford an illusion of privacy. All Liam was interested in, now more than ever, was protecting her.

She walked into the suite without bothering to announce herself. Devon crossed the sitting room to the bedroom, where she could hear a commotion taking place beyond the door. Colin leaned casually against the near wall, cautiously checking his weapon. At her questioning look, he chuckled.

"I know what my brother's like when he's in pain. They don't pay me enough to go in there."

Brother. Devon felt the breath rush from her lungs. The reaction of shock and panic baffled her. As she stared at him, she asked herself how she had missed it. Although Colin was a little leaner than his brother, they were both big men. Now that she was looking for the resemblance, there were uncanny similarities in their bone structure and features. However, Colin's eyes were gray and his hair was an even jet as opposed to Liam's blue-black with its sparks of silver.

Colin watched their latest client's expressions as she absorbed his revelation of kinship with Liam and knew she was comparing the two of them. He didn't mind in the least. Liam and he were similar in some ways, yet also dissimilar. Colin had far fewer cares in this world than Liam did, and thought his brother took on too much responsibility, sometimes overstepping himself.

It made him the perfect man for this job, though. Liam was probably the only man Colin knew who would aggressively throw himself in the path of Morphates. The team would eagerly follow, of course, but Liam . . . he'd fought Morphate fangs and claws, somehow managing to keep his life in spite of it. That envenomation and attack had nearly crippled him—a fate worse than death to men of their ilk. As it was, the incident had cost him his job in the Service. Yet, he still had the fortitude to take on the threat to Devon Candler.

Colin watched the lady in question contemplate the door to Liam's bedroom and the ruckus beyond. It took him a moment to realize that she wasn't hesitating out of doubt, but was rather squaring herself for battle. He knew the look well and a grin exploded over his face as he waited to see what would happen next.

She plowed past him, completely ignoring his dire warnings, and he quickly turned to watch her enter the battlefield.

Devon opened the door just as Kellen Gordon went flying

back from the bed as if shot from a cannon. She instinctively
shifted her bundles to a single hand and reached for him with
the other. She caught him by the left arm, driving her weight
forward into his back and shoulder to halt his momentum.
Then she jerked him hard onto his feet.

"Thanks," he said, running a hand through his wildly
spiked hair now that he had regained his balance.

Devon ignored him the instant he was no longer in
danger of cracking his head on the floor or furniture. She let
go of him quickly as she turned back to see three other team
members trying to hold Liam down, apparently so Inez
could inspect and tend his wound. Liam had been stripped
from the waist up. His face was contorted in agony and his
entire upper body wore the sheen of pain and fever. She took
all of this in with a mixture of frustration and fury. Not a one
of them had listened to her, and all of this suffering was
completely unnecessary!

"Out!"

The bellow was so sharp and so similar to the irrefutable
tone of a drill sergeant that the soldiers automatically snapped
around to face her. Even Liam settled down considerably,
though she was willing to bet it was because his comrades
had suddenly stopped pressing down on him. An advanced
symptom of Morphate envenomation was hypersensitivity
when touched. Rough handling could be extremely painful
for a victim.

"Devon, you shouldn't . . ." Inez tried.

"I said *out*. This is still my house and you will respect
that," she demanded, her pale green eyes snapping with
warning anger. "If you want your commander on his feet
again, you will leave him to me. Trust me when I say I know
more about this than any of you ever will."

"You . . . ?" Another female soldier snorted in disbelief.
She stuck her hands on her hips and squared a belligerent jaw.
"Look, we can take care of our own. If we need someone to

dress us up in high fashion, we'll give ya a call. But this is our area of expertise and we got it covered."

Feeling she was properly dismissed, the team members reached to recapture Liam.

"Oh? So that means you already know that every time you touch him like that, the pain you cause is just like stabbing him about a hundred times?"

Her words caused all sets of hands to freeze before coming into contact with Liam, who sighed audibly in relief. Devon watched him suck in hard, labored breaths for a second before flicking cold, irritated eyes around the room. She settled on the woman who had addressed her so rudely.

"Just because I need help protecting myself doesn't mean I can't kick ass," Devon said flatly. "If I can beat down a Morphate while shot through the leg, then you can damn well imagine what I can do while completely healthy. Do not underestimate me, any of you. Now if you would please *get out*."

She gave them a moment while they gaped at her. All except for Inez, who'd already known that detail, and who was grinning from ear to ear. She got off the bed and walked away. Devon watched her move, the woman's gait awkward and stiff as she began to feel the beating she had taken. She must have seen the concern in Devon's eyes because the Latina patted her shoulder and shook her head as she passed.

"Kellen will take care of me. Help Liam as you say you can."

Once Inez left, the rest followed her lead, starting with Kellen, who saluted her crisply with a chuckle and a wink. The last to leave was the huffy woman she had all but threatened. Not wishing to alienate any of Liam's people, she reached out a staying hand and the other woman stopped short.

"I only have his best interests at heart. I know you do, too. How can there be an argument here?"

The bodyguard instantly eased, consternation replacing peevishness. "No. No argument. Not if you can really help him."

Devon smiled softly when she heard the loyalty underlying

the prickly doubt. Liam had earned this, and she had no doubt he deserved it. "It normally takes a week to recover from envenomation, right?" She waited for the reluctant nod. "I can guarantee half that time or better, depending on how quickly I work. Okay?"

This time the nod was enthusiastic. The soldier nearly ran out of the room to share the startling information with the others. Devon watched as Inez reached to shut the door, listening to the buzz of surprised voices for a moment before tuning them out.

Humans hadn't yet been able to unlock the secrets of developing an antivenin for Morphate venom. Most venom paralyzed prey for consumption, and this venom was no different. However, Morphate venom was also a weapon. It was meant to create the most agonizing stimulation of nerve endings possible, fluctuating in intensity and adapting like a virus so that the nerves in question never over-fired to the point of becoming insensate. That would defeat the purpose of debilitating the enemy with pain. The venom dwelled in the quick of their claws, ejecting the moment the nails came into contact with a certain amount of pressure. Devon knew it didn't take much at all, and that it was almost always guaranteed that if the claw broke skin, envenomation had taken place.

The severity of the envenomation was the urgent issue. Cutting of the arms or the legs made for an agonizing but, generally, non-fatal experience. The only time Morphate venom was fatal was a direct puncture of a vital organ. The bleeding from such a puncture would be bad enough, but if envenomation began directly in an organ, the rapid necrosis of the tissue would almost certainly mean death.

The human inability to develop an antivenin didn't surprise Devon. Their scientists hadn't yet figured out how many layers of deception there were in Morphate venom. They didn't know of the shifting chromosomes between male and female venom, or the gene that had adapted to its environment to make the best effective poison. Then again, humans hadn't entirely grasped that Morphates were dramatically different from one protocol to the next.

Devon hurried over to Liam, setting her supplies down on the nightstand. She sat gingerly beside him on the bed, on the side closest to the wound, watching him flinch as the bed shifted under her weight. He was feeling pain all over by now, his skin crawling with it and his muscles cramping from poison. The fever would nauseate and dehydrate him before long.

"Don't worry," she soothed in a whisper as he swung pained eyes in her direction, "it will ease soon."

She reached for her toolkit, rolling it open over her lap once it was unsnapped. She took out a pair of alcohol swabs, a syringe, and a small sterile bottle of cloudy liquid.

Morphate antivenin.

She was perhaps uniquely qualified to have created it. Before all of this had begun, when she had been human, she'd been a doctor of zoological study and husbandry. Animals, their makeup, and the genetics that made them so different from one another had been her specialty. She had been in high demand in the best of zoos and high-end laboratories back in her days as a human. It was what had put her on Dr. Paulson's radar in the first place. When she had learned of his monstrous plans, she had refused to take part . . . and had earned herself a place as one of his human lab rats for her trouble. She had often replayed that encounter and her reactions in her head, often wondered about all the ways she could have responded differently, more cleverly, ways that could have saved thousands of humans from becoming what they now were.

But it was an exercise in futility; she'd come to understand that. She could not change what had already happened by pounding her head into woulda-coulda-shouldas. But she had the brains and the wherewithal to create countermeasures that would protect the more fragile humans the Morphates lived with. The idea had not started with her, neither had the research, but she was the one who had succeeded.

All because she had courted the military and that military had told her about the claims of a Secret Service agent named Liam Nash. She had gained the military contract to explore the truth of this claim and its effectiveness, and to develop a safe, efficient delivery system for use by soldiers and, perhaps more important, law enforcement nationwide. She had explored and entertained the method that Liam and his people were using now, and had found it subpar and dangerous to the humans wielding the weapons. She had noticed the radiation detectors they wore on their holsters, had no doubt that they had to undergo exposure treatments on occasion. It worried her to think of them taking such risks.

She took out the needle and tubes necessary to start an IV on him. The antivenin couldn't be introduced all at once, in an injection; she needed gradual access. Also, by starting a saline drip, she could try to head off the dehydration that often came with envenomation.

"Liam," she said quietly, knowing his hearing was also becoming sensitive, "I have to start an IV drip and it might hurt more than normal, okay?"

"If you're trying to poison me, you're too late," he quipped roughly, surprising her with his lucidity. She shook her head, asking herself what she had expected and why she should be so astonished. She turned the smile he'd earned on him and laughed softly.

"Actually, you may zink eet eez zee venom zat eez causing zis, Meester Bond," she affected with exaggeration, "but eet wuz zee poizun leepsteeck from zee keess of my leeps zat haz done you in."

"Your leeps?" Liam laughed, instantly scrunching his entire body in pain.

"Hey, easy does it," she soothed with a soft laugh. She waited a moment before pulling his arm over into her lap. She gently stroked her fingers over the inside of his elbow and forearm, knowing the motion would calm any cramped muscles. She listened to the change in his breathing, the exhalation that signaled his relaxation. She tore open an alcohol pad and quickly swabbed a vein. "I love buff men," she remarked in mellow, distracting conversation. "You never have to look for a vein. They are all nicely mapped out. Very juicy and almost impossible to miss."

"And here most women just think it's sexy," he marveled.

"Bulging veins?" she quizzed doubtfully.

"No, buff men," he chuckled.

She grinned as she worked with nimble, efficient movements, her warning turning out to be entirely unnecessary because next he knew she was taping the tubing down gingerly, trying to avoid the dark hairs on his arm.

"*I*," she enunciated as she gave his arm a final pat, "am not most women."

"Thank God for that," he muttered, making her chuckle as she connected the long tubing to a large unit of saline. She hoisted it up, taking down a picture in order to hang the plastic bag on the hook. "Did I ever mention I find resourceful women a turn-on?" he asked as he watched her act with such efficiency and decisiveness, as if she did this sort of thing every day.

"You've mentioned nothing of the kind," she noted.

"You know, you actually look like you know what you're doing," he remarked as his eyes narrowed on her with speculation. "Are you going to tell me you're a doctor now, too?"

Devon contemplated her answer, knowing she couldn't be honest with him. "I'm not going to kill you if that's what you are worried about," she teased, giving him a crooked grin.

"No. I was just curious. Where'd you learn how to do all this?"

"I was an EMT while I was in college," she said with a shrug of a shoulder. "It paid the bills."

"You mean you weren't born into this?" He glanced up and around at the richly furnished and professionally decorated room. "How the hell old are you?" he demanded.

She laughed, flushing as she injected air into the anti-venin equal to the amount she was going to withdraw. She'd never administered it to someone of such a significant stature and weight before and she was going to have to make a calculated guess on the dosage. Luckily, the calculations would also help her dodge the question he'd asked. "How much do you weigh?"

"About 236, I think. Are you going to answer me?"

"I don't think I ought to. It's rude to ask a woman that."

Liam was on to her. Devon was incredibly good at lying, but he'd picked up her tell. She didn't *like* to lie, so she dodged or tried to be evasive first, trying to put off what she felt was a need to fib to him. It was noticeable only because she was so quick to be blunt and truthful the rest of the time. He tried not to frown when he realized she'd lied to him about being a medic. Why would she do that? Where had these skills really come from? What was she so reluctant to reveal? Or was that even it at all?

Frankly, Liam was in too much pain to fully trust his observations at the moment, so he relaxed and let her attend him. He wasn't worried she'd hurt him. She could just let the venom do that on its own if she wanted to. Considering the present threat she was living under, he didn't blame her for being naturally cautious.

All he cared about was that she was safe. That she was within his reach and right where he could see her. He was hurting like he'd been hit by a locomotive, but he could and would move if he had to for any reason.

He was just damn glad he didn't have a reason.

"Shit," he groaned irritably.

Devon injected the filled syringe into a short port leading to the I. V. tubing near his wrist and looked up at him from beneath her lashes. He could see the worry and concern in her eyes.

"Liam, this is going to burn. Considering how you feel, it's likely to hurt like hell. It's going to take an hour for me to inject the first dose, and I will try to help in any way I can. You may even need a second injection if one doesn't take effect properly. You're a big man and I'm . . ." She hesitated, shaking her dark head.

"Just do what you have to do, Devon," he said gently. "I can handle it."

That wasn't at all what she was worried about. She didn't even know what she was worried about. She knew he'd been through far worse than this event. That he hadn't had her expertise that time to help him.

She cleared her throat and lowered her head again as she paid overly close attention to her control of the injection. "You're bleeding again." She reached to touch gentle fingers to his inside arm, just above the IV port. With extreme care, she began to stroke him rhythmically in a single direction along with the flow of the entering liquids. Cramping muscles and arteries twitched in irritation, and then seemed to relax into the comforting stroke. "I'm going to have to stitch that shoulder. You might consider being extra charming to me."

He snorted. "I'm not the charming sort." He reached across with his good arm, mostly because he couldn't seem to resist the impulse, and brushed his fingertips against the side of her neck, pushing back her espresso colored hair. "But I will make an effort since you are the one with all the sharp implements in her lap."

She gave him a laugh, glancing up from under sly, sexy lashes. "Men are impressed by the strangest things," she teased.

"This is true," he admitted. He shifted slightly, grunting in discomfort. He watched as she instantly hastened to straighten pillows, draw up covers, and drop that disturbing stroke of her fingers over the highly sensitive skin of his face, chest, and belly. She'd struck him instantly as the passionate sort, but this tantalizing, tender touching didn't fit his image of her, and it was driving him absolutely mad.

When the team had touched him, it had been pure agony. Hell at the hands of his friends, literally. When Devon stroked him with that slow, thorough shaping of each muscle contour, following each dip and crest the smooth plane of his skin led her to, it was the wildest combination of ultimate solace and blatant eroticism he'd ever known. How he could be feeling any such thing in this situation baffled him. He remembered his last experience with Morphate venom, still had the occasional nightmare in recollection of it. The hallucinations, the pain . . . it was an experience that had taught him to grimly appreciate the vast reaches the human imagination could achieve.

None of it had been pleasant and at no single moment during those dark, horrifying days that followed had he found any measure of peace. Yet, she was drawing him away from that pit of black experience with just a touch. The injection she was feeding him was barely begun, so he knew it wasn't that. It was her.

Liam watched as she continued to fuss over him, alternating between the injection, packing his wounded shoulder, and softly stroking him to relieve the slightest sign of cramps. She had just settled back beside him when he reached up to suddenly seize her by the back of her neck. She gasped softly in surprise at the clamp of his fingers, quickly seeking an explanation in his eyes.

He didn't speak. Instead, he let her see whatever it was she wanted to see in his gaze and in his aggressive hold. He knew nothing about her, yet he'd sworn to trade his life away for hers. And he was fine with that. Prepared for that. But she destroyed his calm, his equilibrium, and his code of ethics, in ways he could never have been prepared for. The least she could do was provide him with a little insight into that carefully controlled mind of hers.

She began her confession with a telltale trembling he could feel vibrating through the entirety of her long, lithe body. Her breathing picked up in tempo and she tried twice to look away from the directness of his gaze, and twice came back to it. As if she couldn't stop herself, those fingers still found absent contact stroking his skin, along the forearm that held her imprisoned. Her nails trailed lightly and torturously over him, sending stimulating shocks zipping all over his hyperactive nerves. Her eyes deepened in shade, becoming that bottle green that was so clear and so strange all at once.

"Liam," she said softly, his name a kick in his gut as it flowed like a purr over her tense vocal chords. "What is it about you that . . . ?" She took a deep breath and tried to shake the thought out of her head, but he held firm and forced her to look into him. He saw her rising panic easily because he could taste it on his own tongue. Morals and ethics and good intentions be damned, there was something between them and it was screaming mightily for attention.

"Tell me something," he demanded in a low whisper. "Why are you doing this? Why are you stretching your neck out so far?"

"Somebody has to," she said on a rushed breath.

"Yes, but why *you*? Why is that somebody you? And don't bullshit me about your company and contracts, because your people barely touched this project of yours."

"I don't owe you any explanations," she said touchily as she tried to shake off his locked hand. He forced her to face him. He wouldn't let her dodge; he wouldn't accept her vague lies.

"I think that when a man willingly allows himself to get poisoned in order to protect your life, you *do* owe him an explanation."

Her eyes widened incredulously. "Are you blackmailing

me because you did your job? What I pay you to do?" she bit out. "Let go of me, Liam. You're going to hurt yourself!"

She was right. The cramps she had soothed away were already returning in force, and if he pissed her off enough, it wasn't likely she would repeat the holistic touch. But as was usual, Liam was willing to take his chances.

"The last time I went through this, I suffered eight days of tremendous agony, horrifying nightmares, and the break-down of just about everything in my life that held value for me. Now you sit here with a professed cure in your hands and I know with every instinct I own that you're telling the truth. That you have the power to cut this hell I'm facing in half, which in and of itself deserves about a thousand questions. So think about what I'm willing to risk in order to get some kind of truthful answer out of you."

The statement made a tremendous impact on her. Liam could see it exploding in her eyes and over her horrified ex-pression. To his surprise, the sudden liquid of withheld tears glittered on the edges of her lids.

"I would never withhold treatment from you just be-cause . . ." She paused, swallowing hard. "But of course, we're strangers, and you wouldn't know that." But Devon could see how he would make that mistake. He came from that sort of world. For the first time, Devon felt intimidated by a human. His fearlessness and his determination were a daunting package. Add to it his skills and training, and she was extremely glad that he was on her side.

She only needed to keep him there.

"My reasons are actually personal," she said quietly as she pushed down the plunger to the syringe a bit more. "And extremely private," she added.

Liam relaxed his hand when she acquiesced at last, letting it drop onto his belly, glad she'd given in before the cramping had become any worse. Frankly, he was about as daunting as a baby harp seal at the moment. "I'm not known for my willingness to give out information willy-nilly, personal or otherwise."

She found a reason to snicker over that. "I don't see you as the sort to do anything 'willy-nilly.' It has a whole skipping merrily through the meadow feel to it that just doesn't suit you." She smiled when he chuckled, lowering her attention to the injection, once again avoiding looking at him directly. Some people did that when they were going to lie. He was learning that she did it when she was going to be fearfully honest. "Morphates," she said tensely, "those like Ambrose and most of his clan, often disgust me. They see humans as inferior domesticated animals. But unlike the way you might feel about a cat or a dog, they hold no love or fondness for human intellects and personalities. Morphates and humans look the same, appearing to be alike in most every way, and yet they know the difference instantly and react with prejudice bordering on ferocity. In some instances . . . even violence. It's intolerable and they deserve to be brought down from their self-proclaimed superiority."

"Why you, Devon?" he persisted gently. "Tell me why it has to be you."

"Because I'm . . ." Liam watched her grit her teeth tightly together, her jaw clenching hard as she struggled with whatever it was she didn't want to admit to.

But neither of them was going anywhere anytime soon, so Liam was more than willing to wait her out. She was so blunt and determined, but here she was bottled up tight and he dreaded what it was that could possibly be so hard to confess.

"How much do you know about the creation and evolution of Morphates?"

The question was unexpected. Liam looked at her with a wary sort of surprise, shifting in the bed until he had achieved something resembling an upright position. Her inquiry was tricky. She *had* to know the answer already, since she knew so much about his professional history. Was she fishing for data?

The idea of her working him for information flooded him with frustration. The heated irritation vanished instantly, however, as she began to stroke comforting fingers over his injured arm again.

"I know pretty much everything," he said evasively.

"I figured you did." She nodded grimly. "So do I. You can't create weapons to kill and incapacitate unless you completely understand the target," she explained needlessly.

He ought to have realized that a government contract would have given her access to a lot of secrets. Liam felt instantly crappy for suspecting her of manipulation. He counteracted the feeling by laying his hand over hers and toying with her fingers. Devon's hands were long-fingered, capable, and graceful. While he ran his thumb over the soft contours of her knuckles, he imagined them painstakingly creating weaponry to fight a formidable enemy. An enemy that wanted her dead for daring to do such a thing.

"Very few people have a true concept of what it means to make a weapon," she said very carefully, as if she were contemplating the impact every word would have. "There is a responsibility to it. A philosophy even." She depressed the hypodermic of antivenin a few millimeters more. "When I created this antivenin, it was a task I took enormous satisfaction in. I believe eventually it can be refined to the point that recovery will be a mere two days if the venom is caught early enough. I'm especially glad I can use it to help you."

It wasn't until she turned the stark pale green beauty of her gaze directly onto him that he realized how intensely he had been waiting for it to return. There was a tenderness in her eyes that completed the meaning of her words and her gentle hands.

"Liam, when I created the weapon prototypes in the armory downstairs, I knew they would be used to threaten and possibly destroy a specific race of people. In my heart I wish they would only be used to provide protection, balance, and equalization, but I know humans too well to blind myself to the truth."

"Yet you still made them. *You* made them. No one else. You saw to it that it was your hands alone that molded and crafted these weapons. Devon, I have been in this business too long not to know that that is as personal as it gets. What did the Morphates do to you that makes you want so deadly a form of vengeance?"

"No," she sighed, the breath long and deep as he felt it rush warmly over his bare skin. "Not vengeance, Liam. A long-overdue punishment. The Morphates in question will come to heel. I swear it. If I have to pick up arms myself, they will be made to feel fear and caution. They will come to understand what it feels like, being alive just because it suits the whim of someone more powerful than they are."

"That sounds . . . tyrannical," he noted in a stunned tone. Her passion floored him. Even though she had numbed it with flat tones and even breaths, her fury went bone deep and he could feel it radiating off of her like the building energy of an impending explosion.

"Call it what you will." She stood up suddenly, breaking all personal contact with him as abruptly as she extracted the now empty syringe. She discarded it, moving efficiently about as she checked things that didn't need checking. Her body was tense with unspoken anger and frustration. "For all their airs of superiority, these particular Morphates are wild, undisciplined children running loose and threatening not only humans, but every future opportunity for them and others like them to be a civilized race among the other civilized races of this planet. Don't you see? There is a war coming, Liam. And trust me when I say that without my weapons to stop them, the worst of my people will cut a swath through the very best of yours unlike anything you have ever conceived of. Humans will barely be able to blink before they will find themselves subjugated by the likes of Ambrose and his clan, used as slaves for purposes you don't even want to envision. I know this because it already happens. I've seen it with my own eyes!"

Overcome with emotion and memories that flooded her features with horror, Devon sat down hard on the bed once again, shaking violently. He could see her hands trembling as she covered her face with them.

He sat up, ignoring the pain in his shoulder and the warning warmth of fresh blood soaking into the bandages. He reached out and grabbed her by the chin. With a hard tug he forced her face out of her hands and made her meet his hard eyes.

"What the hell do you mean by '*my people*'?"

Chapter Seven

"By Christ, Devon . . . *are you a Morphate*?"

Devon instantly lurched up off the bed, dismay at her unchecked confession written all over her. She staggered away from him, but Liam launched himself out of the bed and caught her by both arms. Unfortunately, the venom had taken its toll on his strength and his balance, and they toppled back onto the bed when both gave out on him. Liam's IV catheter popped out of his arm under the duress of his movement, sending a fresh river of blood out from the puncture site.

He ignored that, along with everything else, and rolled Devon facedown beneath the significant weight of his body on the bed, trapping a wrist in each hand and pressing them in close to her shoulders. He might not have much in the way of strength and balance going for him, but he still had his brain, and she'd have a fine time trying to buck off a man of his size.

She wasn't going anywhere until he was damn well ready to let her go. And that wasn't going to happen unless she began answering the flood of furious questions running through his mind.

"Answer me right now, Devon! Are you a Morphate?"

"Get off of me!"

"Devon!"

"What if I am?" she shouted furiously, her head turning so he could see the angry flush of her cheek through a cloud of mussed hair. He felt her flex under him, her round bottom lifting up into his groin as she tried to find leverage with her knees. The contact sent a flurry of explosive input throughout his entire body that split up in two responses. One was an intense cramping of just about every muscle he had, and the other was a rush of male awareness that left his skin humming and his senses drawing all the more sharply to attention.

"What if I am a Morphate," she demanded between gasps for breath. "Will you pull that gun on the nightstand and shoot me into vapor?"

Liam closed his eyes and gripped his teeth tightly together, his forehead touching her shoulder for a brief moment as he tried to push down his outrage. He was breathing so hard, his body shaking with such a fury of spasms and emotion, it was a wonder he didn't fly apart.

Instead he lifted his head and pressed a hot whisper against her ear.

"I am no murderer. And I told you before, killing is against the law. That includes the death of a Morphate . . . whether the law recognizes the possibility of it or not. The only reason I have not, and will not report the death of your assassin tonight is that I have sworn to my country that I won't be the one who reveals the nature of the relationship between mercury and Morphates to the public. Explaining the assassin's death and lack of body to the local cops would kinda go contrary to that promise. When you give me a way to incapacitate Morphates without killing them, Devon, you can bet your sweet ass that I will be using *that* instead of deadly force when given the choice. But since you were in such a goddamn rush to stick your neck out in public tonight without giving us the opportunity to prepare ourselves better, we had no choice in the matter.

"And if you're implying that I'd up and blow away any Morphate that crosses my path, Ms. Candler, just because I am one of the few who know how to do so, I'm going to be forced to remind myself really, *really* strongly that you don't know me well enough to realize that an implication like that would dangerously piss me off. And Devon, the last thing you want to do right now is piss me off. Are you getting that, or do I need to make the point clearer for you?"

He felt her shudder hard beneath him and he closed his eyes again briefly. He'd fantasized about feeling her shudder beneath his weight more often than he'd care to admit the past couple of days, but never had he wanted it to be in fear or anger or whatever the hell it was that she was feeling right then.

He wasn't expecting the emotional rasp of breath she drew in, so rough that it was close to a sob.

"Morphates used to be humans," she coughed out. "Eric Paulson created the Phoenix Project in an attempt to unlock the secrets of pushing back the aging process. He never intended on the immortality I have heard some refer to as an 'undesirable side-effect.' His intention had been to destroy the thousands of living results of his Phoenix Project. Discarding them just like he might have euthanized a lab full of rats that were part of a failed protocol. Only we refused to die. His undesirable side effect was immortality, and we refused to die even though he did everything from poisoning us to shooting us in the head."

She laughed with a breathy sound of bitterness that sounded tragically painful coming from her. Liam could tell she was visiting something or someone she had been in the past. Someone far more jaded and wounded than the woman he had been coming to know.

Liam had learned all of what she had told him and much

more than he'd ever wanted to know during his service. He'd had to learn about the Morphates in minute detail because he was charged with protecting humans from them. Really, it had come down to how hard and how fast a human could wound a Morphate. Wound them bad enough that they lost consciousness as their ravaged bodies regrouped. Up until his accidental encounter with a Morphate in which that creature had ended up dead.

Truly, finally dead.

He'd been treated like a hero. A messiah. All because he had solved a deadly mystery. He'd been attacked in a lab during a visit by the President of the Federated States he was protecting. He had been there, one on one, his weapon thrown across the room and nothing but bare fists and ingenuity to protect him from the rampage of a Morphate male bent on killing him and his principal. He had been grabbing blindly for something, anything to use and all he had come up with was a vial of unidentifiable fluid. He hadn't even cared what it was, he'd only wanted the glass vial. He'd shoved it into the Morphate's eye, ramming it home as deep as he could, the vial shattering under the pressure. He scrambled free of his attacker, intent on using the distraction to get away and find his gun or more backup. He didn't know. He didn't know. It was a fluke. Only a goddamn fluke. By the time he'd gotten to his weapon, the Morphate had been screaming and then . . . poof. Like a magic trick. Now you see him, now you don't.

It had sickened him at the time, both the death itself and the way he had been revered afterward. All for a stupid fucking accident. It had strongly motivated him in his decision to resign to the private sector.

But that wasn't what was at issue.

"Five thousand, two hundred and thirteen men, women, and children," he murmured gently against her temple.

Liam dug a knee into the mattress and lifted his weight. He turned her over beneath himself so he could see her flushed features. He pushed a mess of hair away from her face and took in the dampness around her eyes and the way her hands balled up into fists near her shoulders. She'd let them fall there even though he no longer held her, the position submissive and yet unwelcoming in its defensive and hostile tension. He couldn't blame her. He had been the one to unlock the key to finishing the genocide that had been so impossible the first time humans had tried it.

"And you were there," he realized quietly. "You are one of the original Morphates." Not one of the new generations, those strange children that were hidden away from the public in the Dark Cities. "A lot of things have gone right and wrong since then, too. People are unpredictable, and nine out of ten are really damn stupid, but that's true for all the races on this planet, Morphates most definitely included. But they don't mean shit to me right now, Devon. All that matters is what you and I are going to get straight between us."

Liam reached to palm her cheek, wanting so badly to touch her. But since he was bearing weight on his good arm, he reached with the bad.

"*Shit.*"

They cursed in tandem when he caught himself just in time to keep from dripping blood all over her face and hair. Liam flung himself back away from her and she scrambled for her kit the instant she was free of the cage of his body. He was sitting on the edge of the bed and she turned to stand between his knees as she put pressure on the wound left by the IV. Once she had taped that up, she leaned in to check his shoulder, pulling away the saturated bandages. The instant that sweet smelling hair brushed past to torture him, he reached out and secured his hand to the curve of her waist. He felt her hesitate. She went extremely still, under the guise of studying his wound, but he felt the tension in her every muscle.

"You need stitches," she said after a moment. She stepped back a bit, clearly testing the determination of his hold on her.

She cocked her head to the side and looked so purely puzzled, Liam had to resist a strangely powerful urge to scoop her up close and kiss the expression right off her face.

"Can you do it?" he asked instead, his gaze falling briefly on the complex and professional kit she'd been using so skillfully.

"Yes, but . . ."

"Then, you stitch and we'll finish talking while you do." He couldn't help his next impulse. "Is it better for you from the front or the back?"

He'd asked the question with just enough innuendo to get himself slapped. But this was Devon, and she wasn't exactly the shy and retiring type who got easily affronted. Her eyes widened a bit as she absorbed the intent of the remark, and he could swear he saw her mouth twitch at the corners.

"I think both," she said softly, a tilt to her head adding speculation to the answer. "We can start from the front, and . . . assuming you don't get too worn out, we'll finish from behind."

"And if I do get worn out?" he asked with a chuckle.

"Then I'll just have to lay you out flat on the bed and do you like that."

She turned to get her kit, but he saw the smile and impish victory in her eyes. He grinned like an idiot and didn't hide it when she turned back to him.

"Turn your shoulder toward me," she instructed. He did and she went about cleaning and disinfecting the area in preparation. He watched her prep to use another syringe.

"Now what the hell are you injecting me with?" he asked, rolling his eyes with exaggerated trepidation when he saw the new needle in her hand.

"Subcutaneous anesthetic. Stitches, remember?"

"Don't bother. A needle stabbing into my flesh repetitively won't exactly be noticed among the burning, cramping, and screaming pain."

"I hope you're being sarcastic," she said as she set aside the anesthetic and pulled on sterile gloves. "Isn't there any relief now that the antivenin is on board?"

"Yeah, actually," he agreed. "I'm moving, right? Coherent. And if I sit still and let you do that touching thing, the cramps ease to bearable levels. I wouldn't mind more of that after you do this."

Devon tilted her head, her eyebrows drawn down in so troubled an expression that he felt his chest constrict in empathy. "You . . ." She stopped and cleared her throat, straightening her posture as if she had felt too fragile in appearance. "You don't . . . aren't . . . bothered by the idea of me . . . h-helping you?"

There was a deep and tragic lifetime of pain and fear woven into that awkward statement of insecurity. Liam also knew she hadn't meant to say helping, and that she really wanted to know if he minded her touching him. In that instant he understood completely why she would hide herself away from the world, and hide what she was from those she let in. The scorn, the prejudice, and the hostility she suffered from millions who feared and hated her had to be a daunting existence. Who knew what she had experienced in her lifetime? Hell, Morphates were *immortal*, for God's sake. If she was one of those original five thousand, that would make her over seventy years old.

Christ.

And it wasn't just Paulson who bore blame for atrocities against the humans that became the Morphates. However unwittingly, the government had given Paulson an unending supply of bottom-rung citizens on which he could experiment. And then after they had been liberated from the hell of the Phoenix Project, the Morphates had had to endure a second imprisonment by their own government as the Federated States tried to figure out who and what they were. Only

Nick Gregory's stellar gambit of bringing the press onto the Phoenix Project site during their liberation kept them from being swept under the rug altogether like some dirty little secret. Just the same, how must it have felt? To go from Paulson's prison to the 'interment' labs, these ones government run? It was rumored that the government of the Federated States had tried, over a period of months, everything they could possibly think of to test just how far Morphate immortality went. And while it was damn near impossible to kill a Morphate, they felt pain as keenly as anyone else. They had psyches and they had memories, and Liam had realized long ago that they had a whole hell of a lot of good reasons to detest and distrust humans.

But here she was asking him if *he* detested *her*. She was wondering if he would shun and repel her just because she was . . .

She was a Morphate.

It actually made sense, he thought. She was stronger than the average woman. She had that wicked sex appeal that seemed to cling to Morphates both male and female, and she had sensed trouble tonight well before he had, even though he was highly trained for it. She'd done a fair job of covering her own tracks, too. He might have figured it out eventually, but now he'd never know for sure. Did this mean Carter Spencer was a Morphate? The household staff? Maybe not the staff, but Spencer sure had that holier-than-humans attitude.

He realized he was taking far too long to respond to her query when she took a step away from him, her expression struggling for impassivity but her hands shaking tellingly. Liam reached out without thinking and caught her at the small of her back, dragging her forward between his knees. She bumped breastbones with him and it forced her to exhale in a warm breath that spilled over him. He hadn't quite intended such a macho gesture, but the minute she was there, her warm breasts and softly curved body dragged up tight between his thighs, he realized it wasn't at all a bad experience. Neither was having her fine mouth so close to his as he looked into those sweetly surprised eyes of hers. She held her hands away from him, protecting the sterility of her gloves, and the gesture made him smile. Damned if he knew why, but something about the restriction imposed on her had the strangest effect on him.

"Now, I'm going to answer that question," he said, intentionally drawling out his words as he took his time openly inspecting her mouth. She instinctively parted her lips and licked them. "But I'm only going to do it once. You understand me? I won't answer it again, because I'm going to make damn sure you comprehend me."

Plotting his actions carefully, Liam used his injured arm, now dressed and cleaned of blood thanks to her care, sliding his fingers around the curve of her waist with a slow, purposeful caress. She glanced down as his fingertips stroked the skin left bared by her short sweater. Once he held her firmly with his wounded arm, knowing she wouldn't make any sudden movements that might hurt him, Liam then withdrew his healthy hand and reached to palm the nape of her neck. She stood there held in his hands, motionless, her hands spread away from contact, and her breath coming just as fast as his was.

"Are you surprised I'm touching you?" he asked, anticipation roughing up his voice. "Now that I know?"

"I don't . . ."

"Some believe that your kind can suck the life out of a person just by touching," he interrupted when it was clear he wasn't going to get the yes or no he wanted. "Are you sucking the life out of me?"

"No," she ground out, telling him she'd heard that ridiculous idea before.

"Yeah. If you ever suck the life out of me, I imagine I will be very much aware of it," he mused.

Her gasp was quick and soft, her formerly irritated gaze widening into shock first and then a confused sort of amusement. She didn't know what to make of what he was doing.

Gently, ignoring the cramps and aches it caused him, he slid his fingers under the hem of her sweater. He watched her face very carefully as he traveled over the silken skin covering her ribs and touched the incredibly soft underside of her breast. She made another of those breathy sounds of expectation and Liam relished it. He drew her so close to his mouth that they had to turn their heads to avoid bumping noses. Their rapid breath exchanged quickly as he slid one large hand around the full weight of her breast. She was heavy in his hand, her nipple instantly standing to attention at the stroke of his thumb. She exhaled the tiniest sound of pleasure and he felt it vibrating against his lips. His body exploded in response.

"When you said I wasn't your type," he growled abruptly, his lips nipping at hers as he spoke, "did you mean it because I wasn't your type, or because I was a human?"

"I meant because I was a Morphate," she breathed.

The distinction made sense. To her. It wasn't a matter of her not wanting to be with a human. She'd simply believed a human wouldn't want to be with her. Not if they knew what she was. And clearly, she wasn't the type who would pretend or lie when it would matter most.

"Why did you kiss me?" It was what he liked to call a dumb-ass question, but he had his reasons for asking.

"Because I wanted to." She reached to lay her hand on his face, remembered her gloves at the last moment and pulled back away. She made a sound of frustration as she turned to sweep her lips damply across his.

Liam let her invite him with the light teasing touch and

taste, neither accepting nor rejecting. Just feeling her irrepressible need as it overcame her thinking mind. She pulled back suddenly, a gasp escaping her so softly it was barely audible.

"Did you . . . are you angry that I kissed you?" She found his eyes, bravely needing to know his true feelings on the matter. "That I didn't tell you what I was and let you—"

"Let me!" Liam pulled back to bark out a brash male laugh. "Sweetheart, there wasn't any let in that kiss. I took." His hand at her breast squeezed firmly around her, his thumb and forefinger tugging at the gorgeous crest of her nipple. *Let him?* Christ, didn't the woman know he was only two minutes shy of molesting the hell out of her? Man, she felt sweet in his hand. He itched to have more of her under his touch. To lower his mouth to her sweater so he could taste her right through it. And when he felt these things, as heat and hormones swept through him, pain and tension disappeared to a dull spot far behind his awareness.

It didn't calm him down any when she responded to his manipulation of her body with an eager groan and an undulation of her body against his. Her breast came to snuggle forward into his palm, her thighs shifted between his as she used her body to do what she couldn't do with her hands. She used her mouth to take what he wouldn't give.

She surged forward to catch him in a kiss so much deeper than the teasing touches they'd been torturing themselves with these past minutes, and Liam groaned with the relief of it when her sweet tongue finally returned to his mouth where it belonged. She was so damned aggressive, so hungry, it was more than he could resist in his weakened condition. Or so he told himself when he impulsively slid his palm down the long line of her spine and cupped a fine, firm cheek of her ass. He made another throaty sound as he drew her closer and tighter against himself. A pulse pounding erection was probably the very last thing he needed at the moment, but he was fairly certain he didn't give a damn.

Devon went to touch him, to hold him to her mouth and taste him so deeply he would never escape, even though he hardly seemed to want to. She was drawn up short by her gloved hands yet again and she jerked her mouth free of his with a gasp.

"Liam! Your shoulder!"

"Fuck my shoulder," he growled. "Give me your mouth, Devon."

But the doctor in Devon was already overriding her hormones. She wriggled in his hold, trying to escape him, but having little luck. In fact, Liam seemed to be enjoying her struggles. He even chuckled.

"Liam, please. Let me stitch you. You're getting blood everywhere. All over me."

It was as though she'd spoken a secret code. His arms unlocked from around her so quickly that she stumbled back. He caught her by her waist though before she went any further than his knees, his darkened eyes inspecting her rapidly. He frowned when he saw his blood smearing her sweater in places. She smiled to comfort him and leaned for the curved needle and silk she'd set up. She picked up forceps for herself and handed him a pair of surgical scissors.

"Hold those for me," she said, somehow managing to sound steady in spite of the fact that the feel of the fingers still against her bare waist was driving her nuts. He had such rough, capable hands, and he sure as hell knew how to touch a woman. The way he stroked her and clasped her with such proprietary need made her feel wildly wanted. And she was wildly wanted, she thought breathlessly and with wonder. He knew she was a Morphate, and Liam Nash wanted her. He wanted her to help him, to touch him, and . . .

She shivered and took a deep breath. If she was going to stitch him without butchering him, she needed to calm down and stop the shaking in her hands.

"Liam," she said after a rocky breath, "I'm sorry I didn't

tell you the truth when you took this assignment. I would understand if you withdrew NHK services."

The jab of the needle into his wounded flesh kept him from turning on her furiously, but she felt his hand grip into her soft skin intensely.

"Why in hell would I do that?" he demanded, looking like he would turn her over his knee if he thought he could pull it off at that moment. "Being a Morphate instead of a human doesn't change a damn thing about your needs and our services. You made sure we knew the score up front, and keeping your race a secret doesn't nullify a contract. It doesn't have anything to do with it."

Devon bit her lip, chewing it in thought for a moment.

"Actually, it does in a way," she argued. "There are quite a few Morphates in this world that would consider me a traitor, Liam, for taking part in the construction of the weaponry to subdue and kill our kind."

"Well, that's just too bad, isn't it?" he said sharply. "There are gun and ordnance manufacturers all over the world, Devon, and plenty of people who don't like the fact that those things are made to kill humans, but that doesn't give anyone the right to hunt and kill the creators. Especially not in this country. We aren't always stellar in our behavior, and your people know that better than any, but our intentions as a society are generally good and sound. Unfortunately, society is made up of all kinds and like I said before, some people can be damn stupid."

She nodded and paused in her work to clean the wound of blood. The bleeding had slowed considerably, but she knew he'd already lost too much. Any was too much when it came to fighting off venom. She didn't know what he was using to stay upright at the moment, but when it wore off he was going to crash extremely hard. For the moment, though, she relaxed against him.

Devon felt as though a huge weight had been lifted from

her. She felt she was a terrible liar, mainly because she hated deception so very much, and she'd despised lying to him. But he was quick to reassure her that he understood on a professional level and that it didn't matter one way or the other to him or affect the contracts they had signed.

Did that mean his touches and kisses meant the same thing, but on a personal level? Lord, were they *having* a personal level? It was a terrible idea all around, and they both knew it. They had both said as much only a few hours ago, but since that kiss in the limousine, and just now when he'd held her . . .

Devon snuck a peek at him through her hair, only to find him completely focused on her face and now looking dead into her eyes. She licked her lips and turned her attention back to her task, pretending she hadn't seen him smile with a rather male smugness. The man was far too confident and outrageous for his own damn good. He never seemed at a loss for what to do in a situation. How did someone so young manage to pull that off? Well, not so young by human standards, she supposed, but it had taken her a couple of lifetimes, a few careers, and a drastic genetic alteration to find the kind of confidence he exuded.

Liam now understood the medical kit and the efficient care she was giving him. Even her manner as she worked was subconsciously full of that arrogance that only an experienced medical professional acquired. She had been a doctor.

A doctor and who knew what else. Christ, she was an older woman. A much, much, *much* older woman. He swallowed hard against the tension in his throat as he thought about that for a moment.

She was a Morphate. An immortal. Her body perpetually healed itself and shed all signs of aging so that she remained forever young and forever beautiful. It was Paulson's ultimate achievement. Because of it, she might have had half a dozen careers. An untold number of lovers.

The lurch of hot, negative emotion surging to life within him at the thought of Devon in bed with a parade of other men had him sucking in a hard breath through flaring nostrils.

"Sorry," she murmured soothingly near his ear, mistaking his tense reaction as a sign of pain. "You're lucky. She didn't get you too far beyond the fascia. No muscle damage and the tendons and ligaments were all spared, otherwise you'd be in surgery right now. In the end, all you'll have is a nice macho scar to tell stories about."

He already had enough of those. He didn't give a damn about scars or injuries.

Not his own.

Liam suddenly reached for the hem of her skirt, his palm dragging the material up high along the warm skin of her thigh. He heard her gasp, felt her jerk, but her hands were completely occupied and there was nothing she could do about it.

"Liam!"

He ignored her protest, took a moment to enjoy the tremble that shuddered through her as he gathered the material up against the curve of her bottom, and then leaned as far as he could around her to see her opposite thigh where she'd been shot.

"Liam, sit still! Let go of my skirt!" She squirmed a little, and then when he let go of her skirt so he could slide his hand around the smooth skin of her previously wounded leg, feeling for remnants of the injury, she squirmed a great deal more.

Liam didn't blame her. He wanted to do a bit of squirming himself. Her skin was on fire, but that was nothing compared to the heat of her nearby sex. She was mere inches and a turn of his wrist away. Suddenly he could smell her as well as feel her, his senses knowing without a doubt that she was wet and musky hot from their earlier play. She wore no panties, he realized as his thumb strayed over the contours of where her ass blended into her thighs.

Devon fell heavily against him and moaned close to his ear. "Please, Liam," she begged him, "I can't help you like this."

"Answer a question, Devon," he instructed her as he drew back to stroke her over the mildly safer territory of her thigh. "Did they shoot you with mercury? Is that why the wound still wasn't healed when we first met?"

"Yes," she replied quietly, her smooth thighs shifting restlessly against his hand and arm.

Liam tightened the grip he had around her legs and bottom for an instant, closing his eyes as his teeth clenched in spasm. "Through and through?" he demanded roughly. "Is that why you survived? It went through and the mercury didn't have a chance to discharge?"

"Yes. Only small traces were left. Enough to hinder healing. Please sit up and relax, Liam. Let me finish this. It's okay now. As you can see, I'm perfectly healed." He did as she asked so easily that she was surprised, but after smoothing her skirt back into place, he returned a possessive arm around her waist, fingers pressed into her side firmly. "Liam," she scolded with a laugh, "this is a little awkward." She indicated how he was keeping her cuddled close like some kind of favorite toy.

But when she met his eyes and saw the cold glitter within and the thin line of his compressed lips, her amusement floated away. She held her hands poised mid stitch as she stared at his black expression and tried to understand it.

"How much does it take, Devon?" he asked in a low, flat voice that seemed so alien coming from him when she was used to the depth and richness of his normal speech.

She blinked. "I'm afraid I don't understand."

"Mercury. How much does it really take? What's the process? The science? We put about a half a cc in our bullets, and we haven't had enough experience to really figure it out, but I know you know, and I want you to tell me."

Devon felt an icy chill walk her spine and she turned to look at her hands, though she was too blinded by emotion to move them. "I'm not supposed to—"

"Don't spout that confidentiality bullshit to me, Devon. I'm the one who figured this out in the goddamn first place! Now answer me! How much does it take? I know one bullet isn't usually enough, unless maybe it's the luckiest shot in a lifetime. Tell me."

"It varies, depending on the sex and size of the Morphate," she said quietly, "but fifteen milliliters will guarantee death in any Morphate."

"A tablespoon?" he said almost numbly.

"Yes, but . . . bullets are also doing damage and spreading the contaminant, so it can take less in those circumstances. For instance the damage you did to kill your original Morphate. The mercury and glass went straight into his brain, that was why it worked so fast and so thoroughly even though there wasn't all that much in the vial."

His hand slid from her waist, down the curve of her buttock and curled around her formerly injured thigh once again, the stroke all about tenderness and nothing sexual. It stole her breath away and she looked down on his bent head with bemusement. She automatically continued her stitches as she waited to see what he would do next. He seemed to shift in such odd directions so suddenly, she simply couldn't figure him out.

"What happens if it's not enough mercury? Poisoning?"

"A tablespoon brings instant vaporization once it floods the major organs. Just about anything less than that simply kills more slowly with poisoning. It would have to be less than a teaspoon in order for the Morphate to survive."

"A single bullet."

"Just about," she agreed with a nod. "Depends on the caliber and the load in the particular bullet."

"So someone came at you with an Uzi full of mercury and you managed to get out of that alive?"

Thinking she saw where he was headed now, she took the scissors from his other hand and neatly trimmed her work, inspecting it as she thought about what to say to him. She was not going to tell him any more lies, but she sensed he was already broiling with temper.

"I would be dead if he'd just shot me while I slept," she said carefully, pulling off her gloves and tossing everything over to the nightstand with a noisy clang. She pushed back a little so she could frame his face in her hands and tilted up so she could meet his hard eyes. "However, the sight of me naked in my bed gave him other ideas first, thereby giving me the advantage."

"Motherfucker!"

The evil expletive exploded out of him as he tried to find his feet. Devon knew he couldn't help himself. He was a man used to action and motion. In a temper, he no doubt wanted to stalk and pace to vent his emotion.

However, that wasn't going to be an option for him this time. She set a strong hand down on his good shoulder, exerting her strength against his as she held him down. It was far easier than it would have been had he been in good health. Regardless, Liam was furious on so many levels it was a wonder he didn't split right apart. Keeping him still wasn't helping matters. Devon shrugged and smiled just a little before she used her free hand to catch his face and turn him up to the fall of her mouth.

Liam was too combustible to take her gently, his entire psyche roiling with feelings he couldn't name, never mind grasp. He damn well didn't appreciate her strong-arming him, and her tactic to distract him was the oldest trick in the book! He used the arm around her waist to yank her into his body, lay back and rolled with her until she was once again under him. Liam's goal was to take the dominant position and get up once she no longer had him caged in. Although, the moment he settled into her long, soft body, he found he suddenly wasn't in so much of a rush anymore. Her mouth was damp and lush and he was channeling anger like hunger into her kiss, and she was returning it to him measure for measure. Slowly he became aware of the true heat of her body, the awesome womanly scent of her flowing all over him as he drew away from her mouth just enough to look down into pale jade eyes clouded with need and swollen lips gleaming with the mark of his kiss.

Then he realized he was too damn tired to put up a fight anymore. He ached from head to toe with pain and pent up passion. His shoulder was throbbing and he felt like Quasimodo with an enormous hump deforming him.

He was nestled snugly between the thighs of the most outrageously sexy woman in all the living world, and all he wanted to do was lick every succulent inch of her until he satisfied the seemingly insatiable need he had to taste her. And that was only the start of a long list of insatiable needs he had concerning her.

Devon watched Liam very carefully and felt when the weight of his body began to increase exponentially on top of hers, pressing her deeply into the mattress. His lashes lowered over dimming dark eyes and she heard him sigh just before he stroked his mouth over hers in a slow, steady kiss that was thoughtful and skilled rather than wildly emotional, as it had been a moment ago. Either way, he was one of the most incredible kissers she'd ever known. He took such care to search and search, craving the knowledge of every inch of her mouth, but never overwhelming or intrusive in his passionate hunt. Slowly she felt the change from his trying to arouse her to just taking pleasure in the softness and taste of her mouth.

By the time he lifted his head again, she could barely

breathe beneath his weight on top of her, but she made not the slightest complaint as his lashes shadowed his cheeks and the tension washed out of his facial features. He stared down at her and reached to toy with a lock of her hair, gently sliding the silky texture between his fingers.

"I know what's happening," he mused in a voice roughed and slurred with sudden exhaustion. "Promise me you won't go out of the house without me."

"Liam . . ."

"Promise," he demanded, lowering his head to kiss the pulse along the side of her neck. "I trust my people, but don't risk them yet. I need time. Promise."

"Okay," she breathed against his ear, her fingers sifting through his spiky hair, feeling the dampness of perspiration in it. "I won't leave."

Satisfied, Liam laid his head down on her shoulder and fell asleep.

Devon let an entire thirty minutes pass, letting him reach a deep sleep and, to be honest, relishing the weight of him on her. Then she gently rolled him off of her body, arranged him comfortably in bed, and left the room to update his waiting coworkers on his condition.

Chapter Eight

Liam woke three days later feeling like he'd been on a three-day bender. A shave and a shower improved matters greatly, but didn't shake off the killer headache pounding behind his eyes. He kept having the urge to touch under his nose to check for blood. Surely his sinuses were beyond pressure capacity and would explode at any moment?

Devon found him sprawled back crookedly over his bed, clutching his head and groaning in a whisper. She suppressed a laugh, drawing attention to herself when it made her snort. Liam opened a single eye and glared at her.

"You find this funny?"

"Come on, you're just dehydrated," she scoffed at him as she grabbed for his hand and tried to pull him upright.

"I'm not going anywhere until my brain fits back inside my skull."

"I wouldn't be contrary if I were you. I won't be kind to your head if you make me force you. Let's go. Up, up," she coaxed.

Liam did as commanded, rising to his feet and leaning against her a little when the blood in his head pounded. Once everything settled, he followed her out of the suite. He kept his eyes mostly closed, trusting her to guide him as he flinched away from the daylight. She kept hold of one of his big hands with both of her smaller ones. She brought him into a morning room, making him realize that it was well into the afternoon because there was no direct sunlight in the eastern facing windows.

In spite of the time, however, the table in the room was set with the makings of a hearty breakfast and lots of fruit and juices. Liam was suddenly famished and he practically threw himself into one of the chairs. Devon began to lift covers off of eggs, ham, mounds of toast and bacon. "Cook would be happy to make you a steak if you prefer that to—"

"No, this is great," he said quickly.

Devon had served him a large plateful of everything before he realized it; then she sat down with tea and toast for herself. He picked up his juice, emptied the glass in just a few swallows, and then refilled it. She was right of course; he was hellishly thirsty. "You know," he said after picking up his fork, "you aren't required to serve me. Or keep me company. I'm not here to disrupt the way you live any more than is necessary for security reasons."

Stillness shimmered over her, her genuine smile fading into something less readable. Her eyes turned to focus on her teacup and toast. "You're so right. I'm sorry. You also have a total right to be alone and at peace when you wish it. I don't know how I could be so presumptuous."

Devon stood up hastily, but Liam was already reacting. He had her by the wrist with the lock of his hand and jerked her forward as he came out of his chair. The result was full body contact. It happened so fast that the ring of his fork hitting his plate was still in the air.

"Liam," she protested.

"No. Look at me, Devon."

Devon did, her eyes snapping up with irritated fire. He had to suppress a smile, lest she think he was laughing at her. It was just, her spirit charmed him so much at the most unexpected moments.

"Devon, I didn't mean that to sound so damn cold. It was a scripted remark, one I've used before in the workplace with my principals, and it came out automatically. I enjoy your company a great deal. I didn't mean I wished to be alone. I only meant that I didn't want you to feel you are required to wait on me."

"Liam, I'm a powerful, independent woman who does whatever she likes, whenever she likes. There's nothing about you that would compel me to change that. I'm here because I wish to be, not because it's required."

It was a compliment and an insult all wrapped up together. Liam stared down at her, completely bemused. Finally, he lifted her hand and kissed the back of it, briefly enjoying the clean scent of her skin. "Then let's eat," he invited.

Devon stepped back, peeling her body away from his as though they were two static filled socks fresh out of the dryer. The moment she understood he wasn't trying to scrape her off, she felt that instant attraction that continually pulled them together. He'd done little more than sleep these past couple of days and though she'd spent almost every minute caring for him, she had missed his vitality and the electricity of his waking presence.

Missed him. When she'd only spent so few hours knowing him. It was insane. It was silly. It was . . .

Undeniable. She had lived long enough to know the truth in the things she felt. The truth of the matter was that she was flushed with lust for a human male for the first time in decades. She knew she was hard to please to begin with. Ever since she had left the Morphate enclave of Dark Manhattan, encounters with Morphate males were few and far between. But the move had been very necessary. Her Alpha, Nick Gregory, had deemed it so. And whatever else she was, she would always be loyal to Nick and Amara Gregory. So that had left her with a very rare selection of Morphates living outside of the Dark Cities to choose from, and those males tended to be walking the wrong side of the law and the wrong side of their loyalty to Nick. Despite her voracious Morphate drive and appetites, for her, sex was far too personal an exchange to waste on the untrustworthy and the arrogant.

As far as human males went, she'd always been a little afraid of breaking them. Even the strong ones. She knew she could damage them if she got carried away, and what fun was bed sport without the option of getting carried away? Then there was simply the short-sightedness and rampant immaturity than ran like water through humans in general. It was a turn off.

But Liam was something entirely different. He was that pure Alpha male personality that attracted her madly, with the build and body to damn well back it up. She wasn't afraid of breaking him, that much was certain. She might be the stronger of the two of them, but strength wasn't everything, and Liam practically hummed with confidence in his prowess. That and the way he moved, with a purely male ease of contained power, perfectly balanced and tautly controlled. And just the smell of him. The excellent masculine aroma of heat and soap and sweat. Add to it the chemistry between them, and they lit up like the Las Vegas strip every time they came close.

Oh yes. She wanted this man in a bad, bad way.

But the fact that he was fresh out of his sickbed was only the beginning of the host of problems this particular desire would create. She knew her body wanted his with an incredible intensity, but there were things to be considered. There were reasons why she should be cautious and careful. There were always reasons why she needed to be cautious and careful.

She sat down slowly, smoothing her skirt and taking a careful sip of her tea.

"Have you been getting along all right with my crew?" he asked after a few minutes of relishing his first meal in days; looking around himself as if his crew would be somewhere within sight just because he was talking about them.

"Quite well. They're efficient and they take great pains to explain everything they have to do. We've been practicing some procedures for public outings. Inez is a wonder—"

"Good afternoon! Or should I say morning?"

Devon watched Liam's entire body stiffen, his demeanor changing instantly as Carter Spencer entered the room. Carter bent to kiss Devon's cheek, his hand sliding beneath her hair at the back of her neck in a possessive gesture. He kept it there as he stood to face Liam.

"Breakfast at 2 P.M.? Devon, it's so very continental of you."

"Carter," she greeted, "you know that one of the rules of this house is that I don't adhere to the conventional if I can get away with it."

"Well, I've come to scold you yet again. You've been positively neglectful of your work these past three days," Carter said, pointedly sliding a disdainful glance at the cause of her truancy. "We're behind on everything. You know the world can't revolve without you."

"Carter, really," she reproached sternly, flushing with embarrassment at his behavior. He was acting like a total ass, confirming Liam's dislike of him and shaming her defense of her secretary. Carter was purposely trying to make Liam feel a cut below Devon. It irritated her. It was the story of her life, it seemed, to be surrounded by obnoxious intolerance.

"Spencer," Liam put in calmly, continuing his breakfast as though nothing had disturbed him. But Devon could see the hard gleam in his amber eyes that told her exactly how Liam felt about Spencer and his intrusion. "Give me that smart phone you're always carrying around." There was no asking. It was an order, no matter how casually it was put.

Spencer went rigid. "That's private and no business of yours," he said in clipped tones.

"Actually, it *is* my business. Anything that concerns Devon, now concerns me. The slightest endangerment or whisper of a threat will be met by me until I'm satisfied that it's eliminated." Devon felt Carter's entire body tensing all the way to the fingers around her neck. "Right now," Liam continued, "that threat is you and your open-house style of information storage."

Liam settled back in his chair and extended his jean-clad legs under the table until he was framing Devon's calves with a shin on either side. She could feel his warmth right through the denim and the large muscles flexed against her, drawing all of her attention to the solidity of them. For some reason, it sent chills up both of her legs. She hid a shiver under the guise of sipping her tea, but she knew Carter would feel it regardless. She wished he'd remove his hand from her neck. She didn't want to correct his behavior in front of Liam any more than was necessary. It wouldn't do for this to become—

"Devon, really! Are you going to let this . . . this . . ."

Devon's eyes snapped up, freezing whatever disparagement was forthcoming from Carter's lips with her look alone. She reached up and brushed away his hand with annoyance. "Be very careful what you say, Carter," she warned him icily. "You know how I feel about that. Will you please give him the smart phone?"

Carter shifted narrowed eyes from Liam to Devon and back again. Devon saw his nose twitch tellingly and it was all she could do to suppress a growl of dominance to kick his ass back in line where it damn well belonged. How dare he! Sniffing around to see if she and Liam were combining scents! As if that would have anything to do with the matter! If Carter thought that taking a human lover would lead to her falling under the influence of that human, well, then he didn't know a damn thing about her. After so many years. It was all she could do to see straight, she was so incensed.

Beneath the table, she felt Liam's legs press against hers, a covert sort of hug that brought her attention back to him with a start. He had a lazy expression on his face, his lips quirked up on one side.

And just like that her anger was gone. She didn't understand why, but his amusement over the entire exchange knocked her temper off at the knees. Suddenly she felt relieved, as though finally there was something she could allow someone else to worry about for her. Liam was doing exactly what she had hired him to do. What she had hoped he could do.

He was helping her breathe. He could have easily turned this into a pissing contest with Carter, and Carter was clearly willing despite his age and supposed maturity. But Liam had no desire to prove who was in charge.

He already knew who was in charge.

Apparently, Carter caught up with that understanding a few seconds later when he grumbled, "At least allow me a few hours to back things up and remove my personal business from it."

"Of course. No one is out to disturb your privacy, Carter," she said easily, though she could feel the fleeting tension in Liam against her legs. "Turn it over to Liam by five. I'm sure he only means to secure it."

"Whatever makes you safer, Devon," Spencer said stiffly before he pecked her on the cheek again and left the room.

Liam watched the small demonstration of affection with dark, brooding eyes. He decided instantly that he didn't like Spencer behaving so familiarly with Devon. He hardly thought Devon was the type of woman to be so casually affectionate with her employees. She placed definitive boundaries on those in her sphere, pigeonholing them into certain behaviors and acceptable interactions, and she made it quickly clear what she expected from an individual. She had certainly made it clear to Liam that she was breaking all rules where he was concerned, and it hardly even fazed her. From the start she had scattered personal boundaries between them to the four winds.

"You have a talent for that, don't you?" he asked, picking up his coffee cup. His headache had faded already, only a dull throb in the back of his neck remaining. He stretched out the small kinks that yet remained as he spoke.

"For what?"

"Taking care of multiple problems in one fell swoop. You got me that smart phone, avoided Spencer meeting a horrible death at my hands, and got him out of the room posthaste." He grinned devilishly. "I'm impressed."

"Really, Liam," she scolded sternly. But he saw her hide her smile behind her teacup and her amusement was sparkling in her eyes. "I don't think I've ever enjoyed being in the middle of a pissing contest." She was serious now. "I'd like it if you and Carter could find a way to be civil."

"You might help me out with that by telling me if Carter Spencer is a Morphate."

Her movements quieted noticeably, a single fingertip touching the edge of her cup thoughtfully. "Why? What difference would that make to you?"

"It means I will know what to shoot him with if he turns out to be a threat to you." Liam held up a hand to stay her automatic protest. "I'm not making snap judgments, trust me. I will do a great deal of research on everybody who comes anywhere near you. Equal opportunity suspicion, I promise." He laid his hand over his heart and aimed that troublesome smile at her again. Devon sighed a soft laugh, resisting an urge to throw something at him because he so easily confused her feelings. "Tell me who in this house is Morphate and who is human, Devon. I'll have Colin leave a list of names with you and you can return it to me later."

"I don't know if I like this request, Liam," she said with a dark frown. "It seems so . . ."

"What it is, Devon, is caution and logic. I'm not going to pussyfoot around your hang-ups with racism. Morphates can only be killed with irradiated mercury and I want to know how to kill your maid, your butler, and your damn poodle before the day is out. You understand? Anything that can hurt you, I have to know how to hurt first. It's as simple as that. And if you're worried about that pompous ass you call a secretary, you damn well ought to be, because he is high on my list already."

"Just because he is being careless with his smart phone doesn't give you cause to suspect him! Or is it because he's careless *and* a Morphate?"

"I suspect him because I was standing next to him in a room with at least five others when I learned enough about you to find plenty of opportunity in which to kill you." He ticked examples off on his fingertips. "I know you're going to Milan in October. That you'll be attending the runways in Paris for the new fashions. Oh, and you're giving a charity speech at the Crescent Foundation Ball in November. Screw the smart phone, Devon. The idiot is blabbing your private schedule from here to Timbuktu because he's a thoughtless, bragging piece of shit who makes himself sound better than he is just because he's riding your sexy little coattails."

Devon had visibly paled, her bottle green gaze turning quickly contrite. "I see," she said softly. "I hadn't realized. I apologize."

"Stop apologizing. All I'm saying is it's a problem that needs to be fixed. As soon as possible. I know it generally sucks when you trust someone and that person makes mistakes, but your life is in danger, Devon. Mistakes cannot be forgiven right now, and they cannot be ignored as potential threats in disguise.

"Someone is making it easy for your enemies to find you.

You were out of the house for barely three hours this most recent night you were attacked. I know we weren't followed by any conventional means, so how did an assassin find you so easily? Unless they knew your schedule in advance, I can't figure it out. And as sharp as their senses are, Morphates can't track without following a path. We would've seen them. You would have seen them. Sensed them." He sighed heavily. "I'm going to have your phone lines secured. You ought to use landlines only. It's easier than you think to trace cell calls. Keep the cell with you always though. Even in the house. You never know when you might need it and I want you to get in the habit."

"This is impossible!" Devon jerked herself out of her chair, her hands slamming down on the tabletop. China bounced and clattered as she flung herself away, marching over to the windows so she could look outside. "I can handle inconvenience, Liam, but they will win this war if I become paralyzed by fear."

"Not paralyzed. Cautious," Liam corrected as he quickly came up behind her. His large hands engulfed her shoulders, sending warmth up over her neck and down her arms until she shivered. She felt his face gently nuzzling the top of her head and she forced herself to resist the urge to lean back into his strength. She had a long, dangerous road ahead of herself, and she couldn't afford to depend on anyone. Especially not a human. He'd already risked death once thanks to her overconfident behavior.

"My freedom is being destroyed, and it will only get worse," she whispered, her pain tightening Liam's insides like wet leather left in the sun. "Whoever is targeting me is only the first to know about these weapons. Imagine when other Morphates begin to find out what I've done."

Liam sighed, long and low, knowing she was probably right. He couldn't resist the urge to pull her back against himself, one of his arms crossing her chest from shoulder to shoulder. She reached up to clasp his forearm, accepting his comfort though she wouldn't look away from the view outside the windows.

"Believe me, we're going to make it clear to your enemies that you are off-limits. Once you make a mark on them, everyone else will think three times before facing you down. Then, after the weapons enter mainstream production, there will be nothing they can do about it."

"Except to exact revenge. Morphate clans never forget a slight. They live a very long time and have very long memories."

"Maybe if you make a strong enough and shocking enough show of force, they will never bother you again," he suggested, the silk of her hair brushing against his lips.

"What could be shocking enough to quell Morphates? Not even my weapons will change their unmitigated thirst for revenge, believe me."

"Discover which Alpha is after you and destroy his clan," he suggested softly. Devon whirled completely around in his hold, her eyes wide and horrified. "Hey, you wanted a mercenary," he reminded her. "That's a mercenary solution. I don't particularly like the idea any more than you do—it'd kick up a hell of a hornet's nest if we screw up—but I don't see much in the way of a resolution otherwise."

Devon felt ice running down her spine, her heart aching as it sped along violently. She pushed away from him, wrapping her arms around herself. She was furious with her people, enough to have created weapons of death and debilitation, but Liam was suggesting a form of genocide. She couldn't blame Liam for his cavalier attitude. Her people had given him no cause to think well of them. But she couldn't do what he suggested. She might be willing to cut a swath with mercury through them to make a statement if she was forced to, but she could never permit extermination.

"I could never authorize something so brutal. I haven't the

authority or the right. Only the Alpha Council does, but even they shouldn't do so." She looked at him with stunned jade soft eyes. "How can you even suggest an act of genocide?"

"Honey." Liam narrowed thoughtful eyes on her a moment. "I said destroy, not murder. There's a huge difference."

"I . . ." She shook her head hard, as if trying to resettle her brain. "You need to explain."

"I'm talking about a multi-level assault that would incapacitate the clan. The eventual goal being dispersion. If you can weaken the cohesion that holds a clan together, you can destroy it. And that will show the remaining clans that you mean business and that you aren't going to run and hide." He grinned when her already wide eyes went even rounder as she began to understand. "I'm not saying we are going to pull it off with a zero-gas-cloud count. You wanna kill a beast, you gotta chop off its head, and that means going for the Alpha."

"Tell me," she demanded, springing over to him and clutching at his shirt. "Tell me what you mean by incapacitation!"

"There are three things that give Morphates power. Their money, their physical prowess, and their confidence in their superiority. Take away the first two and the last one takes care of itself. Once doubt and fear begin to erode the connectivity of the clan, the members will start to peel away like layers of an onion. Once the Alpha loses face . . ." He trailed off, knowing that no one knew better than she did how the hierarchy of an Alpha-run clan went.

"Oh my God," she breathed, delight rushing up over her entire body. "Of course! It's like a hostile takeover! You buy the stock out from under them. Sneak up and woo away the employees . . . Liam!"

"If you think you can identify the Alpha, I think my guys can handle the rest."

"Yes! Oh, yes!" She leapt at him, her arms wrapping around his neck as she hugged him. He chuckled, sliding his arms around her and cuddling her close, enjoying her squirming enthusiasm. It didn't bother him that she'd momentarily thought him capable of such barbarism as genocide. It came with the career. And she did not know him well yet in spite of the incredible connection they seemed to have developed between them already. But she was learning.

Meanwhile, he was able to take in the scent of her hair and the feel of her warm, soft body as she laughed happily in his ear, making him smile that he could help her and please her. It'd already become important to him. Dangerous, to be sure, to start to feel attached to one's principal. It had the potential to lead to mistakes. Emotions clouded a man's reactions and clarity of sight.

Still . . . she was a special woman. It took a special being to take the assault she was facing and yet not desire ferocious retaliation of her own. What she wanted was that a lesson be learned. Equalization. An awakening, however rude it might be, to the wrongness of superiority among intelligent beings.

They were all fine ideals, but Liam wondered about the human half of the equation. Human unpredictability could make this weapon into the most volatile invention in history since the atomic bomb. Just because Devon wouldn't lower herself to the level of her enemies, didn't mean that others wouldn't. It tautened his nerves just thinking about it, making him realize he had unintentionally signed NHK on for a potential war. Granted, bodyguards were always in the middle of two factions, determined to protect one from the other, but this had the potential to ripple out into the world with a huge effect. Taking an active part in the controversy was not something he could choose to do on behalf of his people. Fairness required him to tell them the truth of things and ask them straight out how far they were willing to take themselves in this game.

Liam stepped back, releasing Devon as he went, feeling his skin tighten when she looked at him with a touch of bewilderment. She was so damn sensitive that she had already begun to feel his tension.

"What?"

"I have to tell my crew, Devon. Who you are. What you are. Everything to do with this. They have a right to know: to choose if they'll stay on for this. I've also been out of the loop around here for three days and I gotta get back in." He reached to run a distracted hand over his hair, unknowingly making it spike and curl in all directions.

"I don't mind if you tell your crew. You're right, they deserve the choice. However, please ask them not to repeat the information. I . . . The staff's completely human and they don't know I am Morphate. All except Carter, as you guessed," she said.

"Not a problem. Thanks for breakfast. I have a lot of work to catch up on, okay?" he said, reaching to brush a thumb over her chin and jawline. "But at sunset, you and I are going to start playing with those new weapons you keep promising to show me, okay?"

"I'd be happy to," she laughed.

Devon watched as he hesitated, his thumb clinging to her skin just below her cheek. Then he shook his head in bemusement and that thumb moved slowly back to the sensitive pout of her lower lip. Liam's fingers curled up snug beneath her chin and tilted her head up ever so slightly, his mouth playing with a frown and small lines appearing between his brows.

Then he turned and left the room quickly, almost as if he were afraid that if he tarried, there would be developments beyond his control. Devon wrapped her arms around herself, a little quiver of thwarted excitement rocking through her.

That man, she thought, was just too damn tempting for his own good. Certainly too damn tempting for hers. The question was, what was she going to do about it?

Torque lowered his binoculars and leaned back against the trunk of the enormous oak. The tree had been generous enough to provide a well-concealed perch for himself and

Rhiannon as they observed the compound. Rhiannon was on a nearby branch, straddling it with muscular thighs encased in riding leather. She was watching him, waiting for his latest observations with the patience of an adolescent. She was plucking at her Harley T-shirt's decal irritably, and she was pissed off that they hadn't yet found an opportunity to get to Devona.

But he was working on it.

"She has this estate of hers well thought out," he observed. "And these private security people really know what they're doing. If we were humans, it would be impossible for us to get into that house."

"Right, but we aren't humans," Rhiannon drawled, rocking her hips so her legs swung a bit on either side of the branch. She set her hands on the bark in front of her, the entire position and movement looking as if she was riding a hobbyhorse.

Torque grinned. Rhiannon always had to have something between her legs. Tree branches, her Millennium Edition Harley-Davidson motorcycle, or just about anything or anyone else that crossed her path. Torque got a hell of a kick out of that. He and Rhi had worked in groups together before, but most dispatchers for Ambrose Clan worked alone. It was the first time they'd ever been paired up. Despite her impatience, she was all business, and he liked that.

"Yeah. There's also a good chance those aren't regular bullets in those guns either. They're expecting someone like us to show up eventually. Ambrose hasn't exactly been sending subtle messages."

Rhi rolled her eyes in agreement. "Not to mention that the traitor whore will sense us if she is awake when we get close enough. This will be a waste of our time if all we do is kill a few humans. They will just find more to replace the dead ones. They always have more."

Torque agreed with that observation with a grim nod. "We have to wait until she moves off the property then."

"We've been here for nearly two days and she hasn't left yet," Rhi observed.

"She will. Then we follow and we watch and we wait. I'll go for the mark, and you can lay waste to the rest of them, clearing the field for me."

"Mmm," Rhi purred eagerly. "Look at the size of some of them. They will pop like nice, fat, juicy grapes!"

"Yeah, well, there's only one that worries me, Rhi. That big bastard right over there."

Rhi narrowed her eyes on the human male she could easily see striding over the lawn. Like the rest, he wore all black, a shoulder holster and a hip weapon besides. He was a center point. A leader. Most likely the man in charge of the security detail. He never got more than a few feet at a time without someone running up to him to ask something, or his electronic devices calling his attention. But all the while those eyes would roam not only the property but as far beyond as he could manage. Those sharp eyes had encouraged them to move their vantage point back deeper into the tree line.

He'd come out of nowhere. In all the time they had been surveying the situation, they had never once seen him. Not until about three hours ago when he had walked out of the house for the first time. There would be no mistaking or missing a man of his size. He was huge. And while that meant little to a Morphate, this was apparently the human who had set up this situation well enough to keep even Morphates away from their target within. That deserved some respect and some caution.

"So you want me to take him out first?"

"That would be the best, though we'll stay flexible to the way the situation presents itself." He raised his binoculars, studying the giant. "You know, here's what I don't get. If Devona has invented all these bright and shiny weapons, why are these guys only armed with bullets? Wouldn't it make sense to arm your own protection forces with the new proto-types?"

"You mean so we can kill the puny humans and steal the weapons off their corpses?"

He grinned at her. "Exactly."

"I don't really care why. Bullets and guns are something I can handle real easy. So we just thank our luck, you know?"

"Yeah. I know."

"How damn lucky can you get, I ask you?"

Inez glanced up from her kneeling position at his feet, where she was helping him clean and inspect equipment. She frowned, her hands going to her hips as she squinted her eyes against the setting sun.

"What in hell are you talking about?"

"I'm talking about Liam," Kellen said with an exasperated indication of his hand. "Look at him! Healthy as a horse after getting envenomated only three days ago! What are the odds that he would get thrashed and end up in the care of the only person in all the world with an antidote? Hmm? Tell me that's not luck."

"He's also the only one of us to get tagged twice in their lifetime. Is that lucky, you think?" she countered with a snort meant to express her obvious feelings about the ridiculous things that impressed men.

Kellen frowned and looked down at her darkly. Inez cocked her head and waited for his comeback. Instead, he went just a little bit still, and stared at her for a long minute. Inez lifted a brow at him in curiosity, glancing around herself as she tried to figure out what had caught his mind. She usually could tell what he was thinking at almost any given moment, but she was at a loss this time. To her surprise, he reached down and touched her forehead, his fingertips running over her tautly pulled back hair, following the line of her part. Then he seemed to realize what he was doing and he withdrew with a jerk.

Kellen quickly crouched down so he was eye to eye with his partner.

"You got tagged. The only thing that saved you was that vest you had on." His gaze dropped down to her breasts, once again hidden safely behind the light armor. "Whatever you call it, I say it was luck and I'm damn grateful for it." He shook his head once, slowly. "I don't like the idea of telling my little buddy his mommy won't be coming home."

Inez gasped in a breath and her hands balled into fists. "Kellen Gordon, don't you dare! Christ! You are the only man I have ever worked with who hasn't treated me like some special case just because I have tits and a kid!" One of her fists struck him in the shoulder where she knew it wasn't protected. The strike knocked him off balance and he sat down hard on the ground.

"Hey!"

"Shut up! I swear to God, Kell, if you start opening doors for me and jumping in front of me to protect me from danger, I'm going to kill you myself!"

"I have always protected you! Just like you protect me! It doesn't mean I think you are weak or a special case." Kellen ground out an especially ripe curse as they both rose to their feet. "Inez, we're best friends and partners! I'm allowed to be a little upset when you get hurt or have a close call. Wouldn't you be?"

"But it was three days ago! Why are you doing this now?"

That made him pause, his entire face shuttering into an expression so blank, it was obvious he was hiding his feelings. Inez bit the inside of her cheek in regret. She'd yelled at him, and now he didn't want to share his feelings with her. She didn't understand why she'd been so sensitive. Why they were both being so sensitive. It was probably because they'd been separated when it had happened. Kellen had been positive that his presence there would've somehow protected her and Liam. But that was just Kellen. Taking responsibility for everyone in the world.

"I'm sorry."

They both burst out laughing when their apologies came out in tandem. It was so like them, so normal a thing to happen. And just like that their uncanny harmony seemed to return, settling over them calmly and surely. He reached out and hugged her to himself tightly.

"You know I can't pretend you don't have a kid when the little booger is practically a son to me." He grinned against her ear. "And with tits like yours, I can't possibly pretend they aren't there either."

Inez instantly made like she was going to knee him, and he laughed as he caught the threatening uplift of her leg safely in his hand. He squeezed the arm wrapped around her tighter and kissed her loudly on the side of her neck in punishment. He knew it tickled her, and she hated to be tickled.

Inez squealed and shoved him away.

"Hey. No fraternizing on my time."

Inez stumbled as she whirled around to face their Leader. As always, her perfectly attuned partner reached to provide the exact amount of counterbalance she needed to keep herself upright.

"You know, you don't look very intimidating to the outside observer when you're hugging on each other all the time," Liam remarked dryly. He looked down at the drop cloth spread out on the lawn and the dismantled guns and equipment lying on it. "My weapons don't look very intimidating in all these pieces, either. Sun's dropping, kids, and the shift won't end for you until this is done."

"Yes sir," they said.

"But since you two are taking a break, it gives me a chance to talk to you about something." Liam's face was set in such a way that he needn't tell them that it was something serious.

By the time he finished explaining exactly how serious, Kellen was pacing hard, back and forth, in a short concise circuit. His hands were curled around his weapon belt, the leather creaking in his agitated grasp. Inez watched him, knowing exactly what was bothering him. She folded her arms beneath her breasts and took Liam's measure for a moment. Her boss was standing fast, as still as a monument. He was waiting for their responses and their input as well. Negative or positive, he would listen to it all.

"Am I getting this right? You want us to jump into the middle of a war with the entire populace of Morphates?"

"We're already in the middle of it," Kellen ground out, gesturing to Liam. "Didn't you hear him? We're guarding a woman who, in essence, is public enemy number one in the world of Morphates. I mean, I knew she'd invented things and the Morphates were peeved, but a lot of them are going to think she's a traitor to her people. And the ones who think like that are all going to want a piece of her hide. And you want us to stand in the middle of that?"

"That about sums it up," Liam agreed grimly, a muscle ticking tightly in his jaw as he repressed the urge he had to argue and press. Every man in his unit needed to make this choice for himself, not because he felt ordered to or obligated to out of loyalty to him. This was a cause now, and they had to believe in the cause in order to dedicate their lives to it with full enthusiasm.

"If we're going to be fulfilling this contract here for a while," Inez mused aloud, "we're going to have to do something or we'll be forever on the defensive."

"We are fulfilling this contract no matter what," Liam informed them. "The nature of the principal and the identity of the enemy changes nothing contractually. I will expect each and every one of my people to continue on with this assignment just as they would any other. Personal prejudices have no place here if that is affecting either of you. Fear has no place here either, if you plan on surviving. This is no different from any other assignment with the exception of what's at stake, our weaponry and that the need for caution is jacked up to the extreme. The question I'm asking is about what will go on above and below those obligations. Above and below the law, perhaps." Liam shrugged and glanced at the low sun. "But as you know, when it comes to Morphates, certain laws have . . . gray areas." He dusted off his hands, although they were not dirty. Not yet. "I'll leave you to talk it out. There's a meeting at ten tonight where the day shift can discuss it with me. I'm giving you time to think about it. In the end, the goal is to safeguard the life of our principal while keeping our own heads attached. I'm not out to take unnecessary risks, but there will be risks out of the ordinary."

"That's putting it very diplomatically," Kellen grumbled a few beats after Liam had turned and walked away. "Christ, this is insane."

"Actually, I think it's pretty clever," Inez argued with a shrug when he looked at her. "Look, in the end we're going to be beating Morphates off with everything we have, and they don't exactly go down easy, as you know. If a show of force does the trick, then I'm all for it. It's less risk in the long run. And there's something poetic about the weak human mortals bringing the immortals back down to earth."

"Man, I want to know when you became the insane one in this partnership," Kellen sighed. "I mean, I'm as gung-ho as any other maniac in this outfit, Inez, but this isn't the same as beating down a crazed stalker or even outfoxing the mob." Both of which their outfit had done in the past. "That Morphate in the alley was the first one I've ever heard of getting killed by anything, and I've heard of some rough stuff getting thrown at them. If you hadn't told me you'd seen it with your own eyes, I probably wouldn't believe Liam had pulled it off, as disloyal as that sounds."

"I understand your concerns, Kell. I really do," she said

sympathetically, laying a soothing hand on his arm. "I also hear what you aren't saying." She met his dark eyes pointedly. "If you pull out of this, Kell, I won't do it either. I can't fight this fight without my partner to back me up. I won't trust my ass to anyone else but you. I won't risk my son's mother unless you're there to back me up all the way."

Kellen chuckled under his breath, dropping his head and shaking it ruefully.

"Damn you, Inez, you can't put the decision all on me like this. If I get us into this mess and something happens to that fine ass of yours, you know I'm going to be mentally scarred for life, don't you?"

She grinned widely, striking a Marilyn Monroe pose, hands on her thighs and her lush bottom thrusting in his direction. "It is rather fine, isn't it? Come on, partner, you'd never let anything happen to my ass, so what are you worried about?"

Kellen quietly watched her playful display, that shuttered frown falling over him again. She sighed and leaned into him with a nudge. "Come on, handsome," she needled gently, "it'll be a wild ride, but I could use the excitement."

Kellen's attention snapped onto her fully and an expression she had never seen on him before darkened his eyes. She made a sound of surprise.

"Be careful what you ask for, Inez," he said, the tone of his voice so deep and velvet soft that it gave her a chill. "You might get more in the bargain than you expect."

Chapter Nine

"Come," Devon called when the knock sounded on her office door. She didn't look up because she was concentrating on finishing the contract she was reading, but she knew immediately who it was and she could pretty much guess what he wanted.

She made Carter wait until she reached the end of the page, her digital pen flying over it to make last-minute corrections as she went. When she was satisfied, she put it aside and looked up. She saw the scowl on his face and had to resist rolling her eyes at his predictability.

"Yes, Mr. Spencer?" she greeted.

"Mr. Spencer? Have I been demoted now?" he asked, a barely concealed sneer edging his tone.

"Only when you piss me off. Sort of like when your mother uses your middle name when you get in trouble?" She sat back and gave him a tame smile. "Relax, Carter. No need to pass around your resume."

"You know, you wouldn't have even made a joke like that before that Nash showed up. What the hell is going on here? We've known each other for decades, Devona. Why are you suddenly acting like I'm the enemy and that . . . *human* is someone you can trust?"

"Because you've been screwing up in ways that are just too careless to be excused in a man known for his efficiency, and that *human* has nothing to gain in his life except payment for keeping mine in existence."

"Are you sure about that?" he drawled, leaning a hand on her desk and bending forward slightly as he narrowed his eyes on her. "You are a rich, beautiful woman with the sexual aura of a cat in heat, and he's no different from any other tomcat, human or otherwise. He's already staked a claim, you know. You can feel it on him like some sort of primitive monkey beating on his chest and screeching to warn other males away. He reeks of possessiveness. You'd best be careful, Devona. This is not the sort of man you'd want for a stalker."

He straightened up, trying not to look too pleased with himself when she frowned thoughtfully. He had known Devon for years. Many long and loyal years. He knew her inside and out, and he knew one of the things that scared her most was the idea of things she couldn't control. It was why she had so few personal relationships. She could not control others, so she often subconsciously went about discarding them almost as eagerly as she picked them up. It was a shame because she really enjoyed the stimulation of others, but she feared it too. She always had and always would. Carter had only lasted this long because he made every effort to understand this about her. He was well suited to her needs. He took great pleasure in being everything she could possibly want or need at any given moment, without ever giving her cause to worry.

When she was displeased with him on the rare occasion, as she was now, it disturbed him deeply. He didn't like the insecurity. Devon was solid and secure in all ways imaginable. Or she had been before the information on how to kill a Morphate had finally come across her desk and she'd taken on the folly of inventing these damnable weapons. And while her wealth, comfort, and position, the things he treasured most highly, had not changed, they could and would if something were to happen to her. So he had to accept this outside influence that suddenly surrounded them and filled every corner of the previously museum-quiet mansion. This . . . NHK. Though he thought very little of the human forces surrounding them, there wasn't much choice in the matter.

Carter didn't mind their self-imposed exile. He didn't even mind pretending to be human. It had its perks and amusements. But Devon depended solely on him, and he on her, as the only Morphate contacts in each other's lives. The only ones sharing the secret of their existence. It made for a very special bond between them.

"I know you and Liam have taken an instant dislike to one another," she said softly, "but it would please me if you could at least try to get along." She stood up and turned to the covered window directly behind her. She folded her arms across her middle, looking at the window coverings as if she could see right through them. "It's a rare human who can welcome Morphates into their circle without feeling fear and prejudice. So many look on us as monsters. Unfortunately, many of them are right."

"I don't know what you were thinking, telling him we are Morphate. No one except other Morphates knew that. Now a small human army is going to know. And while Nash might not be prejudiced, there's no way he can speak for his entire workforce. It's impossible. These are well-armed and well-trained killers, Devona. They have access to your house. Your bedroom. You. Mark my words, you are risking your life trusting these people. What's more, I resent you telling them about me without even asking me!"

"I didn't tell them, Carter," she snapped, whirling to face him down with angry fire in her eyes. "Your holier-than-thou superiority gave you away long before I could ever have done so. Liam probably suspected you were a Morphate even before he knew I was one! You have no idea what a pompous ass you can be sometimes, you know that? And you talk about racism among the humans? Look at yourself, Carter. One day just watch and listen to your behavior and you'll see what it is that has me so damn disappointed in you!"

Spencer jerked back at the accusation as though she had slapped him in the face. The change that washed through him was phenomenal. He practically deflated before her eyes, his arrogance streaming out of him. He was tall and handsome in a narrow sort of way, so much leaner than Liam that he almost seemed scrawny in comparison, though Devon knew it was unfair to compare anyone to Liam's outstanding physical stature. But as his bravado left him, Carter looked very small all of a sudden. And very young. If a Morphate could look vulnerable, then he had achieved it. He had been careless, but she knew he would never betray her.

"I'm sorry," he said, and she believed him. "I know I do have some obnoxious behaviors sometimes."

"When you are threatened," she agreed, not quite ready to let him off the hook. "What is it about Liam and his people that threatens you?"

"Jesus, Devon, they have mercury!"

He said it like it made all the difference in the world. And she supposed it did. For the first time since Paulson's labs, Carter was facing the only human beings who knew about that vulnerability and had the means to use it against him, and it wasn't bringing out the best in him. How could she not understand that? When one treasures immortality for so long, only to have it so suddenly destroyed, it was bound to make the fear of death prominent, and ten times as daunting.

But nothing should live forever. It simply wasn't a natural part of the lifecycle. The universe was all about life, death, decay, and rebirth. From the smallest bacteria to the exploding stars so far away, the same rhythm existed.

So she simply accepted that she did, indeed, exist, whether

or not it was a natural existence. She enjoyed that existence in her own way, managing it the best way she knew how. Devon figured that was the freedom of being an intelligent being. Unlike her brethren, she believed she would die one day. The price on her life had only reinforced that feeling. Perhaps that was why she saw things so differently. She believed it enough to want to give her people a dose of the feeling.

"I have mercury," Devon said gently. "And I explained to you some time ago that this day was coming. Didn't you prepare yourself for it at all?"

"I . . ." Carter shrugged and looked away. "I thought you'd change your mind."

Devon actually laughed aloud at that. "When did you ever know me to change my mind?" she wanted to know.

The truth was on his sheepish face. He had been fooling himself because it had given him temporary comfort to do so.

"Now, please," she said gently, brushing her hand before herself as if to brush away all these issues, "let's focus on the present and the future and the things I desperately need your help to accomplish. In all fairness, Carter, you've been unforgivably careless with private and secure information and it stops right here and right now. You will obey every directive regarding security that Liam Nash gives you. Understood?"

"Yes, Devon. If that's what you would like me to do."

"It is." She smiled. "Thank you. Now I need to fix my schedule and organize a few more meetings before things get any worse than they are."

"You're going to continue meeting with the members of the Morphate sects, Devon? Are you crazy? After what happened last time?"

"All the more reason to do it," she said firmly. "I am making my propositions to each and every one of them, the Alpha Council as well, until each one sees this situation properly. And in the process, I'm watching for evidence of who my enemy is."

* * *

Devon and Carter finished moving back her schedule the recommended two weeks. It meant reneging on some important appointments and withdrawing from some events she had agreed to attend, but not very many. She was not known for her public persona as much as she was the power of her position. As for the night meetings with the various Morphates she was trying to court, she would design her future meetings to be even more impulsive. No one but herself and the other party would know the time and location and she would even put off naming the location until the last minute. She would warn Liam, of course, but only to give him minimum time for preparation. It wasn't that she didn't trust him. She was simply tired of learning her lessons the hard way and she refused to make any further mistakes.

Outside of the safety of Dark Manhattan, there was no one she could trust except herself. She had known that for decades now, but this was going beyond even the precautions of the past. Devon stood up and turned to the windows behind her chair. She pulled the drapes open now that her desk was cleared of sensitive data and she wasn't sitting with her back to the glass. She hadn't needed Inez to warn her about that vulnerability. She'd been aware of it already. Still, with a corner office, it was hard for her to find anywhere in the entire room that wasn't somehow exposed to the outside. And with infrared scopes, drawn curtains would do little good. If someone wanted to kill her badly enough, they would eventually find a way, and there would be very little she could do about it. Inez's recommendation had been to substitute the glass with something bulletproofed. She had agreed with the idea. The glass was being replaced later that week.

She sighed and leaned her forehead against the glass in question, watching down below as one of the men romped on the south lawn with two of the K-9 shepherds that had arrived early yesterday morning. The soldier was fast and spry, and the dogs were like big puppies as they played. But she had also watched them do training run-throughs that proved them to be the vicious sentinels they really were. Inez had warned her never to approach the animals.

She wouldn't anyway. Many animals, like those dogs, recognized a dangerous predator by instinct long before humans could. This was what made them so valuable in service. That same instinct made certain animals, like dogs or wolves, go ballistic when a Morphate came near. They sensed the beast within, the animal senses and instincts, and the extraordinary thirst for the hunt, be it sexual or otherwise. They sensed kindred beings, and therefore a threat to their own dominance. It would be easy for her to win them over, given time, simply by presenting herself as an Alpha and exerting her dominance. She would just have to go out of her way to see that she did.

Devon felt a quiver slither over her neck and back and she looked over the lawn again. Her breath caught when she recognized Liam's virile form on the edge of the drive. Colin was talking to him, showing him some kind of a schematic or blueprint, but Liam was looking up at the house. His full attention was on her. She knew it without any doubt. This was the reason her body had shivered on instinct. This was why that thirst for the hunt was suddenly stirring in her belly, looking eagerly for her target.

She drank in his presentation of himself, those powerful legs braced apart, hands on his waist, and biceps flexed. Though his hair was close to military cut, it was long enough on top to allow the wind to ruffle through the black strands, the sun glinting off those touches of silver. She rubbed her fingertips together, remembering the feel of his hair, the only thing on his body besides his mouth that she had ever known to be soft. The rest of him was rock solid hard with muscle, vitality, and outrageous masculinity. Just watching him made her palms sweat.

"Devona, you've got it really bad," she chastised herself.

Then again, it'd been a very long time since she'd been with a male. Was it any wonder she lusted after so fine a specimen of one? It didn't help that Carter was more than right when he said Liam clearly lusted after her in return. Oh, she was used to the attention her Morphate chemistry attracted from all males, Morphate and human alike, but Liam more than held her attention in return. Few in either race could make the same claim.

Devon reached back and lifted her hair off the back of her damp neck, not even realizing she was doing it because she was so absorbed in her fascination with him. She had no idea what she looked like to the man watching her from the lawn.

A goddess would have been a good starting descriptive, Liam thought tensely as his fingertips tightened at his waist. She stood in the light of sunset, holding her hair in both hands until her short top rose up to the high arc of her ribs. Her entire belly was exposed between shirt hem and skirt waist. Sunlight pierced her skirt, showing off the full shape of her legs in sultry shadow. In his mind he could so easily fit the pieces of the puzzle together and envision her naked form. God, why was it that she was wearing the most conservative outfit he had seen on her to date, yet he found it just as provocative as those awesomely revealing dresses? The worst part about it was he didn't think she gave a single damn as to what she looked like or the effect she had on men around her.

Liam realized Colin had stopped talking and he sheepishly started to apologize for being distracted . . . until he realized his brother was staring at the same thing he was and panting almost as hard as a result.

"Hey!" he barked, backhanding his sibling in the chest to get his attention.

"Oof! Hey, what was that for?" Colin complained, rubbing his breastbone.

"Keep your eyes in your head, Col," Liam growled at his brother.

Colin snorted out a laugh, "Oh, like you were just doing?"

"This isn't a democracy, bro," Liam reminded him. "It's do as I say and not as I do, get it?"

"Yes, sir," Colin said obediently, making a stellar effort not to grin at his older brother. "No staring at babes on the job. Got it."

"You better," Liam grumbled, his eyes drifting back to the window despite efforts otherwise. To his combined relief and disappointment, the drapes had been drawn and the babe in question had disappeared. He sighed and turned his attention back to the schematic. "Okay. Tell me again where the electric is vulnerable."

And hurry, he thought. *I have a date.*

Chapter Ten

As Liam came down the hall to the security room, he heard a laugh that sought out every small hair on his body, causing them all to rustle swiftly to attention. Like everything about her voice, it was low, melodic, and alluring as hell. He had no doubt that it was Devon. There was no mistaking that voice. Not for him.

He'd dreamed of it for three days. Speaking words of comfort, soothing him as he fought through the venom, and even singing softly to him to pass time and distract. He hadn't needed Carter Spencer to tell him she had spent nearly every minute of the past three days tending to him. He'd known it all along. He had the healed body and soothed spirit to prove it.

Liam couldn't help his curiosity as he came around the frame of the door, wondering what it was that had her pealing out laughter so robust he felt it vibrating sensually throughout his entire body. His appearance caught Devon by surprise, her laughter skidding to an abrupt halt the moment she saw him in the doorway. It was a reaction he wasn't too certain he cared for.

She was braced back against the console, night-vision camera angles panning on bisected screen monitors behind her, and Malcolm Coffey in one of the two station chairs. The second chair was empty, since Liam was behind on his scheduling, and Devon was idly rolling it back and forth with a single foot on the seat. The motion drew his total attention to her leg and the realization that she had changed her clothing. She was now wearing gym shorts and a mini tank top that once again drew attention to her flat midriff and the perfect silk skin spread over trim muscle.

"Hey, Nash." Malcolm greeted him quickly and uneasily. He'd been caught doing too many things wrong not to expect a reprimand, and Liam didn't disappoint him.

"Coffey, I suppose you're looking for a transfer back to compound? We have plenty of paperwork to be done and lots of secretaries to flirt with, if that's what you'd like to do," Liam said coldly.

"No, sir," Malcolm said, automatically rising to his feet as tension whipped through his frame. "I'm sorry. It won't happen again, sir."

Liam glanced at Devon, who was standing up straight now as she bit on her lower lip. He suspected she was biting that lip to keep from intervening, and Liam's respect for her ratcheted up on several accounts. One, that she would be compelled to protect Malcolm, and two, that she would refrain from interfering in his disciplinary methods. The fact that she was used to wielding power in her own home but knew when to take a backseat impressed him most of all.

"Good, because as pretty and charming as she is, she wouldn't be either for very long if you allow a killer to get by you because you're not watching the monitors." Liam held out his hand to her, his expression stern as he beckoned her forward with a flick of his fingers. She was extremely contrite as she slid her hand into his and let him lead her out of the room. Properly chastised and flushing a deep red, Malcolm resumed his seat with a far more attentive manner.

Devon began to speak the moment they were in the hall, but

he stopped her with a finger against his lips and a warning
look. She silently acquiesced and he led her into another
room, which happened to be a small prep room off the
kitchen that the cook and the caterers would use should she
ever throw a party on the premises. Liam shut the door behind
them and she turned to him to make her apologies, but before
a word could pass her lips, he had hauled her up against his
big body. Her breath left her in a mighty rush, but she didn't
think the actual force of her chest striking his had anything to
do with it. His large hands were suddenly grasping at her back
and he caught her mouth with a swift dip of his head and un-
erring aim.

Liam's kisses were unforgettable. She'd turned their torrid
encounter in the limousine over in her memory endlessly. The
kiss and his hot caresses in his bedroom those three days ago
had also been in an incessant kind of replay. Yet, as wildly
vivid as her recall was, it still paled in comparison to the reality. His mouth was a storm of fire and possession, fierce
and hot as he skipped over any preliminary introductions and
dove deep for her flavor and tongue. Devon moaned irrepressibly as he shocked her system with instant hunger and volatile
response. He devoured her, feasting on her mouth as though
he would starve otherwise. Her hands flew up to the back of
his head, fingernails raking up through crisp, short hairs. She
felt him shudder in response. He groaned with a deep rever-
beration that exploded into her mouth and rushed to be felt all
along her body. Her nipples went taut against the material of
her tank, the soft cotton suddenly rough and stimulating
against them. A chain of heat slid down the center of her
body, as though she had swallowed it and it had sunk straight
and deep to the bottom like heavy metal through water.

Liam was convinced he'd lost his mind. Either that or he
was having a hell of a dream. What else could explain the
ferocity of desperation he'd felt to kiss her, instead of scold-
ing her as he'd intended to? He was going to remind her not

to interfere with his people, no matter what her outgoing nature encouraged her to do. Not while they were on duty. He was also going to tell her that it was inappropriate for her to be laughing and flirting with another man when she was also busy driving him up the damn wall. Instead, his mouth was fused to hers and he was claiming her.

If he didn't know better, he'd think he was jealous. He didn't get jealous. He thought it was a waste of time and energy and it was something insecure idiots indulged in. He especially wouldn't feel that way about a woman who . . . A veritable . . .

Oh, Christ.

He was jealous.

God, how quickly she'd insinuated herself into his life! What was even more frightening was that he wasn't certain it was all about her lush, sexy body. He was as much a male about those things as any other, but not like this. It'd been a long time since he'd wanted a woman so much. Had he ever wanted a woman like this? With such uncontrollable hunger? Maybe when he'd been a teenager, when he'd wanted *everything* with uncontrollable hunger, but not for a long time since then and not even half so much in all his adult life.

Liam tightened his fingers against the contours of her back, jerking her forward until she was tighter against him, her belly flush with his, her hips cuddled close. Never once did she resist or flinch or even seem to consider the ramifications of her responses. Not even when he flipped their positions against the door and trapped her between it and his body, pressing himself tightly to her and freeing up his hands. He was craving the feel of her. It was making him insane. His drew his fingers gently around her bare ribs beneath the soft shirt. His hands were shaking, he was pumped so full of adrenaline. He broke away from her mouth with a groan of painful need as he slid his hands up beneath the hem of the tank and slowly encompassed the sweet, weighty curves of her breasts.

"Jesus, you don't own a single bra, do you?" he demanded tightly of her as she easily filled his hands, pebbled nipples nuzzling the pads of his fingers invitingly.

"No," she whispered hotly against his ear. She gasped in a shuddering breath as his fingers rolled over the tips of her sensitive breasts. "Are you complaining or complimenting?" she asked on a groan of pleasure.

Liam wasn't sure. What he was sure of was that the sounds she made on that hot breath rushing against his ear and neck were making him crazy. He conveyed that fact with a forward shift of his hips. "What do you think?" he countered, his agonizing erection obvious as he burrowed against her sex. He was burning and still he felt her heat. He rolled against her, swearing mightily under his breath as an attempt to ease the ache of his body turned into an act of torment when she suddenly lifted a leg in a luscious slide along the outside of his, opening herself up to his stroke. His cock was suddenly fully seated between her legs, mere fabric keeping them parted.

Devon threw back her head, her slender throat working to make a sound of ecstasy that would never come. Liam instinctively covered her mouth with a quick hand to forestall her, knowing that the security room was extremely close and Malcolm would hear her. He lifted his head to look down into her response-laden eyes and he felt her trembling hard against him with excitation and need.

"Shh," he soothed her softly, torn between teasing the hell out of her like she'd been doing to him, and stepping back and giving them both room to breathe. And yet, how divine it would be to feel those sweet, supple legs wrapping around him, opening her more . . . "God, you're going to be the death of me. I just know it," he accused her roughly.

He had meant it as a figure of speech, but the minute he saw the horror in her eyes, he realized his mistake. She squirmed to get away, but he had the advantage and he pressed it, trapping her between his body and the door. He slid his hand from her mouth, burying it in her thick hair and holding her gaze tilted up to his.

"I didn't mean it like that," he said on a deeply felt whisper close to her lips.

"Liam . . ."

She shrugged her shoulder, as if to remind him his other hand surrounded her breast still. He smiled slightly at the idea that he could ever forget such a thing. Very deliberately he drew his thumb over the tip of that perfectly pointed nipple. She was so warm, a heated weight in his sculpting palm. Devon sucked in a breath and he felt her shimmy head to toe with pleasure. She was so responsive. Maybe it was wrong of him to take advantage of that, but he would use whatever method necessary to fix this blunder.

"I have a crazy kind of lifestyle, Devon," he said before reaching to give her a gentle, lingering kiss, "and I know the price I pay for it." Liam slid the palm at her breast upward over her, letting his calluses do all the work of stimulating her. He caught her groans with his mouth and tongue, sensing when her desire to escape him was overcome by her rushing arousal. Her hands fell to his upper arms, grasping his biceps. She closed her eyes and lost herself to him for a good pair of minutes before she gasped for breath.

When she surfaced from Liam's irresistible kisses, Devon found herself wound around his body tightly, her legs holding him captive, her hands clutching at his clothing, and her mouth wet and filled with his delicious flavor. Her brain was afloat in sensations she could barely sort out. What came clearest to her was the way he smelled. Just as a powerful, vital male in sexual arousal ought to: potent, musky, and scorching with heat. She lowered her face against his chest and rubbed against him like a cat marking scent, only she was taking it in.

"Mmm," she murmured, "it's not fair that you can do this so easily."

"Me?" His expression was as incredulous as his voice when she looked up at him. She couldn't help but smile at the genuine amazement in his amber eyes. "This coming from the woman who . . ."

He trailed off, obviously thinking better of his accusation, and she gave him a dirty look. "Coward!"

"Coward!?" He pulled back from her, completely untangling himself from her, looking at her askance.

"Yes," she persisted as she straightened her top and tried to quell the bereft feelings left behind because he'd removed himself so suddenly. "A brave man would speak his mind to me, not edit himself for whatever reason. I don't need edited words or feelings."

"I see. You're looking for truth, then? Pure, blatant, unadulterated truth?" The way he said it, his eyes broiling with burning intentions and steamy desire, made her swallow hard as excited anticipation flooded her. He moved forward again, settling against her hips first, making sure she was once again aware of his needy body. He leaned in close to her ear. "Because," he whispered, "I was going to be a little graphic. I was trying to be a gentleman, or as close to it as I could get. Are you sure you want the truth?" he asked, his lips gliding hotly over her ear.

Since she was suddenly too breathless to form words, she simply nodded. He was so close she could feel him smile against her, as though he had been hoping for that response. She was trembling again, her nerves singing wildly under his influence. He reached up and drew a finger down the side of her neck, slowly wending his way down the low neckline of her top.

"You accused me of affecting you sexually in an over-whelming way, yes?"

"Yes," she managed on a whisper. "And you said, 'This coming from a woman who . . .'"

"This coming from a woman who can make me hard with just the turn of a phrase, the look in her eyes, or the way she laughs," he told her huskily. "This unfair accusation coming from her lips while I'm like this . . ." Devon had no clue as to how or when he'd caught up her hand, but she was very aware when he cupped her palm in his and pressed it against his bulging fly. Her gasp was shocked, but not because the maneuver offended her. No. It was all about the wonderful size and thickness of the erection pressing against her palm and fingers. She heard him hold his breath, the sound of his teeth grinding together very telling as she pressed against him even more snugly than he had perhaps intended. Perhaps he had forgotten the nature of the creature he held in his arms.

"Liam," she purred in uncontainable delight. Her reaction and enthusiastic touch turned Liam's little game against him. He throbbed harder against her touch, his blood pounding until he could barely stay on his feet. "See now how much better the truth can be?" the little vixen taunted him in a voice of pure sexual invitation. Liam had to agree. He surged against her hand and she responded with pressure and friction that extended his already engorged length in hard pulses of expectation. God, her touch felt so good. It was unreal. And if she kept it up, she was going to make him come right in his pants.

Liam had to stop her.

Any minute now, he definitely would.

He groaned when her deft fingers flipped open his belt and unbuttoned his fly. His body clenched in violent anticipation of feeling her bare fingers wrapping around his shaft, stroking him until . . .

"Devon," he croaked as he caught her wrists and pulled her away from his zipper. "I can't do this. You know I can't," he implored her.

Damn it to hell, he was begging, he realized. And he was begging her to *not* do what he oh so desperately needed her to do. He was so hard he hurt, his entire body perspiring under the burn of his heat for her. He wanted her so badly he was seconds away from stripping away those sadistically sexy shorts and taking her right there against the door. God, what he wouldn't do to be burying himself in her right that very instant.

Liam was right, Devon thought as she looked up into the turmoil of his gaze. She shook her head as if coming out of a daze, and the implications of what was happening made full impact. She was in big trouble, she realized. She was living in the same house with a human male who danced across every sensual and sexual tripwire she owned. There was a resounding inevitability to what was happening between them. The impetus would carry their explosive chemistry to the farthest extreme, and it would be likely to happen one day very soon.

The only problem was, she had a great deal of respect for Liam. A respect that grew the more she watched his behavior, listened to his people speak his praises, and witnessed his skills as a protector. She wasn't like others of her kind. She couldn't conceal herself from him if they were going to end up being intimate. Not when she knew all too well how he would feel if he learned certain truths at the last minute. He said he knew everything about Morphates, but did he really know everything? Morphates had hidden enough along the way to assure her that he probably didn't. He would hate her, thinking her the liar and deceitful bitch that she honestly would have become at that point, if she didn't make sure he truly knew what he was getting into.

Panic-stricken and confused, Devon drew into herself, pulling her arms around her body in a brutally tight hug. She saw him watching her with concern and wariness as he neatened up the damage she'd done to his clothing. She almost laughed at how obvious his conflict was. He didn't know what to do with her. He didn't understand her reactions, but he wanted to ease her pain if he could because he feared he had somehow caused it. It was those deep-seated flashes of Liam Nash's heart that strangled her with conflict.

"Listen, sweetheart," he said gruffly, "I don't mean that I don't want—"

She cut him off, and when she spoke, it was as though she had a lash around her throat. "I understand. I honestly do," she said, hoping the truth would override whatever else he saw in her face. "It was thoughtless of me to—"

"Thoughtless of *you*?" He was incredulous. "Who in hell dragged who in here? Will you stop taking responsibility for everything, Devon? It's not your job to make everything right, you know. Why do you do that?"

He was wrong. It was her job to make things right. More than he could ever know. And to that end, she drew up a smile and patted him on the chest in comfort.

"You're right. I just meant that I know we have other things to do that are . . . that take precedence." For some reason she couldn't bring herself to say 'more important.' The sudden light of satisfaction flickering through his eyes told her he understood her omission. This time her smile was genuine as she watched the obvious stroke to his ego flush through him. She didn't mind him knowing he was high on her list of importance, but she couldn't help a little mischief to remind him how easily power shifted between them.

Devon snuggled forward into him, her softer curves instantly settling fully against hard muscle until they were as good as glued together. It was so easy to imagine how the connection would translate should they both be naked. She sighed deeply, the sound of longing washing over them both. She ran her hands around his waist and up his back, her cheek pressed to his chest as she listened to the rise in the tempo of his strong heartbeat. As she breathed in a deep breath, his sun-baked masculine scent of sweat and surging arousal thrummed through her senses and into her blood.

She allowed her fingers to explore him, roaming his back and coming over his ribs again to his chest. He made a repressed sound that combined pleasure and frustration into one.

"Step back," she instructed softly, the flats of her palms pushing gently but using no strength. He obeyed her quickly and she suppressed a giggle as she let him move away from her aching body. Her nipples were so hard they hurt, and she imagined he felt much the same, if not more, in a variety of places. Licking her lips at the thought, she let her gaze drift down the expanse of his gorgeous physique and stop at the noticeable ridge of his erection behind the fly he had forced her to abandon.

She heard him curse richly and Devon knew he was watching her study him.

"Another step," she coaxed him in a sultry, expectation-laden voice.

Again, he obeyed, though this step caused her hands to drop away from him entirely. Her gaze traveled with purposeful lethargy back up his body. Then, when she had met his glittering amber eyes and their ferocious hunger for her, she smiled softly.

"Thanks."

She turned and opened the door, now that she had coaxed him out of the way. It was dirty pool, she knew, but it was worth it for the look on his face when she stood in the doorway and gestured gallantly for him to precede her into the hallway.

"I believe you wanted to see some weapon prototypes? The armory is this way."

His expression of astonishment was too much to handle with perfect calm and a giggle escaped her. Liam narrowed his eyes on her with nothing less than murder in mind and she brushed the threatening expression off by tapping her foot with impatience and grinning boldly at his expense.

"I thought you were anxious to see them," she complained through her humor.

What Liam wanted to do was grab the little tease and jerk her smart, sassy ass back in the prep room and teach her a thing or two about messing with him. But the fact of the matter was she was doing exactly what he had asked her to do. Calling it quits. Her extremely brief and relatively tame tease was a fair enough payback, considering what he'd just done to her. He'd lost all control and started something with her he shouldn't have in a place that was damn inappropriate, not to mention inconsiderate. He gave the devil her due and took a step toward her, but hesitated to very visibly readjust himself, trying fruitlessly to find comfort for a hard-on he feared wasn't going anywhere anytime soon. He couldn't help but grin when she burst into peals of laughter. As he passed her in the crowded doorway, though, he made sure to brush his front up against her front and it ended her amusement on a soft, inward gasp.

He reached for her hand and pulled her to his side, touching her at the small of her back and guiding her toward the armory.

When they reached the reinforced steel door, she punched in the code like lightning, her enhanced reflexes so second-nature to her that she probably didn't realize what a giveaway it was. The door unlocked with a click and a hiss, telling him the room was temperature controlled. It would have to be. Mercury was very sensitive to temperature, another reason why bullets were a primitive delivery option.

The door swung open to reveal a room much, much bigger than he had been expecting. As they crossed the threshold, Liam realized it was because there was a firing range included, as well as a large area of mats for working out with less lethal devices. It would be an excellent venue for training his people in the use of these weapons. The climate control would keep their body heat from affecting the mercury dangerously, allowing for safe practice. He could see the well at the rear of the firing range designed to catch mercury discharge and that there were drains in the floor for disposal. Certainly for safe disposal. She didn't strike him as the type to endanger the environment with improper techniques.

"There's an exterior range as well, but that's only for shooting water laden blanks. The liquid metal is lighter than water, so there is a difference in the weight, but it's negligible, I find, when it comes to basic training in the field. However, weapons calibration should be done in this room."

Liam nodded mutely. He had seen no exterior firing range. Not in person and not on the plans. Granted, he had yet to walk over every inch of the estate, and there was a lot of acreage, but if that range was as state-of-the-art as the one inside, it needed an electrical source and he would have seen it on the wiring charts earlier.

His eyes moved swiftly to the walls. The entranceway had the feel and look of a clean room. Her laboratory and medical background rang loud and clear in the precautions she'd taken. Mounted on the wall in Plexiglas cases, however, were the dark shapes of weaponry.

"Earlier prototypes," she explained, dismissively waving at both walls. There were three rows per wall of both strange and familiarly shaped weapon configurations. Some looked more like medical devices than weapons. He wondered why she kept the failures on display like this, even as he realized he had to be looking at years of work, going well beyond the time since he'd discovered the effects of mercury.

"Damn," he said with a hard swallow as he followed her lead into the deeper recesses of the vault, "I must have seriously pissed you off."

Devon stopped and looked at him with surprise. "Why would you say something like that?"

He gave her a self-deprecating smile. "You were looking for this leverage for a long time," he said, indicating her years of work, "and suddenly some grunt soldier from the secret service stumbles on the answer in a moment of desperation."

It was hard for her to think of him as ever being desperate, but she could easily imagine him in that life or death battle with a Morphate. Fighting a creature three times as strong as even his formidable strength, most likely with poisoned claws, not to mention gnashing fangs and killer instinct.

"I read the report, Liam," she said softly, reaching to lay her hand on his chest, needing to touch him as sudden chills worked their way across her flesh. "What you did was remarkable and heroic. I would never lessen that with something as petty as envy, or feeling somehow cheated of an opportunity I had more than enough time and resources to come up with over quite a few decades. And neither should you with this attitude of nonchalance."

Properly chastised, Liam fell silent and followed her quietly into a second chamber, this one also locked behind a steel door and requiring a retina scan, DNA sampling, and no less than a sixteen-digit pin.

"I am the only one with access to the inner sanctum. I will give you the code to the exterior vault. However, when you wish to work with the weapons, you will need me to get them for you and to return them. This way I can check their status at all times and have a perfect account of all the prototypes."

The inner sanctum, as she had referred to it, was aptly named. This part of the vault was an enormous laboratory also in the style of a clean room: white and perfectly polished floors, lab tables that gleamed brilliantly, and more equipment than he could possibly expect to recognize. Liam wasn't one for staring in wonder, but he did exactly that. Everything on the right-hand side of the door was dedicated to the lab, the refrigeration and storage units and all the analysis equipment.

Everything on the left was sealed in steel containers of every size imaginable. Some stood free like lockers, others were lined up on shelves or wide tables. Each was numbered and labeled with laser etching and each one had its very own electronic keypad.

She walked up the floor between the tables and shelves until she reached the box she was looking for. There were at least three dozen varying boxes in the room, and she walked up to only one as if she knew exactly what it and all the others held. It struck him then that with the safety guards she had in place, no one could enter or exit that lab without her being right beside them. No one else could work in that high-tech and highly specialized environment unless she was right in their pocket, watching over their shoulder or . . . was there even anyone else? When his team had gone over staffing and protection details, had there even been mention of laboratory personnel? Was that because they had already succeeded at their task or was it because they had never existed? Had every piece of this development process come straight from her hands?

Of course it had, he realized. She would never trust anyone else with these kinds of secrets, and she most certainly would not put the responsibility onto anyone else's shoulders. Both of those realizations settled heavily on the back of Liam's neck and shoulders.

He could imagine how it must feel for her.

Liam was moving before he even knew why, crossing over to her in fast, hard strides. She was about to open the box and show him one of her undoubtedly gorgeous weapons and all he wanted was to stop her. He slammed his hand down on the lid of the container, the sound of the metal ringing in the echoing room, the lock automatically reengaging the instant it was closed. Devon turned with a surprised, questioning look in her eyes, and Liam really wished he had the answer she wanted. Instead he was working on instinct, an often good and sometimes bad thing. He looked into the clear jade of her eyes, the color bright in the overhead lighting.

With a very gentle touch, he reached to catch her face in his hand, her chin cradled in the web between his thumb and forefinger as his fingers fanned out over her cheek. He could hear himself breathing too hard, but he was beyond regulating it.

Then the gentle touch tightened to a point just shy of hurting her.

"Are you going to tell me that you spent years locked away in this cold, sterile room all alone for day—no, wait, knowing you, it was for weeks at a time, right? Just for this?" He gestured back and around himself. "You spent this enormous block of your immortality a prisoner to this room for the sake of bringing . . . what did you call it . . . *balance* to the world of humans and Morphates?"

He stepped much closer, towering over her, so tensed with rampant emotion that he fairly quivered with it.

"You tell me, Devon, and don't you dare fucking lie to me this time, or so help me God, you won't like the consequences. You tell me *why you did this*." The truth! Tell me why you buried yourself in this obsession. What drove you into these cold, windowless rooms, day after goddamn day, when you knew it was a path to being utterly ostracized, not to mention a certain death wish."

Liam was looking down into her eyes, his nose barely three inches from her own. As he poured those acidic words and emotions over her, it stripped open the old wounds until she was raw and shaking.

"I d-didn't lie to you," she stammered, her hand instinctively pressing against him to hold him at bay. She could struggle with him and free herself, but that would get them nowhere. He was so clever, so much more astute than he first appeared. How many people would walk into a room and see it the way he was seeing it? See the truth?

"I distinctly remember asking you over and over again why

you chose to embark on this particular task. Omitting is as good as lying, sweetheart, and I refuse to hang my ass out for you if you are going to blow smoke up it!"

"Liam, please, you don't understand! I can't—"

"If *you* can't, then *I* can't." He let go of her roughly and did a sharp about-face. "I'll be damned if I'm going to risk my life and the lives of my crew on 'I can't' when what you really mean is you won't," he threw back over his shoulder as he left the room.

Devon moved, her preternatural speed bursting out as she overtook him in a mere heartbeat, slammed the outer vault door shut and spun the tumbler. She turned to face him, breathing hard not from exertion but from raw fury. It burned in her eyes and clenched tight in her fists and muscles.

Liam had drawn up short in total surprise at what had to be the very first real display of her Morphate abilities. It was strange how it made him feel, seeing the stark, albeit brief, display of what she really was. It made him realize that she had been hiding among humans for quite some time in order to have become so very good at blending in with them. At suppressing what ought to have come naturally for her.

"What the hell is it you think you're doing?" he growled, his hands fisting as he stalked up to her. "If you think you can trap me and try to coerce me into changing my mind, lady, you are looking for a frigid day in hell."

"Always so cocksure, aren't you?" she hissed in retaliation. "Always so *right*!"

"You bet your sweet ass I am!"

"Well, let me tell you a few things you don't know. A few things you've got very, very wrong, *Mr.* Nash," she spat out, her flushed face and bottle green eyes radiating her incredible anger. He was not surprised. He'd stepped into that lab and within moments he'd realized that here was a woman who felt fury with an unquenchable passion. Just like she felt lust, he recalled all too vividly. He suppressed an involuntary shudder when he found himself contemplating what unquenchable lust of this magnitude would be like.

Devon wasn't even thinking any longer. She was only feeling. It was pain, rage, and frustration, renewed betrayal and old abandonment.

"I had a family," she rasped, her voice rough from emotion and shouting. "I had a *life* and they stole me away from it. Eric Paulson and his experimenters stole hundreds of us, from asylums, from workhouses, and right from the streets of the Dark Cities and anywhere else they thought no one would ever miss us. If you had the misfortune of crossing Paulson in the slightest way, say, perhaps, refusing his job offer once you finally realized what that job entailed, well, he couldn't have you running off to report his unethical behavior now, could he? Did they tell you that in your little Morphate 101 classes at the Secret Service? Hmm?"

No. Not all of it. Those, he knew, were the sordid details that didn't matter when it came to how to fight and defend against a Morphate. Who cared who or what they had once been? What mattered was what they were, what they were capable of, and how nearly impossible they could be to stop.

But this answered a question for him. She *was* one of the original lots of Morphates. She had lived life on this planet for at least fifty years as a Morphate, almost twice as long as she had ever been human. He didn't know how old she had been to begin with, but she didn't look a day over thirty. She would never look a day over thirty.

And with that horrendous over-ninety-percent mortality rate Paulson's lab rats had suffered, it was a wonder she had survived at all. It was a wonder any of them had. How could he begrudge her a single day of her life when she had come so close to losing it?

"How old were you?" he asked, his own voice now hoarse with conflicting emotions. A huge part of him wanted to hold her tight and run a soothing hand down the wild mass of her espresso hair, to be gentler than he had been so far as he coaxed his answers from her.

"Thirty-one. Old enough to remember and to mourn. To feel so much fear and betrayal and anger I sometimes thought I would choke on it!" She was shaking so hard, her fists clenched so tight, she looked as though she would do just that.

Liam stepped closer to her on instinct and, although she jerked at the movement, she didn't step away. She did watch him warily though, looking unsure as to whether she wanted him that near her. Looking for the first time like the dangerous animal so many of his kind liked to accuse her kind of being. He supposed that made it easier for humans to take away their rights and not feel guilt about it. But he'd never been the sort to throw the baby out with the bathwater. Even when he'd been pinned to the wall of a lab very similar to this one, Morphate claws skewering him through his chest and his vulnerable human principal, the President of the Federated States, cowering under a table with the bodies of his dead Secret Service contingent bleeding out all around him, Liam had known that particular Morphate was not a representative of the Morphate people as a whole.

"Tell me what this has to do with that room inside," Liam coaxed, the demand gentled by the look in his softened amber eyes. Devon saw the empathy there and tried to ignore it.

"I'm making a point, Liam," she told him, her tone clipped. "There are so many things you don't know about the Phoenix Project. So many things you don't know about the Morphates. And how much information do you have, really, on what happened after we liberated ourselves and entered this world as aliens? Or rather, reentered." She shook her head and ran frustrated hands through her thick hair, mussing it into even wilder disarray than his own hands had created only minutes earlier. "And then the new tragedies began. The hate and bigotry, the supercilious superiority, people treating people like things. And there was nothing that could stop it. There was nothing I could do to stop it."

"Devon." Liam closed the space between then, grabbing her wrists where her hands were fisted in her hair as though she would rip it out of her scalp. "What in the world did you think you could do to stop all of that?"

"I could have killed Eric Paulson!"

There it was. Decades of frustration and guilt tumbling out. What she thought she ought to have done to save them all. To prevent an unpreventable madness.

And what she had on her agenda still.

"When he was still mortal. Sitting across from me at dinner like a civilized monster, offering me fame, glory, and money . . . and me so eager to accept all of the above. So *thrilled* to be in his lauded presence." She all but spat the words.

And light suddenly dawned on Liam.

This was why she had done all of this. This was why she had gone underground in human society, why she had taken on this task so many of her kind would look on as traitorous. She was gunning for the man who had started it all, determined to do what no other had been able to do in the fifty years since the Phoenix Project had come to light. Liam was very well aware of the rumors that, upon his escape, Dr. Paulson had chosen one of his own protocols and had changed himself into a Morphate. That he was still alive and crazy out there somewhere, with God knows what motivations driving him. And for some reason she felt it was her responsibility to put an end to him.

And now he understood so much more about Devon. He finally could see why she was so driven. She carried around elephantine guilt that was weighing her spirit down. There was no way he could possibly undo so many years of damage with simple words, so he wouldn't even try. But he could try and ease her burden just a little.

"Okay," he said, drawing in a deep breath and exhaling it slow and loud on purpose as he drew her against himself with a hand at the back of her head, cradling her against his chest as he breathed again. She picked up on the third breath, following him perfectly through a fourth until he felt the tension unwind slightly from her frame. Enough to let her sink more softly against him. "Okay," he said again. It was simple, accepting if not quite agreeing. He understood her passion. Her fever. He had once been filled with a similar fever. When he had been young, Colin's age, he'd wanted nothing more than to use his training to bring justice to those who deserved it. He had been fortunate, however, to have had the right hands to guide him, to shape him. Hands that had taught him the best ways to funnel his furies and his frustrations. Considering who she was at her core, considering the wild nature of the creature she was harboring inside of herself, it was a wonder she hadn't burned down half the world in her fever to find and destroy Paulson.

But there was much more to her than that. She was too exquisite and too refined, too intelligent to lose herself so utterly and blindly. So completely. So she had saved the obsession for her moments in this lab. Channeled it here. Alone? Had there been no one for her? What of her fellow Morphates? Which City had she been released to? Had she made no connections among them? Bad enough to be so ostracized, but to be ostracized and alone?

Liam tilted her head back between his hands, lifting her chin between his thumbs as he raised her eyes to his.

"It's late. It's been a long day," he told her softly. "After all of this time, I think one more day won't make a difference."

It took a moment for his meaning to sink in, and when it did, he could see the tears burning wetly across her eyes. She made a sound, like a sad, wounded little creature, and then hitched in her breath. Watching this proud, strong woman dissolve into tears was more painful to him then he could possibly have expected. It took his breath away, the way it affected him. He didn't have the opportunity to examine the feelings or worry about himself and the integrity of his own perspective. He was far more focused on what she so clearly needed in that moment. He didn't rush her to the door, because he knew she wouldn't want to be seen by anyone in such a state. She would probably be wishing he wasn't seeing her either, but there was nothing he could do about that . . . nothing he would want to do about that. As far as he could see, she had been on her own, stoic and burning beneath the surface, for far too long as it was. And with what, that jackass Carter as her only touchstone?

He rather surprised himself with his instincts to hold her and calm her. The closest thing he'd ever had to a sister was Veronica and he'd never invested much in his relationships with women. His was not the sort of career meant to foster those kinds of things.

Regardless, he'd learned enough along the way to keep from making a mess into a disaster. Enough to help her find calm after a few minutes and feel proud of himself for managing it. He helped dry her cheeks with his thick fingertips and somehow managed to get her to leave the vault.

As he brought her to her rooms, he very abruptly realized that he was in over his head. That all his principles were in jeopardy. All the rules he was so comfortable adhering to were quickly dissolving.

He was incredibly screwed.

Chapter Eleven

Ambrose's brow was knitted in concentration as he watched the live feed of Devon's well-protected grounds, sent to him by his agents in the field. The relay was a very sharp image with well-controlled audio and his dispatcher on the other end was adept at zooming in on details he thought Ambrose might find interesting. It was quite thought provoking, all those humans being used to protect a creature three times as strong as any of them and a thousand times more indestructible. In the past he might have had his people simply tear a swath through the little mortals to get to his target, but the game had changed dramatically thanks to Devona. Mercury and its application via bullets had become the ultimate game changer.

In the past he had not hesitated to send out his agents to keep the unruly in check, both mortal and immortal, and had not put much thought behind it, but now . . . now that Devona had succeeded in her decades-long quest to figure out how to end Morphate immortality, there were much more serious ramifications to be considered beyond being called into check by the nosy interference of the Alpha Council.

He had shaken them off years ago, and he would find a way to deal with her just as well.

There were many ways for Ambrose to achieve his goals, other ways of penetrating her defenses. He merely needed to be smarter than she was. As he watched, though, he didn't see any of the usual markings that identified the group of mortals she was working with. Normally humans advertised themselves at every opportunity. On the sides of their vehicles. On their very backs in the form of T-shirts or jackets. But this group was clever enough not to do that, to remain as nondescript as possible.

"Follow the humans to their headquarters. Follow her to wherever she goes. Don't engage her unless necessary. Not yet anyway. I know the assassin in you chafes, Rhiannon, but right now I need the thief in you. I need what she is trying to protect so desperately. I need it before anyone else gets it."

"I thought she was trying to protect herself," Rhiannon said with a bit of confusion. "These are bodyguards."

"These are a distraction from the real target," Ambrose corrected her sharply. "She's very, very clever, and never forget that. She doesn't need protecting. Anyone who knows her knows she couldn't care less if she lives or dies. No, it's something other than herself that she is protecting. Or . . . something else she is planning. I haven't quite figured it out yet . . . but I am certain it will be of great interest to me and all other Morphates. Just obey me. Watch her steadily, stay out of sight until I say otherwise."

Rhiannon shut off the connection to her boss with a frustrated sound. When Torque had the audacity to chuckle at her in a very "I told you so" manner, she flipped him off.

"Don't act so smug. You're just as tired of sitting here as I am," she groused.

"On the contrary. I take a lot of pleasure sitting and working a problem out to my best advantage. Ambrose is right, you know, we can't go in guns blazing anymore. While mercury and its applications haven't hit mainstream human knowledge yet, it's guaranteed Devona has seen to it her humans are armed with it. I have no desire to end up a huge gaseous cloud."

Rhiannon snorted out a derisive sound. "So suddenly you're afraid just because she has weapons that could actually kill us? Frankly, immortality made things a little bit boring," she sniffed. "I like the idea of the challenge. Of living by my claws and my reflexes. There's more to being Morphate than our ability to heal and regenerate at a phenomenal rate."

"This is true," Torque agreed. "And it isn't fear, Rhi. It's reasonable caution. I will face those gun muzzles head on, mercury and all, when the time comes, but there are many ways to reduce that risk. And given a choice, I'd much rather bring down my risk level as much as possible."

"Hmph. Never thought you'd be the sort to blink at a challenge," Rhiannon goaded him softly.

"And I never realized how reckless you could be," he mused in return. "Go on then, if you think you're so indestructible."

Rhi shrugged a shoulder. "I may not be afraid of humans or Devona, but I won't fly in the face of my Alpha's orders. That's one thing even I won't do." She smiled wickedly at him. "But I know our Alpha well enough to know that he frustrates easily when it comes to Devona Candler or her masters, the Alphas of Dark Manhattan. I will have my way soon enough." She rolled her eyes as she plucked at a leaf and began to shred it into bits in frustration. "I just hope it happens before I go stark raving mad from boredom. What a way to waste my immortality."

Torque narrowed his eerily fair-colored eyes on his companion, taking a moment to reevaluate the pairing he found himself a part of, as he had several times since this had begun. With his life on the line he didn't need anyone dragging him down and into danger.

He promptly began to formulate the ways in which he

would sacrifice his partner to protect his goals and to cut away her dead weight at the same time.

Devon stood just inside the balcony doors leading to the small private deck that wrapped around her bedroom. She had left all of her lights off and had opened both the door and the screen and now stood in the doorframe, staring out into the night without truly seeing the vast array of stars that usually gave her comfort.

It was cold, a sure sign of the changing season, and her skin rippled in gooseflesh. Superior she might be, physically speaking, but the silk kimono robe went no farther than her knees and it was no protection against the sharp bite in the night air, even for her.

Devon laughed wryly to herself. Some great and powerful experiment she turned out to be. All of her pain and regrets, all the guilt she had borne for decades and all the work she had done to right it, and never once had she shared any of the emotion behind her struggle with anyone. Not even her Alphas. Yet she had spilled all the worst things about herself to a man who was little more than a stranger. A man who meant nothing to her and to whom she meant nothing as well. She had fallen apart and shamelessly turned herself over to his care, let him carry her to bed like a child, taking comfort in his hushing and gentle kisses against her temple.

She clutched the lapels of her robe tight against her throat as she shook her head with regret for her idiocy. Foolish, ridiculous woman. She had stood against dozens of threats and dangers, from the time of her original capture to her time as Amara's Beta, and on to her self-imposed exile among humans and her fight to survive against the Morphate assassins. Why, after all of that, would she choose now to fall apart? And what had been the threat? A man had threatened to walk out on her. Walk out of a *locked door*!

She laughed at the joke on herself, taking a sip of the drink she'd poured some time ago but was still nursing. She heard the occasional bark or footfall from the night crew patrolling the grounds, not surprised to find how quickly their presence had become normal to her. Since her bedroom was on the third story, it wasn't likely anyone would see her there. She was in total darkness, so she could pretty much guarantee they couldn't. Not unless they were using night vision, which was entirely possible. She didn't much care either way.

Liam hadn't gone to bed yet. Considering the hour and the fact that he was still healing, it had been a long day for him. She wondered what could be keeping him so late, then caught herself and wondered why she should even care.

"Devon, you're losing your mind," she berated herself sternly.

It was one thing to want the man physically, but something else entirely when she started leaning on him when she didn't even have to. Maybe it was the sexual tension between them that was messing with her mind and her attitude. She should just take him to her bed, get good and tired out on him, and then get back to what was important. But that would require more disclosures and she wasn't certain she could deal with any more disclosures. Who knew what he thought of her now. He'd been kind, even sweet, but he'd had a hysterical female on his hands and wasn't that what men were supposed to do to get rid of them? Be kind and gentle and tuck them into bed so you could run for the high hills.

Devon groaned and bounced her head lightly against the doorframe. Now she was being bitchy. It sure as hell wasn't Liam Nash's fault that her life was a roller coaster of mistakes and unfortunate treacheries. None of this was his fault and none of it should be his responsibility, but here he was, he and his people, protecting her life. Bad enough the idea had rankled in the first place. How the mighty had fallen, to go from one of the most feared Betas in all the clans to cowering behind the fragility of humans.

It wasn't that she was afraid to die. By all means, she thought, let death come. Only it had to wait. Just a short while. She could not leave humans at the mercy of rogue Morphates and she couldn't leave Ambrose or Paulson alive and loose upon the world. Only she truly understood the horror of what these men were willing to do in order to obtain power.

Once her task was done, let it come.

Liam made a final circuit of the house before heading to bed around 1 A.M. Overall, the day had gone well . . . at least as far as the job was concerned. He was annoyed that he was three days behind, but pleased that Inez had taken over for him and done an excellent job at it. It might be time soon to consider promoting her in the ranks, but it seemed a shame to extract her from her partnership with Kellen. They worked really well together. He wondered which Inez would prefer, especially when Parker was taken into consideration.

When he reached the floor he shared with Devon, he noted quickly that her light was out already. He'd already gained permission to make her bedroom part of his nightly rounds, since she'd admitted that locking doors and windows wasn't one of the things on the top of her mind most nights. He imagined tonight that would be especially true.

He turned his Maglite toward his body and gingerly turned the knob to her door. She had to be exhausted, considering the time she'd spent caring for him and her emotional upheaval earlier, and he wasn't about to wake her and disturb the first peaceful sleep she'd probably had in a while. Focusing the light to a narrow beam and keeping it low, Liam made his rounds of her sitting room. He then slipped into her bedroom.

He already disliked the room. It had a high percentage of glass, which left her very exposed, to his way of thinking. The decking wrapped around from western glass doors to northern ones, then on to include the bathroom as well. Since the house was in the mountains, surrounded by nothing but trees and vast lawns, there was no need for curtains, blinds, or even tinting. She was on the third floor and isolated in the mountains, so, under normal circumstances, why should she worry about exposure? He checked the bath doors and windows, giving the deck a scan, then moved to do the same for the bedroom.

He could hear her breathing deeply and evenly, a heavy, restful sound shadowed by a purring feminine snore of sorts. It made him smile, and like so many things about her, it titillated him sexually when least expected. He absently checked the lock on the door as his gaze drifted over to the bed. As his eyes adjusted fully to the darkness, he could see her sprawled face down among mounds of bedding and a half-dozen pillows. He stepped closer and brought her into better focus.

The first thing he noticed was the spread of dark hair over the pillows and mattress. He followed the bare expanse of a long, beautiful spine right up to the upswept curve of her bottom, where a sheet and comforter concealed the rest of her from sight. Her hands were above her head and he could see the swelling of her breast squeezing out from between the weight of her body and the press of the mattress on the side nearest to him. There was something submissive about the pose, the antithesis of her powerful personality and steady strength. As erotic as he found her strength, this was equally stimulating, proving to him that she truly was sex incarnate. Even when she wasn't conscious of it.

At least, she was to him.

Her skin glowed just about iridescent in the moonlight, even though it wasn't very strong moonlight. As he stared at her, all he could think was that she looked so warm. So incredibly warm. All of that skin. Soft, warm, promising responsiveness that he already knew too well. And yet not well enough.

Liam crossed to the bed in two strides, gently standing his flashlight on the bedside table.

Liam Nash, this is known as a betrayal of trust.

That inner voice in his head was telling it like it was, no doubt about it. She trusted him to come into her room while she was vulnerable and asleep. What he was doing was no better than what that animal had intended to do before shooting up her hotel room like a carnival gallery.

No. It was even worse. Worse because she depended on him. He knew she depended on no one, yet had chosen to trust him to guard her back. Not to ogle it and think far too luridly vivid thoughts of sex and lust.

What in the world had gotten into him?

She had. She'd crawled under his skin and was putting down roots. She wore insanely provocative dresses, spoke incredibly intelligent observations, and sat by his bed for seventy-two hours, spending most of that time soothing him. She had survived the unthinkable fifty years ago. She made him laugh, made him think, and invented weapons no other man, woman, or Morphate could or would.

Yeah. He was in big trouble all right.

The part that sucked was that a man like him thrived on trouble.

He could also thrive on satin smooth skin, given half a chance.

Liam kept his breathing soft and even as he leaned over and reached for the center of the bed. His fingertips touched her back and he swallowed down a groan of pleasure. She was so supple it was like running his fingers through piles of silky, yielding talc that clung to you no matter which way you turned your fingers. He followed the curve of her spine,

feeling the light chill of her skin because the room air was
so cool.

Devon made a low sound reminiscent of a purr and he felt
her move as if to follow his touch, seeking more. She sighed
when her shift brought his entire palm onto her skin. Her
movements were like those of a woman being made love to,
slow and sensuous, receptive to the roaming touch of her
lover.

God, how Liam wanted to be that lover. There was no use
in denying that any longer. His body was singing with readi-
ness in answer to her influence, blatantly hard as if to pro-
nounce boldly what was expected of him. All it had taken was
a touch, a sound, and the smallest movement.

Devon suddenly rolled over, her breast sliding fully into
his hovering hand as she settled. Liam found himself with a
dark, tempting nipple between two fingers, the tip already
pointed toward the ceiling. Any sane man would have drawn
the line right there, pulling back and thanking the powers that
be that he hadn't gotten caught with his hand in the proverbial
cookie jar. Why, oh why, he wondered, couldn't he be that
man? He'd never before let his cock do the thinking for him.
What was so damned different this time?

"Liam . . ."

The low murmur of his name was spoken in the dead of
sleep, he was convinced of it. He squeezed his eyes shut as his
entire body thrummed hotly in response to it. Did this mean
she dreamed of him? Did she fantasize about his touch on her
body, just like this? Liam gently squeezed his two fingers together, pinching that pert nipple ever so slightly, and thrilling
in her instant moaning reaction, the arcing of her back, the
raising of her knees in restless invitation.

Liam abruptly jerked himself away from her, twisting into
an about-face and sliding down to the floor with his back
pressed to the mattresses. He groaned with frustration and

disgust, covering his face with his hands. What in hell was he doing? This was a violation! Pure and simple. There was no room for interpretation. He shoved himself to his feet and grabbed for the flashlight. To his surprise, his hand hit air. It wasn't on the table where he was positive he'd left it. Thinking he had knocked it over, he bent to check the floor.

Suddenly, a straight beam of light blinded him in his unprotected eyes. While he shouted at the unexpected pain, he felt strong hands grabbing him by his shirt and throwing him over and down onto the bed. He was about to retaliate when he felt long legs swinging over him and framing his hips, and familiar feminine weight resting on his belly. Her hair brushed his face, filling him with that scent that was so sweet and so Devon.

"Devon! What the hell?"

"I might ask you the same thing," she pointed out huskily, her torso lowering across his until he felt her breath rushing over his lips. "What are you doing, Liam?"

"Checking the locks," he said hoarsely as he realized he could feel the heat and weight of her bare breasts through his thin T-shirt.

"Are there locks on the floor beside my bed?" she queried, whispering the rushed words over his lips, every syllable a teasingly light kiss.

"Devon, please," he groaned as her hands roamed over his hair, neck, and chest. It was too much stimulation all at once. Her swaying bottom was rocking against his fly, taunting him with the knowledge that she was completely nude and rubbing herself against him. He grew so hard he could have pounded nails. It was gorgeously painful, agonizingly wonderful.

"You know what I think?" she asked, her body lifting so her hands could slide down his chest and marble-hard abdomen, following each defined muscle with smooth surety. He felt her smile lightly against his mouth when his belly flinched beneath her fingers. "I think you were sitting there watching me. Wondering," she breathed, her tongue dipping to lick between his lips. Liam groaned as his head spun with pleasure. Her aggression was maddening. Hot. "Wondering what I feel like here," she swayed her breasts across his hidden nipples. "Wondering what I taste like there." Devon shifted her hips over him, riding him in a silky sway that nearly unmanned him. When his vision finally cleared of starbursts enough to see her riding astride him, head back in bliss, breasts thrust out for his pleasure, he grabbed her arms and sat up with her, forcing her weight down on his overtaxed body as he held her off balance.

"And what if I was?" he rasped roughly. He swung her around, driving her down into the bed beneath him, playing her game by grinding his hips forward between her splayed legs. She trilled out a long low moan of pleasure, her head rolling as her fingers gripped his arms madly.

Liam broke under that response. He reared up on his knees over her and stripped off his T-shirt. He came back over her, his mouth swooping first for her breast, seizing the nipple. He rolled and sucked the hard tip between his hungry lips. He flicked her with teasing tongue strokes, bit with light scrapes of teeth.

"Liam!" she gasped. Devon felt her entire body combust. From that one point he started a ferocious fire, causing licking flames and molten liquid to drip from her body. He surged up to catch her mouth and ravaged her with breathtakingly seductive kisses. Her hands roamed his broad bare back with hunger and delight. They slid into his hair, over his neck, eased over his injured shoulder. Dipped deep below his waist, bumping over his weapons belt to curve over his buttocks and draw him closer down.

Liam had craved the feel of her body too much to be rushed, but he was on fire. Her breasts filled his palms to perfection again and again as he tried to learn her beautiful, writhing form.

She felt every touch with incredible intensity.

"Your hands burn," she breathed into his ear on a moan as he was spreading that conflagration down her hips and thighs.

"Your entire body is burning," he growled as she proved his point with a chain of gasps and something muttered about 'calluses.' Liam smiled slowly when he understood what she found so incredibly stimulating. His rough fingers could do things she couldn't even imagine. Often they were a point of complaint, but he should have known she'd never be usual. He ran the rough edges of his fingers over both her nipples and rode with her when she lunged up off the bed. "Ah . . . liked that, did you?"

Her vivid eyes flew open as she panted and stared into his eyes as if seeing him for the first time. It was an unsettling thing to be on the receiving end of. For a moment he was afraid she'd come to her senses and he was about to be booted out of heaven.

"Liam," she uttered roughly, making his cock twitch just at the sound. "Liam, I couldn't bear if I hurt you," she whispered.

He didn't understand. He didn't understand what her arousal was doing to her, what it was taking to rest calmly beneath him, to pull back and try and emulate what she had once been when she had been human. She could be so dangerous to him. Didn't he realize that?

And why wasn't she pulling away? Why wasn't she doing everything in her power to protect him?

"I can't resist you," she gasped, her hands grasping and stroking over his smoothly furred chest. She raked her fingernails through the hair. "There's something about you that makes me throw myself open to you again and again. Liam, I want you so much and I don't understand why."

"Join the club, sweetheart," he soothed her gently as he took up her mouth in a languorous, deep kiss that went on and on until he felt her calves wrapping around his thighs and her fingers deep in his hair.

"You could hate me one day," she whispered against his lips. "So many people hate me now. I feel it all around me . . . except when I feel you all around me. How do you do that?"

"You think I have the answer to that? The only thing I can tell you is that I'm really glad this is mutual. You do things to me that I never thought were possible." He kissed her again, coaxing her back into that quickly heating frenzy that made her writhe beneath him. "Feel me, sweetheart?" he breathed hotly, rotating his hips so she would know her power over his body. "Tell me how it feels," he demanded as she moaned softly.

"Hard. Hot," she gasped, her breasts heaving with every breath. "Dangerous." She reached to grip his weapons belt, running her hands around to unbuckle it. Before it could be pulled away, though, she would have to undo the second fastening around his thigh on his holster side. She anticipated it quickly and ran a purposeful finger down his inner thigh until she had deftly undone it. She let it fall away, let it tumble off the bed with a loud thump. They both knew how dangerous it was to let the bullets within be treated carelessly, but neither was considering caution in that moment.

Liam began to slide his hands over her again, covering her breasts, belly, and hips. He worked his hand down between the press of their bodies, petting her hairless mound and feeling the viscous cream of her heat already wetting his fingertips. He closed his eyes tightly for a minute as he fought for control. When he opened them, he pinned her down by his gaze alone. He wanted to see her eyes as he touched her and brought her to pleasure. He wanted to watch her seductive, sly features contort in bliss.

Liam slid his touch between her folds and let his calluses run ever so lightly over aroused, anticipating flesh. She soaked his fingers. Devon sucked in her breath as he easily found the swollen bead of flesh that could manipulate her into passion. That was when he realized she had been right. Just like she had said, what he wanted most was to have her against his hungry mouth. Among so many desires overwhelming him, that was the one ringing loudest and truest in that moment.

"Oh God, Liam, you're killing me," she cried when his light, absent-minded touch taunted her. Liam flicked a firm thumb over that sensitive bud, rolling around the edges of it in slow, lazy circles until her hips were swirling with the rhythm. She moaned in response, erotic expressions crossing her beautiful face. In the end, that was why he stuck to his original desire. He wanted to watch her come. He licked a nipple and blew across it. Then he slid farther down her body and parting her labia to expose her clit to him, he was able to lick her just as tauntingly across her clit. Once. Just once. A lick and a long chilling blow before the relentless thumb returned.

"You taste like a dream," he groaned, burying his face in her belly as he rode out the surges of screaming demand that he free his strangling cock and bury himself balls deep inside of her. Yes. Oh, God, yes he wanted that.

"You don't know me," she breathed, her legs clutching at him restlessly, her hands pushing against his chest. It was as if she were trying to hold on to him and push him away at the same time.

Devon closed her eyes, tilting back her head, trying not to let the beast inside of her out as it suddenly came knocking at the door with raging, pounding fists. In this, it refused to be controlled. This time she did push him away, shoved him, actually, using her preternatural strength to do so. She sent him nearly off the far edge of the king-sized bed, even as she rolled blindly away and dropped to the floor. She scrambled to her feet and lurched toward the bedroom door, but he had recovered himself with amazing alacrity and grabbed hold of her before she could so much as touch the knob.

"What the freaking hell?" he demanded as he hauled her about, forcing her to face him, both of them banging her backward into the door.

She couldn't bear being near him. The smell of him lured the animal inside her much too strongly. She held her breath, looked away . . . curled her hands and held them away as best she could. It was all fruitless. There was no pretending Liam wasn't there. Not with the heat of his body so intense from lovemaking and anger, the blend so potent and fierce.

"What is this?" he demanded, giving her a little shake as he tried to see her face in the darkness. But they had moved away from the windows so there was much less moonlight to help him. "Some kind of tease? Are you playing some kind of game?"

Even as he said it, Liam couldn't make himself believe it. Her responses had been too genuine. Too abandoned. Or so it had seemed.

Liam continued to trap her against the door with the heavy press of his body, but he recalled how only instants ago she had proven to him that she could put up a very powerful fight if she was of a mind to. If she was strong enough to send his full weight flying, then she was as strong as they came.

Come on, Liam, think, he commanded of himself.

Then her recent words finally sank into his awareness.

I don't want you to hate me . . . You don't know me.

He reached for her face. Gripping her chin and tilting it up, he forced her to look at him. He focused on her through the darkness and countermanded her when she tried to get free again. Light shone on her left cheek, chin, and lips . . . and the white gleam of the fang that had grown to peek through them. He moved a fingertip up to touch it and she fought a bit harder this time to resist him, forcing him to lay all of his weight against her, digging his feet into the floor to keep her from squirming free.

"No! You show me! You find that courage that I have seen

in every cell of your being and you show me what you think will make me shun you!"

That managed to quiet her like no show of human strength could possibly have done.

"It's not cowardice," she insisted, the words having the softest of lisps because the anatomy of her mouth had been restructured and she was sporting deadly white fangs. She was holding her chin up and looking him in the eye as she did so, as brave as she'd ever been. "I . . . you're human. And I am not. It is very rare for Morphates and humans to be well matched. It . . . it takes a particular kind of human to be able to withstand what we are when we're aroused. Especially when aroused to the point that you have brought me to, Liam."

Logically and intellectually he knew that. He had known it every time he had entertained thoughts of having her when in a calm and reasonable moment. But he tended to forget all of it when he touched her. No. She wasn't afraid. She was protecting. Protecting him. From herself.

But he had asked himself these questions already. Dozens of times. In the secretive, speculating parts of his brain that had considered crossing the line with her, he had imagined what it might be like and had found himself insanely titillated by the thought of it. But he had known for quite some time that his sexual tastes did not run toward the mild or mundane.

"And you didn't think I had ever considered that?" he asked her with amusement poured into his voice as liberally as syrup onto pancakes.

"Well, I . . ."

He could almost envision the gears turning in her head, as well as the soft flush rising on her skin as she began to breathe a little more quickly. However, he knew she would overthink, just as he would overthink if given enough time to do so. It was intriguing to realize how much they had in common. And if she was like him, then she worked best thinking on her feet and in the moment.

Liam darted forward to catch her mouth, kissing her powerfully as his hands swept down the front of her body, over her breasts and ribs and belly and around her hips to the backs of her thighs. He roughly hauled her feet off the floor by sliding her up between his body and the solid press of her bedroom door. The wood clattered in its frame as he did so, but all he heard was the ragged inhale of her breath as he wrapped her legs around his waist.

"Now I think I'm going to fuck you right here. Because I'm tired of waiting for it. And I know you are too. There's only one restriction I'm going to put on you, Devon. When you mark me, as I know you will, don't do it where my men will be able to see."

Devon was not offended by the request in any way. It meant enough that he was breaking all the rules to put his hands on her. He wasn't the sort to fly in the face of his own ethics easily. That made the feel of his hands and the urgent press of his body all the more arousing. Once her legs were locked around his hips, he gripped her around the throat with the left hand and pushed his right back between her legs where it had been before she'd thrown him off her.

"I'm going to make you scream until I see those fangs of yours flashing in the moonlight," he promised roughly against her lips as he swept his thumb against her clit and boldly thrust two fingers into her body. She was more than wet enough from their earlier play and he went in easily in spite of the incredible muscular resistance that greeted him because she was taken off guard and because, he imagined, she was Morphate. Every inch of her was custom designed for strength. And it only took a few moments of touching her to understand that every inch of her was designed for mating as well.

She came alive like something dormant suddenly granted consciousness. Her long legs gripped him, her body curved against him, and he felt the sharp bite of her strengthening claws pricking into the skin of his shoulders.

"Within the borders of a T-shirt?" she asked him breathlessly and a bit belatedly.

"That'll do just fine," he agreed as he began to work her clit and her channel at the same time, in an aggressive rhythm sparked by the arousal claiming him as her true nature was finally unleashed. There was no longer any hint of passivity in her. She grabbed onto him like a thing gone wild, working her own body into his touch, her breath coming quicker and quicker as she took an insistent part in her own stimulation. It made him hard all over again and then some to feel her come alive like that, to discover all the promise of potential sexuality that he had seen fulfilled at last.

Devon growled raggedly against his ear, her whole body writhing, forcing him to bang her back against the door hard in order to keep them on balance. She was gasping for breath, her head cocked back, those gorgeous fangs on wicked display. Somehow the sight of them made her even more beautiful than ever. Almost as if they had been missing all along, the last thing needed to perfect her. And that was probably because on some level he had wondered where they were and how he could get her to show them to him. Knowing Morphates as he did, he knew it would take either extreme violence . . . or this. The height of lust and passion. Her eyes, glowing yellow-green in the darkness, slid closed as she began to moan, punctuating that ever-persistent, underlying growl.

Devon had not felt this level of pleasure in so many years that it had been forgotten. It had been so powerfully dismissed because she had chosen to live among humans and had lived a life where few could be trusted even to know what she was, never mind to bring this out of her. She ought to have resisted even now. She shouldn't trust herself *or* him. It was an act of insanity. But right then she needed to be a little insane. She needed to let herself run wild more than she had ever needed anything in her life. And even though she had had couplings with other Morphates since her alteration those fifty years ago, none of them had attained the degree of intimacy and wildness that threatened her now.

She began the fall into orgasm as if she were falling off a bridge, giving herself over to it completely, welcoming the inevitable. Liam let her fall, holding her securely in every other way so she didn't have to worry about anything else but rolling back into her pleasure. She shuddered mindlessly, amazed at what she was feeling, at the power of it even without penetration of her body, or her fangs.

She reached to grab the back of his head with one hand, the short spikiness of his hair crackling beneath her fingertips even as the long tips of her claws tapped against his scalp in a way that made an erotic shudder skip down his thick spine. She was panting hard in his ear, feeling the ache of her protruding fangs and the savageness of her hunger. Her tongue felt like it was sticking to the roof of her mouth with the thirst she had for him. For his blood. But she needed something else even more. The hollowness of her body was exacerbated as he pulled his hand free of her and moved to make hasty work of his belt and his jeans. In her haze of need she wanted to claw into him, forcing him to her and inside of her. Forcing him to move faster to his goal. Then she remembered his only request for reserve.

There could be no marks for his people to see.

Liam felt her hand suddenly scraping down inside his jeans over his left buttock, her grip sharp and painful as she urged him forward, pushing the denim down and away at the same time. She would better be able to control her hunger later on, after it wasn't so keen, but for now . . .

He was of no mind for slowness or patience either. They'd danced around what they had really wanted long enough. His cock in one hand and her weight supported in the other, he lined himself up to enter her. All it would take was a single savage thrust. But there was something about holding on to this ferocious little wildcat, her nails digging deep into his backside and scalp at the same time, her breath chuffing out of her in staccato growls of demand that made him want to savor the moment even more.

"Do it! Fuck me. Do it hard, Liam, and fast," she demanded in fierce little gasps.

He thought about toying with her, but he was fast reaching his own breaking point. Rubbing the head of his cock all around her wet slit for a moment, dousing himself in creamy wetness, he then moved straight to the cusp of her vagina, nudged, and then in a great forward surge, he rent her eager yet resisting flesh. That she wanted him there was no question, but he could tell with strange surety and immediacy that she had not seen use in quite some time. The thought was fascinating and compelling. It made him thrust harder into her, banging her back into the door and making her cry out.

His name. She cried out his name. He would never forget the sound of it in that animalistic growl, accompanied by the further press of her claws into his flesh. The pain was a perfect sort of pleasure. And it propelled him into one thrust after another. Each one slamming their fervent bodies against that shuddering door. He was risking their discovery with such noises and racket. It promised to attract the attention of the guards walking the other levels of the house. He reached out a hand to add balance to their weight against the door, pushing it steadily into the jamb even as their coupling continued to bring them back and forth against the wood. It didn't eliminate the noise, but it brought it down several notches. And it was a fix he didn't have to concentrate on. A fix he could use to bear into her harder and deeper. She was tight and burned like fire around him, her body heat unbelievable. He couldn't give her but the briefest of hot kisses, his attention fully focused on other connections. But she had little interest in kissing now. She became undeniably fixated on his throat . . . on the powerful pulse she saw beating there in his strong, thick neck.

He promised to be oh so delicious. He promised to be explosive and hot and divine. But she had made him a promise as well, and she was forced to drag her attention down from the exposed length of his neck to the more easily concealable yoke of his shoulder. It was a thick, meaty spot. As good as any, when it came down to it . . . and a delicious access to a rich supply of the fevered blood within him. Leaving the control of the thunderous rhythm he had chosen up to him, she shot forward like a cunning little serpent honed in on a perfect target. The perfect morsel to be devoured.

Liam felt her jerk forward, but it took a moment longer for him to register the sudden burning pain of being bitten. His first instinct should have been to rip free, to tear away from the source of such piercing pain, but instead all he could feel . . . all he could do . . . was come. The violent need to ejaculate was on him and beyond him before he could even think to control himself. He threw his head back and gritted his teeth to keep from shouting the overwhelming pleasure out so loud that the whole of his protective detail came running. He pinned her hard to the door as he jetted into her in long, scalding streams of release. He was aware of her open mouth on him, the warmth of her tongue swirling over his skin to cup up the blood he was losing into her. The sound of her swallowing was somehow the most erotic thing he'd ever heard in his life.

She was climaxing as well. The power of it trebling with every mouthful of Liam she took into herself. She did not throw herself fully into it as she would have loved to have done. A Morphate in true release became almost vicious sometimes, a single bite not always satisfying. Their partner often surfacing with multiple bites and a body tracked with random, fervent claw marks. But she knew she could only go so far with a human lover. Especially when that lover wished to keep evidence of the coupling secret.

Just the same, she rushed with pleasure. Pulsed and clenched with it. Burning off her need and craving for him well enough to satisfy herself. Well enough to satisfy him. As she panted for breath, slowly licking at the worst of the wounds she had created, she found herself smiling against him.

"Jesus God," Liam growled out against her ear, his breath coming hard and his big body actually trembling within the vise of her arms and legs.

Her smile grew wider. He felt the exposure of her teeth against himself and felt in his spirit just how well pleased she was with herself . . . and perhaps the situation at hand as well.

"I can feel the shit-eating grin, I'll have you know," he whispered against her ear, his own smile irresistible. He seemed to have rediscovered the expression since getting to know her. Not that he had been a sad or miserable person, but quite a serious one. Given the nature of his job and his life and all the lives he became responsible for, it wasn't any wonder. But something about her had brought back his ability to smile, even so. It was a daunting idea. The implications of which he wasn't quite ready to sort out.

"Is there anything wrong with my being pleased with myself? Or with you?" she asked him coyly.

His smile grew.

"Not in the least. I wouldn't have it any other way."

He had never spoken truer words.

Chapter Twelve

When Devon woke the following morning, it was with an automatic smile on her face before she even opened her eyes. She felt warm male all along her body and under her cheek. She opened her eyes to find Liam sprawled over a large percentage of the bed on his stomach, and she was lying over him like his own personal blanket, her cheek nestled in the center of his back between his shoulder blades. She tilted her nose up and she could see the fine hairs that had grown back since his barber had last neatened the cut of his hair on the back of his neck. Her left leg was thrown over the backs of his thighs, her belly curved over his backside. How he could sleep comfortably with almost all of her weight lying along his back was fascinating to her. She was also surprised to realize she was quite comfortable herself. She smiled against his skin and reached up to brush her fingers over the previously noticed hairs on the back of his neck. They were soft and prickly at the same time and she gently stroked them into the same direction.

She had never made a habit of sleeping with males. Perhaps when she had been younger and more trusting, but once she had begun to learn the hard lessons of the world they lived in, she had grown very cautious. Yet it seemed caution had abandoned her along with everything else as far as Liam Nash was concerned.

A human male. And yet she had felt more pleasure under his kisses and engulfing hands than she could remember ever feeling with the unmemorable Morphate males she'd encountered since her change. That was saying a great deal, considering the extent of her lifetime. What was it that made him different? Certainly the acts had been familiar enough . . . and then again, not. Her entire body tingled to life with the mere memory of how Liam had burned her body with his combination of passion, humor, and candor of response.

Devon breathed in deep the warmed scent of their bodies. They combined well: Liam smelling of maleness, grass, and the lightest trace of gun oil; she of her own femininity, herbal shampoo, and the touch of her favorite perfume. Among all of that was the unmistakable eroticism of their sexual activities the night before, a heady musk as classic as time and mating itself. The remnants of perspiration and arousal were tangled in the laundered scent of the bedding.

For a species that thrived on its senses, it was a banquet of pleasure all in itself, stimulating and easily stirring the sensations of the night before back to life. Devon slid her palm down over Liam's shoulders, careful of both the dressing she had placed on one shoulder and the fresher wound she'd created on the other, gliding along his back and the smooth expanse of tight, firm skin and muscle. There wasn't an inch of fat on him that she could find last night or even now. Every pound was pure sinew, shaped for form and function both, tempered for flexibility and speed as well as power. She sighed with contentment and delight as her hand slid into the narrowing of his waist and the lower dip of his spine. She went on easily to the rise of a firm, wonderfully shaped buttock. She smiled with satisfied pleasure as she fondled the sexy shape, the marks she had left there as well, and then smoothed her way to his thigh.

"You know, in some countries taking advantage of a person while they are unconscious can be construed as rape."

Devon snorted out a laugh at the idea. Liam had mumbled out the accusation from among his pillows, but she didn't stay her exploration. She reversed her path now, and, since he was awake, added the lightest touch of nails to her travels.

"I guess that makes me a criminal then," she mused as she lingered over the now-flexed muscles of his backside. One of these days, she would have to take a bite out of his extremely gorgeous ass. She licked her lips in anticipation of the very idea. "And you my hapless victim," she added.

"Oh, no you don't," he said, quickly sounding fully awake. His hand slid back and seized her at the waist, but she had the advantage since he was pinned down under her weight. "Devon, I can tell by looking out the window that I'm late," he tried to reason with her. "The kids'll be looking for me soon, if they aren't already."

"Mmm, and finding you naked in my bed would be a bad thing . . . for all involved, or so you say," she chuckled. "But I have to tell you, it seems to be working pretty good for me. You too, I think." She supported the observation by sliding her hand between his hips and the bedding, fingers seeking evidence of her claim. She purred in contentment when she found him suitably hard and heated, her hand curling around him as he absently lifted his hips to accommodate them both. She didn't think he was even aware of making the movement and it made her laugh in soft triumph.

"Hey, that's . . ." He stopped long enough to groan at the play of her hand. "That's not fair. It is morning you know, and men just wake up that way."

"Yes, I know. How accommodating of you."

Liam grinned into his pillow, feeling her wriggle along the length of his body. He timed his reaction just right, waiting until she partially lifted her own weight as she tried to move. With a single arm he pushed them both up. Normally he would have done it already, but he had to be cautious of his stitched shoulder. Besides, he was amused by the idea that she thought her weight was capable of keeping him pinned to the bed.

However, he proved her wrong, hauling himself up so fast that she was dumped off of him with a squeal, rolling right off the edge of the bed. He left her there, swinging up to his feet as she scrambled to hands and knees with an indignant sputtering of curses. Liam stretched, grinning ear-to-ear, and walked into the bathroom without so much as a backward glance.

"You are going to pay for that!" she promised his back furiously.

Devon got to her feet, dusting off her indignity with a frown of consternation. Men! One minute it's flat out seduction and lust, the next they threw you off as if you barely existed! She looked at his scattered clothing on the floor and contemplated throwing it out a window, but his belongings were right across the hall, and she didn't think it would faze him in the least to cross the hallway naked.

Well, fine, she thought as she snatched up her robe, *two can play this game*. She drifted into her robe and marched across the hall to his bedroom suite, smiling when she thought of him emerging from the master bath and wondering where she'd disappeared to. She went into his bathroom and stripped again, taking a moment to survey the masculine tidbits of a shaving kit, aftershave, and comb. He'd find her soon enough when he came in search of a shave. Meanwhile, she'd enjoy a shower.

Devon drenched herself under the multiple sprays with a sigh of exultation. The hot water felt good as it worked out the kinks of her unusual sleeping position. She regretfully washed away the traces of their night together, feeling as though it hadn't lasted nearly long enough, wondering if Liam would want to return to her bed tonight as well. The pure fact of the matter was she enjoyed him. Like no other before him. And she longed for him even now. It would be interesting to see if he would continue to fascinate her and her carnal appetites. Honestly, she didn't see his humor or personality disappointing her anytime soon, so that left the simple question of whether his human stamina would bear up under her very inhuman sexual needs.

Devon's Morphate hearing picked up the sound of the bedroom door opening and she smothered a laugh. She heard his footsteps padding across the carpet, but she didn't notice anything wrong until just before he reached the bathroom door. Too late, she realized the step was lighter than Liam's and encased in heavy boots. She certainly didn't think Liam would put his boots back on just to cross the hall . . .

"Hey Liam, the troops are wondering where you are. Shake a leg, bro!"

Colin walked into the bathroom without so much as a knock. And why should he? It was Liam's room and he was Liam's brother. Apparently privacy was not expected between the two siblings.

Devon hit the taps and turned just as Colin screeched to a shocked halt in the center of the bathroom floor. He stared at her through the transparent glass, his mouth dropping the long distance to the floor and his gray eyes going incredibly wide. Devon slicked back her wet hair and smiled when she saw the color rushing up the soldier's neck.

"Morning, Colin," she greeted, stepping out of the shower. "Could you toss me a towel?"

Colin took a long beat, then reached for the nearby pile while he continued to stare at her. She didn't think it had anything to do with her body, because his eyes never dropped from her face. It was merely the inconceivable idea of her being in his brother's shower that floored him. Colin tossed the towel at her just as Devon heard Liam enter the bedroom. She quickly wrapped herself up as he approached the bath.

"Hey, babe, where'd you . . ." Liam stepped through the door, a towel around his hips, and stopped short when he caught the tableau before him, ". . . disappear to," he finished automatically and unnecessarily. His gaze swung from her to Colin and he frowned in a way that darkened his eyes deeply. A tick developed in his tensing jaw almost instantly.

"Colin, my hair," Devon scolded gently, snapping her fingers to grab his diverted attention. Colin dutifully grabbed another towel and threw it at her, his aim off as he divided his attention between her and Liam.

Liam couldn't believe his eyes, or his luck. Of all the people to catch him in illicit behavior, Colin was the worst choice. Devon could clearly care less as she casually made a towel boy out of his brother. Amusingly enough, Colin obeyed her without so much as a questioning blink. Now over his initial surprise, Liam hid a smile and took Devon's cue for casualness.

"Morning, Colin," he greeted easily as he reached behind his brother for a second towel as well. He moved to his shaving equipment, drawing the towel through the steam on the mirror. "I'm running a little late, I know," he said. "Surely you guys can survive without me for a few more minutes?"

"Of course they can," Devon said as she settled herself on the vanity seat and dried her hair in squeezes and pats, crossing long, shapely legs. "They aren't children, Liam. And, after all, they functioned for three whole days without you."

Liam threw her a look over his shoulder, knowing full well she was being a wiseass because he'd thwarted her earlier attempts to seduce him. "That they did," he acknowledged. He glanced at Colin as he prepared for a shave. "Unless something is wrong?" he prompted, wondering when his brother was going to snap out of his speechless shock.

Colin shook his head.

Liam sighed.

Devon snickered through her nose, covering it under a poorly disguised cough. "Well, I have a busy day ahead," she said breezily. "I'll see you boys later."

Devon got up and waltzed out of the room, stifling the urge to giggle as she rounded the door. However, her amusement ebbed a bit when she thought of what would pass next between the two brothers. Liam had been so specific about his desires to keep his travels across the line of his ethics quite private. She had just ruined all their attempts to do so. Of course, crossing the hall in nothing but a towel, displaying the tracks of her passion on his body, was not exactly the highest form of secrecy on his part. It made her smile a little. Subconsciously, Liam could give a damn about being discovered as her lover. But it was a measure of carelessness neither of them could afford.

She sighed and looked at her bedroom door, opting to linger and make use of her excellent Morphate hearing.

"So this is why you didn't want me staring at her!" Colin blurted out first thing when he heard the door shut behind Devon. "Liam, I can't believe you're diddling the client!"

"Keep your voice down," Liam snapped in warning. "And for that matter, watch what you say. This isn't an invitation for you to speak about her disrespectfully."

Colin swallowed, knowing full well how serious Liam was about issues of respect. Despite the issue at hand, Colin would not disrespect anyone or anything . . . least of all his brother's wishes. "You're right. Sorry about that." Colin shook his head. "If I hadn't just seen otherwise, I'd swear that woman has a set of rocks on her the size of bowling balls. She didn't bat an eyelash when I walked in and found her—"

"What do you mean 'seen otherwise'?" Liam demanded, turning around to glare at Colin.

Colin stammered and flushed. "I thought it was you in the shower," he said in a voice barely above a squeak. He cleared his throat, improving his pitch. "Honest, Liam, I never thought in a million years . . ."

"No, you didn't, did you? You never think about my privacy. You've been strolling in on me since the day you learned to walk. And I've gotten used to it." Liam picked up his razor and sighed. "In a way, this is my own fault for not making an issue of it sooner. And, obviously, there's no reason why you'd expect to need caution in this particular venue."

"How about we not make this about me?" Colin countered. "Liam, are you out of your mind? Skipping the fact, for the moment, that you look like you've played the part of a chew toy, what's the first tenet of this work that you ever drilled into me?" he demanded.

"Not to get personally involved with your principal. And I don't need you to remind me of that, Colin," he retorted sharply. "Besides, it's not like I'm out to marry the woman."

"Oh, so it's just a sex thing?" Colin clarified sarcastically.

"Not that it is any of your business, but yeah." Liam focused on the path of his razor for a moment. "Look, I'd have switched out with Julian or Kadian before this, the moment I began to realize I was attracted to her, but they are already on assignment."

"That's a pile of bullshit. You could have traded assignments. Julian has been established long enough with his principal to make a command switch easy enough."

"Colin, why don't you get off my back and just deal with it, okay?" Liam snapped irritably as he threw down his razor and splashed cool water over his face. "And I'd appreciate it if you kept your big mouth shut while you're at it. I don't want Devon being treated with disrespect or as a source of troop gossip."

"Then I guess you shouldn't have fucked her, huh?" Colin groused, irritated by his brother's slap down.

Colin didn't even hear his own mistake until after the ring-

ing in his head stopped and he found himself up against the wall
with Liam's huge forearm pressed furiously against his throat.

"I swear to God, Colin, brother or no, if I hear you talking
about her like she's some kind of whore I will make a quilt out
of your hide. Do you copy?"

"Yes! Jeez, I didn't mean it like that!" he squawked crossly.

"What I do is my business and no one else's, not even
yours," Liam growled irritably as he released his baby brother
none too gently. "You just watch your step. Genetics will not
save your ass if you screw up, Colin."

"Yeah, well, they won't save yours either," Colin grumbled
as he followed Liam out of the bathroom. "I'm just concerned. You don't have to pitch a fit. I'll be waiting downstairs
with the others."

Liam paused to watch his brother storm off, then cursed
low under his breath. He ran a hand through his damp, spik-
ing hair and glanced across the hall at Devon's closed bedroom door. He had half a mind to turn her over his knee as
well. It was really stupid of her to use his rooms like that.
Colin wasn't the only one who didn't think twice about using
barracks manners while they were on assignment. It was
rather the nature of his position to not expect much in the way
of privacy. The idea of keeping her marks on his body out of
sight was, when he thought of it, rather ludicrous.

Well, he wasn't going to apologize to everyone for his
lapse in his own code of ethics. He would have to deal with
it on his own terms and the troops would have to cope. They
knew him well enough by now to know this wasn't the norm
for him, and that if he broke code it was for a good reason.

Liam just needed some time to figure out what that reason
was. He had a hard time believing it had just been about sex,
as he had claimed for Colin's benefit. It wasn't Colin's business what his reasoning was.

It was Devon's, however.

Liam drew on some clean blacks, leaving his feet bare

but for socks as he went in search of his boots, knife, belt, and
gun holster. He knocked on the door to Devon's rooms and let
himself in when he didn't hear anything from within. He
walked over the threshold with a mild amount of caution. His
clothes, boots, and belongings were neatly folded and stacked
at the foot of her bed, but he saw not even a glimpse of
Devon. He supposed she had gone to her office already,
though he had not seen or felt her departure. He was very
sensitive to the movements in the house, especially hers, and
it bothered him that he had been so embroiled in his altercation with his brother that he had not been aware of her exit.
He picked up his knife and spun it between his fingers.

He heard her clear her throat, the sound surprising him as
he spun about, wondering how she'd snuck up behind him.
She still wore only her towel, and despite her sexy posture
leaning against the bathroom doorframe, her expression was
a serious one. She must have been sitting quietly in the bath.
He raised a brow, curious as to why she hadn't responded to
his entrance before this.

"I'm sorry. I messed up. I wasn't trying to flaunt this. I just
wasn't thinking."

"It's not your fault," he sighed as he laid down the knife on
top of his clothes. "It's natural to feel you have the run of your
own house. Also, it's easy to feel free when it comes to sharing things with a lover. Actually, I *want* you to feel free like
that. It's another form of honesty." He walked over to her,
reaching to frame her face with his hands, his fingertips
stroking through her wet strands of hair. "It's just a new complication in this job that I'm going to need to find a way to
work around. I'll find a way to deal with it. I've got good
people. They'll adjust."

"I'm not worried about them," she said softly, leaning her
weight against him and burying her nose against his clean
T-shirt. He nuzzled the top of her head so he could breathe
in the scent of his shampoo on her hair. Something about it

excited him and his body responded with long, tense pulses of awareness from head to toe. He exhaled a rough sigh as her hands slid around his back.

"One day you are going to explain how you do this," he noted with no little consternation.

"Do . . . this?" She sounded perplexed.

"Turn me on without even trying," he clarified, tilting her head back so he could study her mouth with care.

Devon laughed at him, the sound only serving to worsen his condition.

"Let me get this straight," she said with amusement. "I had my hand wrapped around your very hard cock this morning and you threw me off like yesterday's garbage, and *now* you're turned on? By what, for heaven's sake? Clue me in so I know what works so well on you!"

"You work well on me," he rumbled beneath her ear. "And I had every intention of making you finish what you started with that mischievous hand of yours, babe. However, Colin kinda blew my plans out of the water . . . so to speak."

"Oh? Planning on showering with me?" She smiled slyly as she nestled sexily into his body. He groaned with obvious pleasure, not realizing there was method to her wiggles. As her breasts rubbed across his chest, the tuck of her towel loosened and the linen subsequently slid off her bare body. Liam suddenly found himself holding a naked woman. To say she had a body that wouldn't quit was something of an understatement, he was learning. The woman herself wasn't much of a quitter either, for that matter. "Hmm," she hummed, "you feel very good," she flattered deviously, knowing full well the power she was wielding.

Liam couldn't suppress the reactions of his body as she wound herself around him like a sensuous python. He flash-burned like 100-year-old tinder, a thin sheen of sweat shimmering over his skin. "Devon," he whispered in her ear, "I don't have time for this."

She laughed at that, her hands sliding around his chest and over his belly as she held him tight with a long leg snaked around one of his. "There isn't a man on the planet that doesn't have time for this," she scolded softly, her teeth nipping at his throat.

"Devon . . ." Liam sighed and chuckled at her relentless play. "Okay, then I'll rephrase. I don't have time to do this *right*."

"Liam," she reprimanded him on a sultry whisper. "All I need is you inside of me for it to be right. The thought of it has me halfway there already. See for yourself," she invited. She took a hand from his chest and slid it down her own body, leaning back in a provocative arch as she drew his hand past her breasts, down over her taut belly, and then directly below her navel. Her fingertips rested on the backs of his as she curved them over the soft warmth of her mound, and threaded their mutual touch directly into the moist flesh at the crest of her thighs, all under his riveted stare. She shivered with pleasure from her own caresses, and Liam remained entirely passive because it was suffocatingly arousing to see and feel her touching herself. It made him harder than he'd imagined possible, but he was hardly surprised she was capable of it. She was likely able to turn cotton balls into rocks with just one of those sly, sexy looks of hers.

Devon slid her fingers free of her hot folds, shuddering again as she stimulated her clitoris in passing. Her finger gleamed with the honey of her sex, the proof she'd been determined to show him. Liam's amber eyes were hooded with a dark intensity of desire as he watched her raise her hand. His lips parted in hungry anticipation, but it was her own mouth she touched her fingertips to, running them over her bottom lip until it shone. Then she slid her tongue out and touched it to that shine.

"Oh, man," Liam whispered hotly, just before he reached to seize her mouth so he could share that exotic flavor with her. He sucked her lips and tongue in a wild kiss that was full of his sudden passionate need. She tasted of salty sweet, feminine ambrosia that had his head reeling. Liam reached for her hand and brought those teasing fingers up to his mouth so he could suck first one, and then the other, between his lips. He heard her panting with growing excitement. "Devon. Sweet, tasty Devon," he murmured huskily. "Your wish is my command," he offered wickedly in a low voice. "If there's one thing I know, it's how to take an order."

She felt his palm turning away from her, the backs of his knuckles rubbing her as he unhooked his belt and worked to unbutton his pants. Then he was kissing her again and she lost herself in the mastery of Liam's divine mouth until she felt hot, smooth flesh bumping against her belly. He rubbed his hard erection over her slowly, sliding like hot steel encased in fine silk against her.

"Come here, babe," he commanded on a growl as his fingers moved to curve over her bottom and his huge hands tightened their grip. Her feet flew up off the floor as if she weighed no more than a child. Devon followed those coaxing hands until her legs were wrapped around his waist, his erection sliding through the slick valley between her legs. She wound her arms behind his neck as she gasped for breath in anticipation. She was trembling with excitation, her inner body throbbing with the empty ache of need to be filled.

"Liam," she begged him, tears smarting behind her lashes.

Devon wasn't lying. She seemed on the edge of orgasm and all he'd done for her was kiss her and promise to be inside of her shortly. Her mind was a powerful sexual stimulus, her desire for him so intense that she made it far too easy for him.

But he'd never been a man of leisure.

Liam took a single step forward and Devon's back came up against the wall, mere inches from the door they'd abused the night before. Liam smiled slyly when her brows arched. "What can I say? I like a little counterforce," he whispered teasingly against her lips just as he slid himself into position to enter her. She squirmed in anticipation, drawing the head of his shaft into her grasping sheath. That destroyed the last edge of his patience and he surged into her in one hard thrust.

"Oh, God yes," he groaned heatedly as she surrounded him in an embrace of fire. His entrance, however longed for and anticipated, still came as a shock to her, and her entire body was clenched tight with it as a soundless cry hovered in her open mouth. Her eyes slid closed in bliss and Liam had to catch his breath just from looking at her.

Liam forgot about everything but Devon. Now that he had her happily impaled on him, he had plans that weren't necessarily the same as hers. Using the wall to support her weight, Liam freed up a hand and sank a cunning thumb into the place where their bodies joined. He found her clit, already swollen and ready for pleasure, which he was more than glad to provide. Devon gasped when the first circling touch impacted her, and then moaned when Liam backed it up with a long withdrawal of his cock from her body and a lazy return.

"Mmm, Christ you feel so nice and tight." He exhaled the heated words near her ear, his tongue running around the edge of it and giving her shivers. "And those pretty little nipples of yours are just begging for attention, aren't they?"

However, in spite of the observation, Liam didn't change his hold on her for a second in order to give them the attention he obviously knew they craved. Still, just his suggestive tone and words had the power to make her nipples stiffen tightly in excitement.

"There now," he whispered as he rotated his hips and thumb in different directions. "How's that feel, baby?"

Devon let her head fall back against the wall, her throat working on one sexy moan after another, each sound slamming through Liam like lightning. Liam shifted into long, slow strokes, feeling every inch of her every time he moved, every flutter and reflex. Devon's legs flexed around him, drawing him forward as she caught on to the torturous tempo. She began to gasp and moan in an alternating cadence, her walls tightening around him more with every thrust. Liam slipped his touch away from her, now stroking her belly, her sides, and her magnificent breasts. Her frustration at the change was very obvious and he watched a single tear squeeze out of the corner of her eye. He also watched in fascination as her fangs slowly stretched into place. There was something so perverse in the look of fangs so deadly in a mouth so goddamn sensual and femininely beautiful.

"Liam," she breathed, knowing how much his name in that irresistibly seductive and longing tone drove him to distraction. "Liam . . . Liam . . ." she chanted between moans, so that his name eventually became her exclamation of pleasure all on its own.

She was rising to orgasm quickly, and again he could sense it in her body and the chaos of her vocalizations. Liam suddenly shoved a powerful arm between her leg and his hip and broke the vise of her legs as he pulled out and away from her. Devon's reaction to the abandonment and abruptly finding herself on her own two feet was volatile and furious. Indignant eyes of jade highlighted her passion-flushed features.

He didn't give her much time for any other reaction.

Devon felt strong hands all over her body, turning her, spinning her dizzily as if she were a doll being posed by a playing child. She suddenly found herself bent over her dresser, the polished wood surface cold against her over-heated breasts and belly. Her hands were shackled above her head in one of Liam's and she felt his thighs nudging her open for his approach from behind. This time when he entered her it was with violence, the power of the thrust crushing her thighs against the side of the dresser, the hardware on the drawers rattling. Liam grunted with long, low satisfaction, and after a moment released her hands to push his hands against her shoulders, effectively holding her down while he caressed her. Every nerve, every emotion in Devon's sphere of knowing was raw from Liam's game of torturous delight. After another hard thrust, Liam's hands moved to bracket her hips, shaping them and her bottom for a long moment of stroking. Then he gripped her tight, tilted her entire pelvis so that her backside was inclined high in the air, and thrust once more with a mighty heave of his body and the pulsing shaft within her.

The man was a sexual genius.

That was all Devon could conclude as her body lit up like fireworks and flares all at once, the explosion starting at the spot deep inside herself that Liam's cock had just stroked so intensely. She shouted out, reaching to grip the dresser as the room began to spin with every ferocious thrust Liam worked into her primed body.

"Yes," she heard him hiss, his voice tight with his own mounting need, the position clearly taxing his control as well. "Scream it, baby," he commanded roughly. "Scream my . . . uhn!"

Liam cut himself off as she clenched like a vise around him on his down stroke. He had not planned to finish until he'd brought her to pleasure at least twice, but he had teased her a little too long and been caught by his own snare. She was even tighter in this position, and the constriction as she rose to orgasm was unbearable.

Devon ignited with incendiary force, her entire body shuddering and shaking on the approach, and releasing in Liam's longed-for screams of his name. Her body shook as though she was seizing, and he might have worried about it if he hadn't been roaring out a violent release of his own. He dragged her hips back tight against him so he was as deep within her as he could humanly manage as he spilled in powerful spasms that seared his heart and lungs into paralysis.

"Oh God," he gasped. "Oh God." Liam bent forward, his damp forehead resting on her spine at the base of her neck. "Devon?" He reached to scoop a hand beneath her torso and lifted her back against himself as he straightened up. Her head fell back against her shoulder, her body hanging completely limp, and her eyes closed. Liam kissed her cheek gently and scooped her up into his arms. "Hey, babe," he whispered as he walked over to the bed. He laid her in the center and, after a quick clothing adjustment, Liam sat facing her on the bed and rubbed at her hands and wrists, chafing them gently as her lashes fluttered. "Devon. Hey, c'mon . . . full day of work ahead of you and everything," he teased her softly, watching as her lids opened and her eyes began to clear. Her gaze swung to him and her face exploded in uncharacteristic color. She sat up swiftly.

"Oh, God, please don't tell me I fainted from a climax! Oh, lord, I did, didn't I?"

"It was your position, honey," he soothed her, though he was unable to prevent the cocky tilt to his lips. "A head rush, spike in blood pressure, and the immediate crash after. It happens, sweetheart."

"Not to you!" she snorted in disgust.

"Yes, it does. We just disguise it with snoring."

That made a bright laugh bubble out of her. The more she saw of Liam's sense of humor, the more she liked it.

Devon sighed, nuzzling her cheek against his fresh-shaven face until they were both purring soft sounds of contentment and reaching to draw one another closer.

"I have to go," Liam whispered helplessly, as if she held him in chains.

"Me, too."

They stayed cuddled chest-to-chest and cheek-to-cheek.

Her fingers painted absent patterns on his biceps; his tugged and tangled into the ends of her hair. Pressing engagements became less pressing and everything around them turned soft and quiet. Truly serene. Liam closed his eyes and sighed, kissing her skin wherever he could reach along her nearby hairline. It was the most peaceful moment he'd had in years, and he didn't want it to end. However, someone else would end it for him if he didn't get on with the business of his job.

But he decided to give himself just a few more moments.

Chapter Thirteen

Liam sat in a squat at the top of the mighty brick wall surrounding the property, his attention split between watching the rhythmic pan of the newest camera and the exercising dogs and their trainers. There was plenty of property to work the animals on, and he had told the handlers to keep them down near the walls of the south lawn. The dogs were familiar with all the team members, but they weren't familiar with Devon and he wanted them kept as far apart as possible.

Liam rose to his full height and walked the wall carefully. Installers were in the process of adding razor spikes to the smooth, flat top he now walked on too easily. Unlike razor wire, spikes were not visible from the ground. The perpetrator wouldn't know they were there until he began to get hung up on the three-inch triangles of honed blades. It was particularly vicious, but Liam was not about holding back the tricks of his trade.

"Hey, Liam."

Liam keyed his radio in response. "Yeah?"

"Our principal would like a word with you when you get a chance."

Liam automatically looked up toward her office. The

drapes were drawn as usual. "Tell her it'll be a while. I'm in the middle of something."

"Uh . . . I think maybe you should see her sooner than that, boss. I have a feeling she's thinking of going out."

"What gives you that feeling?" Liam asked sharply.

"She's wearing one of those dresses that ought to have a lot more fabric considering what they probably cost her."

"Shit." Liam didn't even bother to respond. His temper was on instant simmer. She had to be out of her mind. First of all, she hadn't had anything planned, so this was too little notice for him to properly prepare for an outing, especially considering what had happened last time. What could possibly be so important? Another business 'meeting' with an uptown jackass?

Liam's temper spiked from simmer to boil at the very idea of her sitting with and dancing with another man who would stare at her with lust in his eyes. What manner of business was she conducting anyway in dresses that left her half naked and required a meal and wine? Lunches maybe, but dinners where these bastards were manhandling her?

Liam crouched down and leapt off the wall.

Devon was sitting at her vanity with her maid styling the finishing touches of her hair in an elegant upsweep. She looked up in her mirror to apply lipstick and saw him behind her, a heavy presence in black standing like a steadfast sentinel. She pulled the earbuds from her ears, the dissertation from the latest name in biophysics continuing on without her attention as she smiled at him.

"Hello," she greeted. "I'm sorry to give you such short notice, but I need to go out tonight."

"I don't like this, Devon. I don't like having only a couple hours to prepare," he said darkly, his frown creasing his features deeply.

"Nonsense. You've been preparing to protect me for the

better part of a week. Unfortunately, I can't put this meeting off. I needed to make it last minute and I need it to happen without delay."

"Fine. Have your meeting here then."

"Impossible," she said with a shrug, as if it explained everything.

"Why?"

Devon couldn't answer that, of course. Nor should she have to, according to her way of thinking. "Because I say it is," she said with an even chill in her tone. She turned, dismissing her maid with a wave of an impatient hand. "Are we going to have an argument every time I want to go out now?"

Liam's eyes narrowed on her as she crossed her legs. She was definitely wearing one of those dresses again. This time, it was midnight blue silk that made the jade of her eyes stand out. The material wasn't transparent anywhere except across her middle. However, the plunge in the front reached to just below her breasts and was held in place by a single bar pin of gold right between them. Unlike the other dresses, this one had only a swath of sparkling midnight blue for a skirt, the short, snug material showing off every single inch of her legs. This included the sheen of black thigh high stockings. She wore elbow-length evening gloves in black and strappy heels that accented the shape of her calves. A diamond cuff bracelet wrapped one wrist and he saw matching earrings and a necklace waiting on the vanity table.

"I just don't understand what would be so important that you would risk your life on it," he snapped.

"No. You wouldn't understand because you have made no effort to acknowledge the political shit storm I'm trying to negotiate among my own people, have you?" she sniped back at him, irritated he would treat her so unreasonably. "Look, I refuse to argue about something that an argument will not change," she said tightly as she rose. She walked past him to one of her closets and decided on a wrap. With the weather

turning cooler, it didn't surprise him that she chose an exquisite double lined, reversible fur cloak to counterbalance the
brevity of her outfit.

"Devon, I'm only asking you to think about this," he tried
again, attempting to erase the anger from his tone. Provoking
her would not help him win his argument for her safety.

"And I'm asking you to stop harassing me about it and just
do your job, Liam. Please."

The stiffness that whipped so suddenly between them was
hard and harsh. Just as harsh as her cold treatment.

"Right. Got it. One mindless grunt, coming right up," he
barked furiously. He turned hard on his heel and stalked out
of her room like a thundercloud on the move.

Devon sighed in frustration, wishing she could explain the
unexplainable to him. She would just have to find a way to fix
this problem later. There was no time or opportunity to do it
now. Perhaps there never would be. Unfortunately, she had to
make that sacrifice.

Just as she had made so many others.

Liam and Inez, and Kellen and Victoria, were dining on
opposite sides of their principal. Colin was positioned in the
limousine and Malcolm was strolling the restaurant perime-
ter. It was a smaller place than before, more intimate, and
easier to take everyone's measure. However, as far as Inez
could see, Liam wasn't at all pleased. He wasn't even making
a pretense of eating, and he was being far too obvious in his
glaring attention toward Devon. It wasn't like him to make
those kinds of mistakes. Still, all he did was stare coldly at
Devon and her handsome date. Ms. Candler looked utterly
stunning in the dimmed lighting as her dress shone and jewels
flashed brilliant fire. In Inez's opinion, Ms. Candler's date of
the evening seemed a little better behaved and somewhat
more sophisticated than the last one, albeit in a strangely
rugged way. There was a familiarity in his body language that

picked at Inez's attention, though she couldn't immediately figure out why. The conversation between the two never waned and Devon barely once looked away from her companion, her focus and attention completely riveted.

And the more intense Devon's conversation and body language toward her date became, the darker and more thunderous Liam's presence became across the table from Inez.

And that was how Inez Flores figured out her boss had the hots for their client. In a huge way. She took it pretty well, considering how potentially disastrous the situation was.

Devon's date reached to cover her hand and Inez felt the table tremble when Liam tensed with poorly contained fury. The female soldier was once again faced with the boundaries of friendship versus professionalism, but quickly opted for instinct. Her hand reached out to take hold of her boss's, her fingers squeezing his clenched fist as his amber eyes flew from his obsession and locked with her meaningfully focused gaze.

"Liam, I'd be much more comfortable if you tried to neutralize your emotions. Considering what happened last time, I want you to be aware of the danger we're all in." Inez's gentle redirection took a moment to sink in, and in that moment his eyes were back on Devon. "I don't know if this helps," Inez continued casually as she rubbed her fingers in a relaxing rhythm against his tight fist, "but as a woman, I can assure you that she has no interest in that man."

Liam's gaze slammed back to her and he frowned. "How do you know that?"

"The same way you would if you weren't letting emotion cloud your reasoning," she scolded gently. "Look at her body language, *mi amigo*. Even though she is leaning forward toward him and holding his hands, she is not in any way being flirtatious. She's a very naturally sensual woman, I've noted. Almost like a spicy *Latina* I know." She smiled at him when he chuckled softly. "So I think for her it's almost second nature to try to attract everything male in the room. However,

none of her energy is being devoted to that man. The eager-
ness you see is almost . . . familial. As if he were an old
friend . . . or even a brother."

"Then why dress like that? Why be here at all?" he demanded with a frown.

"She dresses consistently. She always wears provocative
clothing. I believe she does it for herself and no other. I doubt
she has any concept of the effect she has on men. Either that
or she's so used to it, it has become passé for her. She has no
insecurities about her body. That is rare in this day and age."

"No. She isn't shy or self-conscious. I like that about her,"
he said offhandedly. Inez wondered if he even realized he was
confirming his feelings to her. "It's a quality that many men
would find irresistible in her."

"Yes, but what's important is what *she* finds irresistible in
a man. She never notices any of the team and barely acknowl-
edges her dates except in these intense conversations she
seems to have with them. The only male I've ever seen her
pay special attention to is you."

Liam snapped out of his preoccupation like a lightning
strike. He shook his head and had the grace to look chagrined.

"I'm sorry, Inez. This has been totally inappropriate. I'm
all right now." He frowned. "Remember never to get personally involved with your clients, Flores. I know I've been
saying it for years, but it's the best advice I ever gave."

"Shame you didn't follow it yourself," Inez chided gently.
"Mind if I ask what—?"

"Yes, I mind. I also mind gossip, okay?"

Inez laughed. "Please, tell me you know me better than
that."

"Well, yes, but it needed saying. Bad enough I broke the
number one rule already. I don't need it becoming a running
goddamn joke in the ranks for the next ten years."

"Wouldn't think of it, Liam." Inez hid a grin behind a piece
of bread before popping it into her mouth. She also wouldn't

tell him that she thought there was far more trouble ahead of him than a few jokes among his men, not if he was already this tied up in knots. It was funny, but Inez had always thought Liam would go for the tough, athletic type. Devon clearly had the brains he would require, and more than enough beauty and sex drive. She had a certain bravery, that was for certain, but she seemed a little too pampered. Liam needed a feisty woman, a sparring partner as well as a companion. He thrived too much in his work for it not to come home with him. If Liam would even consider settling down at all. There were advantages to remaining single in this line of work.

Liam didn't strike her as the type to answer to anyone but himself. Then again, men like her commander never did go looking for love on purpose. It usually came up behind them and bit them on the ass.

"Devona, I think it's time you came home," Nick said softly to her, reaching across the table with his palm facing upward . . . warm and welcoming and oh so very tempting. Nick Gregory was a beautiful man. When he had been human, he had been very much like Liam. A Federated cop, he'd been all about doing the right thing, no matter what it cost him. In the end it had come close to costing him his life. It had most certainly cost him his humanity. He had stumbled on Dr. Eric Paulson and his unethical ways long before others had, and he'd been caught, captured, and thrown into the lab with the rest of the rats for his trouble. Now he was Alpha of Dark Manhattan and the leader of the Alpha Council. He had been and still was Devona's Alpha. She had been devoted to him and his Alpha mate, Amara, since the very start of things. She had believed Nick and Amara would lead the Morphates to a better standing in the human world. They had most certainly led them to carve out a piece of it.

"You've finally finished what you and my brother set out to do five decades ago," Nick said with a soft modulation of his voice. He had learned and grown so much in the five decades since becoming Morphate. Proof positive of what a person could become if only they had enough time to learn the lessons life could teach. He'd once been bullish and hotheaded. Now he was the quintessential leader, and the quintessential friend. "You've learned how to kill our own kind. You've developed the weapons to curb what would otherwise be uncontrollable creatures."

"Much to Ambrose's displeasure. And I don't doubt that Paulson is still out there somewhere, steaming that I got to it first."

Nick flicked sharp, assessing eyes over her. "I know you went undercover all those years ago to avoid detection from the fractious Morphates, but making this a contest of wills between you and the man that made us was never my intention. I would never have had you give up a normal Morphate life for that. Paulson is a ghost. You can't find him. No one can unless he wants to be found. Surely you've learned that by now?"

Devona reached up with her free hand to massage the growing tension in her temple. "Of course I realize that," she lied to her Alpha. She believed with all of her heart that Paulson would be the first to hear of her successes. Especially once she was through leaking the information to the right people. Secrecy had served its purpose; now breaking that secrecy would serve an entirely different purpose. Unfortunately, it would also put innocent people in the line of fire, she thought as she slid a tense glance over to the bodyguard at the next table who was trying with all his might not to glare at her. She could sense he didn't care for her physical contact with another handsome male. He might be human, but he had powerful Alpha tendencies. Had he been Morphate, he most certainly would have ruled a clan. As it was, he was ruling the clan of humans intent on protecting her life; they followed his every command and trusted his every executive decision. Just as all the Morphates in Dark Manhattan trusted Nick's proven leadership abilities.

"I am not doing this in an attempt to ferret out Paulson," she lied smoothly. "I am doing this so Ambrose and the others who think to defect from the Alpha Council will know there are permanent consequences for crossing the line." That, at least, was truthful. "I am doing this to force them to reconsider their lawless positions. Humans and Morphates alike will now have the ability to call them into check. Their days of invulnerability and anarchy are at an end. You put me to this task. You and your brother Kincaid. Fifty years ago you both knew the fractiousness and mayhem of some Morphates would only worsen over time. You had incredible foresight."

"As did you. I believe you were the one to advise me on this point all those years ago."

"It was collaborative," she said dismissively. It no longer mattered who had come to the understanding first. What mattered was what they were going to do with the power they had acquired. And all because one human had accidentally stumbled on a solution they had sought for decades. Her human, she thought with no little sense of pride and respect as she glanced from under her lashes at Liam. She took a breath and leaned closer to Nick, increasing the intimacy of their conversation. "Nick. A word from you and I will destroy them all. Every last weapon. If you think this is a mistake . . ."

"I don't. My mind has not changed on the matter. And anyway, it would be rather like trying to put the genie back in the bottle, don't you think? The power is out, unleashed on the world. If not you, someone else will come up with weapons. No doubt less sophisticated ones." As was proven by the dangerous and volatile bullets Liam's team had designed and now were armed with. Devona realized it was very much time to arm them with her more graceful weapons. Especially since they were going to be in so much danger in the coming days. Morphates were gunning for her, trying to wrest the power of her inventions for themselves. They had proven as much with their previous attacks on her.

Nick closed his fingers around her palm, drawing her hand closer to his side of the table. It was a gesture of insistence. It made her look into his intent eyes.

"Come home. Come be with your people again. You've done well. Sacrificed much. Hidden what you are. Come home and embrace life as a Morphate once more."

"Not yet," she said softly.

"We can protect you in Dark Manhattan. While I respect the reputation and power of these humans you've hired from NHK, they can't protect you like we can. And when this goes public, as it promises to do any moment now, you are going to need Morphates to protect you from Morphates."

"I disagree. I think the whole point of this was to level the playing field. To give humans a fighting chance against Morphates. I think my guard detail is a perfect way to prove that."

Nick frowned and she could tell he was tempted to argue further. She could tell he was tempted to throw his weight around and command her as her Alpha to return to the fold. He knew very well that she would be hard pressed to countermand a direct order from him. But Nick was a great believer in personal freedom. It was what made him so good at what he did. He knew when it was appropriate to pull rank and when it was just being dictatorial. True, an Alpha driven society was very dictatorial in nature, but Nick did his level best to hold on to the fairness and ideals of his past humanity.

"I think you are putting them in needless danger. Risking their fragile mortality."

"I have considered that," she agreed a bit stiffly. The idea of Liam coming to harm . . .

She couldn't resist cutting her eyes toward him, though she knew it was a mistake. She knew she couldn't hide the distress of her thoughts in that moment. She saw his entire body go rigid with suspicion and hyper-focused attention, saw the way he was already glaring at Nick as though he would put a mercury riddled hole in his head any second. This wasn't likely to go unnoticed by Nick, who could still access his cop instincts.

He did not disappoint.

"Your watchdog looks like he'd like to bite a chunk out of my ass," Nick mused without repressing a rascally smile.

"Do not goad him," Devon warned. Political leader of a species or no, Nick wasn't above goofing off and stirring up mischief.

"I think he has a crush on you," Nick observed keenly. Too keenly. It made her look at Nick sharply and her body stiffened with telltale guilt. "Holy shit! Are you screwing your bodyguard? Do you have any idea what a frigging cliché that is?"

"Shh! Keep your voice down," Devon hushed him frantically. Then she squared her shoulders. "I don't give a damn about clichés, Nick. Just like Liam doesn't give a damn about stereotypes. And considering that Morphates have tried to kill him on more than one occasion, I respect him for that."

Nick had to nod in grave agreement. "Humans have been growing more and more prejudiced against us over the past years. That's a nerve-wracking thought, considering we were never merrily accepted in the first place. In the beginning we were able to play the victim card. Now people are forgetting about that and are being flooded with negative news stories that the Morphates of Dark L. A., Dark Phoenix, and their splinter groups have been causing. I won't even touch on the subject of our . . . unusual offspring. And it's only going to get worse. All the more reason for you to come back behind the safe walls of Dark Manhattan, Devona."

She just shook her head.

"Not yet, Nick." She looked back at Liam. "Not yet."

Nick could have pressed her. He could have teased her

quite a bit more, too, he realized as he read her distracted attention toward her bodyguard. But he did not. She was in danger, dancing on a precarious sword's tip. She certainly didn't need any more flack from her Alpha. He'd have Amara contact her in a day or two and let his mate work on coaxing her Beta back into the fold. If anyone was going to succeed, it would be Amara, Nick thought. Their friendship had been forged in the hell of Paulson's laboratory. Nick's mate deserved the right to command her lieutenants. He would not interfere. In fact, he was only there at Amara's behest. He would not have presumed otherwise. Being Alpha did not mean walking all over the rights of his mate. Not in his mind, anyway.

"Okay then. Not yet," he agreed with a nod. "But I don't have to tell you this request isn't going to stop with me."

Devon smiled. "I am well aware Amara is using you to soften me up for the kill. I will expect her call."

"She loves you," Nick reminded her, "and misses you. She won't mow you down and force you to come home . . . unless she thinks you're in too much danger. So stay safe, okay?"

"I'm trying," she insisted as they both rose from their chairs and Nick used their joined hands to pull her close for a warm, lingering kiss on her cheek. If he had not said outright that she was missed, his gesture of affection would have said it all.

Nick was barely out of the dining room before Liam was by her side, his hand resting protectively and possessively in the small of her back. Devon had a bad headache, tension and stress taking its toll even on her Morphate body. She didn't show any outward sign of it, however, knowing she was under scrutiny in more ways than one. Devon wanted to go home more than anything, but she suddenly couldn't look up at Liam and ask him to bring her there.

Despite Nick and Amara's support and obvious love for her, she felt all alone in the world. All alone in her endeavors. She didn't know if Liam would understand that. How could he when she'd never given him any explanations? She understood why he thought she was treating him like some ignorant soldier sometimes. He was an intelligent man and deserved explanations. His patience in waiting for honesty from her was finite and she should not test it too much longer, she knew.

She wanted to go home, but going home meant she'd have to face him in private again, and she didn't want to argue anymore tonight. Time was growing short for her very quickly. She was burning all her last remaining friendships among Morphates into ashes. She felt scorched and dirtied by the coarse smoke left behind. She had never in a million years thought she would one day be orchestrating the possible death of a species.

How far she had come.

Or fallen.

Liam watched her escort leave, and then turned his careful attention back to Devon. He would never be certain when exactly it was that he began to sense the wrongness of her mood, but he knew with sudden certainty that she needed him. That she needed his patience and understanding, not his censure or jealous attempts to control her.

When she looked up at him, he saw a weary sadness in her eyes, and then steel as she prepared herself to deal with him. He slowly reached for her hand.

"Hey," he greeted her gently, letting her know with just his tone that he'd no plans to attack her again.

"Hey," she replied softly, her gaze training steadily on his as she tried to figure out what he wanted from her. Liam imagined there were a lot of people wanting things from her lately.

"I'm never going to be okay with anything I feel puts you in danger," he whispered so only she could hear him, "but I shouldn't have hassled you like that. I might have been overcompensating a little as I tried to prove to myself that our sexual relationship would not change our dynamic as protector and protectee."

Devon looked away, turning her face from him, but she didn't have the fall of her hair to hide behind, so she lifted fingers that shook just slightly to cover her mouth.

"Devon . . ."

"I'm very tired," she said, clearing the quaver from her voice.

"Then let's bring you home." He turned his head, engaging the mic. "Okay guys, let's wrap this up. Col, front or back?" He nodded to himself as he received Colin's assessment on preferable exits. "Nez, you're with me. Kell, walk the route. Tori, stand back and watch."

Victoria and Kellen stood up and went in opposite directions. Inez crossed the floor to join them. He took Devon's hands in his and drew her close, pulling her against his body briefly, protecting her within the comforting circle of his arm. The maître d' brought Devon her wrap and thanked her when she signed for their tabs with a generous tip.

Devon took a deep breath, as though bracing herself for her exit, but what she was doing was trying to scent for other Morphates in the area. She was only aware of Nick's lingering trail. It was no guarantee, however, because there might be human assassins as well, though she felt less threatened by them.

Liam's hand rested on her waist at her back and he guided her from the restaurant.

The intruders knew very well that there were cameras covering almost every inch of the compound. That both visual and heat spectrum projections were sent back to the control room. They had watched guard rotations and movement for so long that they had finally come to understand the order in the chaos of their schedule. Whatever clever prick was in charge of these guys had trained them to never patrol the grounds or house in exactly the same way. They had been taught to change it up constantly, and yet be very thorough every single time. Sometimes they started at the security room. Sometimes they started on the top level. East wing bottom floor. West wing top floor. East wing top floor. West wing mid floor. And the exterior guards did the exact same thing. Sometimes in teams. Sometimes solo. They even had a shadow maneuver where a team split up, the first member beginning a circuit and the second waiting five minutes before following and shadowing his partner's path and checking behind him.

The point was it was impossible to predict how much time they had or what things they might have missed despite their long wait in the woods, watching every detail as shrewdly as they could. Infrared technology and visual cameras did not faze them in the least. It was the human factor that was the wild card.

That humans could be something to fear stuck in the craw. And that was why they were there. They were going to burn Devona Candler to the ground and her weapons with her. Maybe they couldn't erase knowledge of the effect irradiated mercury had on Morphates, and maybe this was only an act of postponing the inevitable, but striking at Devona would have a twofold effect. It would set her project back quite a few years and it would rob the humans of the genius of Devona's intellect. Plus, it would be giving the traitorous, presumptuous bitch what she deserved for betraying her own people. Perhaps Ambrose would order them to do the same to the next and the next who thought themselves brilliant enough to create such a weapon, delaying the development for decades.

Delaying just enough to allow Morphates to move out of the shameful banishment of the Dark Cities and into positions of power all around the world. No more of this illicit bullshit, as if it were a crime to live as free as the humans did. And why couldn't they? Because they were immortal? Because they were stronger than humans? Because of the way they made love? Because of the ferocity of their children?

The thought made Rhiannon smile ferally as she paused for a moment. She was one of those children. As was her partner in this endeavor. In her opinion there was nothing wrong with either one of them. They were even better than their Morphate parents in every way, their genetic code more refined, arranged with a finesse that only nature herself could possibly add. Their Morphate parents could never have breached the security in this house. It would be the new generation of Morphates that would save their race.

The idea made her smile as she stealthily moved into final position.

She waited, hoping a human stumbled across her, so she would be forced to silence her enemy.

Liam followed Devona up the stairs, watching her slow steps very carefully, a frown tugging his mouth. Devon never dragged herself. She worked with irrepressible energy that simply could not be subdued. Seeing her like this, so withdrawn and looking so tired, simply killed him.

"Do you mind if I ask why you were having a meeting with the preeminent Morphate in the Federated States?" he asked quietly. She stopped mid-step and turned to look at him, her soft jewel-like eyes suddenly smiling down at him.

"Of course. You used to be Secret Service. You would be very well versed on who Nick and Amara Gregory are."

"I think every Joe Shmoe at the corner deli in Lightning, Kansas knows who Nick and Amara Gregory are. When you think of Morphates, generally their faces are the first you imagine. They are very public figures, fighting for Morphate rights in this country. And abroad, ever since the Traveling Act was passed. We let Morphates travel out of this country much sooner than other nations began to allow them into theirs. A lot of Morphates did what you are doing if they wanted to travel. Passed themselves off as humans."

"I am posing as human for much more serious reasons than the right to go to the Bahamas," she said heavily.

"Well, maybe you ought to go to the Bahamas. You certainly could use it. Push these weapons of yours onto your human developers already. Fulfill your contract and be done with it. It will take you out of the crosshairs, for the most part, and let you go back to a normal sort of life."

"Just what is a normal sort of life?" she asked, the weariness in her voice suddenly sounding incredibly heavy. "I've been searching for the key to Morphate mortality for fifty years. Almost every day since the day we were liberated. There were those of us who knew instantly what absolute power was going to do to some of us. We saw the types of people, the dregs of society that Paulson was using for his test subjects. From gangsters to psychotics . . . it was only a matter of time before one of them needed to be put down. But how do you put down an immortal psychotic?"

"So far imprisoning has done the job."

"Only if a Marshal Force of Morphates is engaged. Until you, no human force has ever been able to catch and retain a Morphate hell-bent on its freedom."

Liam nodded. The Marshal Force had a reputation for being the baddest asses in the world. Putting the best of fighting-tactics training in the hands of an elite, indestructible force of Morphate men and women had been a brilliant and terrifying move. It had been, as he understood it, the brainchild of another Gregory. Kincaid Gregory, Nick's brother. But that was beside the point, he knew.

"You're changing that. You're making it possible for human forces to stop a monstrous Morphate in its tracks."

"Somehow those human forces will lack the prestige and glory of the Marshals. But at least they'll be well armed."

She turned to go back down the stairs. He followed her

suddenly swift gait away from the west side of the house to the center. Her goal became obvious as she took him to the vault. As she breezed past the safeguards it was all he could do to keep up with her. When they entered the prototype room, she went straight back to the box she had initially wanted to show him. She keyed in the code and lifted the lid.

She reached in for a small, light, metal and poly fabric object and instantly Liam was fascinated. He had expected a gun. Something with the highest tech in laser sightings, like what was strapped to his hip.

"Here," she said, reaching for his hand to affix the device. The fingerless glove slid on easily because of the stretch in the poly fabric. The metal was over the back of his hand and there were sensors across the palm. There were four small holes like launch tubes. "Micro darts. The sensors require simultaneous pressure inside the palm and with the thumb pressing the outer first finger knuckle. It might seem complex, but it prevents the darts from releasing accidentally or . . ."

"Or if you're throwing a punch. No one with any training . . . hell, any instincts . . . would throw a punch like that. You lose all strength and physics. Well thought out," he marveled.

"It had to be. It had to be deadly, quick and, more important, not be able to go off accidentally. The micro darts hold minuscule amounts of mercury and this metal plate along the back of your hand protects you from the radiation. This indicator will turn red if radiation or mercury leaks, even a single microgram. The darts are heat sensitive so they will not inject into non-flesh targets. In the event that some go astray or the shooter misses, the surrounding objects will not be unnecessarily contaminated by irradiated mercury."

"Is it enough mercury to kill?" he wanted to know.

She grimaced. "The only way to truly test that is on a living subject, so you can imagine it is as yet untried. But using my own experience . . . I think you'd have to hit a vulnerable area with four of the twelve darts this contains, in, say, the carotids, to cause death. You get three rounds of four and it reloads with this cartridge, like so." She rapidly ejected the loaded cartridge in the weapon as he might eject a clip from a 9mm, only horizontally. Then she loaded in the small clip with just a push of a fingertip. It was auto-loading, the mechanics grabbing onto the clip and sucking it into place. The load light turned green.

"What's your jamming ratio?"

"Only when damaged or if you try to force it yourself rather than letting the machinery do the job. That's its only flaw, I would say, because I've not known very many patient soldiers in my time."

"Hard to be patient under the gun," he shot back with a grin that was so unrepentant, she laughed at him. "But you haven't known my soldiers. They are trained to think, not just react."

"That doesn't surprise me, considering their trainer." She let go of his hand, allowing him the movement to cock up his wrist and play with aiming the darts. To his surprise, the moment he did a 3-D transparent holographic targeting field appeared in a three inch square over the top of his hand.

"Holy shit. Are these bad boys guided?" If he sounded impressed, it was because he was.

"Next prototype will be. This is just to help you aim. The one I'm fine-tuning now lets you shoot a tracer, then decide to follow it with guided darts. It keeps you from wasting ammo."

Considering the toxicity of the payload, it was a brilliant idea. The finesse of it put NHK's crude mercury bullets to shame.

"Veronica's going to shit herself," he said under his breath.

"Veronica almost underbid me for this weapons contract. Unfortunately for her, finances weren't an issue for me. Tell her I am sorry for that. I have no doubt she would have done just as well given the right resources."

"I wouldn't say that. Brilliant as my partner is, she's known about the mercury for quite some time and the bullets were the best she's developed so far."

"Again, I have unlimited resources, access to labs and minds far beyond this room. You've done well enough on your own." She turned to a second box and keyed in a code. It was longer and clearly different from the previous one. This box also required her retinal scan before opening. She reached in and pulled out the last thing he would have expected.

"A knife?" How the hell was a knife . . . ?

"A wasp knife," she said as she walked over to the lab and pulled forward a beaker with a membrane stretched over the top of it. She pushed the knife through the membrane, explaining every step of the way. "It's a play on a diver's wasp knife. The tip has a sensor that arms it when it undergoes more than five pounds of pressure. Then, if you use the knife, sending it hilt deep into a target, it triggers the CO_2 cartridge in the handle. Divers use it to inject an explosive hit into a shark, causing it to blow up. I've put mercury in front of the CO_2 delivery, so basically you're stabbing and forcing an explosive dose of mercury into your target."

"And if you don't hilt? Most people can't sink a knife that deep . . . or in the heat of a fight . . ."

"Pounds of pressure will compensate. Provided the sensors in the knife are covered up to two inches deep, impact will set it off. The injectors are in the first two inches of the knife, so as a safety measure they won't eject into open air." Liam watched the knife hilt hit the membrane and a forceful silver spray filled the beaker. The membrane bubbled, threatening to rupture, but Devon expertly turned the knife, widening the slit enough to allow excess CO_2 to escape. The contaminated metal was heavier than the air and remained inside the beaker. The knife was soiled so she didn't withdraw it, just left it in the membrane and continued to show him the ejection ports, the armored handle, and how it could be thumbprint encoded, allowing only the designated user the ability to change the cartridge and reload the mercury as well. It also locked the injectors so a man's knife couldn't be used against him. The technology around the handle was so sophisticated it could be programmed specifically to a soldier, or more loosely to a soldier's unit, using DNA identifiers.

"How do you keep it from going off when sheathing it?" he asked as she went steadily and expertly about cleaning up the knife, recharging the cartridges and making it user ready—making him one of the users by having him grip the handle briefly for a DNA read. "Wouldn't that technically meet all the injection criteria?"

"You don't sheathe it." She reached back into her magical box, withdrawing a clip for his belt with a magnetic grip. He could just slap the knife in as he did his gun. Only the clip wouldn't release the knife again, unless the right DNA was touching the handle, keeping him from being disarmed. She reached for his belt buckle, undid it in a slow and careful way that became quickly erotic, and slid the weapon onto his belt. He heard his breath growing louder as his heartbeat began to race. Her fingertips brushed over his belly as she pushed aside the jacket he had hastily donned in order to look decent at dinner that evening. "There. It's coded to your DNA and ready to use."

"I can't keep it. It's your prototype."

"It's the lab prototype. The one we use for tweaking and testing and for developing the next stage. We have perfected models somewhere else. Somewhere much safer," she informed him absently, her fingertips lingering on the belt she ought to be refastening. Instead she was brushing them lazily over the warmth of his taut belly. She could still smell the atmosphere of the restaurant on him, combined with his signature scents. Seeing him armed with her life's work was a powerful, potent thing. And yet her immediate urges were to summarily disarm him. It made her smile wickedly, turning her eyes up to him in dark, beautiful need.

"There are more. So many more. And I'm going to show them to you. But, right now, I need a bath."

She turned then and left him. Walking out of the vault and leaving him to stare after her. Never had anyone turned him on with the promise of weaponry and wetness all in the same breath. Realizing he was falling behind, he hurried after her, slowed down only by properly resealing the vault.

Chapter Fourteen

Devon walked into her bedroom with a much brighter energy to her step, her body moving with its usual automatic seductiveness, heavily enhanced by her anticipation of Liam's arrival behind her. The very thought of him made her smile, made everything seem so much brighter and lighter. Funny, that. He wasn't what she could call a man full of optimism and faith in his fellow man, but he provided the validation she needed for the work she had done, for the path she had chosen, even when she was wavering and not necessarily so sure of it herself.

That had not been her intention when hiring him, of course. Nor had it been her intention when she had taken him to her vaults just now. The intention had been to arm him and protect him to the best of her ability. She would not have him thrust into the middle of a brewing war inadequately prepared for it.

But she let thoughts of war and weapons fall away as she moved into her bathroom and touched the tap control panel inside the door, immediately setting water to fill the tub in a wonderful, heated rush of sound. She reached up to the back of her neck where her dress was tied but her hand froze short of the mark. Thinking her mind was playing tricks on her, she very cautiously turned back toward her bedroom, still standing half in it and half in the bathroom as she did so, and took a slow, searching breath in through her nose.

The Morphate peeled away from the wall, her body perfectly blended into it and not visible to the untrained eye until she moved. But when she did move it was with speed and a furious strength that drove into Devon in a crash of flesh and bone. Devon's head smashed into the doorframe, sending stars across her vision. Her breath left her body as she was yanked off the frame and driven down so hard onto the bathroom's marble flooring that she would have grunted in startled pain had she the breath for it. Her attacker was resolving, still looking partly like the bedroom wall and partly like a lithe, less-than-pretty woman with the bright, joyous eyes of a creature reveling in its element.

Reveling in the kill.

"Just to be clear," the assassin said with a wicked grin. "Some of us don't take kindly to you playing God, Dr. Candler. We think you need to remember how it feels to have someone else toying with your life." She moved in closer, her face hovering nose to nose with Devon's, a fine set of fangs on display. Devon could hear claws ripping and popping through the fabric of her dress where the Morphate gripped her. "Because apparently the first few messages weren't clear enough."

"They were clear enough," Devon huffed as she grabbed the other woman by her shoulders in return. "They made it all the clearer how much in need some Morphates are of being put down! Just like the rabid dogs they are!"

The assassin growled, her naked body strangely warm and deceptively vulnerable as it pressed viciously down on her. Devona realized that in order to blend with her surroundings, the woman had divested herself of her clothes. No normal Morphate could do what this assassin could do. No Morphate from the original lots of Paulson's guinea pigs.

This was Morphate offspring. Devon was face to face with the second most dangerous secret among the Morphate clans. That their first generation of children was developing the strangest of abilities as mutated genetic codes began to mix. However, that was nothing compared to the second generation of children, whose volatile mental states were sometimes deadly. The touch of crazy dancing in the assassin's eyes attested to that.

"Time to play!" she announced.

She hauled back and punched Devon in her face, the pain of it exploding through Devon's head in an excruciating blossom of hurt.

Liam wanted to hurry up after Devon, but as tempting as she was, she couldn't break him of the habitual need to check doors and see that everything was locked soundly for the night on his side of the house. The others were responsible for their sections, but the final check on the west wing side was his chore. He would not rest easy without seeing to it, and when he finally caught up with Devon, he planned on taking a great deal of time with her and wanted no distractions. Keeping her safe was his job and his promise to her, and he would not fail her because he didn't take the time to check a simple window lock.

Devon flailed blindly with one hand, her vision blurred by the dizzying impact of incredibly powerful fists. As a Morphate, she could take a fairly good beating and shake it off relatively quickly, but there was a strength in this slim creature that went well beyond the norm even for a Morphate. It began to make sense to her now why the assassin had thought she could walk naked into this house and kill her.

Or maybe she wasn't going to kill her.

It didn't matter. The attacker's end game wasn't Devon's concern. And as Devon finally got hold of a fistful of her hair, she smiled through swollen lips and yanked the bitch off of herself, cracking her head into the bathroom's marble floor just as the creature had done to her.

"Enjoy that!" she spat, wrestling the slippery bitch under herself and smashing her head into the floor once again. "And that! You come in here calling me a traitor, but what you are is proof and validation that my work is sorely needed!"

The girl regrouped before Devon could smash her down a third time, back-fisting Devon across the face so hard and with such force that she flew off of her and crashed into the doorframe. Devon coughed, blood spewing out of her mouth. The assassin's initial attack had broken one of her ribs. This hit had sent the rib through her lung. She had not felt anything so agonizing in her life. She could barely draw breath. Just because she was physically capable of healing herself from beyond the brink of mortality did not mean it wasn't the most excruciating process known to man or Morphate. This was nothing like a shot to the leg. Breathing affected everything, all of her capabilities. The room was spinning as her opponent got to her feet and loomed over her, her wide face looking strangely reptilian as her cold black eyes, the pupils indiscernible from the irises, regarded her from the left to the right and back again. The movement was slow and graceful, almost rhythmic, but it was so reptilian that it was menacing.

"The thing about our healing abilities? It takes *time*," she noted, a feral grin on her lips. "And in that time, I'm going to fuck you up some more. Then, when you're good and tenderized, I'm going to drag your ass back to Ambrose and he's going to see to it you're tried for your sins against your people."

Ambrose. So that was who was at the bottom of this! At last she knew who to focus on, who was gunning for her so relentlessly. Of course, he had been high on her short list of suspects, if she were going to boil down the entire Morphate race to a brief list of people who had the most motivation for her destruction. She had been meeting with high placed members of all the clans, one after another, these past weeks, trying to get a hint. A clue. If she hadn't been in a fight for her life, she would have taken a moment to cry out in victory.

It would make her victory doubly sweet when she kicked this Ambrose Clan whore's ass.

The Ambrose assassin couldn't possibly have known the magnitude of the mistake she had made.

Devon lurched up from the floor in one powerful, extreme movement, her body like a battering ram, plowing down the startled assassin. Rhiannon had thought her opponent beaten and crippled. But how ironic that the creature from reptilian Ambrose Clan would forget that having both hands around a deadly snake is no guarantee it won't whip back around and bite you dozens of times in retaliation. Even if injured.

But Rhiannon fast learned her mistake. Devon was spitting a savage spray of blood across Rhiannon's face as her hands closed around the other woman's face and with a rapid-fire extension of claws viciously raked them down over it, slicing through both eyebrows and transecting her eyelids. Only the right eye itself was damaged as Devon's claw-tip sliced through her cornea the way paper might slice through the tip of a finger. Swiftly. Painlessly. And with an effect that wouldn't be noticed for several heartbeats. But all it took was a further stressor on the wound to make the damage come screaming to the forefront of attention, and that was what happened when Devon elbowed her hard in her eye socket.

"I've had fifty years to learn self-defense, whelp," Devon rasped between blows and the screams of her stunned victim. "Genetics don't make you a badass. You have to work at it. That's what your generation will *never* understand."

They had become Morphate the easy way. They were born into it. They had never known anything else.

"They threw us away like the rest of the human refuse they didn't know what to do with," Devon spat in staccato breaths as she grabbed the assassin by her hair, climbed her body, grinding a knee down into her crotch and another into her gut to keep her pinned in place. "Gangsters. Drug-dealers. Pedophiles. The criminally insane. Not just a few, but enough to fill the whole of Dark Manhattan! By the time you were spawned, it was all made pretty again. Made nice so you wouldn't stab your baby feet on the thick refuse of dirty needles and broken crack vials! *I* cleaned that up! *I* lived that every day for decades! What the fuck did you ever survive?"

She would have screamed it in the whelp's face had she been able to draw breath, but instead her words came out as the most savage and frightening combination of gurgle and growl ever heard. They were teamed with clawing and fisting at the girl's face and body in rapid-fire beats of savagery.

By the time Liam ran into the room, the assassin was fleshy pulp, barely recognizable as a woman at all. Certainly no longer dangerous. But he could tell Devon was badly injured. The only act of bravery left for him to do was to reach out and touch her shoulder, inserting himself into a violent berserker episode.

She turned on him with a growl of pure savagery and only his fast reflexes spared him her claws as they swiped at his face and belly. When her slashing hand came back at him for a second go, her eyes blinded by coats of blood, he caught her wrist and slapped his gun into her palm. The feel and weight of the hard steel triggered things in her mind, made her react with logic rather than limbic systems. Emotional, knee-jerk reaction melted away far enough for her to recognize that the thing in her hand might help her achieve her goal.

Devon rose to her feet, her body shaking with the overdose of adrenaline it had been using. Without an instant of hesitation, she pointed the gun at her assassin's head and fired it twice, the amazing accuracy of the second shot near the first something only he would ever have the opportunity to appreciate. Even as Devon was stepping away, turning her back on her victim, the body seized once and exploded into a gaseous cloud.

Devon stood there, shaking, raising blood doused eyes to his, only the briefest of fears hurrying through her slowly stabilizing mind. As she looked into his eyes she realized that her savagery would never frighten this man. Never once had the nature of who and what she was caused him hesitation.

"Come," he said softly, holding out his hand and beckoning her forward with the flicking of two fingers.

With her heartbeat raging in her ears still, her blood burning furiously in her veins, and her breath choking in and out of her lungs with every breath, she did as he bade her to do. She moved into his embrace. Devon felt him take his weapon from her sticky hand and heard him click it into his holster as he pulled her tight to his chest.

Liam held her to himself, simply stood there and acted as an anchor for her, ignoring his own surges of fury that she had been up here, alone and injured, fighting for her life while he had been out of reach checking the stupid windows. Once again she had had to fight for her own life, a blood-strewn room the terrible evidence of how desperate the battle had been. But when he had heard the sounds of struggle and come running to her, he'd hit the threshold of the bathroom door and stood there an entire heartbeat, staring and asking himself one very clear question.

What the hell did she need *him* for?

Yes, she was injured. Yes, she could have been the one on the bottom side of the fight. But he doubted it. His practiced eyes took in everything in the room and realized the only one who had ever been in danger had been the would-be assassin. The words spinning from her lips had only reinforced his instinctive knowledge. This woman had probably forgotten more about self-defense and fighting than he had ever learned.

What?

What the hell did she need him for?

* * *

Liam was not the whiny, needy type. Nor was he the type who could only function as the dominant personality. He preferred to train his principals to take care of themselves. And he had signed on with the understanding that Devon had fought against death all on her own once before. But what he did need was to understand his true role in any situation. He recalled she had been quite straightforward about her needs. That she wasn't interested in simply being protected. She wanted to eliminate the threat altogether. He had agreed with her approach.

But since then he had learned she was a Morphate, and that her enemies were most likely other Morphates. Very seriously pissed off Morphates by the look of it. So did Devon need his team merely as disposable muscle to wield her weapons? He imagined getting her kind to carry mercury would be a little bit tricky. Then again, she had made it safe enough for anyone to use.

Liam tried to quiet his mind a little as he saw her struggling for breath, blood and flesh congealing on her skin. He felt his own issues and questions fading quickly as he reached out to touch her temple, his fingers brushing her gently, calmingly.

"Let's get you cleaned up."

Had it been anyone else, any human, his priorities would have been very different. He would have been rushing to apply first aid and get her to the nearest E. R. However, he knew he couldn't do that. Not just because she would heal on her own. But because it was illegal for Morphates to imitate humans, he would blow her cover and potentially send her to jail.

He drew her out of her bathroom and into his own suite. He led her back into his bathroom, keeping one hand on her at all times as he used the other to rummage in one of his smaller supply bags resting on the vanity. He pulled a syringe out of the first-aid kit he found, used his thumb to pop the top off it and exposed the pressure needles. He moved aside the ruined fabric of her dress, the tissue-thin fabric now plastered to her body in a macabre papier-mâché of silk and blood. The pressure needle engaged the moment he applied strength to it, injecting her with painkiller. Nothing much, just enough to get her through the worst of the healing process, he guessed.

"I'll metabolize it very quickly," she murmured, blowing that idea out of the water.

"It'll help in the meanwhile," he said with a shrug. It would have to. He couldn't stand the idea of her being in such pain for much longer.

"There are longer-acting ones. Made for Morphates."

"I didn't know that," he said, frowning as he gave her a once-over. "Do you have any here?"

She laughed a raspy sound without any humor. "I have a factory full of them in Kuala Lumpur. I invented them with the help of a brilliant scientist named Genesis Gregory about forty-two years ago. Genesis is Kincaid Gregory's wife. We've been manufacturing the drugs 'illegally' for several decades. Waiting for the Federated Drug Association to approve something that could cause a human being to over-dose is . . . well . . . something of an uphill battle."

"So . . . weapons . . . and now drugs. That's starting to make you something of a cliché, Devon," he said, his tone in no way judgmental. He was aware of how Morphates had had to work outside the law to make even the smallest strides forward.

"Seems if there's a Morphate centered law to be broken, I've broken it," she acknowledged grimly. "That is why I dis-tanced myself from Nick and Amara. They are working so hard through legal and proper channels to see to it that Morphates can one day find equal standing in our society. Everything they do must appear completely aboveboard or everything they have struggled for will collapse. I won't have that. Someone has to get dirty, and it can't be them." She raised her eyes to his, her lashes stuck together in pointy clumps. The red on her face made the green of her eyes jump out in startling contrast, the sadness in them causing an instant knot in his throat. "I'm Amara's Beta. It's my job to protect her at all costs. It always will be. Even if that means leaving her and the only people who could possibly accept me for what I really am."

"I accept you for what you really are," he told her softly, his fingers curling under her chin to make sure she didn't look away from him. To make sure she saw the steadiness of his eyes. To make sure she understood that it wasn't just words, and that he was including every bestial layer within her. "I accept the Devon that bites and claws at me when she comes. The Devon that is so brilliant I doubt I'll ever be honored to know her equal in my lifetime. I accept," he said, firmly gripping her chin when she went to shift her gaze aside, "the Beta. The vicious assassin who is second to the most powerful female Morphate in the world. Who just handed that joke of an assassin her ass. I accept it all, Devon."

He didn't so much as twitch as she searched him for a glimmer of uncertainty. A dash of overconfidence. But he was not speaking randomly or handing her platitudes. He was reminding her that if any human out there was capable of fully comprehending her, it was he.

"Devona," she rasped softly after a long series of heartbeats.

"Excuse me?"

"Devona. I was born with the name Devona Chandler. It's funny how dropping a single letter here and there can help you disappear into our society and become an entirely different person. I am Devona Chandler. I am Amara Gregory's Beta. I am one of the wealthiest women in the world. I am Morphate and I am deadly. But you know all of this. You accept all of this. And I don't doubt you. What I find so hard to believe is why you haven't even so much as hesitated. You

watched me pull that girl apart and your only action was . . .
was to hand me a gun. In what world does that make sense?
To discover you are sleeping with a killer. What makes you so
okay with that?"

"Because *you* are sleeping with a killer," he reminded her
gently. "Isn't that really why I'm here? I'm a killer of
Morphates. But also I'm a killer of men. Isn't that what a soldier boils down to? Someone who has it in them to be okay
with taking the lives of others. A career soldier even more so.
I am in no position to judge you for who and what you are any
more than you are to judge me. I see a kindred spirit in you.
Although to be honest I find you a bit out of my league."

"A better beast than you? A more savage animal?" she
queried bitterly, punctuating it with a terse laugh.

"No, babe. A better person than me. More refined. More
intelligent. Tomorrow you could decide to change everything
about you and you'd have the wherewithal to do it. Me, I'll
always be a soldier. In one form or another."

"I can't change everything," she pointed out in a whisper.
"No matter what, I'll always be a Morphate. I'll always be an
animal."

"Don't let the blood fool you," he said softly as he began
to peel away what remained of her dress. "We are all of us animals, sweetheart. It's just whether we let that part of our
nature show or not. All I see here is a woman who just fought
for her life. More importantly, one who won."

He hit the taps and the tub quickly began to fill while he
finished pulling blood-soaked silk free of her skin. He steered
her into the shower first, tuning those taps as well before
moving her under the water. When she grabbed hold of his
shirt and wouldn't let him move away from her, he kicked off
his boots and shed the rest of his clothes just as quickly. His
hands ran over her, the tile rushing red around their feet as he
rinsed off the worst evidence of her nature. By the time he'd
rinsed her hair satisfactorily, she was breathing easier and

began to exhale soft sighs of release. She was letting go of the savage instincts she'd had to call on and returning to the Devon he knew.

Devona, he corrected himself. But now was not the time to split hairs about why it had taken so long for her to be completely honest with him. Frankly, he understood. He had lied and omitted his fair share of information to other lovers in his life. It was the nature of his job. It just felt a little strange being on the other side of the equation for a change.

She turned around in his hands, facing him and turning her eyes up to his.

"In a little while I am going to be healed as if this never happened and I am going to want to make love with you just as fiercely as I just fought for my life. How do you feel about that?"

"I think we're going to take a bath first, let you crash and calm. Let's wait and see just what you're in the mood for later."

She smiled then, the expression in her saying he was so silly to doubt her. Liam's heartbeat jolted into a little quicker pace. Her confidence as a sexual being would never cease to floor him. As unsure as she might be about the rest of her life, here she had found perfect footing with him.

And frankly, nothing had ever rung truer for him, either.

Chapter Fifteen

Devon relaxed her head back against Liam's shoulder as his fingers smoothed shampoo lather through her hair. She was already half asleep as she lay beneath the hot, tumbling water with her back to his chest, her bottom settled snugly between his thighs. Despite the openness of their nudity and the sensuality latent in their contact, he'd made no sexual overtures to her, content to let her set the mood and pace. She might have let this passivity worry her, except there was nothing passive about his biological reaction to the feel of her slick, nude body nestled up against him.

Liam enjoyed the way she relaxed under his hands, the way her breathing evened out, and the way she absently curled her hands around his knees to hold on to him. He was aware of the exact moment she fell asleep, but he finished washing the soap from her hair just the same. He slid soapy hands down her shoulders and arms, stroking her gently and slowly. He continued to bathe her, his hands sliding over her throat, her chest, and underarms. He moved on to her breasts, his fingers slipping over her nipples, the aureoles puckering tightly as he swept past. She stirred when he traveled over her belly. Devon turned her head so her face was pressed to his neck, her lips rubbing over him as she smiled sleepily.

"You're better than a maid," she murmured.

"Yeah. I can think of one way I'm much better," he teased her.

"So can I," she sighed, her hand slipping behind her to seek the erect flesh nestled in the curve of her back.

"There we go, thinking alike again," he said, his breath catching mid-sentence when her slick fingers encircled him. "You know, you can just relax and sleep if you want. I won't hold you to earlier promises," he told her tensely. "I know you had a headache before all this started. It can't have improved much."

"I never said I had a headache."

"You didn't have to say it. I could tell," he whispered.

"Mmm, and that's how you're so successful at your occupation, where observation is everything." Devon made the remark absently. She was far more interested in discovering the extent of his arousal and just how hard he really was. Her inquiring fingers alone improved matters, and she could feel him swelling and pulsating with a rush of excitement when she closed her fist around him and stroked him.

"Ahh, baby," he groaned, his legs shifting restlessly around her. His hands anchored to the tub sides. "Your hands . . ." he breathed with rough pleasure as she rubbed fingers over and around him. "Do you have any idea how good that feels?"

"Mmm, I have some idea," she told him, a smile drifting over her lips. She turned around, sliding like a slippery eel until she straddled his hips and had her hand back around him. Her breasts moved against his chest provocatively as she stroked him in several long, stunningly arousing pulls. "I could make you come, yes?"

"Easily," he growled as his hips began to press up with her caresses.

Devon leaned forward to kiss the corner of his mouth, a butterfly flick of her tongue touching him there. She reached her second hand between his legs and cupping his stones she gently tugged on him and fondled him expertly.

"God, it's as though we didn't make love at all," he said with amazement, "the way I react to you. It feels like the first time. That keen, beautiful feeling of first getting to be with a lover. There's nothing about you that doesn't fascinate me. Thrill me."

"I know," she sighed, excitement rising as she watched his face and reactions to her touch. "Even when we're fighting," she whispered against his ear seductively, "I keep thinking how sexy you look in that outfit you wear when you work. About how sexy you'd look out of it."

"Hmm . . . if I'd known that, there wouldn't have even been an argument." She laughed, highly doubtful of that. "Or I would have ended it sooner. Watching you at dinner with another man, watching him simply touch your hand . . . it made me a little crazy, you know. Didn't help that I kept getting an occasional flash of garters through the material of your skirt."

"Liked those, did you?" she chuckled with sinful sensuality as she stroked him in quicker motions.

"Devon . . ." he moaned, his hands reaching to seize her shoulders. "Let me take care of you before you bring me too close," he said, his voice like sandpaper.

"What's too close?" she asked curiously as her nails ran over him, forcing nerves into harsher attention.

"A couple more seconds of that," he said on harshly falling breath.

She laughed, the sound miles away from the pain she'd been forced to feel at the hands of another just a short while ago. She leaned forward to kiss his shoulder in her delight. "Just making sure I have your attention," she murmured against his damp skin.

"That has to be a joke," he laughed abruptly.

"Mmm, nope. Here, is this better?"

She removed her second hand, grasped the edge of the tub

over his shoulder and before he could blink, she had guided him into her snug, hot little body.

Definitely better. But damn, he couldn't get a single word past his throat to tell her so. Luckily, his body spoke for him. His hands clamped onto her hips and he surged up into her.

"One of these days, we're going to have to try and do this slowly," she mused impishly as she felt the desperation in his grip.

"Son of a bitch," he managed at last. "How do you always do this to me?" he demanded. A better question might be 'why.' She always seemed so unconcerned with her own pleasure. With her eager, slippery body all over him, however, it was easy for him to be selfish as she commanded his focus. Liam realized that was partially because she seemed to take a great deal of delight in manipulating him until he was out of control. It turned her on, her body growing hotter with each passing moment, her hard nipples sweeping across his chest, her head falling back as she moved with the rhythm of his hands and hips.

"Mmm, Liam you feel so good," she purred. "You always feel so good."

Feeling good certainly wasn't a problem. An excess of feeling good was becoming an issue, however. She had reached out to grip the tub on both sides, giving herself a wicked leverage with which to move. The water washed away the natural lubricants of her body, and friction grew by leaps and bounds.

"Devon, look at me," he demanded in short, bursting breaths. She lifted her head and opened slumberous, passion-hazed eyes, assuring him that she was just as caught up as he was. "Good girl. Now let's try something before you have your way with me."

She laughed at that, the throaty sound vibrating completely through him. Still, he made good on his proposition by insinuating a hand between their bodies. Taking his thumb and forefinger, he caught up that sensitive bud of her flesh between them and rolled it into a tugging pinch in time to her next slide down his shaft. She jerked hard enough to send water sloshing and her inner walls clamped down on him in her surprise. Liam groaned, feeling his coming climax threatening to boil over. Regardless, he dragged on her clit again until she gasped, then soothed her in quick and slow circles. He kissed her open mouth until they were both moaning and sighing against each other's tongues.

"Oh, yes," Devon gasped, her hips jerking in a quicker rhythm over him. Now all Liam could do was hang on for the ride and pray he held on long enough for her. He gripped her so hard he probably left bruises, but he couldn't help himself as he was lost in her luscious tongue and divine body. Her cries increased, rasping into his mouth as everything about her began to tighten up. It was too much, more than he could handle, and he burst over the edge in wild, gutting release. He heard his grunted shouts echoing off the tiles, felt her riding him for all she was worth, her back snapping into a sudden arch as she followed him in detonation.

When Liam became aware of himself again it was to find his forehead buried against her breastbone and her arms wrapped around his head and shoulders. Then the strangest thought crossed his mind and he laughed aloud before he could check the impulse. She pulled away to look into his eyes with a satiated smile in her eyes.

"What?"

"It's not important," he said dismissively.

"It is to me," she countered.

Liam smiled at that and reached up to cup her face in both hands. "It's just that, when my parents were alive, they'd have these terrible rows. Or so it seemed. Loud and Irish, more bluster than anything. I once got very upset and I remember my mother comforting me. She said to me, "'Tis not the fighting that matters, darlin', but what comes after!'"

He chuckled along with Devon. "I never understood what that truly meant until just now."

"It was a good lesson," she sighed in agreement, hugging him close again with a little shiver.

"Yup. And now it's time to get out of here. You're cold."

"I don't get cold," she denied, shivering again as she lay heavily in his arms.

"Yeah, right," he snickered. Liam anchored her slippery body as best he could and hauled them both out of the water. He impressed himself with the feat, considering he could barely feel his legs after such a devastating orgasm. She aided his efforts by wrapping wet legs around his hips and her arms around his neck. He managed to step onto the bathmat without slipping and breaking both their necks. He grabbed towels and halfheartedly covered her and himself with them as he walked her into the bedroom.

"I think I might keep you a while," she sighed. "You're very handy to have around."

"Thank you," he chuckled, smacking her bottom lightly, the wet sound echoing loudly. But she hardly budged.

Liam dumped her onto his bed and she went willingly. He wrapped her wet hair and then took his time drying her warmly glowing body. Devon's sighs and blissful movements began to arouse him all over again as he ran the soft towels over every inch of her skin. Her flawless, unbruised skin. No one who walked in and saw her would know she'd been beaten viciously just under an hour earlier. Liam was going to give himself a passing once over with the towel, but she suddenly came awake and took a fresh towel from him in order to tend to him herself.

He remained standing and she easily came to him to brush over every hard muscle and delightfully furred inch of skin. She stroked him everywhere, slowing her pace so she could enjoy every inch and every discovery. She was aware that he was becoming more and more excited with every passing second. Men made it easy for women to know these things, she thought with a smile as she dried his thrusting penis too. She kneeled before him to run the towel down his legs and she heard him try to cut back a groan as his fingers pushed away the towel around her hair so he could tangle them into the wet strands.

There was something about having a beautiful, highly sexed woman kneeling before him that just sent a man's brain into sexual overload. Especially when he knew the highly sexed wench was well aware of her effect on him. Had she been ignorant, she wouldn't have nuzzled her face against his rigid member and subsequently licked him. Not once, but several times.

"Forget it!" he growled suddenly as he jerked her to her feet and threw her back onto the bed. "Before you start in on me again, woman, you are going to have at least three orgasms. Got it?"

She got it. At least *four* times before he let her come anywhere near him to return the favor.

It wasn't long after that she crashed utterly and completely. The spikes and falls of adrenaline finally caught up with her, allowing him to extricate himself from her without hands of protest trying to pull him back. The moment he had clothes on his back he was in contact with his people. In the morning the guard on Devon's home would be doubled, though perhaps not so obviously to her. In the wings, he was mobilizing a few other things.

Devon's war with the Morphates had just grown to a new level. They'd become so bold as to stroll into her property. How they had gotten past his people was an issue to be dealt with and examined later. Otherwise, there was nothing more he could do until daylight, when he could interview her a bit more thoroughly about her attack. The devil would be in the details, he knew. And the best way for him to craft a force at her right hand would be to understand the tactics and nature of the beasts they were dealing with.

For a couple of days further into the week they fell into a strangely quiet sort of routine as Liam trained his team to use Devon's new weapons. Every night Devon would fall asleep exhausted in the arms of her human lover, always more and more aware that Liam satisfied her in ways she had never experienced before. In the mornings she would be awakened by a soft kiss and whisper before he got out of bed to begin his workday. Then he would roll her over and tuck her in warmly so she could fall back to sleep. The routine developed a familiarity that brought her the first comfort and security she had felt since it became clear to her that Ambrose Clan was gunning for her.

She would spend the day at work, just as she always had; only now she looked forward to closing the day's business. She knew that soon Liam would supervise the shift changes and then come spend the evening with her before securing the house for the night. At sunset every day she would open the drapes to her office and watch the dogs, or the 'pups,' as Liam called them, exercising on the south lawn with their trainers. Liam would always be there, within sight, and he would always look up and see her there watching for him.

While Devon was feeling comforted by this routine, Liam was unsettled. He was disturbed by how easily he was falling into a pattern that bordered on domestication, he who had thrived on the challenges every day brought him. He ought to be more resistant to it, but he was happily panting after Devon like a well-trained puppy. Every smile, every kiss became a reward. His main crew had slowly but surely become aware that something was going on between the boss and the client. It had somehow become a quietly accepted fact. He'd been a little obvious about it, he supposed. Also, he was working a bit out of character. Normally he'd have sent his original insertion team on to secure her other offices, starting with the first one on her travel agenda. But this time, he'd refused to send any of his key people to secure the London office, keeping them close for obvious reasons. Usually he sent his own people because they were the ones he trusted best to get the job done, but instead he kept the entire primary team on Devon, disliking the idea of anyone else being responsible for her. Still, they had accepted his decision as if he did it the same way every time. Besides, her jet needed securing for the upcoming trip to London. Or that was the immediate excuse he had used to try to explain his reluctance to part with Kellen, Inez, and the others.

He might as well not have bothered trying. He could tell they all knew what was happening even though they never let on. However, he knew his people. He'd never be seen being anything other than professional with clients. But in Devon's case, Liam's people had suddenly become entirely too social. Devon was on a first-name basis with the day crews; even the K-9 leaders and the dogs were fawning over her. He'd never seen the shepherds fawn over anyone other than the NHK family before. They were even wary of their fellow workers from time to time, but with Devon? Puppies. Somehow, with Devon, they immediately got over their natural suspicion of Morphates, sensing something in her nature that let them know she was friend, not foe. They rolled and frolicked around her whenever she stepped onto the lawn. He supposed those were good terms to describe the human soldiers' behavior too. Frolicking and rolling, fawning happily, making friends. In a nutshell, getting entirely too comfortable.

Yet, how could he correct the problem when he was the most comfortable of them all? He hadn't slept in his own bed almost since the night he'd arrived there. Even the realization made him smile when he shouldn't be at all happy about his own deportment. On the plus side, Devon hadn't left the estate for any more 'business meetings,' so he hadn't had to deal with that danger.

Liam watched her office window.

The sun was setting earlier every day, but like clockwork, at the point where the last true moments of full daylight still lingered, she pulled open the drapes. Still, he smiled when he saw her appear as usual. He ought to discourage anything that smacked of routine, but he'd come to enjoy seeing her like this every day just as he was winding up with one shift and about to debrief another. Autumn was digging in. The trees around them would grow bare and make it ever harder for a would-be assassin to sneak up on the property. A normal assassin, in any event. Devon's description of her attacker had been notification of a game changer. He'd been brooding for days on how to see an assailant that could blend into its background. Were there more like her? Devon didn't think it was likely. She explained a little more about the Morphate generations, spinning a wild card into this whole mess that he frankly could have done without.

He could see she was wearing a rather conservative outfit of a business skirt and matching cream-colored blouse. Conservative by her standards, at least. It was a mid-thigh miniskirt, showing off her incredible legs, and with the sunlight hitting her just right, the silk blouse showed the shadows of her skin color and the fact that she never wore a bra. He had a running fantasy involving that window, a whole lot fewer men and animals around, and a striptease under glass, so to speak. She was already a tease, always looking so damned desirable without trying, and then each night when she saw him at last, he would see a change ripple through her. Then she *would* be trying, and it would show. Everything about her body would tune toward him, tempting him until he checked his damned watch to find out how long before he could secure the shift change and get up to her.

And tonight was no different. Her hands slid over her hips

as she zeroed in on him. His body was becoming too readily trained to respond to her, he thought with a wince as it began to do just that. Pulse and breath, heat and rushing blood, all of which were out of his control. He had never known such lust in his entire life. It was almost what he would describe as all-consuming. He found nothing tiring, mundane, or routine about sex with Devon. Quite the opposite. She knew tricks he'd never heard of to stimulate a man. Others he'd heard of, but had never found anyone uninhibited enough to actually use them. Devon had no shame and no inhibitions. If there was one thing he could call predictable about her, it was that she would never complain about his being too rough, too big, or too anything. The more he was exposed to the bestial Morphate inside of her, the more he was discovering his wild side. He hadn't realized it before, but when the partner was as willing and enthusiastic as Devon was, all sorts of things began to come to mind.

Not that her mind wasn't working overtime as well, because he knew it was. Last night he'd had a fast, hard and primal lesson in just how little control he had over his own body, should she decide to take command. Liam smiled wolfishly when he recalled giving the lesson back to her rather handily.

Now, he watched her lay her palm against the glass, as though she wished she could reach out to him. He'd noticed that she was looking tired. Between work, playing most of the night, and the incessant thinking and fretting she was doing, he shouldn't be surprised. He didn't need as much sleep as most people, but it was beginning to wear on him too. He was a human trying to keep up with a Morphate's stamina and wildness. Of course it was going to wear on him. But he'd be damned if he was going to roll over and cry 'uncle.'

And though she glowed with her usual energy, Liam could tell something was not right with Devon. What he ought to do was leave her alone for a night. He could sleep in his own room for a change, give her peace and rest.

"You're weak, Nash," he muttered aloud when he realized that he wasn't likely to follow his own advice. How could he? He looked forward to seeing her all day long, to touching her and hearing her voice.

"Talking to yourself again, bro?" Colin asked, giving him a smirk before following his gaze up to the window. "Ah, the lovely walking distraction. You know, everyone else might be afraid to point out the obvious to you, but there's a reason why we don't get attached to our principals, Liam. I seem to recall you beating those reasons into me at every opportunity."

"I am not going to discuss this," Liam said shortly, turning his attention away from Devon and shocked to find just how difficult it was. He didn't need Colin to tell him he was in trouble. He knew it every moment of every day.

"I kind of think you have to," Colin pressed. "You're going to get killed, Liam, if you don't get your whole head back in this game you're plotting."

"And just what do you think I'm plotting?" he asked his brother sharply. "I'm doing what I was hired to do. No more, no less."

"Now that's a big fat pile of bullshit if I ever heard one," Colin snapped off. "I've been working under you for enough years to know you don't call up our reserves for a single job. You're arming us with these fancy new weapons of hers slowly but surely. You haven't hired any of us for our stupidity. Although the lot of them are a bunch of cowards for making me be the one to come and confront you like this. Guess they figure you are less likely to fire your own flesh and blood. I know differently, but I figure I better risk it or risk losing my brother altogether. Feel like clearing the air for some of us?"

Liam looked up over Colin's shoulder and saw all the members of both shifts lingering a short distance away instead of moving into their positions as they ought to be. He supposed this was their idea of an intervention. He couldn't be mad about it. They were only watching out for him. They understood the dangers in what he was doing, even if he couldn't force himself to listen to them.

"What would you have me do, Colin? Leave her out here exposed? Let her get killed by the next assassin to come through?" Not that they'd been much help on this last attempt. He had gone back through the video and searched for the point of entry the intruder had taken. Only watching extremely closely had he been able to see her; her progress was nothing more than a ripple along the walls as she seamlessly blended with her environment. It had prompted him to add more sensitive heat vision to the cameras. She'd been cool-blooded, whoever she was. She'd barely shown up on their previous equipment. But Roni had created something much more sensitive and though it hadn't been through full test trials yet, he'd seen no other option than to test it live in the field. He wouldn't let another one of those reptilian-based Morphates get past him again.

That would be unacceptable.

Liam looked back up to the window, seeing her there, standing with such beautiful perfection like an impeccably dressed mannequin. Only she could never be so cold and lifeless. Not even if she tried. And he understood there were very few things she tried and failed at. The way she was standing, her legs braced but curving up out of the heels she wore, the straight strength of her shoulders but the way her back curved at the lower spine so her backside was so distinctly rounded. So temptingly exaggerated. So begging for his hands on that flawless ass. . .

Perhaps an intervention wasn't such a far-fetched idea, Liam thought with a grim little smile. He was afraid he was quite addicted to her. But did it follow that the addiction was something harmful and dangerous for him to be indulging in? Well, it certainly wasn't safe, he admitted gravely to himself.

"I don't want you to leave her unprotected. However, I think you need to hand over your command." Liam's attention snapped back to his brother ferociously, his anger at the thought quick and hot. Leave her safety to someone else? Absolutely not. But Colin was anticipating that reaction from him and so had a calming hand raised between them. "Jackson White Feather. He's wrapped up his present job, or close enough to it that he could make himself free for this. You trust him, don't you?"

Of course he did. Otherwise Liam wouldn't have entrusted him to manage his own security details. But . . .

"I'm not leaving. Get used to the idea." He snapped it out like the badass drill instructor he had once been for the Secret Service and the Federated Special Forces. It was a part of himself he only tapped into when he wanted to frighten others into submission.

"I didn't say leave. I said have Jackson take over the teams. Do I look stupid to you? I know you're too much of a control freak to put her safety entirely into the hands of someone else. Plus, I kinda think you're sweet on her," Colin dared to tease him. He held up a hand again to stay the threatening growl that bubbled up out of his brother. "I'm saying you can focus on being one-on-one with her while Jackson takes over the big picture. You know he'll take any and all input you want to add to the detail work. But you said yourself you were pissed off that you were downstairs closing windows when she needed you to be by her side. She needs a one on one. That much is very clear. Make yourself a one on one. Let's keep you right on top of her . . . officially as well as . . . well, far be it from me to assume what you two like to do position-wise."

Liam reached out and cuffed his brother for the smirk on his lips. Colin let him make contact. He'd do whatever it took to rearrange things to a safer, better detail. Including let his big brother get a hit in.

The thing was, Liam knew his baby brother was right. He'd known it from the moment he'd first pulled Devon into his arms. And he'd felt it most keenly when he'd walked in on Devon fighting for her life. He'd been armed with the best in anti-Morphate weaponry and what good had it done her? She'd been forced to fight barehanded. Alone. Wounded.

Liam exhaled long and slow.

"I'll put a call into Jackson later tonight. But don't think you won any points over me," he said sternly to his brother, lest the kid get a swelled sense of importance. "I was planning to call him in in a few days anyway. Him and his whole team, now that they're free. I have a feeling we're going to need them."

The information made Colin frown. Liam was definitely girding up for a war. Colin was okay with going to war for his brother. He'd follow him into any fight. Hell, that was his job. But he was worried that Liam hadn't thought through the ramifications of this particular war. Colin and the rest of the team had their suspicions on where this was going. They weren't stupid. Nor were they afraid to follow Liam into whatever hell he chose for them. He just hoped his brother was thinking with his head and not his dick. He gave his head a mental shake. He'd never thought he'd have to question Liam on a matter like this. But everything about this job had been sideways from the start. Not the least of which being the way their commander had fallen flat for their principal.

Colin wanted to confront her. He'd do whatever it took to get her to back off so his brother would go back to being the sharp, flawless soldier they were all used to. But while he was willing to press his brother, he knew it would be incredibly out of line to interfere with her. Liam would instantly shut down and block him out. He'd probably punch him in the head while he was at it. It was hard to say for sure because he'd never seen Liam act like this, never seen him break all of his own rules before. Honestly, it was like dealing with a stranger. A stranger ten times more human and flawed than the unshakable, untouchable Liam.

"Hey, Liam," Colin said absently as these thoughts rolled through his head.

"Mmm?"

"I'm glad to see you happy."

And in the end, that's what it came down to. Liam was happy. Happy in a way they'd never seen before. In a way that was delightful to witness.

Colin wasn't going to be the one to fuck that up. Happiness was so fragile in this environment that it was very likely to fall apart all on its own.

And that was going to be a damn shame, he thought, as he turned away before Liam could respond to his remark.

Devon had given Liam all the outward appearance of things going back to normal these past few days. No mean trick, that. Liam was a very shrewd man. But things were far from being normal. If Ambrose thought she was simply going to sit here while he took pot shots at her, he was sorely delusional. She was the female Beta of Dark Manhattan. As Liam had pointed out, she was the second most powerful female Morphate on the planet. She had bided her time long enough, played victim long enough.

Now the time had come.

And was the L. A. Alpha involved as well? Were the two in collusion as was suspected? It was one thing for her to entertain taking on one Alpha. But what if there were two? To fight with only humans and mercury at her back might be the hugest act of stupidity. Then again, all it took was dead aim and steady shots. They could potentially wipe out an entire Morphate force from a distance. They certainly couldn't expect to do well if they were drawn in to hand-to-hand fighting. But when she faced Ambrose . . . she could not kill him. He had to be taken captive. He had to be made an example of. The human populace had to believe that the Alpha Council served its purpose. That it could police its own. If humans began to doubt that, the moment they had this weaponry she had created, it could very well become open season on all Morphates.

The future of the Morphates was in her hands, and her heart was heavy with the responsibility of it all. And all the while she had to continually check her morals. She had to make certain she was doing things for the greater good and with respect for the lives teetering on the line . . . both Morphate and human. She'd had to weigh that knowledge every moment her hands and mind spent crafting weapons meant to kill the unkillable.

Liam sat across the table from her watching her as she went through the motions of eating in total silence, her mind completely and obviously preoccupied. She had been drifting into these obsessive states frequently ever since the attempt on her life. It was actually quite fascinating to watch her mind working, watch the expressions that creased her beautiful features. But he had to stop being fascinated and think more practically.

"What didn't you tell me?"

"Hmm?"

She looked up at him as if he had suddenly appeared, rather than having been sitting across from her for the past half hour.

"What didn't you tell me?" he asked again, this time softly, his voice like a stranger's as it fell to a coaxing timbre. It amazed him, the depths of tenderness he had suddenly found within himself. He'd been so hard for so long, he had no idea where it was coming from or why it was coming at all. But it came just when it needed to, it seemed. The deflation of her shoulders as she exhaled told him so, even if she opened her mouth and flat out lied to him with her next breath.

"I don't know what you mean," she said, her gaze shifting to her food rather than meeting his.

"Liar," he said baldly, making her start. He could see her scrounging up a bristling response, but it was all an act. She was going through the motions.

"I am not a liar! What a horrible thing to say to me!"

"From the day I walked in your front door I have been nothing but brutally honest with you. And you have done nothing but lie to me," he said quietly. There was no accusation in his voice and there was a reason for that. "I understand why. You were protecting yourself and you are protecting others. I was a stranger not yet worthy of your trust, and considering all you have on the line here, I don't blame you for it at all. But we are no longer strangers, Devon. And I would like to think I have proven myself trustworthy. Or at least worthy of your confidence."

She deflated again, her eyes turning up to him and a sweet little crinkle of distress appearing between her brows.

"Liam, I'm sorry. Of course you have earned my confidence. And my trust," she added, almost as if she were reminding herself of the fact. He waited as she paused a few beats, settling her own mind. "That girl . . . I know who sent her," she told him softly. "She said Ambrose of Dark Phoenix had sent her. I have Carter out looking for his whereabouts now because it is quite clear to me that he is not in Phoenix. I doubt he would kidnap me, throw me on a plane, and try and control me for a cross continent flight."

"She was going to kidnap you?" he said, his disbelief obvious. "To what end?"

"A question I will ask Ambrose when I see him. She blathered on about my being a traitor to my species, but I know Ambrose. He is not emotionally driven. He never has been. In fact, I suspect him to be a psychopath."

"Psychopaths can imagine a cause for themselves," he said. "Even if for no other reason than the fascination of carrying it out, and watching others act and respond to it." Liam frowned. "I don't like this. And what were you going to do? Rush after him without telling me?"

"I wasn't trying to eliminate you from my plans, only trying to figure out how best to approach the situation in my own head before involving anyone else."

"And what conclusions have you come to?" he asked, trying not to let his temper boil up. She was used to being on her own. Used to being in total control of everything with no one but Carter to bounce an idea off of. There was no reason he should feel slighted by her actions.

So why did he? Why was he so angry?

Devon was too sharp not to notice the change in his tone and the tension in his body language, however much he tried to conceal them. She didn't understand his temper, but she did know she didn't want to alienate him. She didn't want Ambrose to come between them.

"I haven't come to any conclusions as yet." She reached out for his hand where it lay fisted on the table. "I was wondering what you thought of all of this. You once told me you were willing to take an assertive approach, to take the fight to Ambrose's door. Do you still feel that way? Knowing you and your people would be facing powerful and unpredictable Morphates from several generations, will you still offer your help?"

As she spoke, her fingers had begun to stroke the fine hairs and skin on the back of his hand. Unbelievably, the simple contact began to unravel his anger, soothing him with remarkable speed.

"I have complete faith in my people and their capabilities, but I admit, when we first came here I would never have offered them up in a war with one of the most powerful Morphates in the Federated States. However, armed as we now are with a series of game balancers and knowing how true your weapons' aim can be, I'd say we're very much even at this point. I especially like the compressor gun. A large baby like that will certainly level the playing field. And your rapid-fire handguns put ours to shame with those glass bullets."

"They aren't glass," she argued instantly, making him smile because he'd learned any inaccuracy regarding her weaponry was always met with correction. "They're a special—"

"—hematite and glass polymer that holds the mercury safely inside of it long enough to make it through the force of a pin, the ride down the barrel, and the hit into a target. The composite cracks and breaks up on impact, parts of it melting away and allowing the mercury inside to poison the target quickly. A single expert shot can put a Morphate down like a dog. All the while the bullets are perfectly safe for handling and for carting around as ammunition. You did your job very well there," he assured her. "And I think it might not be a bad idea to give these surprises of yours a thorough field test."

"So your thoughts remain unchanged then," she realized out loud as she stood up and came around to his side of the table, all the while holding his hand. "You'd take this right to Ambrose's doorstep. You'd use these weapons to make your way past his people."

"Only those who threatened me or didn't have the good sense to stand down and let me reach said goal. What is that gorgeous smell?" he asked distractedly as she leaned her body against his shoulder. And just like that, the focus of their dinner together shifted once again.

"It's a perfume I created. A little hobby," she said with a shrug that relegated it to a place of unimportance.

Liam turned toward her, his face at breast level as she stood beside him. The aroma seemed to eddy over him on the waves of warmth she was exuding with increasing heat.

"Hobby or not, I find it very appealing." He took in a deeper breath and was surprised and delighted by the instant warmth he felt rushing through and around his chest. The fact that it then shot directly down into his sexual organs was not a factor to be missed. It was rather like being hit over the head with a sledgehammer without even feeling the pain of it. And just like that he found himself hard for her. From the promise of her perfume and the memories of the ways he had discovered the aromas of her body in the past.

"It has a pheremonal axis. It toys with your inner beast, rousing it to attention by titillating those parts that lie dormant, slumbering in wait for a mate to stir them." She smiled. "Well, anyway, that's what the advertising would say."

"It wouldn't need any advertising," he said, his voice low and intent. "It does its job at the first whiff." He leaned forward and placed a kiss at the very top of her cleavage, a slow tasting touch of his lips. Then his tongue made contact. Just enough of a touch to make her catch her breath. Her hands came up and threaded through his hair, nails dragging over his skull and lighting his nerve endings on fire. He reached to touch her legs at the backs of her knees, turning in his chair to face her and draw her in close between his thighs. His hands found the hem of her dress and slid beneath it.

His hands dove under the unusually austere fabric, coasting straight up the backs of her legs until he was cupping the shapely cheeks of her backside in each of them. Her knees went immediately weak, her weight falling into his hands. He let it happen, let her drag them both down to the floor. A cursory glance up at the door of the dining room was the only hesitation on his part. But she was suddenly holding him tight, arms and legs both pulling him against her soft, sexy body, her mouth zeroing in on his for a soul-wrenching kiss. The idea that any of her household staff or any of his team might wander past the open door drifted out of his sense of importance.

She was important. The heat of her. The smell of her. The way he knew she would taste if only he could get his mouth on her. However, she was way too thoroughly clothed for that.

Her hands were on his gun belt, deftly whipping it off his hips and letting it fall by the wayside, the weight off his weapon working in her favor as she fumbled for the bottom holster strap around his thigh. Her fingers and palms were riding down the length of his zipper the very next instant, parting ways so one was cupping his balls through the denim of his jeans and the other was making out the rigid line of his cock in slow detailed strokes. Liam groaned into her mouth, pressing his hips forward into her hold, his hands braced on the floor so he could give her all the access she needed. Her tongue worked with sinuous beauty against his, their kiss trading homes between their mouths, often hovering on the cusp between the two. Every savoring taste of her buried him in a hot haze of the most intense need and outright lust he'd ever experienced.

Wasn't it supposed to ease? Wasn't it supposed to get routine by now? Or was that just what it had been like with everyone before her? What was it about Devon that made each time with her wilder, more intense than the last? The way his heart was pounding in his chest and ears, he thought that if things got any more intense he was going to blow his heart out.

"Leader! Alpha Two, we got something funny going on out here, sir!"

The squawk of the radio froze them both in place, their lips clinging as their eyes met for a long, throbbing heartbeat. Then Liam shifted awkwardly away from her with a violent curse of regret and annoyance, and not a little bit of self-recrimination. He wiped a hand of frustration over his mouth and ran fingers over his throat to key on the radio he had made sure to lock for outgoing contact so nothing they said over dinner was accidentally transmitted to all and sundry. He keyed it while watching her sit up and draw her legs close, tucking them under her round bottom.

"Leader here, what's up Alpha Two?" he said, hoping his

voice didn't actually sound as rough and breathless to them as it did to him.

"Dunno sir, the dogs are going crazy!"

And they were. He'd been too absorbed to hear it earlier but it sounded as though every beast on the property was going wild outside the balcony doors. Liam launched himself off the floor, grabbing his gun and mini binoculars from his heavy belt. He kicked open the glass doors facing Alpha Two's circuit. From there he had a far better vantage point than the units on the ground.

"Okay. I see him. Alpha Two, you have an intruder, west wall, three meters from the pillar with the cherub on it. Loose the pups if he runs."

"Copy that, sir."

"Get dressed and let's haul ass to a room that doesn't have a thousand windows in it," Liam commanded Devon harshly as he reached a hand down to her and pulled her to her feet. "That guy has a rifle and it looked like serious business."

Liam kept his body between her and the windows, wrapping her up in a brief hug of reassurance before he hustled her into the hallway between the dining room and first parlor. He ordered the lighting down to dark. "Okay, this is good for the moment." He braced his arms against the wall, covering her with his body. He was breathing so hard her hair blew all around her face. Devon was so dizzy from the changing rush of emotions and feelings that she reached out and clutched his shirt to ground herself. Liam wasn't doing much better. He slid a hand behind her back and drew her close to his body, letting her feel his comfortable warmth and residual heat.

"You and I are having a discussion after this is over about how you need to keep your frigging sexy ass at a proper distance until it's time to retire at night," he murmured in a deep, rough voice in her ear. It gave her a wild case of excited chills. Her body was still humming with outrageous need. Even now, even with the danger that was stalking her, all she could think about was rubbing herself all over that massively virile body again and again, licking him, taking him in her mouth until he gripped at her with wildly out of control need. All she could think about, all she could care about, was her need to have him wild in her arms. Ambrose and weapons and assassins fell completely by the wayside when he made her think and feel these things.

Liam was listening for a transmission on the radio giving the all clear, knowing that even after his team apprehended the intruder they would search for others. He looked down at Devon, seeking the flash of those pale jade eyes he could see even in the dark. The overwhelming voraciousness in her eyes stole his breath away. For a single moment he knew her every thought. It all began and ended with the phrase 'I want you.' She would draw him into a sensual world where he would be blinded to everything but the pleasure she gave him by hand, mouth, and body.

"God, babe, don't look at me like that right now. My hands are already shaking," he whispered in pained confession against the sweep of her ear.

"Leader, Alpha Two. Suspect apprehended . . . sort of. Sweeping areas now."

"Define 'sort of,'" he demanded irritably. Now was not the time for his team to get cryptic.

"Well, Inez kinda had to make a cloud of him. Sorry, Leader, but he had her in his sights. She didn't have much choice."

"Do a double sweep," Liam ordered roughly. "I'll be down when I've secured the principal." Liam looked down at her. She had a strange smile on her face. "What?"

"Mmm, I'm just wondering how you plan to secure your principal."

She made it sound naughty, and clearly by the gleam in her eyes that was the whole idea. Liam slammed a hand into the wall near her head in frustration. "This isn't a game, Devon! This guy wanted to kill you and you're out here . . ."

"Flirting shamelessly?" she supplied. "Fine. Go beat your prisoner," she said with a huffy wave. "I'll go down to the inside parlor and have a nightcap where there are no windows. Should I take a gun?"

"Damn it, Devon! This isn't a—!"

Devon stopped him by throwing herself at him; sealing her mouth over his until he was kissing her so fiercely she was bending back over his arm. Her leg snaked around his, the muscle flexed so hard it was like clinging to a tree. She also broke the kiss off, thrusting herself away from him. She was panting hard for breath and she pressed a hand to her wet, bruised lips.

"I will never think this is a joke!" she spat at him. "Sending any of you to face down a maniac with a rifle isn't funny to me at all!" She spun away from him and ran like lightning down the stairs and into the belly of the house.

Liam sighed, now remembering why it was a bad idea to get involved with a principal.

Chapter Sixteen

He found her exactly where she'd said she would be, a glass of cognac in her hand, an unknown amount in her belly. It was almost 2 A.M.

"Is everyone all right?" she asked him immediately, the tone of her voice stark and quiet.

Liam didn't want to be hard on her because it had been a rough few minutes there, shifting between desire and fear and fury. He knew his brain had taken quite a while to clear, and his body a bit more beyond that, although adrenaline shifted quite well in transition. Plus, it had been yet another attempt on her life. That made two in four days' time. He couldn't blame her for feeling out of sorts because she had a bull's-eye painted on her pretty little posterior.

"Liam, I'm such a fool," she said suddenly, bowing her head and sighing. "I know better than this. It was so stupid."

Liam hadn't expected her to blame herself like that, so he was a little taken aback. But then he chided himself for the reaction. She had never been the sort to put her own pride and her need to be right above the reality of a situation.

Devon stood up, her skirt revealing her curvaceous legs, her bare skin flashing warmly as she began to pace in a short circuit. Her hair swished around in a dark cloud that was still tangled from his fingers running through it. Her breasts swayed gently under the thin fabric of her blouse with every turn, the tips slightly prominent. She was damnably beautiful, Liam thought with a pained groan.

She turned and walked up to him, ditching her glass along the way. "Liam, I'm not the panicky and clingy sort. I admire and respect your work a great deal and I'm fully aware of your ability to care for yourself and others in any situation. I only said what I did because I was confused and angry. I was frustrated and so damned horny I could reinvent the orgasm given half a chance. And yes, that's a damned hint," she finished off, hands on her hips in a way that made the thrust of her breasts more pronounced.

Liam blinked. She was apologizing for having a hissy in a bad situation. *Hell, if he had a dime* . . . and considering how many attempts had been made on her life, she was fully entitled!

And she was . . .

Horny.

"Devon," he said, clearing the sudden catch in his throat. "Firstly, I'm not upset about things getting confused and temperamental. You were overdue by that point. So was I."

"It would appear that danger, passion, and fear are a volatile mix," she sighed.

He laughed at her. "Now that you mention it, yeah," he chuckled. "Which brings me to something else." He rubbed his hands together, the fingers slightly chilled from being out of doors. "We found a nest, as I like to call it. Deep inside the tree line but within visual observation of the property. There were signs of more than one dweller. I'm guessing the female and now this male. He was getting into position tonight, it seemed. The bullets were dirty with mercury so I'm guessing . . ."

Devon wrapped her arms around herself in a hug as she

absently stroked her shoulder. She walked a short distance away from him.

"It's hardly worth pointing out the details. We know where this all originates." She stopped and looked him square in the eye. "And I know you think you're slacking in your job because of earlier. I don't blame you if you want to withdraw from our . . . our physical relationship. I'm a distraction. And you hate it."

Liam wasn't stupid or dense. He could see the weight on her mind in every step she took. She was right. She was a distraction. Every time he touched her it was as though caution just blew away like a leaf on the wind.

"Honey, listen to me," he said softly. "There are reasons why getting tangled up with you is a bad idea for both of us." He watched her turn slowly around to face him.

"I know that. And I understand if you want to—"

"No! No, that's not what I want at all!" he barked, startling her. "Why are you always so accommodating? Hmm? With me, I mean. You push everyone else around like carefully crafted chess pieces, but with me you bend and turn wherever you think I want you to go."

"There is one piece on a chess board you don't push around until absolutely necessary," she huffed back at him. "Right now, you are that piece."

"That is total bullshit! I'm not some king you have to protect! It's the other way around, Devon! I'm protecting you, remember?"

"I know that! But you don't understand, Liam. I'm protecting you from *me*! From things about me I . . ." Devon went mute, shaking her head as words failed her and distress flooded her eyes.

"Don't!" Liam marched up to her and seized her shoulders, giving her a shake. "Don't treat me like this. I'm not some ignorant grunt. I have a brain and know how to use it.

Why don't you just let me decide for myself how to think and feel about you and stop worrying so damned much?"

"I worry," she whispered. "I can't help it. And I don't think you're ignorant, Liam. I'm . . . I'm afraid." She drew a shaky breath and met his eyes. He could feel her trembling between his hands. "I'm a woman of truth, but I cannot be truthful. I'm a woman of honor, and yet I'm behaving so dishonorably." She brought a hand to her mouth as her eyes filled with tears. "I am a woman of passions beyond the measure of your understanding, or even mine, and I know that you pull at me like no other. God, Liam, I'm blinded by my passion for you and I don't even understand why. I swore to myself I wouldn't make love with you, and yet . . ."

"And yet, so much for honor and truth, hmm?" he asked softly. "I know the feeling, babe. I made the same promise to myself and began breaking it five seconds later. That isn't like me. None of this is how I operate, either in work or with a woman. It's actually making me a little crazy. But, you know what? Sometimes crazy is good for you." He drew a deep breath and sighed it out from his toes, reaching to ruffle a hand through his crisp hair. "Devon, I'm a real stickler for rules and responsibility, but if I look at myself and see myself flying in the face of what I usually live and breathe by . . . I have to know it means something. I'm sure it means something." Whether he was willing to speak the words to himself or out loud right then, that was another issue. But he wanted her to know this wasn't all just . . . nothing. Convenience. Irresponsibility. It was none of the things she was accusing them both of.

"And what about the rest?" she asked, reaching to run a warm hand across his chest, unable to keep from touching him a moment longer.

"Mmm," he hummed with pleasure at her touch. "That is a good question. You're a very big distraction, Devon. A dangerous one." Liam reached out and smoothed back her hair.

"But there's nothing I can do about that, now is there? Even if I tried to walk around this house ignoring you, it would still distract me. All I can do is hand over my post to one of the other Field Leaders. It's the best and safest answer."

"Oh," she said quietly.

Liam chuckled softly. "Unfortunately, that means that Field Leader is going to have to put up with me trying to micromanage his every action." He leaned closer and nuzzled her ear to whisper hotly across it. "I'm not going anywhere. You're stuck with me. In every way I can possibly stick to you."

She closed her eyes and swallowed hard as shivers shuddered through her. "What does that mean?" she demanded roughly. "What are you saying? Please."

Liam circled her arms a little tighter, drawing her against his extraordinarily muscled body until she melted in that way that made her fit him with marvelous perfection.

"It means," he growled, "I'm going to make you come until California falls in the ocean."

When they stumbled into Devon's bedroom, they were locked together in a passionate kiss that had started as an aching seduction in the parlor. Liam had a way with his tongue, slow and searching alternating with light teasing flicks, and it drove her crazy. He shut the door and leaned back against it, catching her body's forward motion by her breasts. Cuddling both up tight in his palms, his thumbs and forefingers seized her flirtatious nipples and pulled them into attentive, anxious points.

Devon drew away from his mouth and reached to nuzzle his ear and neck. He lowered his head to accommodate her. "Liam," she purred, "I want to taste myself again in your mouth."

Liam jerked his head back so fast that he smacked it into the door. Devon gasped and reached to nurse his wounded skull with gentle hands and a giggle. "If I'd known it was going to be such a dangerous remark, I wouldn't have said anything."

"Bite your tongue," he growled, jerking her up tight against him. "I love what you said. Want proof?" His smile was crooked and sly and she laughed. She reached out boldly and ran her palms down the length of his fly, feeling how stone hard he was.

"I've got proof," she whispered against his lips as he surged against her palm.

"Well, what do you know? Same as my proof."

"How about that?" she laughed, a twinkle of delight in her eyes.

"Isn't that known as simpatico?" he asked as he kissed the corner of her lips, his hands sliding down her throat slowly.

"Mmm, close enough," she murmured against his mouth, the words rolling like thick syrup off her tongue. "God, your mouth drives me crazy," she breathed as he continued to tease her with light, sipping kisses around her lips.

"Is that so?" he asked, loosing a low, short chuckle. "Fair play, baby, because everything about you drives me crazy."

"Hmm, I'm all for fair play. Equal rights. We shall overcome," she whispered as she unhitched his heavy belt from around his hips, the tools of his trade scraping across a tabletop nearby as she discarded it. She next reached for his snug black T-shirt, drawing it out of the waistband of his pants until she could slide her palms hungrily over the hot skin of his back and shoulders. She felt the play of taut muscles flexing as she moved over them, filling him with tension and pleasure until he sighed out a long sound of stimulated gratification.

Liam felt the slight clutch of her nails when he finally stopped teasing her and seized her mouth in a scorching kiss. Her entire body burrowed up into him, feminine lines and curves matching his masculine ones, softness meshing with hardness. His heart throbbed with excitement, with the cravings she inspired so effortlessly. Liam reached for her skirt, dragging the material up her legs to her hips. His fingertips touched bare skin across her hip and he groaned with delight when he remembered she was completely naked beneath it. A few quick motions and she'd be naked in his arms.

He took a step, the movement sliding his thigh between hers until she stepped back for balance. They began a slightly clumsy trek toward her bed. All the while, their lips clung in long drugging kisses. Even when she laughed at her awkward travel backward their mouths did not part. Devon's lips were bruised and tingling with heat and sensitivity, but it would take a lot more than that to get her to relinquish the mouth of this man who kissed like sin itself. Her legs bumped into the bed at last, one of the posts nudging at her shoulder.

"I've been dreaming about you these past few days," he confessed in a heated whisper, both hands under her skirt and stroking up her thighs.

"Really?" she managed as his fingertips stroked teasing caresses over the fronts of her thighs, a brief slip between them for the heat she radiated like a furnace, a ghosting stroke over her pubic bone, and then up over her hips to the rounds of her bottom.

Liam closed his eyes as he drew her forward, locking her hips against his own and undulating against her fabulously soft heat. "Yes," he rasped roughly. "I was dreaming of the first time I saw you. You were so beautiful that day I met you. You took my breath away. You still do." Liam listened to her soft panting breaths and smiled against the side of her neck. He nipped at the sensitive skin there, feeling her shiver in response. "All I could think about was all the things I instinctively wanted to do to you. Things I kept myself from doing. But in my dreams I don't hold myself in check. In my dreams . . . how many times do you think I've made love to you? How many ways? How often have I heard you cry out in pleasure? God, I hate waking up from that.

"But then when I do," he breathed, "I have reality, and it's always more than the fantasy ever could be." Liam slid his hands high up her sides, bracketing her ribcage and feeling its wild expansions as she dragged in breath after breath. "Your skin is softer, your mouth more delicious and hot, and your scent . . . mmm . . ."

Devon felt him breathe in deeply against her neck as his enormous hands slid up to capture her naked breasts beneath her gathered blouse. "Oh, Liam," she uttered on a shaking gasp as his thumbs rubbed over her sensitized nipples and her breasts swelled with heat and arousal.

"Not many women can claim to be the perfect handful for a man of my size, honey, but you can." He growled the observation beneath her ear just before reaching to suckle the lobe briefly. "Lift your arms," he coaxed her silkily.

She did and the blouse flew off, floating to the floor and forgotten an instant later. Liam took a step back so he could ravage her with hungry eyes. Devon reached out for him, slipping strong fingers around the waistband of his black pants and tugging him forward with demanding insistence. He obeyed when he felt her fingers brush over the tip of his erection. A moment later he was flush against her while she stripped him of his T-shirt and worked open his regular belt and his fly. Her teasing fingers brushed against him again and again, flitting away to a new task the minute he began to make a sound of response.

Liam grabbed her around her mid-back and hoisted her clear off her feet. He dragged the little tease up along his body until her breasts were level with his mouth. Instinctively her legs hooked around his ribs and waist, her hands clutching his shoulders as he lined her spine up against the bedpost. He caught her nearest nipple teeth first, drawing it through light scraping nips and the long stroke of his tongue.

Devon gasped and moaned, her hands clutching his head now, tangled in his crisp cut the best she could manage, holding him to his task. She shuddered against him, her legs tightening around him, drawing his lower belly flush to her hot, wet core. And she was getting wetter all the time, each pull of his mouth on her breast driving her wild with internal fire and aching longing.

Liam abandoned her tender nipples suddenly, his forehead pressing against her breastbone in between the beautifully shaped globes, his breath coming so hard he could barely see straight. "God!" he cried. "You have no idea what you're doing to me!"

The statement was a warning. The only one he could sanely manage. He felt as though he had been waiting for her forever, and he couldn't bear the separation for another second. He reached beneath her bottom to free himself from his pants.

"Yes! Oh, yes," she exclaimed, knowing instantly what his intentions were.

"Relax your legs just a little, Devon," he coaxed her.

She did, sliding down his belly until she held on by his hips and she could feel his shaft sliding up between her legs, the tip plowing through wet flesh until he was notched to her entrance. His hands came to grasp her hips, holding her right where he wanted her.

"I'm . . ." he gasped, his mouth brushing hers between drags for oxygen. "I want your teeth in me when I do this."

"No. Not so soon," she denied him in breathless gasps. But he could tell it wasn't too soon. She could barely close her lips, her fangs were protruding so far. "I like it best," she amended, "when you're coming. It tastes like nirvana. It makes me fly." She shuddered in his hold. "Just come inside me," she begged impatiently. "Please, Liam . . . Liam, please . . ."

She began to chant his name, over and over, against his lips, within his mouth. That low, sultry artistry of his name. Liam couldn't bear it, so he slipped his hand over her mouth as he thrust up into her, feeling the pricking of her upper canines in the meat of his palm. She was tight. Like a fist squeezing snug around him. He heard her muffled cry against his hand, knowing it was an even sexier call of his name and thanking heaven for his forethought. Much more of that and he would have exploded before he'd had a chance to get started.

Liam thrust again, sliding deeper this time, feeling her flex around him as he filled her further. He was only two-thirds of the way inside of her, and he wanted so badly to be buried to the hilt within her.

"Am I hurting you?" he asked breathlessly. He felt her smile against his palm and she shook her head. He looked into her dancing jade eyes, saw the humor there and chuckled softly. "I'm sorry, but I warned you about the way you say my name, didn't I?" She obediently nodded and he felt her stick her tongue out and flick it against his palm. "Okay, baby, one more time and we'll be nice and cozy," he said roughly. He watched her eyes widen as she understood he wasn't through yet, then he felt her smile even wider. She wriggled against him, sliding him in just a little deeper and making him groan. He felt her relax her inner muscles, pull up so he slid partway free, and then that athletic drag and undulation of her hips again that drew him deep, deeper, bathing him in liquid fire every inch of the way, and finally, with one last wriggle meeting one last thrust, he was buried fully inside of her.

Liam felt her moaning as her body pulsed around him in welcoming hugs of inner muscles. She squirmed and he released her mouth so he could support her with both hands. She immediately threw back her head and cried out her pleasure to the vaulted ceilings. "Liam!" she gasped as her inner body began to ripple in waves and pulsations of drawing pleasure. She was so primed that she was already reaching the point of orgasm.

"It's all right," he both soothed and coaxed as he drew away and worked her back onto him tightly, the swollen head of his cock buried inside of her bumping her cervix in this position. Those minor muscle quakes grew and the fist around him began to tighten and tighten. Devon gasped and moaned as he bent to nibble a thrusting nipple.

She darted for his throat like a serpent, completely forgetting herself and his request that she keep evidence of their liaisons to a minimum. But none of that mattered to him the minute hot fangs sank into his neck. It hurt like a motherfucker, was the first thing to race into his awareness, nothing like when she bit his shoulder. But the pain was so violent it was beautiful and exquisite.

Devon lit off like a rocket, coming hard and with a wild scream of his name vibrating into his skin. He had to hold her tight as her entire body convulsed with pleasure. She throbbed around him, milking and milking at his cock and his neck, furiously suckling for his release, and she almost got it. By the time she fell limply forward against him, Liam felt like he'd been through a gorgeous sort of torture. He clutched her close with one powerful arm, bracing against the bedpost with the other. After a moment he turned and sat on the edge of the bed, the action nudging him a little deeper inside of her and stirring her back to awareness of him. She hyperextended her jaw, pulling those needle-sharp canines free of him in a slow, excruciating movement, then lifted her head, shoving away her hair and looking at him with satiation in her stunning eyes and his blood shimmering on her lips.

"Liam," she whispered. And like a Pavlovian response, he twitched inside of her. It made her giggle and she laughed against his lips as she kissed him. He'd grown used to the taste of his own blood in her mouth. Now he couldn't imagine fucking without it. He wondered if seeing himself bleed would forever get him hard after this. Liam smiled and stroked her hair back from her face as he kissed her deeply.

"I'm officially the kinkiest person I know. I never thought I'd be so into the pain and the blood that comes with fucking you, but God, Devon, I can only wonder how I ever understood the true connection between pleasure and pain without that."

She felt him shift and then he rocked back, pushing himself deeper inside of her as he lifted his hips and slid his pants and boxers down his legs. He then wrapped an arm around her waist and leaned forward over the edge of the bed until she was dangling back over his knees. She laughed as he expertly undid the laces to his boots even without being able to see. She helped him out by reaching for the opposite boot and doing a fair job on it.

"Grab my knife, baby," he instructed her. It took but a second for her to understand him. She ran her hand around the top of his boot and found the knife and sheath. She dislodged it and handed it to him. He slid it under a pillow and then scooped her back up against his chest as he kicked away all his remaining clothes, even stripping off his socks with nimble toes. "Now," he sighed with satisfaction, "I believe you were fucking me?"

Devon snickered wickedly.

"You were going to explain how it feels when I do this . . ." She lifted her bottom, just a little, drawing him in and out of her in a partial thrust. She pleasured herself in the process by allowing his cock to rub over the most sensitive spot on the walls of her pussy, humming a low sound of excitement in response.

Then Devon was watching the world spin madly around her as Liam rolled her onto her back. She felt his knees digging into the mattress. "Ah-ha," he breathed with a sinister laugh. "I have leverage now, you little minx."

"Liam!" she laughed.

"Go ahead. Say it all you want, baby. Shout my name to the rooftops. I'm more than ready for you this time."

He proved the point by sliding himself fully out of her body. Devastated by the sensation of loss, Devon cried out and reached for him. He hadn't gone far, just to the outer edges of that hot little tunnel of torture she had. However, he had methods of his own for exacting painful pleasure, and one of them required him to rub his soaking wet cock all over the outer folds of her body, the head especially dancing across her swollen clit, which was already sensitive from her initial orgasm. He pushed at one of her knees, spreading her legs a little wider while he watched himself, glistening from base to tip, as he rubbed and stroked against her. Her thighs began to tremble and she was clawing at his back as he rebuilt the tension of her body, this time affecting her from the exterior.

"That's it, honey," he said breathlessly. "God help me, you are the most incredible thing I've ever seen," he rasped as she raised her hips and sought longingly for him. He had been prepared to take his pleasure, but the more he saw her react, the more he wanted her to lose control. He watched that cool, sophisticated beauty flush with the tousled looks of a wanton and it just about drove him insane. Liam thrust into her in one smooth stroke and she shouted out with exultation as he filled her tight and hot. He licked and nipped at her breasts, then withdrew from her again. The sound she made was akin to fury, her body writhing with frustration and spiraling tension. It was perfection. She grabbed at him blindly; she begged him both with incoherent sounds and with sharp demands. Liam waited for his lover to tremble and moan, near to tears with frustration, then he slid down the center of her body, slipped two seeking fingers deep inside of her, and sought for her clit with his tongue.

Devon was by turns infuriated, frustrated, and obliterated. Every time she came close again to release, he'd shift away, tease with half-promises, drag out every touch and stroke until she hummed and vibrated with need. When Liam thrust his fingers inside of her, she sobbed out his name. When his tongue flicked over the sensitive nexus of nerves at the top of her slit, she launched her hips up into his voracious mouth. Liam devoured her, lapping up her flavor, nipping at susceptible swells until she was chasing on the heels of release.

Her head was thrown back, her breasts heaving with every breath and cry, and the shout was almost always the same.

"Liam!"

Liam felt the peaking tension in her body, her muscles squeezing his fingers tight. He wanted to suckle her right where he was while she came, but he couldn't bear his own absence from her body any longer. He surged up, covering her and finding her in a single motion. He thrust so deep and so hard he felt the impact of their pelvises. She was too far gone to care, so Liam used her the way he wanted to. Deep, hard, and fast, pumping into her in a crashing rhythm that sucked the pleasure from him in brisk, tight strokes.

Devon came in hard, pulsing beats almost immediately. The low, purring moans of pleasure shaped into his name shuddered through Liam and exploded in a violent starburst of release. He thrust into his orgasm until he couldn't do anything but throb and spurt his seed into her hungry body. Liam gritted out a shout of pleasure from between clenched teeth, his body shaking violently until he collapsed against Devon in a rush of weight and muscle.

Devon had no complaints. She felt a possessive hand on her breast and his gasping breath in the crook of her neck, and she felt numb and floating and tingling and just *wonderful*. His opposite hand slid under her head and suddenly he was rolling over, dragging her with him and dumping her body over his.

He turned his head and kissed her cheek in a chain of sweet kisses, making her smile and turn her lips to meet his. He kissed her as though he still hadn't had enough of her, making her sigh contentedly as his arms locked tighter around her.

"You are something else," he said.

"I can't escape the feeling that all I did was lie there breathing hard." She pouted in mock consternation as her hands slid over his exposed skin. "I hardly got to touch you."

Liam chuckled at that, letting his hand sweep the curve of her back and up the slope of her derriere. "Well, it's to be expected when your brute of a lover barely bothers with foreplay."

"Mmm, you actually have a point there," she speculated, pushing herself up against his chest and sliding into a straddle over his hips. "I think I feel even more cheated now," she mused.

"Cheated! Excuse me, but there's a two to one orgasm ratio here. Cheated," he scoffed, his fingers crawling up her thigh. "The whole county knows my first name by now."

Devon gasped, smacking him when his fingers tickled her high on her inner thigh. "You're no gentleman, do you know that?"

"I admit it. I'm a barbarian in barbarian's clothing." He caught her arms and rolled her back beneath himself, hitching himself up her body a little further. "At least, I am when I'm with you." He slid sensuously against her and Devon exhaled a sound of surprised delight when she felt him already hardening against her.

"But you just . . ."

"I told you that you wouldn't believe what you do to me," he whispered hotly against her lips before snagging her up in a heart-pounding kiss. He broke away and found her ear. "You also can't imagine what I want to do to you, baby. How many ways I want to have you. God, you're like a drug." Liam licked a long sensuous line down her neck to her shoulder, where his teeth scraped in arousing little nips.

He bent to suckle the closest nipple, tugging it between his teeth until she arched into him and moaned loud enough for it to echo into the room. He released her, smiling secretively as he gently kissed away the stimulating pain.

"One of these days, I'm going to take a taste of your blood. Just to see what the excitement is all—"

Devon cut him off when she suddenly tossed him off her body, flinging them both over with astonishing strength and force. She landed on his chest with a thump, making him exhale in surprise. Now that she had him where she wanted him, she sat up like a proud queen on a throne, her fetching breasts thrusting attractively within reach.

Liam was always impressed by her strength, constantly letting the softness and delicateness of her rounded curves trick his mind into thinking she was far more fragile than she really was. Liam smiled. It probably wouldn't be the last time he underestimated his woman.

Devon slid hungry hands up over his chest and back down to his belly. Beautifully manicured nails, polished in a dark violet, scraped erotically over his skin, through the hairs over his pectorals, seeking out his sensitive nipples.

He tucked both hands behind his head like a majestic king awaiting service. Devon gave a low, sultry little sound of humor, making him look at her with suspicion in his eyes because it sounded so devious. That was when she leaned forward to seek out one of his nipples with the teasing flutter of her tongue. She switched sides slowly, trailing kisses and sweeps of her tongue over his chest on the way. Liam's hands came forward to clasp her thighs, his fingers tensing against her taut flesh.

She sat up and looked down on him with a wicked smile.

"Tell me, will you continue to keep this relationship secret from your subordinates?" she asked, genuinely curious as she reached behind herself to drag her fingernails up and down his thighs, knowing full well that the slight stretch of her shoulders tempted him with the lift of what she was beginning to suspect was a highly favored body part. His eyes fixated on her breasts as if on cue, his desire plainly set in amber.

"You know, I think I'm in trouble no matter how I answer that question," he observed distractedly.

"What do you mean?"

"If I say yes, you could be offended, thinking I'm ashamed

to be up front about this. And if I say no, you could think I'm flaunting a conquest."

"Hmm. I never thought about it like that. So which is it, Liam? Conquest or confidential?"

"Neither." He touched his fingers to the side of his neck. "Between this and the fact that I'm bringing Jackson in to take over, it's kind of a moot discussion."

"Liam, I didn't do that on purpose," she murmured contritely as she leaned forward to kiss him. "I just . . . you make me forget myself. You've always been able to do that."

"That sentiment is very much reciprocated," he said gruffly. "Why do you ask?"

She paused only a beat and then flicked her eyes to his. "Because I recognize that I am rapidly losing control of my ability to be discreet with you. There is a part of me that throws a tantrum and pouts every time I can't show everyone that you're mine. Deliciously, manly *mine*."

Liam responded to her gentle, flirtatious kisses but as her busy mouth began to travel down his breastbone to his rigid belly, he seriously began to confess to himself that he'd been having the very same sort of internal tantrums.

He closed his eyes in pleasure as her tongue swept down below his ribs, drifting over every muscle in his stomach with attentive licks and kisses. He looked down at her, surprised to find his fingers tangled in her dark hair, hands cupping the back of her head. Every light scrape of her teeth, every exhalation of her breath was torturing him with anticipation and temptation. Her hands were sitting still on his hips, framing him with her fingers curved gently toward his buttocks. Her mouth slipped lower, below his navel, and he felt her breath skipping over his tumescent flesh.

"Devon," he breathed achingly.

He felt the sweep of her hair brushing over his erection

and the taut sac below it, and then her kisses fell to his thigh, completely bypassing the area that craved her attention.

Devon suppressed a smile when he groaned in frustration. She returned her attention to her worship of his smoothly muscled body, loving every contour with her seducing kisses. She was very aware of her power over a very powerful man, and that it had nothing to do with her superior genes and physical advantage. He was in her hands, having placed himself there with amazing trust.

Proving her point to herself, she ran her eager hands and nails up along his thighs, both atop and along the insides. Liam shifted restlessly and he held back sounds of frustration . . . or pleas for her to stop teasing him. Devon slid up his thick thighs and looked at the pronounced thrust of his penis, smiling as it twitched in anticipation of her approach. She pursed her lips and blew a stream of tepid breath across him, watching him in delight as he groaned aloud and brushed anxious fingers through her hair, trying to recapture the head she'd slipped out of his reach as she'd kissed his thighs. She reached for him with a single extended nail and touched it against his shaft, just below the fat red cap at the tip. She drew her fingertip down over his hot, veined skin, so incredibly soft, yet so unbelievably hard just beneath that.

Liam hadn't been bragging when he'd said he was a big man. Even after so many encounters as lovers, she was still impressed by his length and thickness. She smiled, her lip slipping eagerly between her teeth as she stroked him all the way to the base of his cock and then lower, right over the malleable sac beneath. She cupped him there briefly, flicking her fingernails along the back of his balls teasingly until she felt him tighten in her hand and heard him moan out a curse. Then she took a measure of pity on him and closed her hand fully around his delightfully hard erection. She had scooted up far enough to be within reach of his hands and one sank tensely into her hair.

"Babe, you're killing me," he rasped out, the remark a plea.

But it was her intention to make him the victim of a temporary death. And like most victims, he wasn't going to see it coming until it was too late to do anything about it. She dipped her head to hide her sinister smile and the greed for his pleasure in her eyes. She stroked him with a feathery grip, there but almost not, fingers stimulating his skin but not the throbbing flesh and nerves beneath. His hips shifted, seeking stronger contact, and she denied him until he was nearly thrashing with need.

"Oh God, Devon, this is insane," he groaned. "You've proved your point already . . . just . . . just . . ."

"Just what?" she murmured sexily, her smile flashing up at him with all the wickedness of a true temptress. "Just this?" Her tongue snaked out quickly to lick over the swollen head of his prick, lapping up drops of liquid she'd tortured out of him. His taste was divine on her tongue, salt and musk and a touch of herself, which she found to be an incredible turn-on.

"Devon!" he half shouted, half groaned, his fingers flexing violently in her hair.

She didn't wait for him to settle, too impatient to tease and torture him anymore. She'd had a taste of him and she wanted more. Her fingers curled firmly around his thick circumference, and she held him against her lips, drawing him slowly over them, back and forth with little slips of her tongue. She circled her tongue around him, tasting him again as she tempted more from him.

When she pressed her lips against him to form perfect suction, his whole body tensed violently in preparation for the suckling draw of her mouth as she drew him in, at first in short strokes and then longer ones.

Liam was in hell. Or heaven. Or purgatory. He couldn't decide. One moment her mouth felt glorious, and desire pulsed through him from head to toe. The next he was being overwhelmed by the urge to lose himself in delight with no regard for anything else, and he fought the swelling responses of his greedy body. Then it was blindness, bliss so utterly intense that he felt almost numb with the power of it.

"Devon, baby," he croaked out, grateful he could still speak. He tightened his hold around her hair in case she didn't hear him. Just then, her artful mouth swirled snugly around him, her tongue flicking the underside of the head, a screaming sensitive spot. Her hand slid tightly along his length as her mouth retreated, a definite rhythm forming now, one that he lifted his hips into automatically. "Devon!" he barked out as passionate pleasure surged low along the interior of his body. "Devon I want to touch you. I want to make you . . ." Liam gasped as she ignored him and stroked him with hand and mouth working like a beautifully choreographed form of torture. Suddenly she had him so close it was like feeling himself boiling inside. "Baby . . . oh, baby I'm going to come," he growled out roughly as his entire body tensed in preparation. She didn't relent, not for a moment, tightening suction, and stroke, and her flawless rhythm until he could do nothing but feel, and feel, and feel.

The approach of his orgasm was ravaging and hot; the release itself was violent and blissful. Liam shouted out uninhibitedly, his entire body bucking as Devon delighted in milking him until his outcries told her it was too much to bear a moment longer. She released him at last and he grabbed for her with awkward fumbling hands. She smothered a laugh as she accommodated his wishes and slid up his body and into the clutch of his arms. Liam was rasping hard for breath, his hands still tensing tightly now and then, and his body shaking with aftershocks of pleasure.

Feeling content and very proud of herself, she snuggled down against his shoulder, using it as a pillow.

But before Liam even recovered enough to talk, she said,

"Tomorrow we're going to hunt down Ambrose and put an end to this once and for all. I want to go home. I want my family back. I want to live my life again as a free Morphate woman. I want to be Devona Chandler."

Liam took a very deep breath.

"And I'm going to give you that."

Chapter Seventeen

Ambrose was in the Catskills.

So damn close. This whole time. Him and half his fucking clan, Liam thought as he looked down on the site from a nest, similar to the one they had found, high in the trees at a reasonably good position to view a great deal of Ambrose's compound.

"Well, we could always call the local authorities and rat him out," Kellen suggested. "Technically, he's not supposed to be off the reservation."

"Neither is she," Liam pointed out dryly, cocking his head at Devon. "Anyway it's a gray area. They never punish runaways, just send them back to their own Cities. He's guilty of far more than a simple straying charge."

"Human law isn't going to apply here," Devon said softly, narrowing her eyes on the activity around the main house. It was a huge, modern masterpiece, guaranteed to have every bell and whistle money could buy and all the comforts imaginable. Also all the best security. Technology aside, though, Ambrose had a huge crowd of Morphates constantly moving in and out of the main house and huddling around three of the smaller houses on the property. The compound was just about as hard to get to as Devon's property was. "Ambrose has to be made to answer to Morphate law," she continued. "Which he broke the minute he seceded from the Alpha Council. It's also the only thing we have proof of. The only thing that can have him deposed as Alpha of Dark Phoenix and thrown in an Alpha Council Penitentiary. Everything else, the attempts on my life, the attempts to gain the mercury weaponry for himself, his crimes against Morphates and humans . . . we have no proof of them. He's made sure of that. He's always made sure of that."

"Why don't we just cloud this guy," Kellen asked irritably.

"You just answered your own question," Liam said. "Because he'd go up in smoke and be forgotten in a second. Or be a martyr forever."

"The last thing we need is a Morphate civil war with the memory of Ambrose at its core," Devon said bitterly. "But to imprison him and make an example of him, to show other Morphates that his behavior will not be tolerated, that is what is needed. Between his capture and handing over my mercury weapons to humans, we can drastically change the playing field. It will bring others in line very quickly. The Morphates can pursue their rights the way our human ancestors did it. The way women did it. Legally. Politically."

"Christ," Kellen hissed. "You have a lot of faith in humans. That they won't just turn on you and start putting the whole lot of you down one by one. We have plenty of examples of that in our history too, you know."

"I know," she said softly.

Devon left it at that. They didn't need to talk about just how big a risk she was taking. But she wasn't the one who had started this journey. Kincaid Gregory had started it nearly fifty years ago when he had anticipated the trouble Morphates like Ambrose would cause. And with the newer generations of Morphates becoming stranger and more powerful, it was best they had some way to control them.

"So what's the plan, boss?" Kellen asked, looking through his glasses and watching the way the Morphates moved, looking for patterns that would indicate security teams, routines, and shifts.

Liam looked at Devon.

"What's the plan, Devona Chandler?" he asked her softly.

"Well, I was kind of thinking of knocking on the front door."

"Ambrose, you are not going to believe this," Max blurted out as he burst into the main parlor.

Ambrose slid a venomous look at the new generation Morphate and wondered to himself why he insisted on surrounding himself with these impulsive, uncontrollable children. Bad enough his final assassin had not checked in for over twenty-four hours. He'd rather expected Rhiannon would fuck up. Had almost counted on it, really. He'd hoped her attack would make Devona flee in panic. After all, having an attacker make it all the way into the bedroom was bound to shake her confidence in the security and safety of her property. Knee-jerk reaction, especially when protecting a precious payload like Devona was protecting, would be to relocate to a place deemed safer. Out of reach. Different. It would have provided him the perfect opportunity to attack her in force once and for all. A caravan was always weaker than a fixed position. He would have achieved all his goals at once: killing the traitor and acquiring the weapons for himself.

But Devona had not budged. Had barely blinked. She had stayed snuggled into her home with her pathetic human security force. What a joke. That something so weak and so fallible could ever stand up to a superior Morphate. Superior in intelligence, superior in strength, and superior in longevity. In a word: perfect. They were perfect.

"Do surprise me," Ambrose invited the young Morphate darkly, making it very clear that he was thoroughly annoyed.

"Devona Chandler is at the gate requesting an audience!" Max veritably overflowed with the news. And why not? He was right. No one would have believed him.

Ambrose sat up straight, his spine growing long and his shoulders squaring as a sensation of utter delight swam through him. He shifted his gaze to the man seated in the chair across from him.

"Well. What do you make of that?" he asked.

"Hubris," was the reply. "She's no doubt going to try and negotiate with you the way she has tried negotiating with all the other Alphas on the Council. After all, she has no reason to think you have been the one trying to end her life. You've left no proof. No trail."

"It's one of my most sterling talents," Ambrose agreed with a pleased smile. "How exciting. Now I don't have to kill her. I can lock the bitch up and dissect her twice a day for the rest of eternity." Ambrose sighed with pleasure at the thought.

"I rather like the idea," his companion agreed. "The possibilities are endless, if you don't mind sharing access."

Ambrose quickly frowned, then just as quickly shrugged off the covetous craving that caused it. What did it matter who did the poking and prodding? As long as he got to watch it.

"But I am forced to wonder how she knew I was here. Like her, I am using a human persona for my holdings here. I have no choice." His tone was dripping with contempt at being forced to sneak past human laws. But soon that wouldn't matter. Soon humans would learn what it felt like to be lorded over and treated like second-class citizens. A plan that would be ruined if Devona succeeded in handing over her mercury weaponry. No. It would not do at all if the insects suddenly became venomous.

"She is a brilliant woman and no less resourceful than you

are," the other man pointed out. "I doubt it took much work for her to find you."

"She only thinks she is clever," Ambrose bit out. "She's about to learn what a truly superior mind is capable of. Bring her here," he commanded of Max. "And someone get me Tansy and Jacan."

Devona's heart was pounding at a speed that ought to have killed her, had she not been immortal. She walked up to the house, flanked on either side by Ambrose's Morphates. She wondered how this was going to play out. Wondered if she was just plain crazy for attempting this. Liam had only gone along with her plan after she'd agreed to three ground rules: she'd been fitted with a radio comm to be left entirely open the whole time, they had waited for dark to fall, and his teams were already infiltrating the property. They had moved past the cameras, tricked the motion and heat sensors, and snuck in quite close to the house from all different directions. She had made certain they were armed to the hilt with mercury weapons. The rest was up to their stellar training and the man who led them.

As expected, her arrival caused something of a spectacle. News had flown through the compound about who Ambrose's guest was. She was being stared at from all quarters. Morphates were trying to be discreet and failing miserably as they gravitated toward the front porch to get a look at her. That was very much a part of her plan. To draw them all in. The fewer Morphates they needed to corral, the better. It was best Ambrose's people got a very good look at what was about to happen.

Ambrose was standing in the center of the parlor she was led to. There were other Morphates around, some sitting in chairs, some lounging at a nearby bar. One in particular was a tall, stunning black woman not three feet to his right rear.

To his rear left was a very strong and intimidating male in a leather vest with a smaller but tough looking female right at his side.

"Greetings, Devona. Welcome to my home."

Oh, how smug he seemed, Devona thought as she swallowed back a swell of bile in her throat. He was just so confident of his superiority. He had tried to annihilate her in half a dozen or more different ways, and yet he stood there greeting her as if she were the closest of friends. She had wondered, as she had met with the other Alphas and their lieutenants, time and again, "Is this who wants me dead?" And now, here she was standing in front of him, knowing for certain it was Ambrose, and she honestly couldn't tell herself whether she would have been able to discern the truth from his congenial demeanor as he stepped forward and extended his hand.

She wasn't stupid enough to take it.

She smiled to cover her rebuff.

"Ambrose. Thank you for seeing me without announcement. I know it's terribly rude of me."

"Oh please," he waved her apology off. "I'm not the sort to hold the little things against people."

But the big things, like annihilation of their species . . .

She could almost hear the words. She could feel the wall of hatred emanating toward her, thinly veneered with these social niceties.

"I was wondering if we could speak," she said, keeping the façade of her ignorance up with yet another smile.

"Of course, of course." He moved aside a little, his arm extended behind him. "Come join us. I believe you know my guest."

Fixated as she was on the immediate Morphates near her, Devona hadn't initially noticed the male in the chair just behind Ambrose. When she finally did, her whole stomach bottomed out, an eerie injection of liquid numbness washing over her at the same time because she couldn't quite comprehend or accept what she was seeing.

"Doctor Chandler," Dr. Eric Paulson said smoothly as he rose to his feet. "It's been a long time. How have you been?"

Too long. Not long enough. God, help her. She was going to kill him. She was going to die. All of these thoughts and more sped through her mind as she stood frozen in place, staring at him.

"Holy shit, she's in trouble," she heard Liam announce over the comms. "Move in, people, this charade is finished!"

"I'm fine," she said a bit dumbly. "Yes, I'm perfectly fine," she said more strongly, trying to speak to the men lying in wait outside. She was close enough to Ambrose to do what she had come to do, but Paulson was spinning her for a loop. Here was the ultimate criminal. Here was a man hunted by every man and Morphate in the world. In Ambrose's parlor. As an honored guest. If she had not already known Ambrose to be a psychopath, she would have truly recognized it then.

"I'm glad to hear it. I hope you are not like so many of these other Morphates, holding grudges against their creator. They thrive in their new condition, yet still curse me. You are a doctor. A scientist. And though we have disagreed in the past, surely you can agree that there is no value in fussing over what cannot be changed."

"Change is just that," she said, but only the man who had become her lover recognized the strange detachment in her words. Devona without emotion was like a night without stars. And here she was, face to face with the man she despised more than life itself, surrounded by enemy Morphates. It changed the entire game plan for him and he knew it changed it for her as well. "Fluid. Ever-moving. Ever evolving. Everything must evolve or risk being left behind."

Devona lifted her hand, her flowing sleeve falling back as she pointed her fingers at Ambrose's neck, and then closed her fist. The darts filled with mercury shot out instantly, pelting the startled Morphate in the neck. He roared with fury, even as she raised her opposite palm toward Dr. Paulson, braced her feet and shifted her shoulders hard to engage the one weapon she was giving to the humans that meant far more than anything that used mercury. The micro-wiring ran down the inside of her arm, looking no different from a heavy, translucent vein, until it spiraled in the seat of her palm. The trigger was along the back of her arm and shoulder joint, connected to specific muscles that only engaged when contracted a certain way.

The pulse that exploded from her hand hit Paulson dead in the chest, a wall of energy and sound that blew him off his feet, sent him crashing back into the stone fireplace behind him. Ambrose barely got his fingers to his throat, had only an instant to claw at the darts, pulling two of them free.

Too late.

Much too late. His people didn't even twitch as their Alpha evaporated into a gaseous cloud. After he was gone, however, Jacan leapt for Devon, grabbing her in an arm lock that prevented her ability to use her mercury weapon.

"Jacan, careful," Tansy gasped breathlessly as her lover came so close to such a deadly weapon.

"I'm not here to harm anyone else," Devona was saying loudly, her palm still facing the stunned Dr. Paulson, even though he was crumpled up into an unconscious pile at the foot of the fireplace. She heard glass breaking, heard the others arriving at her back, felt the tension in the room ratchet up to a point of violence, forcing her to speak louder.

"The Alpha Council passed sentence on Ambrose alone," she shouted, trying to be heard over the ruckus. "All anyone else will suffer is fines if you don't return to Dark Phoenix or wherever you are from and wait patiently for the Freedom Act to allow us the right to move and live freely in the Federated States. The Council feels confident that once the humans are armed with weapons like this stunner, they will gain more confidence, be less afraid, and more willing to be fair."

Everyone in the room stared at the unconscious man who had started all of this so many years ago with his sick, illegal bid for immortality.

"Let her go," Liam demanded gruffly, his entire demeanor no-nonsense as he aimed one of Devona's new pulse guns at Jacan's head.

Devona looked up over her shoulder and into the dark eyes of the Morphate who held her. This was a very dangerous man. She could feel the power in his body and could see the capability in his eyes. She recognized his face. Jacan. Ambrose's Beta.

"You are Alpha now. You will be recognized as such by the Council," she said softly to him. "You can lead very differently from the way Ambrose did. And you can help us pack off Eric Paulson to the penitentiary he has long deserved."

Jacan looked over her features for a long moment, then slid a glance at Liam.

"How do I know you won't spray down this entire place with mercury once I release you?"

"Because we would have done it already," Liam answered for her. "Instead, your people will wake with headaches from the stunner in an hour or two. An hour after that they will never know they'd been hit. And like she said, we're not interested in you or your people as long as everyone remains calm and behaves."

Jacan took several beats to think. He took in the situation in which he now found himself.

"I am grateful you don't assume everyone in Dark Phoenix is of Ambrose's bent. You understand I couldn't overtake him yet. As much as I would have liked to, he was too well fortified and much stronger than I was." Jacan let her go and stepped back. Tansy hurried to his side even as Liam reached out for Devon's arm and pulled her into the safety of his hold.

Never once did she lower her hand or turn her focus from Eric Paulson's direction.

"Interesting choice," Liam said quietly to her, pressing his lips to her hairline and gently rubbing a soothing hand in circles over her lower back.

"When faced with the two of them, it was the only choice. I could have killed Paulson and stuck to my original plans as far as Ambrose was concerned, but the truth is Phoenix needs a new Alpha and Paulson needs to be held accountable for his crimes. It would have been selfish of me to deprive a great many other Morphates of the opportunity to see this sick bastard locked in a tiny cold cage of his own. They've waited fifty years for this, and he makes, by far, the better choice. I think Ambrose's death and Phoenix's new Alpha makes the point for obeying the Council laws well enough."

"I would have to agree," he said, looking carefully into her eyes. "So let's bundle Paulson up and get him in front of your Council then, shall we? It's long past time you got home."

Epilogue

The face of the world was changing.

She had been instrumental in it.

Nick Gregory watched through the balcony glass as Devona turned over the E-pad in her hands, effectively turning off the news program she'd been watching. He reached out to touch Amara's hand, stroking her fingers in just such a way that, after fifty years, spoke very clearly to her.

"You thought she would be happier," Amara said with a strange smile on her lips.

"She worked long and hard to achieve the things she did. But she hasn't smiled once since coming back into our fold."

"That's because she left something behind," Amara said softly.

"Something?"

Just then the bell to the apartment rang out, drawing its owner's attention out on the balcony. Devona stood up and crossed through the living room, acknowledging her first visitors with a nod of her head before going to let in her next one.

"But now that the Freedom Act is on the verge of passing, I think things are going to change," Amara told her husband wisely.

Devona opened the door and froze in shock to see the frame filled with Liam's presence. He was by far the most beautiful thing she'd seen in weeks. The return to her pretty penthouse home in Dark Manhattan, the retrieval of her identity, the faces of her friends, all of it had been glorious, but nothing had made her feel the way opening that door and seeing his face made her feel.

He looked a little tired . . . a little haggard. But despite that, he was as huge and gorgeously male as ever. He was vital and strong, so intensely alive in front of her that she could almost feel the beat of his pulse emanating off of him. In just a few heartbeats she was wet between her legs and parched against her tongue and craving him in both places.

But they hadn't spoken once since she had returned through the Dark Manhattan gates. Not one call. Not a single email. He'd simply said goodbye to her and they'd left it at that.

"Here's the deal," he said in a rough rasp. "I'm human. I'm going to grow old and die. I love my job. I love my business. I'm not going to give any of that up. But . . ." He swallowed so hard she heard it. "But I'm pretty damn sure I love you, too, and I'm not willing to give you up either. So . . . you're the smart one. Figure out how we can do this."

Devona took a deep breath and slowly, suddenly, began to smile. She reached out to touch him, her fingertips on his chest, her breath leaving her on a sound of great relief.

"Well, nothing says you can't live in Dark Manhattan. And in a few months I can leave the reservation and we can stay anywhere you want."

"I heard the news and I came right here. I didn't want to interfere in the homecoming you waited so long for. Worked so hard for," he said, finally stepping over the threshold and taking her up in his arms.

"It wasn't as special as I wanted it to be," she confessed breathily to him. "It was missing you. This is all echoes of the past, and all I craved was possibilities of a future. Do you really love me?"

He smiled down at her.

"Yeah. I'm pretty well stuck on you, honey. I figured it out after about a week of missing you, wandering aimlessly through my life and feeling like someone kicked my puppy."

"I'm a Morphate," she felt the need to remind him as he started to kiss her with no little amount of heat.

"I think we've established that," he said with a chuckle.

"I won't grow old. I won't die. I'm going to fang you frequently. At this very moment I'm dying to get my claws into you."

"Thank Christ!" he declared hotly.

"And . . . I think I'd like to have children. But I have to unlock some of these genetic anomalies we're seeing. And our child would be a hybrid. I'm not sure there's been a hybrid of human and Morphate before, or if it's even possible. It ought to be, since we work the same reproductively . . ."

Liam sighed and pressed his cheek against hers, his gaze falling on the couple sitting just beyond her shoulder.

"She gets like this sometimes," he said to them with a grin.

"We know," Amara said with a smile.

Liam wrapped Devona up in the biggest, most powerful hug he could manage, pulling her feet right up off the floor.

"Just say 'I love you, Liam,' " he instructed her softly against her ear. "And all the rest will take care of itself."

"I love you, Liam," she said obediently.

And it did.

ABOUT THE AUTHOR

New York Times bestselling author JACQUELYN FRANK is the author of the successful Nightwalkers series, which first introduced the world to her unique paranormal romances. She has since gone on to create two more successful, bestselling series, The Shadowdwellers and The Gatherers.

Jacquelyn Frank has been passionate about writing ever since she picked up her first teen romance at age thirteen. Since then, she's gone on to write over ten bestselling books, with more on the way. Before Jacquelyn became an author, she worked as a Sign Language Interpreter and substitute teacher.

For more information on Jacquelyn Frank and her books, readers may visit her Facebook page at www.facebook.com/pages/Jacquelyn-Frank/371620872548 or visit her website at www.jacquelynfrank.com.

Read on for an excerpt from HUNTER by
Jacquelyn Frank writing as JAX, available now.

It had been ten years.

He turned his face up toward the night sky, feeling the
sharp cold of winter across his skin, seeking the kiss of the
moon as its thin light shone through the veil of clouds skim-
ming its surface. Frost coated the hardened ground; every
step he took crunched into dormant grasses and autumn's discarded leaves as he moved deeper into the woodlands. There
was no snow, neither fresh nor old. Not unheard of, but rare
for this time of year. He wondered if it had snowed at all this
season yet.

He didn't guard his steps, the feeling of being on home soil
relaxing his normal vigilance. The vibration of his power and
presence brought nature to awareness, rippling through it in
some ways, meshing with it in others—as foreign to it as it
was familiar.

At last, he spied the breach between the two slanted oaks
that marked the clearing. When he stepped between the thick
trunks of these two old sentries, he saw the lone willow in the
center of the uneven terrain of the clearing, and he felt his
heartbeat quicken in anticipation. After all, it had been a decade
since he'd last seen the Blessing Tree. A decade too long.

Oh, how he had missed this place!

The magnificent old tree whispered of its ancient power, tantalizing him with its hum of familiarity and homecoming. This was the center of his world. It had been since he was only seventeen. His blood stained the bark of the old willow, and so did the blood of his family. He had roamed very far from this core place, but distance had never changed the fact that his roots were here, just as much as the old willow's were.

It had been the agony within his family, caused by his very presence, which had driven him to abandon his home. He had been in pain, blinded by anger and guilt. All of the turbulent emotions young men are prone to succumbing to. Those feelings had spurred his decision to leave. Even now, years later, the hurt still lingered in his slightly tarnished spirit.

He moved closer to the old tree, the ground lumpy now with the running of its massive root system. Its gnarled trunk shone silvery luminescent in the frail moonlight, even through the curtain of thin, naked branches. He passed through them and headed farther in.

When he reached the base of the Blessing Tree, he carefully stepped up the steep knots of inclining roots. He touched the light gray of the bark, watching the weak moonlight dance with dappled patterns over the back of his hand. His palm warmed and prickled, the energy of the tree flowing through him. He couldn't help the deep sigh that rushed out of him as he was infused through every cell with the blessing and wisdom of the august tree. It swept away all the remnants of poorly managed emotions, lingering bitterness, and the disappointments of the past, giving much-needed succor. His mind and heart cleared; his pulse pounded with joy.

He was home at last.